THE ORDER OF CHAOS

BOOK ONE

BEN J HENRY

Contents

Readers Club Download Offer

The characters in this story explore lucid dreaming: becoming conscious in their dreams. If you are interested in lucid dreaming, and would like to learn how to wake up in your dreams, then visit **benjhenry.com** to download your free short guide.

PART ONE: SIMULACRUM

The greatest war that man shall fight will not lie on the plain.
No spear or gun, no atom bomb, no enemy terrain.
The foe long sought, this evil fought, will share his given name.
The war between and war within will be one and the same.
From fear inane, projected blame: to seek is not to find.
The greatest war that man shall fight will lie within his mind.

— Aldous Crow —

CHAPTER ONE
Blackout

THE MOON LINGERED in the morning sky like someone had forgotten to erase it. Throughout the streets of Godalming, flocks of schoolchildren filed down pavements chatting animatedly with the early-morning energy gifted only to the young. Teachers flicked on kettle switches and stared into space, waiting for the water to boil and the term to end. Summer was fading and on the chill breeze hung the first autumnal leaves: red-gold promises of a change in season. It was the first day of the academic year.

Alicia counted from five to one and gripped the lock on the back of her front door. She turned it counterclockwise, opened the door a fraction and decided that her laces were loose. She bent to tighten the laces while an impatient gust of wind pressed the door against the toe of her trainer. She stood and permitted herself a final count from five as she stared through the thin panels of glass in the door. She glanced over her shoulder at her father sleeping on the sofa, his head facing the entrance and his eyes closed like the world's laziest guard dog, and then swung the door open. Stepping onto the mat, she counted from five to one, her eyes fixed on the corner of the driveway.

She knew she was stalling, and that these countdowns would make her late for the first day of her final year at school. Alicia was never late; she had not missed registration since her mother baked cupcakes for the class on her fifteenth birthday and then stopped the car to give them all to a pair of homeless men on the drive in.

'Honestly, Alicia, don't be mad—they will enjoy them far more than your form group.'

'I'm not mad, nobody brings in cupcakes for their birthday any more.'

'And Lord knows those children don't need any fattening up. I just hope the sugar doesn't kill them. You can't get diabetes from a few cupcakes, can you?'

'We're going to be late.'

That had been three years ago. Now Alicia blinked at the sky—a lurid blue, offensively bright for this time of day—and let out a face-splitting yawn. She had slept through her alarm, which unsurprising given that she had only fallen asleep three hours before it sounded. Muttering 'Zero', she closed the door behind her, resigning herself to the truth: the summer holidays had ended and her brother had not returned. She stepped from the mat, unaware of the eyes watching her from behind the bush across the road.

Winter spied Alicia's yawn through the rhododendron leaves and her body responded naturally. A tremble ran through her fingers and she held the can of paint against her chest as a silent yawn erupted from her throat. Resting the can on her thigh, she pressed the back of a hand to her mouth and watched Alicia turn down the pavement.

'Ready?' she mouthed to Jack as Alicia disappeared around the corner. Winter emerged from her hiding place between the bush and the fence on the corner of the quiet street. Glancing left and right, she marched across the road towards Alicia's house. She did not see Jack follow, but sensed his presence: pale-blue eyes searching the windows as they reached the driveway. Unaccustomed to treading lightly, Winter crunched her feet along the gravel and towards a side gate that led to a sheltered walkway between Alicia's house and the six-foot wall separating the neighbouring property. She flicked a spider from the rim of the can, shifted it into her left hand and tried the gate: unlocked. Jack chased her through and she closed it behind her, feeling the needle-prick of adrenaline now that she was officially trespassing.

Winter trudged along the dark passageway, past the washing machine, lawnmower and a geriatric Christmas tree to reach the back door. Jack's brow furrowed above his twice-broken nose: he feared that they would find it locked.

They've nothing left to steal, thought Winter, trying the door and finding it open. A triumphant smile lit her aggressively beautiful face as she entered the property. Creeping through the kitchen, her gaze swept the family photographs that grinned on the windowsill, glossy eyes following her deeper into their household.

In the living room, she stopped at the sight of Alicia's father asleep on the sofa. Draped in a colourful pashmina, he lay with his head on a cushion and his knees tucked, resembling a young boy. The sofa was angled out from the wall such that, were his eyes open, he would see through an archway to the front door. The gentle snores filling the dark room with a soporific rhythm suddenly broke and his ruddy cheeks twitched. Winter's heart stopped and the can of paint weighed heavily in her hands.

'Mr Harrington?' she whispered, taking a delicate step across the carpet and raising a hand tentatively in the direction of the sofa. Everybody knew that Alicia's father was narcoleptic and dropped into sleep as though someone had stepped on a wire and his plug had come out. But narcoleptics were not known to sleep deeply.

Satisfied that Alicia's father was sleeping soundly, Winter turned for the stairs. Jack thought it was a good thing that he was sleeping downstairs; Winter reminded him to be quiet. She passed two bedrooms and a bathroom before reaching the master bedroom at the end of the corridor. The paint can was heavy, and she wished that Jack would take it. She eased it back into her left hand, shifted the strap of her bag higher up her right shoulder and switched on the light.

The room was tidy, the bed made. Heavy teal curtains were

drawn open and a block of light spilled upon an easel in the corner of the room. On the easel sat a canvas with a half-finished painting of a volcanic landscape. The bed was positioned in the middle of the far wall, and directly above each pillow hung two paintings. On the left was a portrait of Alicia and her mother, Anna, painted in a style that Winter recognised—with more than a little jealousy—as Alicia's work. She wrinkled her nose at the sight of her classmate and art teacher and turned her gaze to the portrait on the right, painted by Anna.

The sight of Alicia's father and younger brother made Winter's stomach churn with acid, prompting Jack to question—again— whether this was a good idea. The pair in the picture grinned in vibrant hues, two pairs of hazel eyes telling lies of an alert wakefulness. Ignoring Jack's discomfort, Winter reached for the postcard in the back pocket of her jeans, and when her eyeline left Alicia's brother and settled on the card in her hands, she was glad to have brought it with her.

The postcard, purchased five weeks ago in Winter's hometown in Sri Lanka, depicted a beach that she did not recognise and a temple that she could not name. It was the text that had caught her eye: *Wish you were here.* She had bitten her lip, smiling at her own joke as she drew a line through 'here' and wrote 'dead'.

It had seemed funny at the time.

'Come on,' Winter ordered, pocketing the postcard and nodding to the space above the headboard. 'Across that wall.'

But Jack did not move. He did not take the can of paint. It was Winter that pulled the paintbrush from her shoulder bag. It was Winter that nudged the alarm clock aside and placed the can on the bedside table. It was Winter that stepped onto the bed.

She wished that Jack was here, but Winter was alone.

The duvet was soft and the mattress creaked. She glanced over her shoulder and down the empty corridor before sizing up the stretch of wall that was to be her canvas.

'Lower or upper case?' Winter asked. Her fingers shook as she placed the lid of the can on the spine of an open book that lay face-down beside the alarm clock.

Comic Sans, said Jack, and Winter smiled. She pictured the thick neck beneath his blond hair, stretching the collar of his rugby shirt: *Henson 18*. With the ghost of a smile on her lips, she proceeded to paint upon the white wall in white paint with careful, measured strokes.

You sure she'll see it? Jack asked as Winter stepped back, trying to discern the white paint against the wall.

'When the lights go out,' Winter whispered with a wink. 'Black-out.'

She left the lights on and the door ajar, carrying the paint can in both hands with the brush on top, to avoid any tell-tale drops striking the beige carpet. She descended the stairs and crossed the living room, where Alicia's father continued to sleep in the shadows. In a distant recess of Winter's mind, she hoped he would not be the first to turn out the bedroom lights. Her message was not for him.

Closing the back door, she stole quietly down the side alley and through the gate. Stepping into the front garden, Winter paused, glancing down at the can. With a grunt, she hurled it over the brick wall and into the neighbouring garden and was about to follow it with the brush when a violent clang assaulted her ears; the can had struck something hard and metallic on the far side of the wall.

Drawn by insuppressible curiosity, Winter hurried along the wall to peer into the front garden.

You said it was abandoned, Jack hissed.

It was.

The can lay on its side on top of a police car, nestled in a dent in the roof of the vehicle. White paint slid down the windscreen. Her chestnut eyes snapped in the direction of the front door, where a boy of her age looked from the can of paint to the brush in her hand. His mouth was slightly open, and a spark of humour lit his green eyes.

'Nice shot,' he said, grinning.

Winter watched the lid of the can slide gently down the windscreen, riding the wave of white paint.

Blackout.

Footprints

ALICIA SAT ON the arm of the sofa with one hand resting by her father's head and the other picking at the wilted leaves of the Caesar salad that she had left out for him an hour before. Since her mother taught art at the school, Alicia was often called upon by reception staff to perform duties for which they were unable to find a willing teacher. Having distributed new students around their after-school activities, she had arrived home late and her father had slept for the remainder of the evening. The only signs that he had departed from the realm of slumber at all that day were a half-eaten ham sandwich on the kitchen counter and a concerning smell of wet paint coming from upstairs.

'It was pretty standard for the first day,' she commented, popping a crouton between her molars and crunching into the silence. 'Just your usual start-of-year bereavement assembly. Big photo of Jack at the front of the hall—that one of him at the Bath Cup? Nothing out of the ordinary. Winter didn't show up, though.'

A snore escaped her father's nostrils.

'Now don't be unkind, Dad. Would you have expected her to turn up, knowing every eye would be on her? Every sympathetic—' she shook her head. 'It's probably best for the new kids that she's taking some time to get her head together. Remember last year, when she tricked those Year 7s into an "assembly" on the sports field and soaked them with the sprinklers?'

She watched his eyelids flicker, and an incoherent mumble passed his lips.

'Your words, not mine,' said Alicia, eyebrows raised. 'She'll be all right, though. She's, well, she's a lot of things—'

Snort.

'—Stop it. Be nice. She's a lot of things, but she's tough. Probably just needs an extra day, without all the questions, and the…' she trailed off and, with nothing but the passage of air through her father's parted lips, her thoughts were punctuated by the ticking of the clock on the wall above the fireplace. Three friends had asked through fragile smiles why she had not responded to their messages and—as though to answer their own questions—whether there had been any update on David's disappearance. Five students and three teachers had asked where her mother was—*Is she unwell? Do ask her to drop me an email about the Fair.* At lunchtime, Alicia decided that she had earned a little break. In the girls' toilets, she had counted down from one hundred.

'She'll be fine. Try not to worry, Dad. Don't want you losing any sleep over it.'

She smiled through a yawn and cocked her head to catch her father's eye, but his lids remained stubbornly closed. Rory Harrington was a great appreciator of jokes, big and small, humorous and otherwise. Alicia and David had been raised on puns and rapid-fire quips, with meals around the dining table descending into improvised comedy scenes, littered with lines from Rory that made the jokes in Christmas crackers sound like profound wisdom.

'What do you think might happen,' Alicia had once asked in a derisive manner while her mother and father enacted a scene in which she was failing a chemistry test; the upcoming exam was playing on her mind, 'if you were to take something seriously, just once?'

Her parents had shared a glance, Anna with her husband in a headlock and a cucumber/Bunsen burner at his throat.

'Divorce, probably,' said Anna. Rory had nodded in sombre agreement.

Presently, Alicia lifted the corner of the pashmina, which her father's snoring had shifted like sand across the skin of a drum, and tucked it back over his shoulder. A somnolent smile twisted the corner of his lips, and Alicia saw dream versions of Anna, David and herself bent double with laughter as he regaled an anecdote from his years at Trinity College in Dublin. A small crease pitted her brow.

She sometimes envied how effortlessly her father departed from the waking world, as though he never had two feet on conscious ground. His narcolepsy had struck, with no warning, when she was eleven. Anna joked with her friends at the uncanny timing of these episodes that tended to happen whenever Rory had a particularly boring task to undertake, like dog sitting for his brother's three dachshunds, or filing a tax return. To begin with, his episodes were regarded with mild amusement rather than frustration. But over the years, the condition worsened. As a husband and father, he remained doting; but as a welfare officer, golfer and volunteer fireman, his days were over. Fortunately, nobody minded if you fell asleep while pruning the hydrangeas, so this hobby had been a late bloom.

'According to rumour,' Alicia whispered conspiratorially as a memory from the canteen surfaced, 'well, according to the Carpenter twins, Winter set fire to a police car. You've got to hand it to them, they're not short on imagination.'

That sounded disturbingly like something her mother would have said, so Alicia decided to end the conversation.

'Good talk, Dad.'

She kissed her father on the forehead and rose from her seat. Neither of them had heard from Anna in two days, though they had both left messages on her mobile phone. Rory had slept more often than usual during this period, as though on strike until his wife returned.

Alicia tossed the salad in the kitchen bin and ascended the stairs in dim light; night had fallen and the bulb above the landing needed replacing. Bulb replacement was a task that fell under the category of 'too dangerous' for narcoleptic Rory and 'I'll do it at the weekend' for Anna. Alicia could not remember the last weekend that her mother had spent at home, and decided that she had better replace the bulb herself, when she next had the chance.

At the top of the stairs, she did not turn left to her bedroom, but right, past the bathroom and directly to her parents' bedroom, without her eyeline grazing David's door: a little trick that she had adopted subconsciously and mastered through habit. The smell of fresh paint was strong and she might have considered that her mother had returned to finish the volcanic vista, had Rory not maintained his position facing, if not watching, the front door.

The light was on and nothing was amiss, except a poorly-made bed. The painting on the easel remained as incomplete as it had been when she checked the room that morning, to see whether her mother had returned in time for school. Glancing over her shoulder towards the stairs with the sting of dishonesty in her chest, Alicia pulled a sheet of paper from her pocket. She thought she had found the last of the 'Missing' posters, but this one had been caught in a hedge at the end of Gardner Road. She unfolded the paper with the tremulous fingers of one receiving examination results.

David's face grinned from the centre of the page, the once-brilliant colour faded to bleached tones. 'Missing' stood in black letters across the top of the A4 sheet, with a description of David and the family contact details beneath the photo. To look into her brother's eyes, it was as if—

No, thought Alicia. *No.* She folded the sheet of paper and sat on the edge of the bed, a surge of emotion rising within her like a tidal current beating against a splintering dam. Tears pricked her eyes and the vision of her parents' bedroom doorway fell to fragments of memory: Alicia tearing a poster from a telephone pole last February and sliding down to sit in the snow; clenched fists against her mouth, screaming until the paper was wet; a crunch of footprints; an arm around her shoulders: *There, there.* Never before had she seen such emotion in her headmistress's face. Never again would she let herself indulge in such weakness.

She shuddered inwardly, took a breath and turned towards the paintings behind her. On her mother's side of the bed hung the portrait that Alicia had painted of them both. Pocketing the poster, she stepped up to the painting, smiling at the immature strokes of her fourteen-year-old self. Dark hair fell down her face, parted symmetrically across her forehead like a waterfall broken by an overhanging rock. Her large eyes, a malachite green, beamed back at her in almost Disneyesque proportions. Alicia sat with her mother behind her, their heads facing forward and their bodies at a forty-five-degree angle. Anna's cropped blonde hair was a field of gold: wild sunflowers and wheat. Her young, elfin face was as pale as Alicia's.

'You have your mother's talent,' said her father, her teachers, her friends. Her mother's talent was what Alicia admired above all else, and she considered it outlandish that anyone might compare the two, as though by complimenting Alicia they were failing to see the beauty that Anna had uncovered. Only in her prouder moments could Alicia see the humour she had caught in her mother's wild black eyes: the promise that nothing is as serious as the world wants us to believe.

Wrinkling her brow, Alicia bent over the bedside table and brushed a finger against a spot of white paint on the spine of her mother's book, *Lucid Dreaming: A Beginner's Guide.* The tiny speck, no larger than a poppy seed, smudged against the pad of her forefinger.

In the absence of her father, Alicia shot an accusatory glare in the direction of his face on the canvas above his side of the bed. Patches of the white wall appeared to be wet. She stepped around the bed and her fingers lifted to the canvas, tracing her father's cheek, as though by following each brushstroke she might discern how her mother had captured that look of innocence that defied adulthood. Beneath ruddy cheeks, Rory's complexion was at odds with his Irish heritage, tan where his children were pale. From him they had inherited only his dark hair, which—considering a summary of his characteristics—Anna joked was a blessing.

And then there was David. How accurately had her mother replicated each freckle on her brother's cheeks? She would like to position him beside the portrait with his back to the wall—and surely, at twelve-years-old, he would stand as tall as it now—in order to compare the image with reality. When painting David's eyes, had her mother made a conscious decision for them to look directly at the viewer, or had this white lie been born unwittingly?

Where are you hiding? She did not voice this thought aloud. David and Alicia had often played hide and seek when he was an infant and she was approaching the age of ten. As a blind child, David was notoriously bad at finding places to hide. He struggled with the concept of glass, and Alicia had laughed tears when she found him crouched behind the patio doors at their grandmother's house, for all the world to see.

'I'm eighteen on Wednesday,' she whispered to her brother's portrait. 'That's two birthday presents you owe me.' Tapping a finger against his chin, she continued: 'I tell you what, come home and we'll call it even.'

Carefully, she gripped the sides of the portrait and lifted it from the wall, angled towards her so that nothing fell from behind it. She took the poster from her pocket and placed it in the recess behind the painting, where it crunched against the others. She then lifted the painting back against the wall.

When her mother had first come home with a poster that she had pulled from the window of a newsagent in Guildford, Alicia had been speechless. She had been unable to articulate the words to express her anger. An hour later, she had stepped into her parents' bedroom and managed to utter three words: 'Put it back.'

Anna had shaken her head, sighed and reasoned that it had been over a year since David's disappearance: everybody in Godalming—everybody in Surrey—knew her brother's face. The posters served no purpose other than to fade in shop windows as a constant reminder that the police had failed to find him. Alicia did not argue with her mother, but when she found the poster in the bin, she decided that was not its rightful place. She would store them for David and show him when he returned, if only so he knew what trouble he had caused.

Her attention was snagged by a muddy mark on the pillowcase. She leaned closer to look at what appeared to be a footprint, igniting her curiosity as to what her father had been up to while she was at school.

The scent of paint was heavy in the air; she stepped up to the window and opened both panes outwards. A full moon hung in a clear sky, so bright that the black canvas upon which it lay was starless and empty. Alicia set her elbows on the windowsill and gazed at the moon. With an absent mother, a missing brother and a sleeping father, she was afforded a level of independence that other teenagers could only yearn for. An overwhelming loneliness rose within her, as though the moon were all that remained in an empty sky, and she all that remained in an abandoned household. Was it this oppressive tranquillity that drove solitary wolves to raise their heads and howl?

Her gaze drifted to the neighbouring house, where lights were on in two of the windows. It had been two years since David's disappearance and eighteen months since the family next door had deemed the neighbourhood unsafe for their young daughter. The house had remained empty until the previous day.

When Alicia's eyes found the front lawn, two things struck her as unusual. The first was that the vehicle in the driveway was a police car. The second was that the roof of the vehicle appeared to be glowing green. She then spotted a similar illumination on the tip of her finger. The paint was not white: it was glow-in-the-dark.

Her pulse quickened as she turned to face the wet marks above her parents' headboard. Suddenly, the muddy footprint on the pillow was not clumsy, but sinister. Striding through each heartbeat, she crossed the carpet and reached for the switch by the door. Her finger paused for a half a second before she turned out the lights.

In bold capital letters, a single word glowed bright against the darkness.

MURDERER.

Dollhouse

GUS CROW HAD spent several hours over the past year faced with teaching staff and school counsellors exasperated by his profound indifference to education. But to be summoned to the headmistress's office on his first full day at a new school? That was a record. The girl beside him appeared as apathetic to her plight as he was, watching the headmistress as though she were a vaguely interesting cartoon. Yesterday had been a memorable start to life in Godalming and today was promising to follow suit.

'You told your uncle that the paint was your idea?' asked Melissa Lawson in a monotone. At forty years old, she was relatively young for her position at the prestigious school, though her grey eyes were as distant as a veteran's. The office reflected her sombre character: no paintings from infant pupils dotted the walls, no inspirational quotes urging everybody to keep calm and do something comical. All that had caught Gus's eye as he took a seat at the mahogany desk was an old dollhouse on a table in the corner of the room. The intricately carved wooden structure appeared to have been attacked with a sledgehammer and meticulously reassembled. With sky-blue paint peeling on cracked panels and bay windows missing tiny panes of glass, the quaint artefact struck such a contrast to the utilitarian office that it looked like an item confiscated rather than displayed.

'I thought she had thrown paint over his car,' said Gus in a soft, Southern-Irish accent. 'Not plastered *Murderer* across my neighbour's bedroom wall.'

The previous morning, Gus had strolled across the uncut grass to assess the damage to the police car and stood beside the young woman, who had not moved from her position at the corner of the lawn. He watched the bag slide off her shoulder and was about to ask why she had taken such spectacularly bold action against the authorities when a guttural cursing issued from the front door. Dressed only in boxer shorts, Sergeant Crow had demanded that the pair step forward and explain themselves. At the sight of the furious middle-aged man in his underwear, Gus and Winter had exchanged a smirk as they approached the house.

Gus had mistaken her open-mouthed silence for bewilderment, and he respected the rebel for not bolting down the street. In casual defiance, he said that it had been his idea to paint the car. The baffled police officer had scratched his bald head, asked for Winter's name and dismissed her abruptly, perhaps realising that he was in his boxers.

'Look at me making friends.' Gus had grinned as Winter tossed the paintbrush into the wheelie bin and disappeared around the corner. His uncle had taken him inside to pursue a line of inquiry that had gotten him nowhere, and Gus was sent to school that afternoon.

'Why would you say that you were involved?' asked the headmistress. Her blonde hair was pulled into a chignon bun at the back of her head, so tight that the skin was stretched thin and bloodless across her narrow face. With the white suit jacket and matching trousers, she could have passed for a marble statue at a war memorial.

Gus shrugged. 'It seemed like fun.'

Melissa Lawson studied the boy across her desk: the collar on his polo shirt half-up, half-down like a dog that had cocked one ear. Beneath a tangle of dark hair, green eyes met hers with a cheerful confidence. She had received a telephone call from Sergeant Crow last night, informing her that Winter Hazelby had allegedly written a threatening message on the wall of her art teacher's bedroom.

Melissa explained the situation between Anna Harrington and Winter, and had offered to deal with it personally. Sergeant Crow considered this an excellent idea, and had asked that she speak with Gus as well. Melissa had found the request odd: the new boy was likely trying to cover for Winter, as had dozens before him. But now she saw why the police officer wanted someone else to attempt a conversation with his nephew.

The headmistress opened her mouth to try another angle, but her phone rang in the pocket of her trousers. She held the device in both hands and two shrill rings sounded as she stared at the name on the screen. Tightening the bun at the back of her head, Melissa stepped out into the hall and closed the door behind her, leaving the pair alone in the office.

Gus shifted in his seat to face Winter, who remained silent. She pulled a slim denim satchel from the floor and flicked it onto the desk where it landed with a thud. She unbuckled the clasp with delicate fingers, her nails long and unpainted. Thick hair tumbled against her white cardigan like liquid ebony. One glance at those fierce eyes and tightly drawn lips and you knew where you stood with Winter: well beneath her.

He had been at school for five minutes yesterday when he first heard mention of her name. Arriving at the end of lunch, he had made straight for the canteen, where a pair of blonde twins were perched either end of a bench straining beneath the weight of the rugby team. Over the boys' heads, the girls exchanged theatrical whispers over Winter's whereabouts. Nearby students paused with cheeseburgers floating before their mouths, staring at their plates and listening intently as the twins warped whatever Winter had told them about her absence.

'When they arrested her,' one girl surreptitiously declared, 'the ash from the burning car fell on her hair like snow.'

As Gus rounded the table on the way to the food counter, one of the rugby boys caught his eye. A loud voice cut through the twins' reconstruction of Winter's struggle in handcuffs.

'Hey, new kid!'

There was the look that Gus had seen before on the faces of the popular and slow-witted, as the boy raked his body in search of a comment that might impress his peers: 'Your shoes are crap!'

Gus had glanced down at his tattered trainers, raised his eyes and winked.

'Your opinion says more about your character than it does about my shoes.'

'What?'

But Gus had strolled off to find a sandwich.

In the toilets and on the back benches, Winter's name circulated the school, spoken with shock and awe, but never scorn. In history class, a thin, breadstick of a boy had told Gus that Winter's attack on the police car was obviously a publicity stunt, since Winter was in the process of renaming the planet. At his locker, he overheard a girl with a voice so plummy it sounded as though she had burned her tongue suggest that Winter had committed the crime in blind rage: the police refused to believe that Anna Harrington had anything to do with the death of her boyfriend.

Now Gus watched Winter open her notebook and continue to brainstorm what appeared to be alternatives to 'Earth'. Moving between three schools over the past year, he had met so many 'Winters' that he struggled to tell them apart. Schools were rife with teenagers desperate to model themselves on popstar Ashley L'Amour, whose latest album, NV Dis, encouraged a ruthless clamber to the top of the social ladder, setting fire to each rung you surpassed. Considering himself invulnerable to the opinion of others, Gus registered bubbles of irritation when faced with the self-obsessed. He could not understand the filters placed between what people thought and what they said, as though they believed their answers to be genuine and their images authentic. He knew that he was different; he had no expectation or desire to 'fit in', but at least he was not pretending.

Winter had affected a lofty, purposeful air as she added ideas to her brainstorm of new names for the planet, and was currently circling what looked like 'Vivador'. Gus quelled the rising bubbles.

'You're very pretty,' he stated.

'You're hopelessly odd,' Winter replied, her eyes not moving from the page.

Gus folded his arms. 'Is that so?'

She made no response. He leaned forward and rapped his knuckles against the edge of the desk, drawing in the scent of polished wood.

'Why do you think Anna Harrington murdered your boy-friend?'

The scratching of the pen gave way to a pregnant silence. Winter sat back in her chair and stared in the direction of the dollhouse as she took the bait.

'Jack was swimming in the school pool over the break, prac-tising for Nationals. He's the best swimmer in school. Best rugby player. And the best—well, he was. They said he drowned. They said Mrs—that woman says she found him dead in the water.'

She turned to Gus and fire blazed in those chestnut eyes.

'She wasn't even supposed to be in school. Alicia—her daugh-ter—thought she was on a pottery course in Bath. Everyone knows Mrs Harrington lost the plot when David ran away. And it's not as if she was playing with a full deck before he disappeared. If I were her kid, I'd have run away too.'

Gus's second and final lesson the previous day had been an art class. At Valmont School, art was a compulsory subject for all year groups, with Year 13s receiving two classes a week. His peers were clearly disappointed to have a supply teacher and the air was thick with whispers: *Where is Mrs Harrington?* An unreliable informer whose face Gus did not recall had told him that Winter had hated the art teacher long before Jack drowned. Alicia's eccentric mother could be harsh when she felt effort was lacking, and had said that Winter's GCSE submission had the 'artistic panache of a squirrel.'

Winter stared into Gus's green eyes in an attempt to gauge whether he believed her.

'You're very pretty,' he repeated. 'On the surface, I mean. Like a cupcake with a Brussels sprout in the middle.'

Winter blinked long eyelashes.

'Some people like Brussels sprouts,' she said.

'Some think they're the epitome of evil,' he replied.

She returned to her pad of paper.

'Let's imagine,' said Gus, tracing the mahogany grain with a fingernail, 'that Anna Harrington was so devastated by the disappearance of her son, she started drowning kids at school. You reckon painting *Murderer* on her bedroom wall will scare her into a confession?'

Winter sighed and continued to doodle as she spoke. 'I don't want to scare her. I want her to know that we know.'

'We?'

She shrugged. 'Everybody.' She eyed him without moving her head. 'This is Valmont. This is my school. And if I say that woman murdered Jack, that's what happened.'

'Methinks the sprout hath a high opinion of itself. You might want to save some time there,' he nodded at the paper, 'and campaign to name the planet *Winter*.'

She dropped her pen and spun in his direction.

'Methinks thath—Me—I will *literally* bite you.'

'Well, I guess that makes me the cupcake.'

The door opened and Mrs Lawson returned to the room. The headmistress stared at the blank screen of her phone before taking her seat.

'Back to class, Master Crow,' she uttered with the flick of a wrist as she drew an organiser from the desk drawer and placed it before her. 'And you're to stay away from Alicia Harrington. She's suffered quite enough.'

Gus frowned, rose from his seat and shouldered his rucksack. He nodded in farewell, realised that both women were studying the papers in front of them, and made his exit.

When the door closed, Melissa adopted a light tone. 'That was our new school counsellor on the phone. I've booked you in for a session on Monday.'

Winter watched her make a note in the organiser with tiny neat lettering.

'You think I'm going to sit back and listen to some hippy tell me it's all right to cry?'

Melissa lay the pen beside the calendar and put her elbows on the mahogany desk. She placed the tips of her fingers together one by one and considered Winter across the top of them.

'Listen, you insufferable little tart. You don't like me and I've more respect for the plaque between your teeth than for attention-seekers like you. But I see no need to involve the police in this any further—an embarrassment that we both know your mother would be glad to avoid. So, you will do a session with the counsellor, we will pretend this never happened, and you can return to whatever social media platform you intend to self-combust on.'

Winter ran a tongue across her upper gums. Melissa lifted the pen and lowered her gaze to the organiser.

'Now get out.'

Same mind, different problems

SHE CAME INTO *this world with a brush in her hand; that girl was painting before she could talk*: such things could not be said of Alicia. It was not until her thirteenth birthday that she expressed any interest in her mother's creative pursuits. In her pre-teen years, it was not indifference that Alicia felt when she saw Anna at the canvas, but resentment. Though too young to articulate her frustration, Alicia understood her desire to leave the room when her mother was painting; to keep the crayons in their box unused and the gifts of slender brushes and tiny acrylic pots unopened. With a blind brother, she could think of nothing so inconsiderate as to spend her time generating images that he would never see. Had she the talent, she might have learned to play the piano and sing, filling his dark world with music. But before Alicia learned that she had inherited her mother's keen eye, she had echoed her capacity for singing in tune. David's ears were to be protected.

So, Alicia described the world to him. The rainbow sheen on puddles that marked the passage of an oily wheel; the manner in which raindrops chased one another down a pane of glass, drawn by unseen bonds. It was on her thirteenth birthday that Alicia realised why her mother painted. To capture the world in its entirety, you had to see the details that others overlooked. The act of painting was not a means to an end: the artist was not driven by the desire to create something new, but to uncover what might otherwise remain unseen. Alicia pulled the unused easel from the back of her cupboard and she painted. She searched for the smallest detail and lost herself in that delicate struggle to replicate it. And then she described these details to her brother, painting his world with every hidden beauty she could find.

On the eve of her eighteenth birthday, Alicia braced herself for another style of painting: the erasing of a threatening message left for her mother. Some details were best left in the dark.

The floorboards under the carpet creaked as Rory carried the can of white paint towards his bedroom. Alicia dashed through the doorway and took it from his hands, along with the pair of brushes in his pocket.

'I'll take these, Dad. Last thing we need is paint on the floor!'

She said it lightly, as a joke, but his hazel eyes crinkled and he pushed his empty hands into the pockets of his pyjamas. The pyjamas, striped in shades of blue, had been a Christmas present from Anna three years ago. Rory and David had received matching sets and when this was described to David he insisted that they wear them at home during the day. Since his son's disappearance, Rory had worn little else. His eyebrows twitched and the doorbell rang.

'I'll get it,' he said quickly and turned for the stairs. Biting down the urge to protest, Alicia carried the paint to the bedroom. Each time her father trundled up and down the carpeted steps a die was rolled. It was only a matter of time before it landed on the wrong number and his narcolepsy struck. Rory refused to move a bed downstairs like an invalid, and his nights on the sofa had become an unspoken compromise while Anna was away.

Alicia placed the can at the foot of the bed and heard two pairs of feet down the corridor. Rory stepped into the room followed by a boy of her age. The boy had one hand scratching his dark, scruffy hair and the other buried in the front pocket of his hooded jacket.

'This is Gus Crow, the boy next door.' Rory beamed as though he had found one of her childhood heroes in the street. 'He's offered to help with the painting.' He clapped his hands together and shrugged. 'I'll leave you to it, then—we've only two brushes.'

Not remotely abashed that he was in his pyjamas, Rory winked at his daughter and left. There were a dozen brushes in a cupboard down the side alley and Alicia had the uncomfortable feeling that she was being set up.

'Thought you might need a hand.' Gus offered his and the pair greeted one another in a formal, awkward manner. His smile was playful, but with the dark lines under his eyes, he might have passed for an undead extra in a low-budget horror movie.

'I was wondering if anyone would ever take that house,' said Alicia. 'You've just moved in, this weekend?'

Gus put his hands in the pockets of his jeans and nodded.

'Green as they come.'

'You're Irish?' said Alicia, gesturing as though to his voice box. 'My dad, he's—'

'Dublin, yeah, he said. My mother's from Galway, I grew up there. So to speak.'

'I've never been. Dublin, or Galway—not to Ireland. If half of my dad's university stories are true I doubt they'd let him back in the country.'

Gus smiled politely and folded his arms, never still for a moment.

'You weren't in school today?'

'I couldn't sleep last night,' Alicia answered.

'I bet. Mum's out searching for your brother, you've crazies writing messages on your walls, and your dad's sleeping for the both of you!'

Alicia tensed, unaware that her mouth was open. He wasn't being obtuse; she heard no malice or mockery in his tone. His expression was placid.

'And what's your excuse?' she asked, cocking her head and mirroring his folded arms. 'You look like you haven't slept in a week.'

'Weeks. Plural,' he said, grinning. 'Let's call it insomnia.'

26

Alicia saw the details that others overlooked. Gus was confident, but his relaxed attitude was feigned. The self-consciousness in his eyes was reflected in his quick movements. He watched her with the manner of a lazy house cat that might leap into action at the hint of a threat.

'What will you do about her?' asked Gus, nodding vaguely at the wall.

'Who?'

'The artist. Winter.'

Alicia would never have told her father about the message. She would have painted over it herself while he was downstairs—made up some excuse about cracks in the wall. But she had screamed and he had woken. Rory had contacted the police immediately and the pair were surprised when their new neighbour appeared at the door two minutes later. Sergeant Crow had spoken in an irritable manner, his face reddening into his bald scalp as he informed them that he knew who was responsible. At the mention of Winter's name, it was Alicia who had suggested that he contact Melissa Lawson. *She's the headmistress—she knows Winter—she'll know what to do.*

'Well,' said Alicia, following Gus's gaze to where the letters lay invisible on the illuminated wall. 'Winter likes to run at night. I was thinking about shaving her head, painting her scalp and giving the bats something to aim at.'

Gus laughed: a sudden burst of merriment, and Alicia's cheeks flushed.

'Winter has issues,' she added softly. 'Her boyfriend just died, so…'

'Same mind, different problems,' said Gus. 'That's what my father used to say.'

There was a curious look in his feline eyes, as though he was trying to discern the outline of the writing on the wall.

'I'm sorry about what she did to his car,' said Alicia.

'That's my uncle's car.'

The curious look vanished in a blink and he stepped closer to the bed, feet either side of the can of paint, as he studied the painting of Rory and David.

'So, the little lad just took off, eh?'

'You've done your homework.'

'Gotta know who's living next door, right?'

Alicia nodded and turned to the portrait. With Gus in the room, she could not bring herself to meet her brother's eyes. She let her gaze hover on his mouth: his lips slightly parted, as always, in anticipation of what was coming next.

'David's blind.' Alicia spoke in a neutral manner, as though the two of them were assessing the evidence at a crime scene. 'Dad had burned his hand on the radiator and Mum was applying some kind of salve. I was at the park, playing tennis. David was playing football in the garden—one of those ones with the bell inside? He was getting pretty good actually. Mum can't remember when she heard the bell stop. The side gate was open. He was just... gone.'

'*I'm sorry*' hovered on Gus's lips, but he knew how trite it sounded, having heard it countless times over the past year. Saying nothing, he crossed to the portrait of Alicia and her mother and picked up the book on the bedside table.

'Lucid dreaming?'

Alicia shook her head. 'Mum got into it when he disappeared.'

Gus read a line from the back of the book: '*Wake up within the dream and meet your subconscious face to face.*'

'I guess everyone needs an escape from reality.'

Gus nodded. 'Can I borrow this?'

Alicia grinned and shrugged. 'Sure.'

Gus studied his neighbour. Dark hair framed a heart-shaped face and her porcelain skin was so white that it made her green eyes luminous, like the glowing roof of his uncle's car. Alicia's eyes were confident and her smile genuine. She was an open book, honest, and—given how readily she had accepted help with this sensitive task—terribly lonely.

Alicia registered pity in the boy's eyes and nodded to the can at her feet.

'We'd better get started. At least one of us might get a decent sleep tonight!'

Gus nodded to the paintings on the wall. 'Let's get these down.'

Alicia stiffened. She waited for Gus to reach out for the portrait of her and her mother before quickly lifting her father and David from the wall. She lowered the painting to the floor with one hand pressed against the posters concealed behind the canvas.

When Gus lifted Alicia's portrait from the wall, something fell from behind it. A small book landed on the pillow with a soft thud. Gus froze with the painting in his hands: something hidden— something private—he fought an urge to look away, his eyes fixed on a symbol embossed on the black leather cover. Alicia stepped around the bed and lifted the book in both hands, tracing a nail across the chipped gold foil in its centre. An oval folded in on itself in the middle to create the image of an eye, and from the top of the inner circle a jagged line struck a bolt of lightning across the iris.

Something hidden, something private; before Alicia could give her rational mind a second to play with, she turned the cover. Scrawled upon the creased pages, in a cursive script that might befit a biblical scroll, names had been crossed out. Gus watched Alicia flick through the book, spanning dozens of names until they ended abruptly, over halfway through, and gave way to blank pages.

Alicia thumbed to the last marked page. Of the eight names, two were yet to be struck through. Her heartbeat found a new rhythm as her eyes locked upon the final name in her mother's hidden book: *Melissa Lawson.*

The house next door

UNOPENED BOXES SURROUNDED the single bed. The white sheet slung across the mattress was untucked and the pillow had been stuffed inside a T-shirt, its pillowcase hidden within one of the boxes. The wardrobe door was open, revealing two wire coat-hangers draped in cobwebs. A hooded jacket and black jeans lay discarded in a crumpled pile by the door. Gus lifted the sash window to coax a breeze into his stuffy bedroom and collapsed back on his bed, dressed only in a pair of charcoal-grey sweatpants. Eager eyes roved the pages of the book in his hands, mining its content as though to unearth the secret to eternal life.

But it was not life that Gus was after. It was the chance to escape the waking world for a few hours each night, to break that interminable cycle before the rising sun cast long shadows, rolling out the carpet for a carbon copy of yesterday's struggles. In the twelve months he had spent in the reluctant care of his father's twin brother, Gus had been expelled from three public schools in Galway and subjected to a string of home tutors, each flummoxed by his attitude to learning. At seventeen, Gus could have found himself a job, or an internship, had he any motivation. Joe insisted that, while Gus deliberated, he might at least attempt to turn his grades around.

'There's something wrong with that boy,' he had heard one tutor comment as she informed his uncle that it would be her final visit. 'He's got the ability, all right—he's not lacking in that department. But I've never met a child with such a complete and utter disregard—'

'Thank you for your time,' his uncle had seen her out, having spotted Gus's feet through the banisters at the top of the stairs. At school, it was his peers that had driven him to distraction: their relentless competition to determine who was the best at everything that could be measured, and then to lord this, consciously or otherwise, over everyone else. Had Gus known that he would be exchanging the tedious displays of his self-obsessed peers with the maddening silence of his tight-lipped uncle, he might have made more of an effort in class.

'He doesn't mean to be difficult,' a counsellor had consoled the policeman during an exit interview at his previous school, speaking as though Gus was not lounging in the chair beside him. 'He's got a lot on his mind.'

That much was true, and Gus was certain that he would have a good deal less on his mind if he were able to process it; and in order to do that, he needed to sleep.

On the box of clothes that Gus was using as a bedside table sat an old lamp that he had found at the back of the wardrobe. The jagged glass rim of a broken shade was visible and the naked bulb glowed with a fervent brightness, straining to prove its value. Under the glare, a small white pot, unlabelled, contained the pills that Gus took each night before he climbed beneath the sheet. The pills promised eight hours of dreamless sleep, and this promise was a lie. His uncle had bent some rules and broken others to source the medication and insisted that they would work just fine if Gus tired himself out with exercise, rather than drifting around the house converting oxygen to carbon dioxide. Rarely one to follow his uncle's instructions, Gus had started running at night in an effort to quiet his racing mind. Yet his mind raced on.

He was reading a chapter on the different ways to initiate a lucid dream, from both the waking and dreaming states, when he was disturbed by the sound of a car. Heaving leaden limbs from the bed, he dropped the book on the desk leaning against the wardrobe and pressed his forehead to the window. Midnight was approaching, and

Sergeant Crow had finally returned from the station. The orange glare from a street light glanced off the policeman's scalp as he ran a hand over the dent in the roof of the vehicle, muttered something inaudible and turned for the front door. A knot tightened in Gus's stomach as he raised his eyes to the house next door. The master bedroom was dark, but light from the corridor spilled through the doorway. Someone was still up.

He had caught sight of the names on that last marked page before Alicia snapped the book shut and tossed it at the foot of the bed like something inconsequential. He had cleared his throat and proceeded to pry the lid from the can of paint, as if he had seen nothing of interest. And so began the charade, with both parties acting like there was nothing suspicious about a list of names hidden behind the painting of a woman accused of murder.

As the pair painted over Winter's message, the air had been heavy with unspoken thoughts. Gus caught Alicia staring at the painted image of her mother, face-up on the floor. It was the only image of Anna Harrington that he had seen.

'Is that your work?' he asked, caught by the equine eyes on the canvas.

'A few years back.'

'You've some talent.'

Painting over the message had not taken long. Two minutes later, Alicia was thanking Gus for his help and—through an unconvincing smile—wishing the insomniac a good sleep. He had returned the smile and thanked her for the book on lucid dreaming before making his exit.

He reached home with a pounding heart, taking the stairs two at a time, his limbs thrumming with adrenaline. Eight names had been written on the page: six struck through and two remaining. He had recognised the name at the bottom of the page, having been in the headmistress's office that afternoon. But it was the last name to be crossed out that had him pulling the phone from his pocket. He keyed 'Jack Henson' into the internet browser.

The first hit, a news report from *Surrey Speaks*, showed a well-built blond boy of his age, smiling with hands gripping the shoulders of his teammates. *Seventeen-year-old drowns in school pool*: the headline was followed by details of the police investigation. *Found by the art teacher, Anna Harrington.* Gus swallowed, his throat dry, staring at the image for over a minute until all he saw was the absolute certainty in Winter's eyes.

Now he looked through the window of Anna's empty bedroom, through the open doorway to the lit corridor, wondering whether Alicia was speaking with her father. Were they talking about the boy next door, fearing what he had seen?

There was a single rap on the door behind him and Gus's uncle stepped into the bedroom. Joe Crow was a heavyset man with broad shoulders and a narrow waist, half an inch shorter than his nephew but twice his mass. Wrinkles ran in lines from his small, dark eyes to the edges of his hairless scalp as he surveyed the scene before him.

His irritable gaze drifted from the pile of clothes at his feet to the unopened boxes before settling on the desk against the wall. Amongst the spoils of an upturned bag—mobile phone charger, micro-USB cable, half-finished pack of chewing gum, house keys— he spotted the cover of Anna's book. Gus turned from the window as his uncle crossed the room in two strides. Keys slid, jangling to the floor, as Joe snatched the book from the desk.

'Where'd you get this?' he asked, eyeing *Lucid Dreaming: A Beginner's Guide* as though it were a magazine filled with obscene material. Gus took a glance at the pristine, navy Surrey Police uniform and grinned, ready to be arrested for possession of dangerous goods. He sat on the bed with his legs crossed beneath him and his hands on his knees.

'Alicia Harrington lent it to me.'

He delivered the line with a well-honed look of boyish innocence, knowing precisely the reaction it would provoke. And there it was: fear in those bullet-hole eyes as control slipped through his uncle's iron grip.

'I asked you to stay away from her,' the man uttered in a low voice. Sergeant Crow had been relocated from Galway to Surrey the previous month. Gus had congratulated his uncle on rising to a rank of such unprecedented importance that the government was relocating him internationally, from one law enforcement agency to another. Oblivious to the sarcasm, his uncle had mumbled something about being trained as a British police constable, and that the return from Ireland to the UK was inevitable. The final twist in this unconvincing tale was that Joe had chosen to rent the house next door to the one girl in school with whom Gus was forbidden any interaction.

'You did mention that, Uncle, I remember now. But I don't think you ever gave me a reason?' *You never give me a reason.* Gus swallowed a bubble of irritation and continued in a low tone: 'How am I supposed to avoid the girl next door when you won't even tell me why?'

'This is why,' said Joe, shaking the book before his nephew's eyes.

Gus held his breath, leaving a space in which Joe might elaborate on the truncated response. He watched the struggle in his uncle's eyes: truth filtered into fiction.

'Her mother—she has funny ideas. She's—' He shook his head dismissively, as if it was too great an effort to generate another lie for Gus's sake. Instead, he flipped the book to read the back cover and sighed.

'What do you want with this?'

If Joe found that book so interesting, what might he make of the little secret that had fallen from behind Anna Harrington's portrait?

The policeman would likely have something to say about a list of names struck through, which included that of a recently deceased teenager. But whatever conclusions he drew would not be shared with Gus. The boy met his uncle's gaze. Both kept their secrets and exchanged their lies.

'You've heard of it then? Lucid dreaming? Waking up within the dream, creating whatever takes your fancy. I thought, since you'll never dance for me, Uncle, I could envisage a glorious stage—an amphitheatre—with you pirouetting under a spotlight in the centre. Wouldn't that be grand?'

'You think this is a joke?'

'A joke? I didn't think you were familiar with the term.'

Joe said nothing. Gus rubbed his eyes and stared hard at the police officer's face—a face that would mirror his father's, had he the dark hair or any semblance of humour.

'Total control of your dreams, that's what the book claims. I thought, maybe if I can take control, then whatever you're so bloody afraid of—'

'Are you out of your mind?' Joe raised his voice and Gus's spine went rigid. 'What do you think the pills are for?'

The pair looked at the white pot on the bedside box.

'I don't need pills,' Gus uttered sourly. He drew both hands down his face, slowly, as though trying to remove a mask. 'I need to sleep. Natural sleep. I can't think straight.'

'Then go for a run.'

Joe tucked the book under his arm and left the bedroom.

Marigolds

THE WALLS OF David's bedroom were painted as the sea and sky. On a coat of light blue, Alicia and her mother had fixed large amorphous masses of cotton wool. The lowest of these clouds, within reach of grubby fingers, had greyed and balded. At the base of the wall, thick, sweeping strokes of dark blue had been coated with varnish, flowing like waves of glass.

Sitting against the waves, Alicia ran her fingertips over the golden symbol on the cover of the leatherbound book. From a young age she had mimicked her brother as he traced objects to study their texture. Most textures felt the way they looked, such as the coarse sandpaper that their mother used on wooden sculptures, and the dusty, warm cavity after a pool cue has been chalked. Others were surprising: the static electricity on the old television screen at their grandmother's house; the loose, dry skin of the toads that nestled between rocks surrounding the garden pond. What did David picture when he explored such things with curious fingers and tentative lips?

With the book resting on her thighs, Alicia flicked through the pages. Dozens and dozens of names—how many had she keyed into the internet browser on her phone? Thirty? Fifty? Each name was struck through with a bold line; each person's death had been unexpected and sudden.

Swallowing down the rising nausea, she turned to the page that she had studied for so long she could see it with her eyes closed. These final eight names were not written in her mother's handwriting—of that she was sure. The lettering on the time-worn paper was looped and slender, like ancient wisdom set to parchment with a quill, left to dry and sealed with a wax stamp.

Of the six names struck through, she recognised only one: Jack Henson. The line drawn through his name was not in the black ink that bled into the page, but the mark of a blue ballpoint pen. A snake twisted through Alicia's gut. Her rational mind struggled to generate plausible alternatives to the most sinister conclusion. Perhaps her mother had found the book and decided to conceal it, rather than show this incriminating evidence to the police? Perhaps Winter had placed the book behind the painting when she left her message, in order to frame her teacher? But each of these explanations was a fantasy, born of a mind unwilling to face the truth: Jack Henson was dead and her mother had struck his name from the list.

The page trembled between Alicia's fingers. On seeing his name, she had chucked the book to the end of the bed and reached for the paintbrush. Surely Gus had spotted his headmistress's name, but had he recognised Jack's? Each had waited for the other to comment, complicit in their silence: *nothing to see here.* As they painted over the invisible word, Gus had caught her staring at the portrait on the floor, her mother's smile promising that nothing is as serious as the world wants us to believe. Images of Jack choking on chlorinated water had obscured her vision.

In David's bedroom, Alicia's phone lay on the carpet with the colourful façade of a sweetshop on the screen. An elderly woman stood in the doorway, hands behind her back and smiling eyes magnified through glasses. Orange flowers hung in baskets either side of the store name: *Marigolds.* Jack Henson was the last name to be struck through, leaving two on the list: Melody Wilson and Melissa Lawson. Alicia had keyed 'Melody Wilson' into the internet browser to find that she was the sole proprietor of a confectionary store in Bristol. Was it jumping to conclusions or was it common sense to assume that this is where her mother had spent the last few days? Through Alicia's sleep-deprived mind, drifting thoughts darkened like thunderclouds. If her mother was in Bristol, was Melody still alive?

She flung the book on top of her phone and was about to sink her head between her knees when something caught her eye. The corner of a loose sheet poked out from beneath the leather cover. She withdrew a sheet of bleached-white paper that had been tucked in the back of the book and, unfolding the paper, found a sketch in what was unmistakably her mother's style. In thin charcoal pencil, Anna had drawn a garden shed. No title in the corner, no words on the front or back; an unremarkable structure of wooden planks with no windows and a narrow door.

Alicia had seen this shed before. She stared at the door as though willing it to open, trying to recall why it was familiar. This shed lay at the bottom of a field, possibly at school. She grasped at the corners of memory fragments, but drew none into focus.

Exhausted by curiosity, Alicia dropped the sheet and pressed the heels of her palms to her eyes, willing the darkness to swallow her and the world to disappear. She sat with her elbows against her knees, palms to her eyes, and listened to the empty silence of her broken home.

Minutes later, she withdrew her hands and watched with curiosity as the cotton wool clouds drifted across the sky. She could not remember how she and her mother had managed to make the cotton wool move, and followed the passage of a cloud from behind a poster in the corner of the room to the window beside David's bed.

She stepped up to the open window, which overlooked the garden. In the centre of a well-tended lawn was the pond that she had requested for her eleventh birthday. Gawking at the inch of water at the bottom, she had wondered if fish could swim on their sides.

'Can't we fill it up more?' she had asked as her mother walled the shallow pit with large rocks.

'Your brother might fall in.'

'He'd dry off.'

'Honestly, Alicia. If he fell in, he might drown.'

'He'd have to lie down flat and try really hard.'

Her mother had laughed and continued building her ramparts.

Overlooking the garden, Alicia saw a sun high in the sky, which was odd given that night had fallen while she and Gus had painted the wall. This peculiarity circled to the forefront of her attention and two thoughts struck her simultaneously: this was a dream; she was aware.

An explosion of clarity—and everything sharpened in the highest definition. Sunlight filtered through the branches of the oak at the far end of the garden, with green leaves that wore spots of russet-brown as they succumbed to the change in season. From the reflection of the hyacinth in the still waters of the pond to the pair of butterflies circling the head of a sunflower, Alicia was stunned by the resplendent lucidity of the dream. Reality was bleak in comparison.

'You can control your dreams,' Anna had said with excitement when Alicia asked about her newfound interest in lucid dreaming. 'You can see anything, Alicia. Go anywhere. You're limited by imagination alone.'

Alicia could think of only one thing that her mother would want to see in a lucid dream, and the thought both thrilled and terrified her. As a child, she had often dreamed that a wolf stalked her. As this fear intensified, the belief grew and the wolf presented itself. In a dream, what you get is what you see. Standing at the window, Alicia felt the eyes on her back. The garden view blurred as a current of fear assaulted her. What if she turned to find the image of her missing brother—to see that freckled face in perfect clarity—only to wake beside his empty bed? Steeling herself, she faced the room.

It was not David that stood in the bedroom doorway, but a wolf.

The beast's head was lowered to the carpet, hackles raised between broad shoulders, spittle on red gums and fangs bared, bright as the whites of its eyes. The snake twisted in her gut, but the room did not tremble. The dream was lucid and her mind as sharp as the claws that gouged the carpet: this nightmare could do nothing but wake her.

Deflated by her resilience, the wolf loped from the room. Alicia followed. The carpet was soft beneath her feet and the banisters smooth between her fingers as she descended the stairs. A silver tail swished through the open front doorway and it was not until she stepped on the doormat that Alicia realised where the wolf would lead her: to Valmont school. She was seeking the shed along the contours of her memories.

The wolf padded around the corner of Gardner Road as she reached the end of her driveway. The street was empty and, though she knew it was a dream, she could not quell the surge of self-consciousness that had her glancing down at her black top and blue jeans, relieved that her imagination had not left her in underwear. She followed the wolf along the pavement, marvelling at the serrated leaves on a rosebush and paint peeling on a fence-post. She was approaching the row of shops that marked the midway point of her journey to school when the wolf slipped down a path to the right. She picked up her pace, disoriented by the change in direction. This pathway led to the park where she used to play tennis, but she could not recall a shed here.

The dirt path was narrow, bushes encroached on either side and sunlight through the boughs speckled the animal's back. When they reached the park, the wolf stalked between the tennis court and football field and to a small green on the far side. Crossing the cycle path to this triangle of grass, Alicia understood their destination. At the corner of this green, a solitary cottage nestled in the trees. Anna's mother, Eloise, had lived there until the day Alicia was born.

It had been empty ever since.

Alicia opened the gate in the stone-brick wall at the front of her grandmother's cottage. She ran her eyes over the weatherworn bricks and down to the marigolds in window boxes that gave the property that quintessential cottage image, like a child's drawing. She had not visited the cottage in years; it was unlikely that the abandoned house would be in the manicured state that she saw it now. The red door was gleaming in the sun as though newly painted, matching the colour of the tiles on the low roof. The wolf was nowhere to be seen.

The bright orange flowers reminded her of Melody Wilson's sweetshop, which in turn reminded her of her mother's hidden book. As this train of thought derailed her concentration, the cottage took on the quality of a gingerbread house. The golden-brown stone was soft and spongy, the stalks of marigolds striped like candy cane. She was losing herself in the dream.

Panic rose within her. Like ink through blotting paper, the acrid emotion tore through the fabric of the dream and she felt the wall of David's bedroom against her back. She latched her focus to the dream environment: the red front door was gone, replaced by the wood-panelled door of a shed. She reached out and twisted the iron handle, pulling the door open. A wolf howled and darkness engulfed her as the dream ended.

She was lying on the floor of David's bedroom. The ceiling light dazzled her eyes, bright as the sun. She glanced at the doorway, almost as surprised as she was relieved to find herself alone. Pocketing her phone and tucking the sketch in the back of the book, Alicia walked down the corridor, chased by the snores of her father from the floor below. In her parents' bedroom, she returned the book to its hiding place and drifted to the window: one last glance to see whether her mother's car had pulled into the driveway. While her driveway was bare, a police car sat outside the neighbouring property. Waiting.

Gus stepped through his front door wearing a neon-green vest and black shorts. Automatically, he raised his eyes to the neighbouring house and met Alicia's gaze through the bedroom window. He lifted a hand to wave and the snake curled in her gut. Alicia returned the wave and watched him slip beneath the glow of orange street lamps and sprint into the night.

She released her breath: 'One hundred…'

Ryan, age 7

I WAITED UNTIL everybody was asleep and I walked past the Leave-It door, where Daddy works. I walked right up to the Locked door and I put the dollhouse on the floor. I lifted the corner of the carpet and picked up the key. That's where Daddy hides it for me. That was the first time I used the key because I was scared before, but now I had a reason.

The stairs were covered in spiderwebs but they don't scare me, so I carried the dollhouse up them quietly. I was at the top of the house, where the walls are like under the stairs. There were broken shelves lying sideways and boxes with brown stains that looked like they were wet. There was only one window in the roof, and I stood right under it but only saw the black sky.

The dollhouse was actually very heavy so I put it down in front of the mirror. It wasn't a mirror like for Mummy's face and brushing teeth. It was taller than Daddy and when I sat on the floor it was so wide that I could only just touch the edges with my toes. I was pretty tired from carrying the dollhouse up the stairs, so I sat down and looked at the Ryan in the mirror.

I hadn't seen me that close before and if I looked at my eyes it looked like another Ryan was looking back. Mummy says that my eyes are going to get me in trouble one day, but she says that with a smile so she doesn't mean jail. Mummy says that I am her special little boy and that is our secret, because Sam does not have a mummy or a daddy. That's why he lives with us, so that Mummy can teach him.

I wasn't actually in the top of the house so that I could look at myself in the mirror. I pulled the torch from my pocket and I turned it on. The light went on and off, on and off, as I shone it in the mirror. Just like Mummy showed us in Science, the light reflected off the mirror and bounced back. I pushed the dollhouse in front of the mirror so that the light from the torch was shining in the windows. I pretended that there were people inside and the torch was the full moon.

It isn't exactly fair that Daddy reads to Sam every night. Sam has epilepsy—that's what makes him special. Daddy never reads to me. He tells me that I should reflect in the mirror instead—that's why he hides the key for me. But he doesn't mean I should throw myself against it and bounce back, no sir. He means that I should think about my problems. He says that the Ryan in the mirror will always help me decide what to do with the feelings that are too big for me.

Daddy gave Sam the dollhouse for his birthday. It wasn't exactly fair because dollhouses are for girls, so I took it from his bedroom when he was sleeping. There are two beds in his bedroom, but I am not allowed to sleep in the other one. Mummy says you never know when there might be another orphan who needs our help.

Dollhouses are for girls, so I couldn't give it back to Sam. This was my problem, but the Ryan in the mirror had an idea. I walked past the Leave-It door and to my bedroom. I opened my window so that the people inside could look out and see the fields and the trees that go on forever. Then I let go.

There was a terrible smash. I heard Daddy's voice through the Leave-It door, yelling Mummy's name—on and off, on and off.

'Melissa!'

CHAPTER TWO
Happy birthday

WHEN ALICIA ENTERED the kitchen to see her father with a fork in each hand and a grin on his face, uplit by the eighteen candles on a birthday cake, she very nearly screamed. She had spent the remainder of the night feverishly attempting to dream of her grandmother's cottage, certain that beyond that wood-panelled door lurked the memory that would unravel her knotted world. Her efforts yielded little over three hours of sleep and no dreams that she could recall.

When she steadied herself against the back of the chair at the kitchen table and admired the Victoria sponge that her father had managed to bake independently and in secret, she very nearly burst into tears. She blew out the candles and Rory hacked at the cake with a fork.

'Happy Birthday, darling,' he said, mirroring her delirious smile. He slid a massive portion onto a small plate and pushed it across the table with both hands. Alicia took a seat, lifted the fork and rubbed sleep from her eyes.

'How did—when? Thanks, Dad.'

She very nearly told him about the leatherbound book; but why spoil the moment? She plugged her mouth with cake. The sponge tasted of baking powder, but Rory hadn't noticed, finishing his equally gigantic slice in thirty seconds. She ate it all while he told her about the time that he and his university flatmate sold brownies at a charity bake sale and the Ultimate Frisbee team had fallen violently sick. His laughter ended with a cough as he caught her staring at the two empty chairs around the table. Creatures of habit, they would each sit in a particular chair. In Anna's chair, on Alicia's left, the central wooden spindle was loose and she would twist it until it squeaked, distracting David from whatever he was eating at the time.

'She'll be home later,' Rory's voice was quiet and comforting.

Alicia nodded, her eyes down as she carried the plates from the table. He would have said if he had heard from Anna; he must assume that she would not miss her daughter's eighteenth birthday. Alicia did not share his confidence. With a bright smile, she thanked him for the cake, planted a kiss on the top of his head and left to shower for school.

She did not go to school. Treading the pavement slabs as she had in her dream just hours before, Alicia's chest was tight, her ribcage a coiled spring. One of the girls would remember: *Happy Birthday*, and then it would spread. Birthday wishes would end in questions. They would ask why her mother was absent, and she would have to lie. They would want to ask about David, just to let her know that they had not forgotten, but they would stop them-selves, and that tiny awkward pause while one of them tried to think of something to say—

She turned down the path that led to the park. A nagging in the back of her mind, the cry of a buried memory: what had she forgotten? She was so tired, her eyes would pop out of her head if she sneezed, but not so tired as to believe that this trip to the cottage would jog her memory. Anxiety pushed her further from school and she counted her steps down the path, fabricating hope: she needed a reason not to respond to her mother's birthday wishes with accusations of murder.

At half past eight in the morning, the park was empty, except for a solitary magpie pecking at the foot of a bin. Alicia crossed the park in brisk steps, unable to shake the onion-skin image of the wolf ahead of her, stalking through her memory bank.

Her grandmother's cottage was the epitome of abandoned. The window boxes were overgrown and the red paint on the front door had all but flaked away. She had tried to describe the colour to David when her parents had painted it during their last visit to the cottage, almost a decade ago.

The rusted gate brayed like a donkey, and she walked down a path thick with weeds. Knowing the front door to be boarded from the inside, she passed under the boughs of trees along a dirt path down the left-hand side of the building. In the back garden, bottle caps and an empty crisp packet faded grey on the ground beneath a swing set. A broken beer bottle poked through a thicket of pampas grass: evidence of teenagers who had found a use for the vacant space. She passed the patio doors, with boards visible through the glass, to the tall bushes crowding the back door. Broad leaves pressing against the glass were pitted with holes: the work of hungry beetles. She had convinced her infant brother that their grandmother hole-punched the leaves to allow sunlight through. David was so trusting. How easy it must have been to kidnap him.

She plucked a loose pebble from what was once a flowerbed and prepared to break the glass panel in the back door. Pausing, she tried the handle. It was open. Old, rotting wood scraped across the tiles as Alicia entered the cottage.

The kitchen cupboards and worktops were clear. There was nothing on the walls but an ugly handcrafted plate that nobody had seen fit to store. A dead woodlouse lay upside down in the sink. She carried on down the corridor.

She was eight years old when she was last inside the cottage, running a pair of her brother's toy cars along the wall and describing the most epic of chases. David had waddled behind her in a nappy, following the sound of her voice and tracing muddy fingerprints in her wake. Now, she brushed a smudge of dirt from the wallpaper and glanced up the stairs. Skylights in the bedroom lit a narrow landing. In comparison, the room at the front of the house was dark and dank, like a cave. Three boards had been nailed across the back of the door, and two across the windows on either side. A small, cracked window beside the mantelpiece received the remnants of sunlight that were not swallowed up by the neighbouring trees.

Alicia scanned the sparse contents of the room as though a useful memory might surface. A sofa faced the door, covered with a dustsheet. The room was otherwise unfurnished. Dents in the brown carpet marked where a television cabinet had stood, and the coffee table that was now at Rory's bedside. Loose wires jutted from the walls where light fittings had hung. Stepping over cigarette burns on the carpet (the work of teenagers that had accessed the property before Rory put up the boards), Alicia walked to the single item on the mantelpiece. An ornamental stone monkey, the size of her fist, pressed both hands to its eyes, playing hide and seek.

'What have you done with my brother?' Alicia whispered, lifting the ornament from the mantel and allowing herself a smile that fell when she heard a voice upstairs. She raised her eyes to the ceiling and a floorboard creaked overhead.

The voice was angry, muffled as it travelled from the bedroom above: *What am I supposed to do?*

Alicia's heart pounded in her temples. The front door was boarded up; her only way out was to pass the stairs. The stone monkey slipped through her fingers and landed on the corner of the fireplace with a loud crack.

The floorboards creaked again, twice—footsteps crossing the room in the direction of the stairs. Alicia picked up the monkey and considered hurling it through the cracked window. She could just squeeze through it, but would shred herself on broken glass in the process. Holding the monkey to her chest in both hands, she listened. No footsteps, no talking. Were they listening for her?

She crept along the spongy carpet back towards the corridor, stepping over the tell-tale floorboard that had creaked during games of hide and seek. At the foot of the stairs, she paused, hearing nothing. She took a step forward and a silhouette broke the light in the landing above: a figure at the top of the steps.

Winter's face was lost in shadow. She wore a loose white shirt and a large leather belt, dressed to impress at school.

'What are you doing here?' Her tone was accusatory as she descended the stairs.

'This is my grandmother's house. Who's up there?' asked Alicia, looking over Winter's shoulder, expecting a second face to emerge.

Genuine surprise creased Winter's brow as she replied: 'Nobody.'

'I heard you talking to someone.'

Winter shook her head, reaching the bottom step, and Alicia pushed past her, marching up the stairs with the monkey in her hands.

'Alicia...' Winter called, irritation in her voice as she chased after her.

The landing was five paces across, with a bathroom on the right and a bedroom on the left. Alicia turned for the bedroom. A mattress that had previously leaned against the sloping walls was now in the centre of the room, beneath a purple, patterned sleeping bag. Light flooded the small room through two skylights in the ceiling, catching the gold chain on Winter's denim satchel by the corner of the mattress. There was nobody in the room.

'Seriously?' asked Winter when Alicia strode to the corner cupboards, opening doors to the bare eaves.

'I heard you.' Alicia straightened up, looking past Winter in the direction of the bathroom. Winter folded her arms, her glare corrosive.

'I was talking to Jack.'

There was a flash of vulnerability in her eyes; a curl to her lip:

49

this was not a lie. Winter was a cornered animal, forced into confessing that she had been arguing with her dead boyfriend. Alicia paused, then dropped the ornamental monkey on the bed.

'Why are you here?' she asked.

'That's none of your business.'

'You broke into my grandmother's—'

Winter closed the distance between them.

'She killed him.'

Glowing green letters flashed before Alicia's eyes. Her mouth opened and closed before she managed: 'You painted that message—do you have any idea—'

'You don't know where she is, do you?'

Winter's head was cocked. Alicia frowned and Winter jumped on the hesitation.

'I don't get the "motive"'—air quotes, eyes narrowed in disdain—'I don't know if maybe she thinks Jack had something to do with David, or—or whoever took him said they'd give him back if she—I don't know, Alicia. I'm not a detective. But I'm not stupid. There's no way he would have drowned in that pool. A cramp? Seriously?' She shook her head and stared up through the skylight. Her eyes were wet. 'But she was there. She was right there, the moment—and you said she was supposed to be in Bath. He was swimming alone in school, and she was right there. She killed him.'

A tear slipped down her golden cheek. The coiled spring tightened in Alicia's chest. When she spoke, her voice was soft, almost pleading: 'She would never kill anybody.'

'You know that? I never thought my dad would drink himself to death. I never thought—we don't know what anyone is capable of. You don't know anything.'

Alicia did not know anything. She thought of a book with a name struck through in blue biro. The memory fragment was chased by another: a cold look on her mother's face as she glued dead petals to the wicker sculpture of an eye.

I would do anything to get him back, Alicia.

She shook her head at Winter, denial in her eyes. But Melody Wilson's bespectacled face beamed between baskets of marigolds. What was her mother capable of?

'Get out,' said Winter before Alicia managed to construct a sentence. Her hands were on her hips, her eyes dry.

'You can't actually live here—'

'I don't live here! I just needed somewhere...' Winter trailed off and swallowed. 'What are you doing here, anyway? Shouldn't you be at school, making up excuses for your mother?'

'I just needed somewhere.'

'Well,' said Winter, leaning down to pick up her bag. 'You can have it.'

Floorboards creaked as she marched towards the door. Alicia blinked heavy lids.

'I talk to David too, sometimes.'

Winter turned on her heel and, for half a second, a sliver of understanding passed between the two young women who had lost more than they could articulate.

'Maybe you should talk to your mother.'

Footsteps receded down the stairs and Alicia stared at Winter's sleeping bag, lying open like a gutted fish.

Tattoo

THE GIRLS ALTERNATED positions with their backs to the window of the art room, the girl on the right taking photos of their three unsmiling faces. The sky was cloudless and the light bold: perfect conditions for the latest silhouette trend, with filters to set their eyes bright against the shadow. Gus had arrived at school early, hoping to catch Alicia on the way in. He had been watching the girls strike identical poses for the past five minutes. It was not the ideal start to his birthday.

Winter walked into the room, flanked by the Carpenter twins. She paused by the empty teacher's desk, the thumb of one hand tucked into her leather belt and the nails of the other drumming her satchel. She cast her eyes around the class as though surveying a hotel buffet. Eight students sat in pairs at the desks and Winter made eye contact with each of them before claiming the empty desk in the middle of the room. She nodded at the girls taking photos, who broke into wide smiles that fell as soon as she passed. The desk was made for two, and one of the identical twins, whose hair was in a ponytail, took the empty seat beside Gus and lugged it to Winter's side.

'You know that abandoned cottage by Fletcher Park?' Winter's voice was loud as she pulled a sketchbook from her bag.

'The one with that creepy shed at the bottom of the garden?' asked the twin with pigtails, while she and her sister scrubbed their seats with anti-bacterial wipes.

'Alicia has been sleeping there,' said Winter.

'Why?' asked the twin with the ponytail, taking a tentative perch on the drying seat.

'Her mum's a murderer, you tapeworm,' said her sister. 'It's not safe in the house.'

'How do you know?' asked the first, laying out coloured pencils on her corner of the desk. 'That she's been sleeping there?'

Winter shrugged. 'I know everything.'

Heels clicked on the concrete floor as a young woman entered the class. Wearing a royal-blue cocktail dress cut just above the knee, she looked as if she had stepped off a luxury yacht. She was tall, with dark hair that fell down her long neck and past square shoulders. The class took a collective breath at her striking appearance: mixed heritage, East Asian and Caucasian, with large eyes that settled on Gus at the back of the room.

'Miss,' said one of the trio at the window, in a Lancashire accent. 'Can you take our photo?'

The woman's face was impassive as she walked over to receive the phone. Holding it before her, she took a couple of steps back until she stood in the doorway. She then extended her arm and dropped the phone in the bin, where it landed with a clang.

'Sadly,' said the woman, clasping her hands as she strode to the front of the room. 'Mrs Harrington remains absent.'

She paused, perhaps waiting for moans of protest. The girls fished the phone from the bin and whispered to one another furiously as they took their seats. Gus shot another look through the window to the quad beyond, but Alicia was not approaching the classroom. The path leading to the art room was bare, apart from some chalk outlines drawn by younger children, giving it the appearance of a crime scene.

'I know how fond of her you all are.' Her gaze flicked past Winter. 'My name is Ms Burnflower, but you can call me Rainn. You'll have to forgive me,'—a self-deprecating smile—'I don't know the first thing about art. I'm actually the new school counsellor, but Mrs Lawson thought it would be good for me to get to know some of the students.'

In the seat nearest the teacher, a girl raised her hand and spoke in a plummy voice: 'We were supposed to learn about Escher this term. That's what Mrs Harrington told us last year. The supply on Monday had us doing self-portraits,' she added with an eye roll and a small laugh.

Rainn inspected the girl at the desk before her like something she had just stepped on.

'No swearing in this classroom,' she said, her voice firm. 'To Mrs Lawson's office.'

Rainn pointed at the door and the girl glanced left and right, wide eyes seeking solidarity, before deciding that a word with the headmistress was exactly what she wanted. Scraping back her chair, she marched indignantly from the room.

Though her eyes had returned to Winter, Rainn's arm remained extended as the girl disappeared through the doorway. Gus's breath quickened as he spotted something on her slender wrist: a tattoo. He blinked. A black oval curled into a lightning-struck eye; it was the symbol on the leatherbound book.

Rainn shook her head and folded her arms.

'This lesson, we will concern ourselves with a subject that is very close to my heart. A subject that will be close to yours every day for the rest of your lives. That subject is fear.'

There was a glimmer in her cerulean eyes. Winter's back was straight, her posture matching Rainn's, mirroring the larger ego. The teacher spoke so quietly that the students leaned forward at their desks.

'I remember what it was like to be your age. Well,' she pursed her lips, 'at your age I fled my home in Singapore and flew to England to determine what had happened to my mother—I wasn't agonising over what to wear to the Ashley L'Amour concert. But context is irrelevant: same mind, different problems. As a child, you fear the dark, the monsters…the offers of old men in new cars; being eaten, stolen, broken—you fear what your parents have the power to protect you from. But as a teenager, these fears move beyond the limits of parental control. Beyond the safety of a locked door. It is not death that you fear, but humiliation. What would they think of you, you wonder, if they knew the truth?'

The question hung over the class, mouths bemused, eyes entranced.

'Perhaps you are scared of being defined as a beauty or a brain?' Rainn continued, trailing her fingertips along the desks as she circled the room. 'A boy or a girl? Being stuffed into boxes that are already labelled?'

She locked eyes with the thin, breadstick of a boy at the desk to the right of Gus.

'Perhaps you are scared of talking to a beautiful woman?'

The boy shrank into his chair.

'It is important,' said Rainn decisively, a finger raised, 'to identify our fears, for it is fear that will dictate the choices that shape our lives. The fear of missing out, the fear of rushing in. Whether we choose to act—to apply, to commit—or not to act—to avoid, to defer—at the core of these decisions lies our fears.'

'What do you fear?'

Rainn turned to the voice in the centre of the room and challenge lit her eyes as she met Winter's gaze.

'A world of order,' answered Rainn distastefully, moving to the front of Winter's desk. She ran a finger through the coloured pencils. 'Straight lines. Checked boxes. A world without chaos.'

Heels clicked as she returned to the front of the room and sat on the teacher's desk with one long leg folded over the other.

'This morning, you will draw what you fear. Not spiders, not snakes—I'm not interested in phobia. In truth, I'm not interested in what you draw at all; I'm looking for the struggle. The courage to override that desire to hide in the shadows like a child with its arms wrapped around mummy's legs. I am looking for honesty.'

The students opened their sketchbooks. Even the girl whose phone had been binned was pressing her pencil to the page, her expression livid. Rainn scanned the classroom and when her eyes landed on Gus, he realised that he had neither pencil nor paper. He left his seat to help himself to the supplies along the bench against the far wall. Passing Winter's table, he saw a sketch of a policeman covering his ears.

Rainn leaned on Winter's desk so that their eyes were level. Gus watched her rub at the tattoo on her wrist and look down as though checking it was still there. She spoke quietly to Winter, asking about the picture, and Winter launched into the tale of her murdered boyfriend.

Rainn squeezed Winter's shoulder and circled the room, pointedly avoiding the efforts of the Lancashire girl, who sat back when she passed in the hopes that Rainn might comment on her work. The teacher stopped by Gus's desk, taking a moment to admire his pencil sketch: a folded oval with a bolt of lightning across the inner circle.

'I'm not much of an artist.' Gus grinned.

'And what do you fear?' Rainn asked as though he had not spoken.

'Tattoos,' he replied, shuddering. 'Needles.'

For five long seconds, Rainn appraised him with disappointed eyes.

'Perhaps you fear people knowing who you are.' Her whisper was a statement, not a question. 'Speaking of which: Happy Birthday, Augustus.'

She flashed a smile and he opened his mouth to reply, but she had already returned to the front of the room. She perched on the desk and rubbed a thumb across her tattoo while students continued with their sketches. Gus tried to catch her eye, but she ignored him. He was about to rise from his seat, to ask her how she knew it was his birthday, when she hopped abruptly from the desk. Rainn drew the lesson to a close, sending the breadstick to Mrs Lawson's office for insolence when he commented that they were only halfway through the hour.

Gus remained in his seat as the other students filed out of the classroom. He watched Winter shoo the Carpenter twins on their way, and they glanced back at her through the window with tight-lipped pouts of abandonment. Rainn shot Gus a winning smile and led Winter from the classroom, chatting conspiratorially like old friends.

They just dropped dead

Happy Birthday my Adult Daughter. Wow. 18 years ago, you were causing me more pain than I'd ever experienced. Still deciding if it was worth it. Home for dinner. Sorry. Love you lots xxx

Alicia held the phone in both hands and read the message three times. Her bare legs were crossed on the bare mattress, her jeans beside Winter's sleeping bag on the floor. The phone had not been silent; her sleep had been deep, and she cursed herself for missing the message that she had been waiting on for days.

Home for dinner—she checked the time to see that it was approaching four in the afternoon. She had hoped that a nap on the mattress might result in a lucid dream of the cottage, but she had slept all day, and she had no memory of any dreams. The sleep had at least cleared her head, and it was with sharp eyes that she read the message a fourth time, picking out phrases.

Sorry—for turning up late on her birthday? For spending four nights away from home without bothering to tell her husband and daughter where she was? For hiding a list of dead people behind a painting above her bed?

Or for murdering Jack Henson?

Her finger hovered over the call button, but she stopped herself. Instead, she typed into the internet browser: *Bristol Marigolds sweet shop Melody Wilson.*

The *Bristol Post* had uploaded a news article at nine that morning. Melody Wilson had died in a kitchen fire. Alicia's head was no longer clear as she scanned the article—*loved by the community;*

daughter shocked; lived alone—but there was no mention of foul play. The elderly proprietor had apparently left the stove on while boiling pasta, the net curtains had caught on fire and she had been asphyxiated by the smoke. Alicia scrolled back to the top, to read the article more slowly, but lowered her hands. The phone slipped through numb fingers and tumbled from the mattress to the floor. Feeling limp and heavy, she stared at the empty plant pot beside the bedroom door, her eyes tracing a deep crack down its side.

She jumped at a thump downstairs. As one waking from a dream, it took a moment to connect the three wooden *thunks* to its context: someone had knocked on the front door. She pulled on her jeans and stuffed the phone into her pocket as she rushed down the stairs. Winter? No—she knew the door was boarded. Crossing the living room, she pressed her hands to the boards and peered through the crack to see her neighbour standing on the far side, his green eyes narrowed.

'It's Gus,' he announced unnecessarily.

'It's locked,' said Alicia. 'Boarded shut. I'll let you in the back.'

Not entirely convinced that she was awake, Alicia walked along the corridor to the kitchen, drawing the phone from her pocket to clear the internet history. She heaved the rotting door over the floor tiles and looked expectantly at Gus, who stood in grey jeans and a grey T-shirt, with a black rucksack over his right shoulder. He lingered on the doorstep like a monochrome vampire, awaiting an invitation to cross the threshold.

'Hi,' said Alicia. 'How did you know I was here?'

Gus shifted his rucksack higher onto his shoulder and explained that he had overheard Winter telling the twins that Alicia was sleeping there. Alicia lacked the energy to be infuriated by this news, and moved aside so that Gus could enter. He stepped inside the kitchen and surveyed the dark, stripped space, from the peeling wallpaper to the ugly ceramic plate above the radiator. On a metal bracket, the kiln-fired plate depicted two deformed hippos swimming in a circle.

'What on Earth is that supposed to be?' he nodded at the plate.

'That's my Year 6 art project.'

'It's gorgeous.'

She ignored the comment and walked into the living room while he described, with a hint of pride, how he had caught the twins in the car park at the end of the day and told them that he had been asked to hand Alicia homework. They had been surprised that he had the gall to talk to them, but were eager to describe the whereabouts of the abandoned cottage that Alicia had been forced to hide in. They had refused to give him a lift.

Alicia pulled the dustsheet from the sofa and cast it on the floor, scanning the cushions for spiders. Gus dropped his bag and took a seat, camouflaging against the stone-grey fabric like a lizard. With a straight back, he turned his head from the crack in the window to the empty fireplace.

'I love what you've done with the place.'

'It's my grandmother's—it was. She died the day I was born,' Alicia paused. *Eighteen years ago, today.* 'I would offer you a cup of tea, but I don't think there's a kettle.'

Gus made no comment, continuing to scan the room as though he were a parent visiting her university digs.

'I don't actually sleep here,' said Alicia. 'Well, I did today, but not last night. I just…' She shook her head and then gestured at the bag between his feet. 'You didn't come here to give me homework?'

Gus glanced at his bag as if he had forgotten something.

'No, no,' he said. 'I wanted to tell you what you missed in art class.'

Alicia's stomach clenched, but it was not her mother's absence that Gus was referring to. He explained how the new counsellor had clearly never taught a lesson in her life, and how interested she had been in what Winter had to say about Jack.

'And,'—a deep furrow appeared between his dark brows—'she knew it was my birthday.'

'It's your birthday?' asked Alicia. 'Mine too.'

Wind whistled down the chimney and flecks of ash spread across the black tiles at the foot of the fireplace.

'That's not all,' said Gus, and Alicia thought he looked evasive. 'She had a tattoo on her wrist. And it was the same as—it was the symbol on that book. The eye.'

Alicia knew which book he meant and understood his caution. She watched dust motes hover in the beams of light that filtered through cracks between the boards. Their unspoken agreement not to mention her mother's secret had come to an end.

'Does your mum have any tattoos?' Gus ventured and her eyes snapped back to his. He flushed, his Adam's apple shifting up and down at the umbrage in her eyes; his question tainted with accusation. 'Have you any ideas, I mean…' he continued, but Alicia sat back against the cushion and folded her arms before she spoke.

'No, she doesn't have any tattoos. And I don't know what that symbol is, or what that book is. Or where she is. Or anything. You saw the names?' A nod from Gus and she continued, 'I searched some of them. Lots of them. These people are dead. All closed cases, unexpected deaths—drowning in riptides, falling off horses. Heart failure. They just dropped dead.'

She could not mention Jack. She did not mention Melody. Their deaths were more real than the faceless names and her throat caught at the thought of them.

'I looked up the symbol,' said Gus. 'But *"lightning eye cult"* didn't get me very far. Nothing.'

Alicia appeared transfixed by the boarded door and Gus felt the distance between them. Her body was tense, her lips firm, and it might have been because she had only met him the night before, or because his uncle was a police officer and her mother a suspect in what she now believed to be a murder case, but she was not being honest with him. He was tired and frustrated and he resented the filter in her eyes.

What do you fear? Rainn's question pulled him back to the lesson in which he had disclosed nothing, shut tight as Alicia was now.

'I don't really have insomnia,' he said, leaning forward with his elbows on his knees. He faced the door as she did, like two reluctant guests on a talk show. 'I take pills to stop me from dreaming. My parents died last September. A year ago, today. My uncle says they had heart attacks—she went first and he was just so damn mortified…' out of the corner of her eye, Alicia watched him chew his lip, 'he followed right after her. They just dropped dead.'

Alicia sat up, mirroring his posture, though nothing but empty expressions of sympathy formed on the back of her tongue.

'I don't know why he doesn't want me to dream,' Gus continued before she might comment, 'but I know it's got something to do with how they died. Something he's trying to protect me from. They're lying to us, Alicia. My uncle. Your mother. But we should be honest with each other.' He lifted his hand as though to grip her knee, as his father would have done, but thought better of it. He stared into her malachite eyes.

What do you fear?

His voice was sombre: 'Tell me something nobody knows.'

Alicia suspected there was something he wanted to tell her. They were strangers, linked by the missing and the dead, but he was trying to forge a connection. Her thoughts turned to the side alley at home, and the five minutes she had spent on Saturday evening staring at the box of washing powder on the shelf above the dryer. There was only enough left in the packet for one load, but she was determined to make it last for two. She had started to guess how many cubic centimetres of powder were in the corner of the box, so that she might halve the amount accurately. But it was dark and she did not like to be alone in the side alley any more. It was no longer safe.

'I started counting things this summer,' said Alicia, looking over Gus's shoulder to the empty mantelpiece. 'I would guess how many days it would be until the phone rang and someone had found David wandering around the back of their farm, living off fruit and berries. I wouldn't let myself change the date, even when it was getting close. And when the days became a single day, I counted the hours, and then the minutes. And then the seconds. I would stop what I was doing and listen for the phone. I was so sure it would ring. I was certain.' She remembered the buzz of a lawnmower or the quarrel of birds building to a crescendo, like seconds ticking down on the timer of a bomb. 'And when nothing happened, I picked something else. Another date—or maybe he would be back by the time my toothpaste ran out, or the sunflower outside the window had reached the third pane of glass.' Her father had asked where the sunflower was. He had not seen her eyes dart to the bin. 'I'm not crazy. I know it makes no sense, counting down. But knowing that it isn't rational doesn't make it stop. Each time I start to count, it gives me hope. That's what I live on.'

They breathed into the silence and Alicia sat back in her seat, pulling up the sleeves of her green cardigan. Gus made no comment, and she was grateful for that; she did not need him to justify or excuse her behaviour.

'Tell me something nobody knows,' she demanded.

'I'm into guys,' said Gus, fighting the urge to break eye contact. 'It's a big deal, coming out to your parents, or so I've heard. I never got to do that.' He said nothing for a few seconds and the wind pressed the leaves of bushes against the front windows. 'I don't think it matters, who you find attractive—blonds, brunettes, guys, girls.

But I would have liked to have known if it mattered to them. And…' he sucked in a breath and Alicia looked away. This was harder to say than he had expected, and she suspected that she was the first to hear it. 'They were murdered, and they never really knew who I was.'

When his eyes met hers, sincerity burned as anger.

'I want to know if they're in that book.'

In the pause that followed, over the thumping of their hearts, they did not hear the footsteps coming down the side of the cottage. Alicia cleared her throat. She wanted to help him. She needed to be honest with him. Or as honest as she dared.

'There was a sketch in the back of the book,' she said. 'It was my mother's. She had drawn a shed, and I don't know where it is, but I know I've seen it before. That's why I'm here—I'm trying to remember, before she gets home. I've got to remember where it is, so I can find it before I speak to her.'

Gus stood up so fast that Alicia flinched. He paced back and forth across the carpet.

'The pigtails—the twin—Winter said about this cottage and pigtails said the one with the creepy shed in the garden.'

'But there isn't…' Alicia's eyes widened. There was no shed in the garden, but in the woodland beyond there was a clearing. In that clearing she had played with her brother, and that is where she had seen the shed.

A well-kept secret

'HOW CAN A dream be dangerous?' Alicia mused, plucking a white petal from her shoulder. She and Gus stepped over the low wall at the back of her grandmother's property, entering the woodland.

'My pills, you mean?' said Gus. Behind them, a breeze caught the swing and a high-pitched moan swept the trees. 'I don't know. I used to wonder if maybe I'd seen something that I wasn't supposed to. Something that might come back to me in a dream.'

'Like a repressed memory?'

Gus shrugged, hands in his pockets, as they strolled between the silver birches. He kicked at fallen leaves, uncovering thistles, and Alicia studied his face in the dappled light. Dark rings lay in shadows beneath a scruffy fringe, giving him the appearance of a boy growing old too fast.

'I had my first lucid dream last night,' she said.

His face lit up: two cat-eyes in a shaft of light between the trees.

'I've had vivid dreams before,' she continued, 'ones where you wake up and it takes a moment to realise you weren't actually late for the test or—'

'Waltzing with a wombat?'

'Sure. But nothing like this. It was just as she described—Mum. Every tiny detail. Each fibre of the carpet, the grain of wood in the banisters, it was…it was like waking up.'

She brushed a hand through her hair, self-conscious at how wonderstruck she sounded. She scrutinised his expression as one might examine a crystal ball: searching for signs of judgement. He was very conscious of his eyebrows.

'What did you do, in the dream? You shaved Winter's head, am

I right?'

She grinned, and told him about the wolf leading her to the cottage.

'It's weird, isn't it?' she added. 'A part of me—some part I couldn't reach when I was awake—it knew the shed was here. It makes you wonder, are all the things that we think we have forgotten just waiting there…sitting on shelves at the back of our minds?'

The decline steepened and they used the lower branches of trees to prevent them from slipping on the leaves. Gus considered what memories might lie forgotten on shadowy shelves, and what his uncle was so keen to protect him from. Alicia, chatting as though she had not spoken to a soul in days, vented her frustration at failing to maintain the lucid dream, and her inability to dream of the cottage since.

'Apparently,' said Gus, 'if you spin on the spot, that helps. It grounds you in the dream, or something like that. That's what I read in that book of your mother's, before my uncle confiscated it.'

Guilt flashed across his face when Alicia frowned.

'What did he want with it?'

'If he's scared of me dreaming, he definitely doesn't want me doing it lucidly. Who knows where a wolf might lead me?'

She did not return his smile, and he wished he had not mentioned that her mother's bedtime reading was now the concern of a police officer. As they passed between the final pair of silver birches and entered the clearing, Gus filled the silence with tips that he had read on how to achieve a lucid dream.

The clearing was twice the size of a tennis court, with a section of abandoned railway line running through its centre. The line was raised on a grassy bank, and beyond the iron girders, a wooden shed stood pale against the trees. Gus shielded his eyes from the light of the early-evening sun, a gleam of orange catching a section of the track like the edge of a blade. The pair walked shoulder to shoulder, treading fallen leaves as they crossed the clearing. Alicia recalled David's squeals as they played on the abandoned track, killing time before her tennis lesson in the park. The shed was a mere whisper in her memory: the door had been locked, and she had paid it little attention.

The door was now open, facing the woodland to their right; they could not see inside from the angle of their approach. Gus's eyes were on the rusted lock hanging from the door, twisted and broken, when he froze at the sound of voices coming from within the shed.

In unison, Gus and Alicia gripped each other's upper arms, pulling down to crouch behind the raised line. Through the wild grass, they watched two figures emerge from the wooden doorway. Winter stepped out first, tears streaming down her face. Alicia did not recognise the woman that followed. She was half a head taller than Winter, her striking face taut with impatience. Her expression softened when Winter turned and threw her arms around her. Winter's shoulders heaved up and down as she wept and the woman patted her back, muttering something about Jack. With Winter's head on her shoulder, the woman glanced down at the tattoo on her wrist and gave it a quick rub as though it had itched.

Gus kept low, motioning for Alicia to follow him towards the right of the bank as the women headed for the other side of the truncated tracks. Alicia waited for them to cross into the trees before whispering: 'The new counsellor?'

Gus nodded, 'Rainn.'

The pair stared at one another, wordlessly transmitting a question they needn't voice aloud: why had Winter led this woman to the shed?

Long grass grew either side of the wood-panelled door, which did not budge when Gus pressed against it; it had been open for some time. He flicked a loose screw hanging from the lock before stepping into the small structure. The interior was bare apart from a stone well protruding from the soil.

'Well, well, well,' said Alicia, following her neighbour into the musty shed.

'Creepy, secret well,' Gus added.

'A well, kept secret.'

Alicia traced her finger around the circle of time-worn bricks. The shed was barely wide enough for her to complete a full rotation while staring into its depths.

'Why would my mother keep a sketch of a shed that hides a well in the back of that book?'

Gus's first thought was that it would be a convenient place to dump a body, but he kept this to himself. The door was east-facing, not receiving the light of the sun that had started its descent over the trees to the west; orange rays through cracks in the roof did little to illuminate the well. A couple of iron rungs descended into shadow. Alicia opened the torch application on her phone and a brilliant white beam spilled into the darkness.

Following the rusty footholds rung by rung, she estimated the shaft to be ten feet deep, ending in the soil used to fill it. She played the beam across the floor of the well, half-expecting to see the outline of a skull staring back at her. She shuddered.

'What's that?' asked Gus, taking the phone from her hands. He shone the light against something caught between broken bricks in the soil. Alicia recognised the postcard instantly, having overheard the whispers that filled the school corridors on Monday, courtesy of the Carpenter twins.

'That's the postcard Winter sent to Jack from Sri Lanka,' she said.

Gus traced the torchlight across the card, struggling to read the writing.

'Wish you were…?'

'Dead,' said Alicia.

'Ouch! Some sense of humour.'

It was their last connection before she died, Alicia thought, dramatically. In the half-light, she saw a ghostly image of Winter casting the postcard down the well. Remembering bottle caps and a plastic wrapper by the swing set, she whispered: 'Jack and Winter used to come here.'

Jack was in the book. And now he's dead.

Alicia left the shed as a cacophony of thoughts jostled for her attention. She took a deep breath, drawing fresh air deep into her lungs and forcing down the rising anxiety. Focusing on the railway track, she distracted herself with memory: David standing on the track pretending that a train was coming; shrieks of delight as he managed to balance perfectly on the iron girder, placing one foot before the other. Alicia had waited until he was standing on the section of track highest up the bank and then asked him to jump. She could only have been eleven; he must have been five. He did not know if she was really waiting beneath him, but he jumped.

He always trusted her.

The trust for her mother frayed like an old rope. Until David's disappearance, Anna Harrington was unfailingly lighthearted and bubbly; it was inconceivable to imagine her playing any part in Jack's death. But Alicia could not accept that this was all coincidence. Her mother's hunt for David had led her into the shadows. What had she found within their depths?

'Jack was in that book,' she said aloud as Gus stepped beside her. 'Do you think he saw something in that well? Something he shouldn't have?'

The pair glanced back through the door of the shed. The well lingered in shadow, its rim barely visible.

Gus's eyes were steady when he met Alicia's gaze.

'You need to talk to your mother. I need to know if my parents were in that book, and why she's hiding it.'

'You need to talk to your uncle. If Jack did find something down that well, Winter just told that woman. And if she knows it's your birthday, she's not just here for Jack.'

'You don't think I've tried? I'd have a better chance of getting Winter to rename the planet after me than getting my uncle to loosen his lips.'

'These deaths must be connected, Gus. Your parents, Jack… and Mrs Lawson's on that list. If they want us to keep our mouths shut, they're going to have to tell us everything.'

Lucid dreaming club

GUS SAT ON the unopened box with a photograph in his hands. His eight-year-old self, with a mop of unruly black hair, held out a parkour trophy as he perched on a low wall between his grinning parents. Benedict stood with a hand on his son's shoulder, his posture straight and proud. His dark hair had been tamed in a manner that Gus was yet to master. The smile on his face was warm as he faced the camera. In Gus's fatigued state, he could almost feel the weight of his father's hand on his shoulder. Sylvie's blonde hair was tied back and her large eyes gazed slightly to the left. Laughter creased the corners of her eyes; perhaps she had caught a joke from a friend in the background. As his gaze oscillated between their faces, Gus wondered what his parents had done to deserve their fate. Had they chased names in a book of murder? Had curiosity killed the pair of them?

The edges of the photograph were faded with fingerprints so he searched the open box beside him and withdrew a framed picture of himself and his grandmother, Blithe. The pair were sitting in a rowing boat on Lake Windermere, the shot taken by his father at the bow as he climbed aboard. It looked as though Blithe was resting her hand on Gus's shoulder, but he was pretty sure she had just told him to stop wriggling and was attempting to hold him still. With not an ounce of affection towards the cold and impersonal woman, he pulled the photograph from its silver frame and cast it into the box. As his parents were placed safely behind the glass, Gus caught his eyes reflected back at him, dark-ringed and bloodshot.

Happy Birthday, Augustus.

His father and uncle had lived in Cranleigh with their parents,

Augustus and Blithe. Augustus died when the boys were sixteen, and Benedict left for Galway, where he met Sylvie. When Sylvie gave birth, Benedict named his son after his late father. But everybody called him Gus. The only person who referred to him as Augustus was his uncle, who had joined his twin in Galway when Blithe passed away.

Perhaps the new counsellor had checked the register before class, noting Gus's date of birth and full name? Or perhaps this tattooed stranger had known exactly where to find the police officer's nephew? Perhaps if his mind was not so harassed by the need for sleep, he might assemble his fractured thoughts and make sense of the situation.

When he and Alicia had returned from the cottage an hour before, Gus was not surprised that the police car was still out; in Galway, Joe had left the house at all hours to settle disputes. He would return in an irritable mood, furious at whatever he had been expected to deal with. Gus was convinced that his uncle had joined the police force to be provided with a constant supply of delinquents at whom he could direct his rage. As Gus waited for Joe to return, a dormant shadow rose with each hollow thump in his chest. While his father had been benevolent and his mother polite to a fault, Gus understood the anger that lay behind his uncle's impatient movements and gruff tones. He had seen himself in those bullet-hole eyes.

A second hour passed and Gus paced the bedroom floor. Thoughts fell like snow on restless animals, unable to settle. Like a panther in an inadequate enclosure, his feet padded the floor while fierce eyes saw nothing but memory. He had worn circles into the carpet of his empty dormitory at boarding school, waiting for his parents to collect him. Enough was, apparently, enough: having scaled the front wall of the boarding block at midnight and speared his roommate's teddy bear on the arrow-headed minute hand of the decorative wall clock, Gus was expected to return home with his parents and discuss whether he saw a future at Beckingdale. Since it was blindingly obvious that he did not, this charade was the school's final message to Mr and Mrs Crow that their son's behaviour was not the sole responsibility of the school. If they could not talk sense into the unsettled teenager, he would be expelled.

When he heard a knock at the dormitory door, Gus had braced himself for a mixed reception. His father, gentle as he was, would be disappointed at having to cut the trip to Portugal short to discipline his son. His mother would be unable to suppress the excitement of seeing him on his birthday, despite the lavish celebrations she had thrust upon him the weekend before. The combination of forced parental admonition and delight would be rather comical.

But Benedict and Sylvie had not come to collect him. It was his father's twin brother who had stood awkwardly in the empty corridor. At the sight of his humourless uncle, Gus's disappointment had been palpable. Send the police: that will straighten the boy out. He had thought better of his parents.

The journey home was endured in silence, broken only when the pair sat across from one another at the living room table. Gus braced himself for another lecture, wondering how 'bad cop' his uncle intended to be. His head was resting in his hands, elbows cold against the knotted oak, when Joe's words fell.

'Augustus, your parents have had an accident.'

Those seven words were about the extent of the information that Joe divulged. Gus interrogated the police officer for details, but Joe had the temperament of a wounded bear, and any mention of the subject was like driving a hot iron into open flesh. The more he demanded—the greater the pressure he applied—the more his uncle withdrew within himself.

The 'accident': two heart attacks, two minutes apart.

Gus found the lie offensive.

At first, he thought Joe was silenced by a grief so total that it numbed his every move. Receiving sidelong glances and irascible tones, he wondered if the officer resented having to welcome his nephew into that grey and joyless home. But as the months passed and Gus worked his way through three schools and four home tutors, he realised that it was another emotion that sealed his uncle's lips: fear.

With his thoughts swirling like the contents of a snow globe, Gus probed the root of this fear. Was Joe afraid that Benedict and Sylvie's murderers were still at large? Did he fear what Gus would do if he discovered the truth? Flurries of thought stole the spotlight of his attention for only a moment, unable to outstage the question that plagued his mind every waking hour: why were his parents murdered?

He stepped up to the window. A large moon supplemented the orange glow of street lamps, illuminating the Harrington's empty driveway. Night had fallen and Alicia's mother had not returned. In the snow globe that was Gus's mind, a storm of competing questions worked him round and round the bedroom floor until the glass cracked.

IT WAS HALF past nine in the evening when Joe returned. He stepped through the front door to see his nephew sitting at the living room table with a rucksack in his lap. The young man fought back a yawn as he straightened in his chair, and Joe wondered how long he had been waiting for him. Closing the door, he pulled something from the pocket of his uniform and tossed it to Gus.

'Happy Birthday.'

With one hand on the rucksack in his lap, Gus raised the other and caught the pot of pills.

'Latest blend,' said Joe. 'Eight hours of dreamless sleep.'

Gus said nothing, twirling the pot in his hand while his uncle crossed the room to the bay window. In the gloom behind closed blinds, he lifted the northern hemisphere of a large wooden globe to reveal bottles of liquor within.

'You're welcome,' Joe muttered.

'My parents died a year ago and you have told me nothing.'

Joe turned, whiskey bottle in hand, and Gus met his eyes: a sliver of blue around large pupils. Joe opened a glass-fronted cabinet beside the fireplace, withdrew a tumbler and set it on the mantelpiece.

'And why do you think that might be?' Joe asked, his eyes on the glass as he poured generously. Gus placed the pot on the table. The bag was heavy in his lap.

'Because you think it will upset me? Because you think I'm too young—that I'll do something stupid?' He chewed his lip, tapping a foot on the carpet. What had he forgotten? Which memories did his uncle strive to keep on the dusty shelves of his mental library? 'I don't know, Joe. Maybe you're responsible?'

Cold eyes held his gaze as Joe crossed the room towards him. The man's jaw tightened, his nostrils flared and a part of Gus was drawn to that anger like a cat to the fire. Joe placed the glass of whiskey on the far end of the table and settled his hands either side. He spoke with the steeled manner of an interrogator.

'Maybe my brother and his wife—the only two members of my goddamn family who deserve to be alive—were murdered, and I was left with the child that they were never supposed to have?'

Gus swallowed.

'Rainn Burnflower,' he said, and his uncle's eyes widened a fraction. 'Who is she?'

Joe shifted his focus to the high-backed chair, manoeuvring himself into it as though the act of sitting required his full attention. Gus gripped the outline of the object in his bag, his palms sweating.

It was not too late; he could still return it.

'I don't know anybody by that name—'

'I'm off.' Gus stood abruptly, knocking the table so that the pot fell on its side and the whiskey sloshed in the glass. He slung the rucksack over his shoulder.

'Where?'

'Lucid dreaming club,' he said brightly. 'Alicia will be waiting for me.'

Gus opened the front door and his uncle rose from the chair. For a moment, the man looked defeated, and then sincerity filled his eyes and a low rumble carried across the room.

'Your parents were murdered by a group of people more powerful than you can imagine. And I mean that in the most literal sense. These people have come for Anna Harrington. I asked her to stay out of it, but she has made up her mind. They will come for Alicia. And if you do not take your pills, these people will come for you. And there will be nothing that I, or anyone else, can do about it.'

The door caught in a breeze and slammed shut.

'Now sit down.'

Gus's chest tightened. He walked back to the table and gripped the back of a chair.

'Why were they murdered?'

Joe swilled the whiskey in his glass, selecting his words like a chess master, calculating each move and their probable outcomes.

'Because they stole a book.'

A tremor ran through Joe's fingers and he took a long draw of the amber liquid. Gus returned to his chair and shifted the rucksack into his lap. He pulled an object from the bag and tossed it onto the table between them.

'This book?'

Joe Crow choked on the whiskey. Suppressing a cough, he reached towards the leather cover, but his fingers did not brush the golden foil. A memory surfaced: his brother drawing an eye in the sand at Salthill beach while Sylvie coaxed her infant son into the water.

'Where did you get that?'

'I'll answer your questions, Uncle. When you answer mine.'

Reality check

THE ALARM CLOCK by Alicia's bed displayed 20:07. She glanced at her open door and then back at the clock. The boxy digits had not changed. Returning through the woodland, she had drilled Gus for information on *Lucid Dreaming: A Beginner's Guide*, and he had described reality checking. Eager to recall what he could from the book that his uncle had confiscated, Gus explained how the dreaming brain has difficulty reconstructing numbers and text. Unlike the natural contours and textures our minds have generated for millennia, these symbols are harder to reproduce; if you look at writing on a poster or the time on a digital clock, glance away and look back again, the symbols will scramble. That's how you know you're dreaming.

20:08. The numbers had not scrambled, but they continued to change: another minute marking Anna's absence. Alicia pushed the door to, leaving it open so that she might hear the front door, and kicked off her jeans. Lying back on her bed, she checked the call history on her phone: *Mum (7) – unanswered*. It was not uncommon for her mother to run out of battery on her phone; Alicia and Rory were not surprised when she failed to return their calls. Anna would disappear at weekends, make up some excuse about visiting relatives or attending art courses, and return with receipts from coffee shops and petrol stations that did not match her stories. When Alicia first suspected that she was searching for David, it had filled her with hope: her mother had not given up, tossing posters in the bin like it was time to move on. She talked herself through Anna's need for discretion: what mother would give her daughter false hope? For months, Alicia swallowed the lies and cradled a flame of positivity in her chest.

At 20:09 on her eighteenth birthday, this flame was a raging fire and the fragile hope a burning desire for the truth. According to that lucid dreaming guide, the more frequently you conduct a reality check while awake, the better the chances of your dreaming mind repeating this pattern. Alicia had been glancing between the clock and the back of her door sporadically for half an hour, having finished sharing a pizza and strained smiles with her father in the living room. Conversation had been stilted, the pair pausing mid-sentence, eyes shooting to the window as each car passed by. Neither had turned on the television. Alicia had not mentioned her mother's absence, and Rory made no comment when she announced at half past seven that she was off to bed.

'A tired body and an alert mind,' said Gus as they strolled up Gardner Road. 'That's what you need for a light sleep, prime for...' two small lines appeared between his dark brows. 'Why do you want to lucid dream anyway? That wolf was leading you to the shed, right? And we found it.'

'Right,' said Alicia. The wolf was a means for her subconscious to remind her what she had forgotten; she had no reason to believe that there were other memories waiting on shadowy shelves. So why was she so eager to return to the cottage in a dream?

Outside her home, Gus had asked if he could come inside. He wanted to check whether his parents were in the book.

'I'll let you know,' Alicia promised with an affirmative nod. 'As soon as I've spoken to her. I—' she peered through the window to see the empty sofa in the living room. 'I don't want to take it out again, and risk my Dad seeing it. Not till she's back.'

Two lines returned between his brows, but Gus did not argue.

'Happy Birthday, Alicia.'

'Happy Birthday, Gus.

It was with a tired body and an alert mind that Alicia climbed under her bedcovers. She lay her head on the pillow and watched the glare of the street light brighten on the ceiling as the remnants of daylight faded. With ears trained on the front door, she considered what Gus had said in the cottage. His parents would never return home. A flurry of guilt and her eyes creased; she could have shown him the book. Rory would have wondered what they were doing, and where they had been—it would have been awkward. But not impossible. She could have checked the list of names while he prepared dinner. The flurry became a dull pang; she could check it now, if she was quiet, but what to look for? She had not asked Gus for their names.

20:17. She rolled onto her side, pulled the plug from its socket in the wall and the digits disappeared. When she closed her eyes, half-formed questions rattled in her skull like a ball across a roulette wheel, spinning indefinitely. A defeated sigh escaped her lips as she opened her eyes and turned to face the green glow at her bedside: 18:18.

It took her a moment to spot the inconsistency.

Allaying the rise of excitement, Alicia focused on her dressing table, where an ornamental stone monkey was draped with the cheap jewellery that she never wore. When she looked back at the clock, the digits were unintelligible: this was a lucid dream. She stepped from the covers and crossed to the door, where the cold brass handle was invigorating in its realism. Knowing that accelerating heartbeat threatened to destabilise her, she rushed down the corridor.

Alicia reached the top of the stairs and a large crow shot over her shoulder. She turned to watch it flap its wings in mid-air like a hummingbird, shedding black feathers on the carpet. The bird disappeared through her parents' bedroom doorway and the hammering of Alicia's heart drew the texture of the pillow to her cheek. In her lucid state, she recalled what Gus had said about spinning on the spot. Feeling the weight of the duvet on her chest, she spun gently in the dream, letting the solid landscape soften and blur. The trick was a success: the weight of the bedding was gone. She had anchored herself in the dream.

Outside, a morning sun peered through the trees, spilling a prism of light on Gardner Road. She crossed the front lawn in bare feet and ran the pad of a forefinger along the rough brick on top of the gatepost. Leaves on the rosebush beside were thick with aphids. With no wolf to guide her, she ventured to her grandmother's house alone.

The red paint was flaking and the window boxes overgrown: her memory had filled in the gaps. Stepping over the low wall at the back of the property, she heard a donkey's bray behind her as the wind toyed with the gate. The fallen leaves of silver birches drifted between thistles and Alicia considered the strength of her memory: she could never have sketched this scene so comprehensively had she been asked to recall it, but the details unlocked one after another as she walked through her mind.

Day had fallen inexplicably to night when she left the cover of the trees. A large moon bathed the clearing in a cold light as she strode towards the open door of the small wooden shed. Inside, the stone well was showered with dust motes that drifted through slender moonbeams permeating the ceiling. She had made it through the shed door without waking, completing a challenge that she had set herself unconsciously.

Still under, still lucid. What next? She was about to peer over the moonlit rim when another compulsion seized her and she took three paces back. Decisively, recklessly, she raced forward, leaped into the air and threw herself down the well.

I am awake, Alicia thought as blades of grass brushed her chin. The light of a midday sun was hot on her jeans and glowed a deep red behind her eyelids. She opened her eyes to find herself on a grassy knoll. At the foot of the hill, a lamb tugged at green shoots.

I am asleep, Alicia thought when she turned her head to see the smooth bricks of a well beside her, rising from the summit of the hill. She pulled herself into a sitting position and drew up her knees, studying the marks that the grass had left on her bare arms. She cast her eyes across an eternity of rolling hills: a still shot of a green ocean undulating into the distance.

When her roving eyes returned to the well, a young man was sitting on it. A daisy poked between the toes of his bare feet and a pair of athletic calves disappeared beneath blue denim shorts. The contours of a defined chest were visible beneath his white T-shirt. But it was his eyes that immobilised her: circlets of a glacial blue so sharp that they contradicted the realism of the landscape.

She rose to her feet, spotting a long, sharp dagger on the brick beside him. The roulette wheel spun, expanding with the questions that it generated. It landed on its primary question and she opened her mouth to speak, but the stranger broke the silence in a deep voice that resonated through her bones.

'Welcome to Vivador.'

Ryan, age 8

ON MY BIRTHDAY Dad told Sam about the dollhouse. Mum had told Sam that she was trying to clean it for him but she dropped it on the patio. She did not want Sam to be cross with me. But Dad said I had spoiled Sam's birthday and it's only fair that my birthday should be spoiled too. He says that people get so much attention on their birthdays that it goes to their heads.

I could tell that Sam was so mad with me. I thought that he might drop me from the window. When Dad was telling Sam what I had done I could not look in Sam's eyes, so I looked at the gold letters on Dad's briefcase: P.S. Lawson. Peter Samuel Lawson. It made me wonder if that's why Dad likes Sam the most. You can't choose your children but you can choose your orphans and I think he probably would have chosen Sam instead of me.

Dad says he chose Sam because he has dark hair so it would be easier to tell us apart. I think he was joking because we look very different. His eyes and skin are darker than mine and he is also taller. I felt bad for spoiling both our birthdays, so I drew Sam a picture of all four of us at Burnflower—that's the name of our house. Sam's hair was black like Dad's and mine was gold like Mum's. I was colouring my eyes when Dad said I should be outside playing like a boy, not drawing in my room like a girl, but I think he just likes it better when he can work upstairs all by himself. Even Mum gets told off when he's working and she sings while she hoovers the stairs. Sometimes her singing goes to my head and gives me a headache.

I told Dad that I can't play cricket with Sam because he's mad at me for smashing his dollhouse. Dad said that a boy needs friends and that friends should not keep secrets from each other, which actually did not make sense. The only secret I had was the mirror upstairs and I did not want to show Sam where Dad hid the key for me. That's when I knew my birthday had gone to my head.

I waited until it was dark and this time I was really sure that Dad was not in his study. Then I went downstairs and woke Sam up.

ON AND OFF the light flashed, faster and faster until I could not tell whether the bright flashes were coming from the mirror or inside my head.

'Stop it!'

Sam's hands were strong against my back and my head hit the metal corner.

On and off, faster and faster—

—darkness.

MUM SAYS THAT Sam had an epileptic fit. I wish I could remember what happened. I wish I knew if it was me that killed him.

CHAPTER THREE

Glass dagger

ALICIA SURVEYED THE foreign landscape. Round and alert, her eyes roved from the patch of woodland visible beyond the crest of a distant hill to the tiny lamb nibbling at the grass by her feet, before returning to the dagger on the rim of the well. The handle of the weapon was white, perhaps ivory; the blade was transparent, crystal or glass. Its brilliant edge glinted in the light of an unseen sun.

Lying awake at night, one ear on the front door, she had contemplated the difference between waking life and a dream. In waking life, one event led to another: cause and effect. If you saw a fish in a store window, you might remember to feed the fish; once home, you would toss pellets of food into the garden pond. In a dream, the mind played connect-the-dots, linking associated thoughts. You might see a fish, remember your fear of drowning, and find yourself in the garden pond, drowning—as a fish. There is no control in a dream, no conscious choices. Imagination plays tag with memory and results in chaos.

Lucid dreams were different. It was not clarity that distinguished them from a regular dream; Alicia had experienced vivid dreams in which every bristling hair of the wolf was visible, every detail from the drop of saliva hanging on its jaws to the bloodstained claws. It was the sense of awareness that differentiated the two: the knowledge that she was lying in her bed while the world around her was a construct of her mind, open to manipulation.

In dreams both common and lucid, the environment was as fragile as smoke, a heartbeat away from vanishing irretrievably. The landscape in which she now stood was unnervingly solid. She raised a hand to her chest, pressed fingers against her vest and felt the acceleration of her beating heart. But the adrenaline pumping through her body did not draw the sensation of the pillow to her cheek; she did not straddle the conscious and unconscious dimensions, walking that tightrope along the impermanence of a lucid dream. The landscape remained as stable as the waking world.

'Where am I?'

The stranger rose from the rim of the well and spoke in a rehearsed manner: 'Through lucid dreaming, the conscious element of your self—your spirit, your soul, however you wish to call it—has detached from the physical mind. While your body remains in bed, your soul has entered a space beyond the waking world. Vivador is the immaterial realm, where consciousness can interact in its purest form.'

Alicia's knees wobbled and she held out her hands, palms down, to steady herself.

'I'm dreaming.'

The stranger's eyes were calm as he lifted the dagger from the rim of the well. The glass blade was long and curved, like a ceremonial artefact. He turned the weapon in his hand and offered it to Alicia.

'Kill the lamb.'

Stepping back instinctively, Alicia bent down and lifted the beast into her bare arms. Its coat was incredibly soft as it struggled against her, its wild eyes searching for the grass at her feet.

'No,' she met the stranger's eyes. The rapid patter of the lamb's heart pulsed against her shoulder.

'It's just a dream,' he uttered. 'It's not real.'

The lamb had given up struggling and bleated nervously, puffing warm air against her earlobe.

'It would feel real.'

He stepped forward and Alicia raised a palm: 'Please!'

He nodded and the hint of a smile played across his face. Alicia lowered the animal to the ground and when she raised her eyes the dagger was gone. The stranger joined her at the bottom of the hill and crouched down, gesturing for her to do the same. She did so tentatively, glancing from the rim of the well to the pockets of his denim shorts in search of the weapon.

'In the physical realm, we are limited by language. Words reduce the world around us to a series of labels insufficient to represent what we see. If I were to describe a rose to you, drawing from every word in existence, the image in your mind could never match the image in mine. I could sketch it, paint it—' he shook his head, '—no tool available could reproduce the rose in my mind's eye. But here...'

He lowered his eyes to the ground between them. The blades of grass shifted as an infant bud nudged its way to the surface before rising upon a strong and thorny stem to burst into flower. Alicia ran the back of her fingers across a velvet petal. Its irrefutable beauty challenged her belief that this rose was anything but real.

'In Vivador, you see what I see.'

Betraying his professional demeanor, delight danced in those glacial eyes. She studied the short strands of hair on his head, flecks of cinnamon-brown amid a tawny-gold, and scanned his flawless, symmetrical face. She searched for evidence that she had unconsciously generated these features based on others that she had seen; but she recalled nothing.

'How did I get here?'

He stood up and faced the well, where the lamb grazed at the long shoots about its base.

'If I say *Red*, you say *Six*.'

Alicia stood and crossed her arms.

'Red,' he said.

'Six,' said Alicia.

'That is a link that we now share: a connection in our minds between the colour red and the number six. A conscious pathway, private to us. If I were to say *Red* to anyone else, there would be no such response.'

He gestured to the top of the hill.

'This well represents one of these conscious pathways. It is a link between two far greater concepts: Vivador and the waking world. Through this well, you hijacked the conscious pathway of whoever established this link—of one who had found Vivador through a lucid dream.'

Alicia considered her body under the bedcovers and looked down at her projected self: the olive ribbed-knit crop top that she wore around the house on warm days; the blue jeans with a hole on the left knee where she had caught herself against a nail. As her mind had filled in the inconsistencies when she visited her grandmother's cottage, so had it generated the details of her outfit. And these had been generated subconsciously, like characters in a dream. She scanned the hills that lay between the well and distant woodland, so bare and unremarkable. A blank canvas.

She strolled to the base of the nearest hill and settled her focus on the blades of grass at its crest. Narrowing her eyes, Alicia summoned a deep, meditative concentration. The hilltop trembled and from it erupted the trunk of a tree. The upper half of the trunk split, unfurling like a plastic wrapper over a naked flame. Branches twisted into thick boughs and buds blossomed from their gnarled fingers. The barren tree shivered under an explosion of leaves: a gamut of natural colour ranging from rusty saffron to olive green. Where nothing had stood moments before, a great oak towered above her.

The stranger climbed the hill, stepping beneath the canopy of the tree to place a palm against its trunk. Alicia watched him study her creation. Fine hairs on the back of his neck disappeared beneath his T-shirt. If he was not the product of her subconscious, then who was he?

She blinked and surveyed the landscape, turning on the spot. No dreamlike quality of light, nothing that might differentiate this environment from the waking world. Except for the words between her ears. While awake, her mind was an inchoate mass of tangled thoughts, a backlog of half-baked, unprocessed ideas, crushed down to make more space like a bin in need of emptying. Here, the space behind her eyes was as clear as the unreal air in her projected lungs.

Jack was here—a reminder, a warning, three words heavy as cinder blocks.

Jack is dead.

'Who are you and what do you want from me?' Alicia demanded of the figure standing in the shade of her tree.

'My name is Ryan. I'm here to take you to your brother.'

Collective nouns

JOE RETURNED TO the living room with a tumbler in each hand, both filled just above the crystal pattern inscribed halfway up the glass. He placed the water beside Gus's pot of pills and settled into a leather armchair by the liquor globe. Resting the glass of whiskey on his knee, he shot furtive glances at the book on the table as though the lightning-struck eye might blink at any moment.

'Take a pill,' he urged, nodding to the unopened pot. 'You're about to slip off that chair. We'll talk once you've slept.'

'We'll talk now,' Gus said, straightening his back. 'Tell me what you know about this book.'

'What do you think it is?'

'Don't start that crap—'

'Augustus.'

Lines of impatience furrowed Joe's brow from his bushy eyebrows to his bald scalp. Gus had studied the book before Joe returned, and his parents were not in it. Like Alicia, he had keyed dozens of names into the browser on his phone and found a string of sudden deaths: healthy individuals who had fallen from horses in Ireland and cliffs in Portugal, drowned in bathtubs in Wales and riptides off the Cornish coast.

'It's a hit list—' Gus stifled a yawn, '—a list of people who are being targeted. One by one.'

Joe nodded, tapping a thumb against the glass on his knee. He had not changed out of his uniform and the edges of the dark fabric were lost against the chair. Gus leaned forward and gripped the table, his fingernails white.

'Who wrote it?'

'Your father used to call it the "Murder Book".'

A block of light through the kitchen door and the glow of street lamps behind the closed blinds did little to illuminate the dark room. Joe leaned across the liquor globe and lifted something from the shelf lining the bay window. From the shadow, he withdrew a large stuffed crow perched on a tree branch. Gus blinked scratchy eyelids over dry eyes as Joe ran a finger over the feathered head.

'You're familiar with collective nouns? Pride of lions, flock of sheep...'

Gus was already there: 'A murder of crows.'

'That book was written by our family.'

Gus returned his eyes to the leatherbound book with a steady pounding in his temples. His mouth opened and closed before he managed to speak.

'My parents?'

'No,' said Joe, and firmer: 'No. They stole it, remember?'

The policeman rose from his chair and returned the bird to the shadows before walking up to the table as if it were an altar. He cradled the glass against his chest.

'It was my grandparents. Your great-grandparents. They are responsible for this.'

Gus's eyes searched the gold-foil symbol, his mind latching to the names concealed within: *Jack Henson, Melody Wilson*. Their faces haunted the edges of his vision.

'You never...' Gus shook his head. 'You or Dad, you never mentioned them. When Grandma died, I thought that was it. Are they...?'

'Still alive?' A grunt. 'Yes. And no—our father never talked about his parents, and neither did we. Now you know why.'

Gus studied Joe's gruff face as though it might spark lost memories. During summer holidays, his parents had taken him to Cranleigh, where they would endure Blithe's relentless criticism of everything said and done by anyone in her vicinity, particularly Joe, her sole carer. Evenings had been spent playing card games on the wooden terrace, with Benedict smoking his father's pipe and Sylvie accusing Joe of cheating just to rile him up. Blithe had interrupted each game with a new demand, from changing the water in the vases in her bedroom to opening the window while she read in the living room, refusing to join their games but seldom allowing her presence to go unnoticed. When the widow passed away and Joe joined his twin in Ireland, Gus had assumed they were all that remained of the Crow family.

'Benedict and I were keen to cut ties,' Joe mused, swirling the remnants of his drink in the tumbler. The air was rich with the scent of whiskey. 'Our grandfather reached out a couple of times, but we kept our distance. At least, until—'

'—Mum and Dad stole that book?'

'Sylvie had this fear that, once you were old enough, your great-grandparents would take an interest in you. When you were young, they paid you little attention; but as you got older, they started to send you birthday cards from their home in Portugal. You never saw them. Sylvie made sure of that. She felt guilty, and so did Ben. They knew what our grandparents were capable of—what family they had brought you into. When you turned seventeen, they went after them. They went to Portugal. And they stole the Murder Book.'

'How did they die?'

Joe drained the glass and set it down on the corner of the table.

'I don't know how they do it. But I know it involves lucid dreaming—that's why you take those pills. I don't know how they killed your parents, but Anna Harrington was there when it happened. They handed her the book and dropped at her feet. They died because they interfered, Augustus. And now Anna—I tried to convince her to give it back,' he picked up the glass again, as if to crush it in his thick fingers. 'I tried to talk sense into the woman.'

Gus thought of the large, equine eyes in Anna's portrait, now haunted by the death of his parents. His leg twitched, seeking permission. Adrenaline urged him to sprint to Alicia's door and wait for her mother's return, itching to glean fragments of his parents' final moments.

'What was she doing there?'

'Anna was looking for her son. Wrong place, wrong time.'

'And she went to Bristol, this weekend, to warn Melody?'

'She failed. Melody Wilson died last night. Kitchen fire.'

Gus pictured the elderly proprietor closing her sweetshop for the evening and turning on the stove.

'Why are they killing these people?'

'I don't know,' said Joe, glancing down at the glass as he spoke. He raised his eyes to Gus. 'But if we don't return the book, they'll kill us too.'

'Rainn,' said Gus. 'At school, I saw that tattoo on her wrist,'—a nod at the book—'She's working with them?'

Joe's face paled and his Adam's apple shifted up and down.

'She's here for the book. And if we give it to her now, there's a chance Anna might be spared.'

His uncle was keeping some cards close to his chest, but Gus understood that the possession of this book put them both in danger. Fatigue pulled at him like an ocean current and his bloodshot eyes sought the pills on the table. A powerful longing surged through him to close his eyes, to let go and to escape.

'If my parents died taking this book, I'm not going to hand it back like a good little Crow.'

As though acting independently of his body, his fingers clawed at the lid of the pot and prised it open. He tipped a pill into his trembling hand, popped it in his mouth and chased it with the water. A naked relief lit Joe's face.

'When Anna gets home, she'll come looking for it,' said Gus, pushing back his chair. 'Alicia will know I've taken it. Until she comes knocking, I'm looking after this.'

Joe made no move to stop him when Gus lifted the Murder Book into his hands and carried it up to his bedroom. He tucked the book at the bottom of a box of hooded jackets and then frowned, pulled it from the box and hid it at the back of his wardrobe. As he sidestepped the box on the way to his bed, the floor tilted as the pill began to take effect.

Eight hours of dreamless sleep.

He collapsed onto the bed and then rolled onto his back, rubbing his eyes. Grumbling, he forced himself into a sitting position, dissatisfied with the hiding place.

He hasn't told you everything.

Gus pulled the book from the wardrobe and cursed, looking left to right as waves of drowsiness drew him under.

He'll ransack this room.

He stuffed the book down his shorts and crashed on his mattress. Seconds, minutes or hours later, a brilliant light burst into the room—bright sparks in his eyes and a distant growl. He sat up to see headlights through his bedroom window. The growl ended as the engine cut.

Gus rose from his bed and staggered to the window. Pressing his forehead to the glass, he watched Anna Harrington step out of her car.

A + E forever

ON THE OUTLYING tree of the forest, something caught Alicia's eye. Letters had been engraved into the foot of the trunk. The scaly bark of the pine had been pried away and a message scored into the wood beneath: *A + E Forever.* The lettering was untidy, cut with deep strokes. Kneeling on fallen needles, Alicia ran a fingertip over the letters, reminiscent of her mother tracing the alphabet into David's palm.

A and *E*? Anna and Eloise? If Vivador was anything other than a profound lucid dream, was it not conceivable that her mother and grandmother had also ventured down the well? But, if so, why take the painstaking effort to cut letters into the tough wood when the message could be conjured in an instant?

'Come on,' said Ryan.

He had asked her to follow him and she had not hesitated. She had asked him where they were going and what her brother was doing in this place; he had kept his eyes forward and his mouth closed. In silence, they had crossed the hills and reached the edge of the forest. Beneath the pale sky, tall pines stretched to her left and right as far as she could see. Since Ryan would not answer her questions, she directed her attention inward.

If you believe David might be here, why aren't you running?

Unbound from their biological shell, her thoughts rang clear between her ears.

Because Jack is dead.

In the waking world, if something was troubling Alicia it might manifest as irritation or impatience, a lack of appetite or sleepless nights. The underlying cause of her unease might lurk on distant shelves, as had her memory of the shed. But here, in this immaterial realm, the spotlight of her attention cut through the shadows. There was nowhere for her anxiety to hide.

She entered the forest with cautious footsteps as she separated fact from belief. Jack had visited the well and died. His name was written in a book that her mother had hidden while she searched for David. The environment was stable and her thoughts clear; but these were weak reasons to believe that this was any more than a dream. It was infinitely more plausible that this was a fantasy born of desperation: the handsome stranger guiding her through the woods to her missing brother.

How can a dream be dangerous? Gus took pills to protect him from his dreams. If this place was real, then Alicia was venturing into the unknown with a man who had been waiting for her, rehearsing lines with a dagger at his side. Keeping her head forward, she stole glances at his wrists, his neck and the biceps that stretched his short-sleeved T-shirt—no tattoos. Though these would not be difficult to hide. Following this stranger deeper into the woods, the cavity between her ears filled with anxious pleas to turn and run.

You have two choices, she thought. *Follow him wherever he is taking you, or wake up and wait for Mum to come home.*

She picked up the pace.

'Who created this forest?' she asked, brushing a finger along a branch sticky with sap. Ryan shook his head: he did not know. She ran her eyes across the upper branches and over the fragrant needles that littered the soft soil. If this forest had been created by another mind, had its creator conjured the image of every tree? It had not been necessary to determine the shape and colour of each leaf when creating the oak. If it were possible to raise a forest from the bare ground, what if she imagined a planet? As the thrill of possibility pulsed through her, a breeze rustled the branches overhead, dislodging pine needles.

'Who creates the breeze?'

'You do. Conscious and unconscious creation: Vivador is constructed through will and expectation.'

Alicia focused on the boughs above and a great gust of wind swept the forest. The trees swayed under a fierce gale and pine needles showered upon the pair. With a bashful smile, she brushed needles from Ryan's shoulders. He fixed his gaze ahead and continued walking.

She scanned the trees, half-expecting to spot her brother red-faced and breathless from chasing squirrels. Half an hour passed, with each line of trees a replica of the previous, devoid of animal life and disturbed only by gusts of wind that she created unintentionally. Her rising impatience was echoed in the intensity of the intermittent breeze. Ryan's face was so peaceful, and his even, plodding steps lacked any urgency. Her fists clenched.

'I want to know where you're taking me.'

'We're nearly there.'

'Nearly wh—'

She stopped and reached out a hand to grip a low branch.

'What is it?' Ryan asked.

'Nothing,' said Alicia. Had she imagined the concern in his voice? 'I just felt dizzy.'

Ryan was calm as he spoke: 'It is likely that someone is trying to wake you. You had better return to the well, else they'll think you're in a coma.'

Who gave him these lines?

'Run,' Ryan uttered.

She raced back through the forest, pausing twice when the ground trembled like the skin of a beaten drum. Her legs did not tire and her breath did not fall short as she sprinted through the trees and over the hills beyond. Two minutes later, she reached the hilltop and flung herself down the well.

Hear no evil

SOMEONE WAS SHAKING her shoulders. Alicia bolted upright in bed, so fast that she nearly knocked the figure to the ground. Her eyes focused and her breathing stopped: it was her mother. She stared hard at the face before her, as though after all she had recently experienced, seeing her mother at her bedside was the hardest to comprehend.

'Honestly, Alicia. Are you drunk? I've been—'

She threw her arms around her mother's neck. Spiky, blonde hair tickled her cheek as the hug was returned, and only then did Alicia realise how much she needed it. For a full second, that coiled spring of anxiety began to unwind, and then she was released.

In the large black pupils of Anna Harrington's eyes, Alicia saw no signs of deception. If the promise that they held remained, it was buried beyond a foggy cloud, obscured by remnants of things that the woman should not have seen.

'Where is it?' Anna asked, her gaunt face lined with panic. Having seen so little of her mother over the past months, having spent so many hours gazing at her own re-creation of that face on the canvas, Alicia met a stark contrast between her mental image and reality. What was elfin and bold in those immature strokes lay aged and troubled before her.

'Where's what?' Rory poked his head through the door. A delighted grin lifted his round cheeks, as if he were thrilled to see both his girls in one room. Anna held Alicia's gaze, the glare of street lights catching the bags beneath her eyes.

'Your father told me you painted the wall above our bed?'

Alicia cast the covers aside and threw her legs over the edge of the bed. Wordlessly, she rose and walked past her mother, past Rory in the doorway and down the corridor. In her parents' bedroom, both portraits lay face-down on the floor. Scattered around the portrait of Rory and David were the posters she had collected. The recess behind her painting was bare.

'Where is it?' Anna repeated over her shoulder.

'Will I put the kettle on?' asked Rory. He tilted his head at the night sky through the window. 'Sure, it's nearly eleven, but still... might be nice?'

'I don't know,' said Alicia, stepping closer to the empty wooden frame. Her jaw tightened as she wrestled with the idea that the one person she had opened up to had betrayed her.

'Honestly, Alicia—'

Alicia spun to face her mother with fury in her malachite eyes.

'Honestly, Mum?' Her voice was raised and Rory winced in the corridor; nobody shouted in the Harrington household.

One January, Alicia had been desperate for a mobile phone: her best friends had both received them for Christmas, and the pair had taken to spending breaktimes discussing their social media profiles while Alicia sketched wolves in her notepad. Anna had been adamant that she was 'too young' to carry the internet in her pocket. As a hormonal twelve-year-old, Alicia considered herself old enough to make her own decisions and accused her mother of isolating her from the group chats that dominated life outside of school. Anna had criticised the inane online chatter she had witnessed having confiscated devices from her students—groups attempting to communicate through acronym and emoticon, flirting and bickering their way into disputes—surely there were better ways for her daughter to express herself? Alicia had expressed herself with a string of curses and the slam of her bedroom door. When Anna had knocked on her door later that evening, she had not come to discuss the phone.

'Your brother is blind,' she had whispered, her large black eyes uncharacteristically sombre. Alicia had lifted her head from the pillow and hissed over her shoulder: 'What does that have to do—'

'He cannot see, Alicia—'

'You think I don't know what "blind" means?'

'I think you understand what the word means.'

'What does *that* mean?'

Anna had walked to Alicia's dressing table and lifted a stone monkey, sat with its hands on its ears. Alicia had taken the monkey from her grandmother's house during their final visit, and it had since been used as something on which to hang earrings and drape necklaces. Anna removed a beaded necklace that was tucked through the monkey's arms and went to her daughter's bed with the fist-sized statuette in her palm.

'How much of our world is visual? How much do we experience through image and colour? David's world is texture—' she brushed a finger across the stone head, '—smell, taste and, above all, sound. If he cannot see the beauty in this world, then he must hear nothing but beauty in his home.'

Alicia had sat cross-legged on her bed, lifted her hand and received the stone ornament. The monkey sat on her fingers, pressing its hands over its ears with a quizzical look on its face.

'Hear no evil,' she had said. Alicia and her mother had continued to argue over bedtimes and household chores, liberties and responsibilities, as frequently as in any mother–daughter relationship. But they never raised their voices. From that January, Alicia made a conscious effort to paint their house with positivity. Through description, anecdote and praise, she helped her mother to generate beauty in a world that David would never see.

Presently, Alicia chewed her bottom lip, checked her anger and levelled her voice, if only for her father's sake.

'Honestly? Do you know the meaning of the word? Where have

you been?'

Anna was fully dressed, wearing a mint-green trench coat and jeans. Beside what appeared to be a gift on the bed, wrapped in white paper with a gold bow, lay her large handbag. Had she just returned, or was she ready to go?

'You've been looking for him, haven't you?'

Anna reached out and took her daughter's hands in her own. The expression on her face was troubled.

'I have one last stop to make. And then I'm all yours.'

One last stop, thought Alicia. *One final name on the list.*

She was no longer in Vivador, yet the words between her ears were so clear she might have played them through headphones.

'Let's take five minutes,' said Rory, still hovering in the bedroom doorway. 'I'll make us a nice brew and we can have a proper chat.'

He strolled off down the corridor.

'I found the book,' said Alicia. 'I found the well. I—' She hesitated. *I found a man who said he'll take me to David—*

'Your father said Winter broke into the house. Do you think she might have taken it?'

'Have you found him?'

Anna looked through the open window, her eyes on the police car in the driveway next door. Her haunted eyes narrowed.

'No,' she replied, stepping past Alicia and to the bed. She lifted the gift and stared at it for a moment, before turning to meet her daughter's eyes. 'But I think I've found someone who can help us.'

As the gravity of the statement plunged through Alicia, her mother slipped past, kissed her on the cheek and dropped the present into her hands.

'Happy Birthday,' she whispered. 'We'll open this when I'm back.'

The shape of the present was unnervingly similar to the missing book, but whatever the white wrapping paper concealed was almost weightless. Alicia followed her mother's hurried steps down the stairs. When the front door opened, her throat tightened. Her mother was leaving, again. Alicia's eyes burned as words spilled from her open mouth: 'I'm still here.'

Anna watched a tear slide down the side of her daughter's nose. On her eighteenth birthday, Alicia was an adult; but she remained the child that Anna repeatedly left behind. Anna swallowed, slung her bag over her shoulder and raised a finger.

'One hour. And I will tell you everything.'

She turned down the drive and Alicia wiped the tear from her chin. She stepped into the open doorway, creasing the paper in her hands as a fraying rope in the back of her mind twisted. Tightened. Taut.

And then it snapped. As Anna opened the car door, Alicia heard her thoughts as clearly as in Vivador. She knew she would regret what she was about to say, yet it did not stop her from calling across the driveway: 'If you killed those people,'—their eyes locked—'don't come back.'

Anna blanched. She closed the car door and started the engine. Alicia crossed to the kitchen doorway and asked her father: 'What did she tell you?'

There was a thump as the kettle hit the floor and Rory slid to the ground. Alicia dropped her birthday present on the table by the door and dashed over to protect her sleeping father from the growing puddle of boiling water.

It's not down my pants

JOE SHRUGGED INTO a jacket and opened the front door as Anna's car pulled out of the driveway. He closed the door behind him, but it opened again a second later.

'Get back inside,' Joe ordered as he unlocked the car.

'Nope,' said Gus, opening the passenger door and crawling inside. Joe lowered himself into the driver's seat and gripped the wheel.

'Get out.'

'Drive.'

Gus blinked until the three images of his uncle coalesced into one: a pair of beetroot cheeks hot with the desire to lean across, open the door and kick him through it. The pill coursed through his bloodstream, leaking into his organs, powering him down.

'Where's the book?'

'Well,' Gus clicked his seatbelt into place with clumsy fingers, 'it's not down my pants.'

Joe hissed through clenched teeth: 'Is it safe?'

'Are we going after her, or not?'

With no time to argue, Joe closed his door and started the engine. He shot a glance at the Harrington property as they slipped past, and did not turn on the headlights until they had reached the end of Gardner Road.

'We're off to Melissa Lawson's, right?' Gus asked as they took a left onto the main road and the shadowy shapes of houses blurred past the window. The policeman took a deep breath through his nostrils and exhaled slowly. Gus folded his arms and tried to put his feet on the dashboard, but lacked the space to do so.

'I'm not giving them the book,' he said. 'Not until I've talked to Alicia.'

At eleven on a Wednesday night, the roads were empty. Joe did not stop at red lights, but continued towards the centre of Godalming, accelerating past cars parked along the roadside. Gus's head rattled against the window as they turned down the cobbled high street. A white building with a clocktower was bleached in moonlight. He raised his eyes to the large moon in the cloudless sky and his breath spilled on the window.

'It's odd, don't you think?' he said, his tongue heavy. 'The moon can pull tides—gallons and gallons right up the shore…but it can't lift a grain of sand? If it can move oceans, it must have an effect on us. Don't you think?'

Joe took his eyes from the road to study his nephew's face.

'I think you should close your eyes and let that pill do its job.'

'Is that so?' Gus grinned. 'Then you can go rifling around, searching for the Murder Book and handing it back to your grandparents and doing the total opposite of what my parents died for?'

The hard look on Joe's face made Gus uncomfortable and he looked away. They were on residential streets again: lights off in the windows; mice dashing between bins. Joe took a sharp turn and Gus's head thunked against the back of his seat. At the sight of Anna's car at the end of the lane, the policeman floored the pedal.

'That's it, Uncle,' said Gus, sitting up to grip the dashboard. 'Hit the siren, quick—'

'Sit back.' Joe pushed him roughly into his seat. Gus shot him an injured look, rubbing his ribs, and Joe glanced down at the young man's lap. 'Is it down your pants?'

'No!' Gus replied, more indignantly than was warranted, given that the book had been down his shorts ten minutes before, while he stared through his bedroom window.

If you killed those people, Alicia's voice had carried through the glass, *don't come back.*

'She didn't kill anyone,' Gus muttered aloud.

Anna accelerated: she had seen the police car. Gus gripped the armrest as Joe flooded the screaming engine. Alicia's mother pulled the wheel to make a left turn, but Joe undercut her. He hit the brakes and Gus was flung forward and caught by his seatbelt. Joe cut the engine, his car blocking the entrance of a long driveway.

Through his window, Gus saw a white house flanked with tall bushes. A blink, and the bushes became fir trees. A Jeep was parked in the shade of the trees, where the moonlight did not fall. In the daylight, this Jeep was a juniper green; Gus had been struck by the juxtaposition of the offroad vehicle and Melissa Lawson's business suit as she parked it at school that morning. He panned his gaze to the right and caught frustration on Anna's face as she abandoned her car in the middle of the empty road.

Joe had already positioned himself between the bonnet of his car and the manicured bushes at the front of the property, blocking Anna's route. Gus hauled his leaden legs onto the gravel and used the roof of the car to steady himself, his eyes on Joe, who glanced at Melissa's house with unveiled apprehension. Anna tightened the cord on her jacket.

'We have the book,' said Joe.

Gus looked down at his crotch, frowned, and realised that his uncle meant possession of the book, back at the house.

'Come back to mine,' Joe added, 'and we can talk.'

'Move aside, Joe.' Anna's voice was calm, but her lip trembled: an expression Gus had seen on her daughter's face, sick with impatience.

Joe spoke so quietly that Gus leaned against the bonnet to catch his words.

'Rainn is here—she's staying with Melissa. They will be expecting you. They will be watching. Come back with us. If you hand her the book—if it comes from you—they will leave you alone. You never asked for it!' he hissed. 'And they will spare Alicia.'

Rainn is here: Gus's eyes roved the dark panes of the stately building, blurring between blinks. In the top-left window, the moon winked back.

'Honestly.' Anna shook her head, thrusting her hands into her jacket pockets. 'You know that's not true. What good is that book to them now? They're all dead. What good is it to anyone? If they wanted to finish me off, they'd have done it by now. It's Alicia they want. Her and Gus. And they won't stop until they've found them.'

She was looking at him—her huge black eyes glossy in the moonlight. Gus resisted the urge to wave, swallowed painfully, and dry words tumbled from his mouth.

'You saw them die.'

Anna shot a glance at the house and Joe took a step closer to Gus, who realised that he had not spoken quietly. He attempted a whisper: 'Why did they give it to you?'

Joe put a firm hand on Gus's shoulder, to steady or warn him. Anna shook her head and sniffed.

'Because I was there,' she said.

In her equine eyes, Gus saw his parents' faces. His legs began to wobble. He steadied himself on the roof of the car, closed his eyes and forced them open. It was like hauling a boulder up a hill, straining under the mental exertion and trying not to lose his grip.

Anna turned to Joe. 'You keep on hiding, Joe. Keep drinking. But this won't go away. They have my son. They have hers,' she nodded at the house. 'You won't help me, but she will.'

She did not wait for a response. In supporting Gus, Joe had left the way open and Anna shouldered past. Small stones crunched loudly underfoot as she marched down the driveway. Joe took half a step and stopped as if a forcefield stretched between the bushes.

Gus was shoved into the passenger seat, and heard his uncle growl: 'We're getting the book.'

The engine purred into action and Gus leaned his right cheek against the headrest, watching his uncle drift in and out of focus.

'Alicia,' said Gus. 'We'll wake her up. She won't be sleeping. We'll tell her what's happening.'

Bullet-hole eyes darted back and forth between Gus's face and the road ahead. Gus's eyelids were so heavy he considered propping them open with his fingers.

Joe's voice was gruff: 'You're into her, aren't you?'

Gus turned his head away and laughed silently. Mirthlessly. And then frowned. Behind his eyelids, Alicia lifted a portrait from the wall.

'I stole her book.'

A churn in his empty stomach. A rush of memories: Alicia on her grandmother's sofa, confiding in him, trusting him; the pair of them outside her house as she refused to let him see the book. Him thinking: What if Anna returned and found a new hiding place? Why hadn't they learned to lock the back door?

His teeth rattled in his skull as Joe accelerated over cobbles.

'Augustus,' warned a voice to his right. 'You can't...Alicia—'

'I'm into guys.'

It might have been the pill. Gus kept his eyes ahead, watching the approach of the clocktower at the end of the street, the minute hand ticking closer to the end of his first day as an adult. His statement hung in silence. Joe's mouth opened and closed in the reflection of the windscreen.

'Oh,' Joe shot his nephew a sidelong glance. He adjusted his grip on the steering wheel and ran a red light. 'I just—you don't seem very...'

'It doesn't really work like that.'

'Right, yes. Okay. Good.'

'Good?'

Joe cleared his throat. 'When my father married my mother, he had a child from a previous marriage. A daughter—Anna. Alicia is your second cousin.'

Seconds trickled by. Gus watched a petrol station blur past, the world brushing against the windows like the bristles of a car wash. He waited for the blurring to stop, for it all to slow down and make sense. Chemicals melted in his bloodstream, dissolving fear, dissolving time. He waited to feel something.

'Well,' said Gus. 'Good thing I'm not into her.'

Blood rushed along his temples, feeding his brain with the remnants of the pill. He slid back into his seat, waiting for Joe to remark on his admission. To ask him if his parents had known, or to tell him they had suspected. To say something.

They approached a roundabout before the Refectory Inn and Joe cleared his throat to speak. Gus sat up and the police officer's phone rang in his pocket. He pulled it out and Gus caught a blur of letters on the screen: Lawson. Joe pulled into the middle of the Refectory car park and jumped out to answer Melissa's call. Gus lifted a hand to open the door but fatigue overwhelmed him; a battery straining on one percent; a blink, and Joe was back in the car.

What? asked Gus, in his head.

Joe's square shoulders rose and fell, a cloud of breath spilling through his nostrils as he stared at the windscreen.

'Anna's dead,' he said.

Gus blinked once more and slipped from consciousness.

Ryan, age 9

WHEN AMIRA MOVED into Sam's bedroom, Mum said I should leave her to settle in while she's processing. But I don't like to go into Sam's bedroom anyway, so Amira draws with me in my room. Sometimes I write numbers and she copies them, like Mum used to teach me in Maths when I was as little as Amira. She is only six and lost her parents in an earthquake in Egypt. I asked her about the pharaohs and the curses in the pyramids, but she's not much of a talker.

Mum laughed again for the first time when we were playing Bingo in the classroom. She asked why Amira always picks the same numbers in the same order and Amira said they were the colours of the rainbow. Amira's special, like Sam. Peter says she has synaesthesia, which means numbers have colours and colours have smells. We sang the rainbow song but with Amira's numbers and Mum was laughing the way she used to when something so silly happens that she never wants to forget it. She holds onto the wall like she's falling over and laughs so hard that she will always remember.

Amira is quiet but she's brave. She's not even scared of my scar, and doesn't stare at it like Mum does. I stared at the scar in the mirror. It looks like someone tried to draw a line from my eye to my ear, but got bored halfway. There must have been about 29 stitches but they're gone now. On the corner of the mirror I could see my blood on the sharp metal leaf growing out of the frame. Or maybe it was rusted.

I was thinking about how Mum used to say that my eyes were the bluest in the whole world when I heard Peter calling my name from downstairs. I thought I was in trouble because he told me not to go in the attic in the daytime now that Mum knows I was in there. But Mum was planting cucumbers in the garden and Amira was playing with the dollhouse in Sam's bedroom so I thought it would be okay.

I hid the key and went downstairs and Peter was standing in the doorway with a puppy. It was this tiny husky, so soft it was unreal. Amira came out of Sam's bedroom and the puppy licked all over her face. She said the eyes tasted like lemon—they were blue just like mine. It made me wonder if Mum had picked the dog as she used to talk about my eyes all the time.

'Your first pet,' Peter said to me. I looked at Amira and she was so excited, like this was the best thing that had ever happened to her.

'It can be both of ours!' I said.

Peter didn't look too happy about that and said I was being ungrateful. The dog was for me and he wanted to know what I would call it. It turns out it's a boy, so I named him Sam.

Me and Amira played with Sam all afternoon. When Amira went to sleep in Sam's bedroom, I took Sam up to sleep in mine. I almost fell asleep when he stopped wriggling next to my leg like a bag of rats, but that's because he had run out of the room. I panicked and started shouting his name all over the house. And then I saw that the front door was open.

I'm not supposed to go in the attic in the day and I'm definitely not supposed to go outside at night. But I could see Sam running around in the grass by the Pagoda. The Pagoda is a tower at the end of our garden, near the lake. Peter says that Buddhists used to keep human bones in them. He built one when him and Mum moved to Burnflower, but Sam's bones are kept on the other side of the garden, behind the vegetables.

After Sam died, Peter stopped working in his study. He started calling the room in the Pagoda his office, because it's really quiet over there. I left the door wide open and ran across the grass to get Sam. He jumped around like it was his idea to play outside and he just didn't know what time it was.

That's when I heard Mum shouting in Peter's office in the Pagoda.

'Why did you give him the damn dog?'—She was so cross with him.

I did not hear what Peter said, but I held Sam tight in the trees when Mum went back to the house. She shut the door behind her and I knew I would have to ask Peter to let me back inside. I went up the steps and I pushed open the wooden door and I was so angry that I didn't even knock.

'What's wrong with Mum? Why doesn't she want me to be happy?'

I was shouting so loud, but you can't hear shouts from the house. Peter closed his computer and told me that Mum finds it hard to love me after what I did to Sam. It wasn't actually very cold that night, but it felt really cold when he said that.

Peter let me back into the house and I took Sam up to my bedroom. With the lights off, Sam looked like a baby wolf. Peter looks like a wolf too, with his black hair and the teeth that you can see because of the bit missing in his top lip. I think that's why he got me the dog. I think he wants me to be a wolf like him.

CHAPTER FOUR
Am I dreaming?

SHE COULD NOT look at the coffin. She saw it when she scanned the crowd, avoiding each pair of eyes that sought her own. She saw it behind each detail that her mind feasted upon, from the sleek pipes of the organ nestled at the end of a wooden mezzanine to the white stone aisle worn smooth by a thousand blushing brides and as many grieving widows—a time lapse of white and black eroding the stone like warm water over ice. She could see her mother's coffin when she blinked her eyes, but she could not watch them carry it through the heavy doors and across the grounds. In the waking world, what you see is what you get. Alicia did not 'get' it, and—with every fibre of her being—she refused to.

Her eyes latched onto the stained-glass window high in the wall of the church. This large, circular window contained tiny pieces of glass, irregular in shape yet tessellating as though shattered and painstakingly reassembled. Each glass fragment, as diaphanous as the wings of a dragonfly, appeared to be a different colour, though this may have been a trick of the light that struck the window from behind. As she ran her eyes across it, she could discern no pattern.

Her mother would have spotted the pattern. Anna Harrington, devout believer in fate, would have understood what it all meant. She would have explained how each fragment had been assembled for a reason, fitting together to form one coherent whole. But all Alicia saw was chaos.

Noses were wiped. Eyes watered under heavy brows and trembling lips offered grave condolences: 'I'm so sorry.' Alicia remembered a time before David's disappearance when there had been other words in their vocabularies.

'Your mum is so weird!' said a friend after Alicia's mother burst into the bedroom to show them a ring she had purchased from a homeless man. Her friend had almost fallen off the bed, recoiling from the iron band as if it were a cockroach. Anna's eyes, wild with enormous black pupils, darted between Alicia's face and the ring as she pointed out marks on its surface: a faded pattern that she was managing to interpret as a story.

'Don't tell your father,' Anna said with a wink when they asked how much she had paid for it. A week later, Alicia spotted a painting of the ring on her mother's easel and asked her where it was. Anna's smile had been devilish.

'I snuck it back in his cap when he wasn't looking,' she had whispered, biting her lip at this devious trick.

Anna Harrington was weird. Not in a disturbing way, like Alicia's biology teacher, who trimmed his fingernails into sharp points and drummed them on his desk when the students were not listening. Not in an irritating way, like Uncle Niall, who found it necessary to explain precisely why his jokes were funny when only Rory laughed. Anna chose not to behave as society prescribed. If there was a more interesting or amusing way of doing something, then that was the preferable option.

At eleven years old, when Alicia's growing self-awareness manifested as acute self-consciousness, her mother's unorthodox character became a point of contention.

'Take it off,' Alicia had hissed when Anna walked through the living room wearing a lime-green balaclava. Her mother had stopped with her hand on the front door and looked back at the sofa, where Alicia was reading to David.

'It's freezing outside,' Anna had remarked.

'People will think you look crazy.'

'Yes, darling. And I will think that they look cold.'

It was not until the age of fifteen, and many such exchanges later, that Alicia realised an undeniable truth: almost everybody adored her mother. And those few that did not like Anna Harrington were awkward, angry characters who had forgotten how to smile.

'Conformity isn't her thing,' Alicia remarked to her friends in class with a shrug. Mrs Harrington was a teacher who believed that, so long as you demonstrated creativity, it was all right—if not preferable—to be as noisy, messy and downright inappropriate as possible. Some of the parents found her subject matter a little mature; some of the governors were still sore from the Ofsted incident with the contraceptive balloon animals; and lazier students had suffered from her frank assessment when effort was lacking. But Mrs Harrington's lessons were inspiring and had fostered a love for art in a school where the subject was compulsory.

As the coffin was lowered into the ground, Rory's hand was so hot it burned Alicia's skin. She stared at a patch of sky between the corner of the church and the tree beside it. This rectangle of blue was so sharp that it appeared to be in the foreground of her vision, with the tree and church behind it, like an optical illusion.

For three days, the world had presented itself to her in this manner. *Look at this!* Her mind had cried at the reflection in the glass as she brushed her teeth. *Do you really think this is real?*

She had once returned from a family holiday in Tokyo and it had taken two days after the flight for her ears to pop. She had not known that her hearing was diminished until her ears crackled and the subtle sounds of her surroundings flooded back. Since Vivador, something had popped. Her thoughts were no longer diminished, and her subconscious had a lot to say.

Not all these thoughts were welcome. Between the grey matter and the roof of her skull, a truth refused to sink in: her mother had fallen down the stairs at Melissa Lawson's house and broken her neck.

But it was reality that had died.

For three days, she had failed to dream lucidly. Following comprehensive internet research, her bedroom floor was littered with Post-it Notes scrawled with every dream she could recall: a process recommended to increase awareness of the dream state and trigger lucidity.

'Am I dreaming?' Alicia asked herself several times each day, a reality check that increased the likelihood of asking this question in a dream. When Rory had caught her asking her reflection in the kitchen sink, he had given her a curious look.

Her mind whirred in a futile effort to separate truth from fiction, reality from fantasy, and the longer she remained in the waking world, the more abstract her thoughts became. The fragments of dreams that lay strewn across her carpet echoed a rising paranoia: crows watching from the boughs of trees that tapped her bedroom window; Gus fighting through a crowd at the funeral with a book in his hand; Melissa Lawson dipping her quill in black ink and scribbling names on wrinkled parchment. She craved the static tranquillity of pine forests and the cool certainty of glacial eyes.

On the evening of the funeral, Alicia looked at the alarm clock, away and back again to find it obstinately glowing 20:42. She threw the clammy bedcovers aside, abandoning her latest attempt to find solace in the immaterial realm. Wearing only underwear and one of her mother's old Bowie T-shirts, she walked to the bathroom. She washed her hands under the tap and wondered how each finger directed itself without her conscious attention. If she was not moving her fingers, then who was? She slunk back down the corridor and recognised the clipped tones of her headmistress.

'—to at least consider it.'

'I'm not sure, Melissa. It's good for her to be at home…'

Her father's voice was tired and troubled. Alicia's bare feet padded down the carpeted steps. Through the banisters, she saw two untouched cups of tea on the table by the sofa. Rory's round face was red and his eyes groggy, like a lost boy at a theme park, waiting for his parents to collect him.

'Good for you, perhaps. But we should put her best interests at heart, and question which of the two of us can offer your daughter the support she needs.'

Melissa Lawson was sitting in an armchair with her back to Alicia. Her clipped tones carried up the stairs.

'She has lost her brother and now her mother. Without intervention, I fear that she may lose her mind.'

Alicia descended the stairs with rigid, robotic steps as the blood in her temples thickened. Through the scream of insidious thoughts, memories surfaced, real and imaginary: Melissa's kind smile as she prised the poster of David from Alicia's blue fingers; Anna's wild eyes as she was pushed down the stairs.

The head in the armchair turned her way and a shadow crossed Alicia's vision. Melissa's lips were parted, her grey eyes wide.

'Get out,' said Alicia.

Her father twitched, his eyes pleading.

Alicia opened her mouth and screamed those two words until her voice was hoarse. She clutched the banisters as Rory ushered the headmistress through the archway to the front door. Alicia's ears were muffled as she drifted through the kitchen, out of the back door and into the garden, where smoke rose from the remnants of a barbecue on the patio. Blinking her eyes, she spotted her mobile phone on a garden chair.

Seventeen calls to her mother, unanswered.

Twenty-four messages from family and friends, unread.

If you killed those people, don't come back.

'Am I dreaming?' she whispered, placing her phone on the barbecue and returning to bed.

I am a Crow

GUS STEPPED BENEATH the shower head, turned the tap on and let ice-cold water envelop him. The frigid torrent drowned out his thoughts, numbing his face, his body and his mind. The pills had stolen him to a dreamless abyss from which he had arisen with a clear head and an abundance of energy. The clouds had lifted and the world lay before him, bare and exposed.

Once showered, he caught his reflection in the mirror above the sink: the dark rings had softened around his eyes. The clouds had lifted, but the storm remained; what had lain dormant, sequestered in the shadows of a sleep-deprived mind, now surged livid through his resurrected body.

I am a Crow.

Was this volatile anger the same pervasive emotion that had driven his great-grandparents to write the Murder Book? His parents hadn't harboured such rage. Gus's father had been passionate and driven by his work, but always in good spirits. His mother had been a peacemaker, hating only hate itself, namely racism and war. And poor tipping, since Sylvie had waited tables at a beachside café. 'Skimp on clothes, but not tips,' she had told him. 'Nobody will judge you for a bargain at the charity shop, but give a bad tip and people talk.'

Could he attribute his anger entirely to the loss of his parents, or was it his birthright as a Crow?

For three days, he had taken his pills and escaped the unpalatable truths of the waking world. When the first pill wore off, he had woken to a remarkably lucid mind and was hounded by a barrage of questions concerning Anna's death and the murder of his parents.

Unwanted thoughts demanded his attention with the fervour of an abandoned dog. He had popped another pill and left his thoughts to chase their tails without him.

Joe had not protested against his nephew spending three days in bed. Gus had woken to glasses of water at his bedside and a tray of sandwiches presumably taken from the canteen at Joe's office in Guildford. In that unconscious abyss, Gus was as safe as Joe could keep him without locking the bedroom door and swallowing the key. It also gave the police officer the opportunity to ransack his room.

At first, Gus had woken to find his belongings as he had left them: the pot of pills at his bedside, the pile of hooded jackets half-spewn from the nearest box, his clothes decorating the floor in their allocated spots. But through a subconscious spot-the-difference, Gus knew that his uncle had searched the room while he slept. Perhaps the socks had lain beneath the green vest; perhaps it had been the blue hoodie and not the grey with both arms hanging out the box.

When the second pill wore off, he woke to find that Joe had abandoned any attempt at subtlety. His possessions had erupted from the boxes and lay sprawled across the carpet, the collateral damage of his uncle's impatience. While his shorts might have proven effective, they were not the most comfortable solution, so Gus had found another home for the Murder Book.

Presently, he dried himself with a towel and plodded down the corridor to peer inside his uncle's bedroom. Joe was out, presumably at work, and the large room was empty. It could have accommodated a king-size bed, but there was a single bed tucked in the corner. As if determined to take up as little space as possible, Joe had positioned his bedside cabinet at the foot of the bed and his wardrobe in the corner beside it. From subtle invasions of his own, Gus knew the bedside cabinet contained five old badges, two broken phones, a severely creased photograph of Joe skiing with Benedict and Sylvie, and an illegal firearm. He had first come across the 9mm pistol at his uncle's home in Galway, while searching for clues concerning the death of his parents.

Gus never entered the room to look at the photograph, but it always found its way into his hands. The trio were sitting on a chairlift, his father in the middle, taking the picture with both hands. Sylvie had her head on Benedict's shoulder, snow lining the creases on her woollen hat. Joe's grin was so broad he looked unrecognisable. If Sylvie had not become pregnant, would Benedict have left his brother alone with their insufferable mother? If Gus had never been born, perhaps Joe Crow would have a brighter disposition.

On the cabinet, facing the bed, Joe had placed an old television on top of an older VCR player. Stacked against the cabinet were a collection of VHS videos, mostly gritty detective dramas. One of the few exceptions was the *Yoga-ta-get-fitta* video that Sylvie had found in a charity shop and bought Joe as a Secret Santa present (a secret that would have been better kept had she not laughed hysterically the moment he tore the wrapping paper). Gus opened the box to check that the book was still inside. It was the last place his uncle would look.

He returned to his room with guilt weighing in his gut like a sack of ball-bearings. Deceiving his uncle was justifiable: Joe was keen to return the hit list to his homicidal family; Gus was not prepared to part with the evidence that his parents had died to extract. It was Alicia's porcelain face that haunted the corners of his vision.

He pulled on his sweatpants and gazed out of the window to see the sun high in the sky. Patting his bare stomach, he distracted himself, trying to calculate when he had last eaten. He clocked that it was now Saturday afternoon: Anna Harrington's funeral.

Alicia had opened up to him, sharing her secrets. He had followed in Winter's footsteps, repaying her honesty with betrayal. He had needed the book; he had needed the truth, and his efforts had not been in vain. He had a right to know what happened to his parents.

As did she.

'What would I even say to her?' Gus asked aloud, resenting his incessant conscience. He could find her at the funeral, find an opportune moment to pull her aside while they buried her mother, find the courage to admit that he had stolen the book hours before the murder. *But it's all right*, he would say, *she didn't kill anybody. Actually, that was your great-grandparents—mine too, funnily enough. We're second cousins, isn't that—*

Joe emerged from the front door of Alicia's house. Glancing left and right, he marched down the empty driveway with a white package under his arm. Alicia was at her mother's funeral and Joe was robbing her house.

The ball-bearings liquified.

JOE STEPPED THROUGH the doorway and made a beeline for the liquor globe. With the package tucked under his arm, he lifted a bottle from the southern hemisphere and turned at the sound of footsteps behind him. There was a violent fury on his nephew's face and the Bushmills Single Malt hovered at a forty-five-degree angle in Joe's hand. Gus snatched the bottle and hurled it against the wall by the front door. The glass shattered and amber liquid stained the wallpaper.

'Did you throw her body down the stairs, Uncle?' Gus bared his teeth, shoulders hunched, his nose two inches from Joe's. 'When you dropped me in my bed and went back to the house, did you and Melissa have to carry Anna Harrington's dead body up the stairs and toss it back down to make it look convincing?'

Joe said nothing. He knew that any attempt to reason would only fuel the fire. Giving his nephew space to calm down, he crossed the living room and placed the white package on the stairs before picking shards of glass from the floor. A pool of whiskey remained in an unbroken corner of the bottle. Joe picked it up carefully and tipped it into his glass.

But Gus did not calm down. His thoughts were focused on his uncle 'investigating' the death of Alicia's mother and fabricating the lies that would protect him.

'Our family are murdering innocent people and you are letting them die. I'm heading to the police station,' Gus stated, marching past his uncle to the front door. 'If you want to shoot me with that gun of yours, please go ahead. If you can remember how to use it, that is. It's kind of like drinking whiskey, really; except instead of hiding from things and letting them die, you kill them yourself.'

Gus opened the door and Joe grabbed him by the shoulders. He was slammed against the wall where the bottle had broken. His uncle's hand pressed hard against his rib cage, gripping his chest as though ready to tear out his heart.

'You feel this?' Joe hissed. 'This is beating because of me. This is beating because I promised to stay out of it.'

There was the anger in his uncle's eyes: evidence that Joe Crow was part of the family.

What do you fear?

Gus did not fear it; he found comfort in that consanguineous rage.

'You're hurting me,' he hissed through gritted teeth. Joe relaxed and Gus's feet crunched on the glass.

'Oh, what fun,' said a voice in the doorway. Both heads turned to see Rainn on the doorstep. She stood with her hands on her hips. There was a cheerful confidence in her blue eyes.

Before the second pill had returned him to the abyss, Gus had asked his uncle what he had seen when he went back to Melissa's house that evening. Joe told him that he had found Melissa aghast, cowering over Anna's body at the bottom of the stairs. Rainn was elsewhere.

Without invitation, the woman hitched up her long dress and crossed the threshold. She strode across the carpet and sat in Joe's leather armchair. The police officer stood tall, blinking his small eyes. In her presence, he appeared to have shrunk.

'But you haven't really stayed out of it, have you, Joseph?' said Rainn, crossing her legs and folding her arms. Her small mouth was pressed into a knowing smile. 'Moving next door to Anna Harrington, keeping young Augustus from us all.'

Barely perceptibly, Joe shifted as if to step between Gus and the woman. Rainn leaned forward in her chair, elbows on her knees and hands clasped together as she directed the heat of her attention on Gus.

'Hello again,' she said. She looked to be in her early twenties, not many years older than him, yet she spoke as though addressing an infant. 'Your great-grandparents send their regards.'

Gus felt cold whiskey on his back and shards of glass underfoot.

'Was it you—'

'Augustus!' Joe protested, his eyes burning a hole into the floor. Gus swallowed his question. He did not know in what capacity this woman worked for his family, but Joe's fear was enough to silence him.

'Was it me that killed Anna Harrington?' she asked with wide eyes and a bashful smile, flattered by the implication. 'No. We have your great-grandparents to thank for that.'

Joe stepped between them, thumbs in the belt of his trousers.

'I tried to convince her to return the book. I want no part in this.'

'Yet you play it so well, Sergeant Crow.'

She held out her slender white hands and waited. Joe lifted the package from the bottom of the stairs and lay it across her palms. A gold bow was curled on top of the white paper: it was a birthday gift.

'So very well.' She toyed with the bow and then placed the gift in her lap, raising her eyes expectantly. 'And the book?'

Gus's breath petrified in his lungs.

'I searched Anna's house,' said Joe. 'Nothing.'

'Not to worry,' Rainn said with a wink. 'Melissa is quite confident that Alicia will be able to find it.'

Returning her eyes to Gus, Rainn whispered: 'You're always welcome to join, you know.'

'Join what?' Gus asked.

Rainn raised an arm to present him with the symbol on her wrist.

'The Order of Chaos.'

Joe balled his fists and growled: 'You can leave now.'

Humour danced in her eyes, as if he were performing a charade and doing a very good job. But she said nothing. Whatever power she held over him, Joe could rip out her throat if he decided to. She brushed her thumb against the tattoo and it was then that Gus understood what it was: a reality check. Had this been a dream, the symbol would have smudged.

She rose from her seat and drifted towards the door, turning on her heel in the doorway.

'I'll tell Aldous and Morna that you send your love.'

Joe closed the door behind her and leaned his forehead against it, breathing heavily. Gus cleared his throat, unused to his uncle displaying any sign of weakness.

'That was Alicia's birthday present?' he asked quietly.

Joe eyed Gus as if surprised to see him there. He nodded and retrieved a new bottle from the globe.

'Anna was writing letters for Alicia. All that she knew. She

planned to give them to Alicia for her birthday, so that she could…'
Soft *glugs* as Joe filled his glass. 'Choose.'

'Choose what?'

'To finish what Anna had started. To find my grandparents.'

Gus stepped closer now, a fierce intrigue burning in his eyes.

'Those letters lead to them?'

'She won't need them anyway,' Joe said, waving his glass and wishing that he had not mentioned it. Gus asked why that was, noting sorry resignation in his uncle's face.

'Alicia won't need to find them. They will find her.'

Gus watched his uncle deliberate.

'There's a man working for them. He will lead her to them. If you want to protect Alicia, you'll warn her against lucid dreaming. And you'll hand that book to Rainn.'

How can a dream be dangerous?

It was time to face Alicia.

You don't have feet

SHE NEEDED TO get out of the house. She was not deserting her grieving father; she would be back in the morning, before he even knew she was missing. For months, Alicia had lain in bed with her ears trained on the front door, listening for the sound of her mother returning. But now, if she were to hear the soft click of the front lock or the gentle squeak of the back door, it would not be Anna Harrington coming to answer her questions. It would be Winter Hazelby, breaking in to paint messages on her walls; Melissa Lawson at her bedside, suggesting that she move in for a while; Gus Crow sneaking up the stairs to steal her mother's book, her birthday present, or whatever else he could get his thieving hands on.

She needed to get out of the house, so she crept past the family photographs lining the corridor, each a parody of her home life. She silently wished her father goodnight as he slept on the sofa—like the world's most useless guard dog—and slipped through the front door.

Her feet faltered. The light in Gus's bedroom was on. Perhaps a guilty conscience kept him awake at one on a Sunday morning? Her fingers twitched as she considered marching up to the door and demanding the items he had stolen, but it was her mother's voice that rang between her ears, quieting her own. Anna Harrington was never hot-tempered, always managing to squeeze that moment of pause between the situation and an emotional response. She would maintain a positive outlook and consider all options before jumping to conclusions; hers was the voice of reason that cut through the drama.

Alicia suspected that Gus had taken the book, since he was the only other person who knew where it was hidden. Or was he? Might Joe Crow or Melissa Lawson have taken it? Gus wanted to know if his parents were on the list, but what would he gain by keeping it?

She stood in the light, staring up at the bedroom window. Even if Gus had taken that hit list, what would she do if she got it back? Hand it into the police station where his uncle worked? The book linked Anna, Melody, Jack and a number of suspicious deaths, suggesting that they were connected; not accidents, but murders. But what else might be drawn from it? It was, after all, just a list of names that anybody could have written, herself included. If she handed in the book, it would likely end up on the desk of the man who had done an admirable job of making Anna's murder look like a tumble down the stairs.

Alicia knew why she deliberated: she wanted to speak with Gus. A shadow obscured the light as he stepped up to the glass. Their eyes locked and she felt nothing but anger and distrust. He opened his mouth to call out to her, but she turned from the window and marched down the road, barely a shadow under the overcast sky. Gus did not have the answers that she sought. Her answers lay beyond the waking world.

In the living room of her grandmother's cottage, the faint light of the now-uncovered moon broke through the boarded windows and fell in bands on the dustsheet on the sofa. She tugged the sheet and gave it a quick shake, wary of spiders that might have taken cover beneath it. Chastising herself for muddled priorities, she carried the sheet upstairs to the bedroom.

Nudging Winter's sleeping bag aside, Alicia removed her shoes and lay down on the cold mattress. She wrapped the sheet around her, tucking it under her feet.

'Am I dreaming?' she whispered at the skylight overhead, where a strip of stars was visible through a break in the clouds. She conducted a final reality check using the clock on her phone, drew her knees to her chest and closed her eyes.

Without intervention, I fear that she may lose her mind.

She had not lost her grip on reality; her fingers had not slipped from that which was real, reaching out to snatch at ghosts. With every ounce of her being, she had pushed reality away, determined to disconnect from the hostile environment that the waking world had become.

With each whisper of wind that caught the front gate, a donkey's bray carried through the walls. The hooting of owls, a set of ghostly footprints down the side of the cottage and a cacophony of illusory horrors pulled Alicia from the edge of consciousness. But when her imagination was finally exhausted, heavy eyelids fell and sleep welcomed her.

So frequent were her reality checks, Alicia's subconscious carried the pattern into her sleeping mind. She was chasing her brother on moonlit railway lines, marvelling at his ability to balance, when she questioned if she was dreaming. She pulled a mobile phone from her pocket and the digits scrambled on a second glance. Once lucid, she latched her focus to the open door of the shed, not daring to see if her brother's image remained on the tracks behind her. She leaped through the doorway and dived into the well.

FROM THE VEINS that ran through the leaves drifting across the fields in a breeze generated by her own expectation, to the ground that stood so firm beneath her bare feet, Alicia felt the intense, living presence of Vivador. She had closed her eyes and fallen awake.

She ran her fingers across the gooseflesh on her lower thigh, just beneath the hem of her sweater-dress. Leaving her body insensate on a mattress in an abandoned house did not sit well with her; she nodded to Ryan on the rim of the well and set off down the hill in the direction of the forest. He caught her by the hand.

'Close your eyes.'

She obliged.

'Picture yourself on the edge of the forest, facing the marked tree. Feel the breeze that travels through the branches of the pines.'

Hair swept her brow and the scent of pine filled her nostrils. A fallen needle brushed the back of her hand.

'Now be there.'

Opening her eyes, Alicia stood at the edge of the forest.

'In Vivador, I cannot take you where you have not been. But it is possible to blink between the places you have visited, as you might move through memories in a dream.'

She gazed from *A + E Forever* in the foot of the pine to the vast forest that awaited them. Was this the purpose of the inscription? So that Anna and Eloise, or whoever it was, might blink from the well to the edge of the forest?

Ryan marched through the trees. He appeared to have no interest in conversation, only in delivering his lines as instructed, and delivering her to whoever had instructed him. She walked behind him, like a dog, anxious thoughts insisting that she realise the danger of following this stranger into the unknown. But—*honestly, Alicia*—what choice did she have? She pushed the thoughts aside and strode behind him, forcing her attention out of her mind and into the forest, where a deep, eternal silence reminded her of the full moon. She chose to break it.

'I'm sorry I took so long. To get back here. I couldn't sleep.'

She had no intention of telling him why. Some things were better left in the waking world.

Ryan made no response, though he studied her for a moment.

Does he think I'm pretty?—What a juvenile thought! How embarrassing to hear her insecurities so clearly. She considered her drop-shoulder chenille sweater-dress: an item she had seen in a store window last month. Had her subconscious dressed her in clothing that she coveted, or to impress this figment of her imagination?

'You must have wondered where I was?' she asked.

Had he sat on that well for three days? How slowly had time passed since her last visit to the immaterial realm? It was difficult to believe, or perhaps to accept, that he was really there, and that Vivador continued to exist while she was awake.

'Have you been waiting here all this time?'

'I have been here all this time,' said Ryan, ducking a low branch. 'But there is no "waiting" here. Waiting would imply boredom. Why would I be bored?'

She could not have created Ryan: she did not understand him. It was his eyes that troubled her, not their arresting beauty, but their absolute vacancy. When David was an infant, she had stared into his sightless eyes and counted backwards from ten to one, believing that, when the countdown ended, a spark of recognition would light those empty pupils and, for the first time, he would see her face.

Mouths twisted and nostrils flared, a myriad of micro-expressions could express and betray emotions. But there was something deeper in the eyes: some indescribable connection that fascinated her, and in them she sought the connection that she and David had been denied. Beauty is in the eye of the beholder, and secrets in the eye of the beheld.

In the eyes of Gus and Winter, she had seen calculation and concern as they delivered their lines and assessed the impact of their words: *Was that funny enough? Was that cruel enough?* In contrast, Ryan's eyes were at peace, without want or need. No ego lay within them.

Faced with his profound serenity, she prickled with irritation: this man could never understand her. Without desires of his own, how could he understand that hers were so painful that, were she to face them head on, they would break her? Ryan could have sat on that well for all eternity, wanting for nothing. She needed to find her brother.

'Tell me where he is.'

'I have to test you first.'

They stopped on the edge of a broad clearing. Shards of glass were strewn in a layer so thick that Alicia could not see the ground beneath. It looked as if someone had taken a million clear bottles and dropped them from a great height.

'What am I supposed to do?' she asked when her guide stood motionless before the stretch of broken glass. Light streaming from above fell upon the razor-sharp edges and split into prisms. The ground shimmered.

'Cross it.'

She looked from his impassive face to her bare feet. Tentatively, she raised a foot and brought it down on the glass. The sharp edge of a large fragment dug into the ball of her foot.

'It hurts,' she whispered, unable to put her weight on it.

'Only because you expect it to.'

Driven in part by his indifferent manner and in part by her desire to prove what she was capable of, Alicia put the full force of her weight onto her foot and took another step. With both feet on the broken glass, her mouth was wide and her eyes watering.

'It's cutting my feet!' she turned her head with a hand outstretched, ready to grab Ryan's shoulder. He took a step back, out of reach, and folded his arms across his T-shirt.

'You don't have feet.'

Alicia faced ahead. She felt the glass in the soles of her feet and knew that she was bleeding. She also knew that she was bleeding because she knew that she was bleeding. Had she not assumed that she was bleeding, she would not have bled. Amid the pain that shot through her feet and up her legs, it struck her as ironic that she was at once trying to believe in this reality—to commit to the idea that

Vivador existed outside her mind—whilst trying to understand that neither the glass nor her bleeding feet were more tangible than the pain she was imagining.

'I have no feet,' she hissed, taking a step forward and cursing the strength of her imagination. She almost buckled as something sank into the heel of her right foot. She thought of her feet in the waking world, curled under the dustsheet, and denied the pain with every step she took. Determined to pass this test, believing that every step took her closer to her brother, Alicia dragged her mind over the matter.

Ryan caught her arm and she lowered her eyes to see that she had walked several paces on bare soil.

'Shoes would have sufficed,' he said, striding on.

'Is…was that a joke?'

Ryan led her through the thinning trees at the far edge of the forest. Alicia picked up her pace to walk alongside him. Bubbles of irritation rose at his staunch placidity.

'How is walking over glass supposed to help me reach David?' she asked as they stepped between the outer trees and reached the edge of a cliff.

'In denying pain, you have shown that you can rise above expectation, and that is essential here. But if you are to reach your brother in Vivador, you must do more than resist it.'

Standing on the lip of the cliff, Alicia saw a flat plain below them, stretching to the horizon. Directly ahead, a stone's throw away, a solitary door stood in the grass. This large wooden door appeared to be attached to no outer structure. Four metres wide and over twice as tall, it broke the empty landscape as if somebody had removed an enormous castle but forgotten to take the entrance.

'The Unbreakable Door was designed to withstand any attack that a human mind can conceive. Your next task is to destroy it.'

Aldous & Morna

THIS IS BECOMING *a habit*, Gus thought as the back door of Eloise's cottage scraped the kitchen tiles. He had knocked on the front door, politely at first and then heavily. If this was where Alicia had fled in the middle of the night, she was either ignoring him or locked in sleep.

It was six in the morning and he had not slept. He had not taken his pills. Waiting at the window for Alicia to return, he had watched his uncle drive off down Gardner Road. Had Joe received another call from Melissa, this time concerning Alicia? The police officer's mobile phone went straight to voicemail. Unable to wait any longer, he had pulled up his hood and left the house to skulk between the last rays of the street lamps.

Fatigue followed the sleepless night. His senses laboured underwater: muffled sound, blurred vision, dampening the fear of facing his neighbour. Pacifying the urge to retreat to his bed.

She was not on the sofa. He scanned the room, furrowing his brow, breathing through his nostrils as his uncle would have done. Had the window to the right of the fireplace been cracked? Where was the dustsheet? In the corridor, his foot disturbed a floorboard near the stairs and he froze, fearing he might wake her, before remembering that was his intention. Unless, of course, she was not here. Unless she was lying at the foot of Melissa's—

She was here. Alicia was curled on the mattress with her knees tucked and her hands clasped beneath her chin as though in prayer. She looked smaller and younger. Fragile. He flicked a switch by the door and a bulb below the skylight cast a stark light over the bedroom. As he approached the figure sleeping alone in an abandoned house, his heart tightened as if someone had given it a rough squeeze. He crouched beside her, balanced on the balls of his feet, lifted a hand to shake her shoulder, and hesitated.

Fine strands of dark hair fell across a face too peaceful for a girl who had just lost her mother. No frown troubled her thin brows, no tension hardened her lips. Would it not be cruel to wake her to a reality she had escaped?

Gus ground his teeth. He was not deliberating for her sake; he feared her accusations. He pushed back his hood, shook her shoulder and whispered her name. Her body was limp and he might have checked her pulse had her chest not risen and fallen beneath the dustsheet. Shaking her shoulder with more confidence, he continued to call her, urging her to return from wherever lucid dreams had taken her.

Malachite eyes snapped open and she sat up abruptly. There was no groggy, hypnopompic look on her face. Focused and determined, Alicia gripped Gus's outstretched arm.

'Where is it?'

He lost his balance and fell onto his backside, landing on the stone monkey. He shifted into a kneeling position and blurted out: 'Alicia I'm so sorry about your mother—I know it's not what you want to hear—I know you just want to be alone, but…'

She looked at her neighbour, clutching the monkey in his lap. In his eyes, she saw sympathy, and deeper still: empathy. Both had lost their mothers to unknown forces. Two strangers, connected by tragedy. Pity left an acrimonious taste in her mouth, but this was not pity; unlike Ryan, Gus understood her pain.

'I wanted to be alone, too,' he continued, unable to stop. 'I wanted to lock myself away from their charitable faces. I know what it feels like to be so…so belittled by their words. Mirroring their wooden smiles. But you can't…here…'

He looked around, from the broken plant pot by the door to

Winter's sleeping bag beside the stained mattress, as if this was how Alicia had chosen to decorate her hideaway.

She rose, standing rigid. The bulb was too bright. The sky through the window continued to lighten as the night ended. Her vision blurred as pressure built behind her eyes, pushing against the walls of a dam, threatening to break. In Gus's hands, she saw a monkey with its palms to its eyes, not shutting the world out, but keeping tears within.

To cry was to submit to reality. This was not her reality.

'Why are you here?' she asked.

Gus stood on Winter's sleeping bag. He had given Joe an ultimatum: tell him everything he knew about the Order of Chaos, or the book would go back to Alicia. Joe had added a condition of his own, that, in exchange for the details he had seen fit to hide from his nephew, Gus would hand the book to Rainn. She would not leave without it, Joe insisted; until she left Godalming, a guillotine hung above their heads.

He had taken a moment to consider the offer. To return the hit list to Rainn was to betray Alicia, but what might be gained from the old book? If his parents had passed the book to Anna Harrington so that she might protect those yet to be targeted, then this had been in vain. Melody Wilson and Melissa Lawson were the only names yet to be struck off the list. Melody was dead and Melissa was presumably only alive because she had promised to help Rainn retrieve the evidence.

It was not the book that Alicia needed. It was all the truth that he could spare.

'My grandfather, Augustus, before he met my grandmother, he had a child with another woman. That woman's name was Eloise Grett.'

Alicia ran her eyes around the walls of the bedroom, searching the pale rectangles where photographs had hung. She had known so

134

little about her mother's mother, and nothing of her mother's father. How much did anyone know about the grandparents they had never met? Was it in this bedroom that Eloise had died on the day she and Gus were born? Gus's lips parted as he studied her response, waiting a moment before adding: 'You're my second cousin. Or something like that. Do you want to sit down?'

'No.'

'Okay. That book was written by our great-grandparents. Aldous and Morna. They—'

'I need some water.'

Alicia stepped past the boy who was no longer just a neighbour and pressed a hand to the wall as she descended the stairs. She took each step with care, holding back the torrent of questions that threatened to trip her. Filling a glass at the kitchen sink, she stared into the pink glow beyond the trees and counted down from ten to one.

She turned to face her second cousin, who was now leaning against the work surface and asked: 'Aldous and Morna?'

'They live in Portugal—'

'They're still alive?'

'Yes. And they're lucid dreamers too. When they were young, our age, they found…' his brow wrinkled, 'a realm. A space—I don't think there's a name for it. Something beyond waking reality.'

A place where you can create dreams together. Joe's sarcasm had been impeccable as the whiskey took effect.

Gus paused, recalling the name that Winter had circled on her brainstorm for alternatives to 'Earth'. A name that Jack must have suggested following his journey down the well.

'Vivador,' said Alicia.

Green eyes locked. What had she seen in a realm so dangerous that it lined his uncle's eyes with fear?

'I would like to sit down,' said Gus.

The living room was dark, but neither hit the lights. Alicia took the statuette from Gus's hands and returned it to the mantelpiece. Gus sat cross-legged on the sofa and Alicia joined him, her back straight and her hands on her knees.

'Go on,' she said.

'Aldous and Morna, they thought they'd somehow managed to merge their consciousness. But it was bigger than that. This space could be found by any lucky lucid dreamer who looked in the right places.'

Lucky, Joe had snorted, drumming his fingers against the oak.

'They knew that if it became public knowledge, everybody would descend on their paradise. Ruin it. So, they started to track people down—people who had reached Vivador, and ask them how they got there. What "portals" they had used.'

'Like the well?' asked Alicia, hands to her elbows in the cold room. Gus nodded, though his uncle had been sketchy on the details here.

'They hid that well in the shed, blocked old pipes, destroyed arches—anywhere a lucid dreamer had found a connection to Vivador. But it wasn't enough. They couldn't destroy all of them, not the bigger ones, like Stonehenge—'

'So they wrote that list?'

A moan slipped through the boarded windows as the gate caught in the wind.

'All they had to do was ask people for their names,' Gus uttered, his throat dry. 'Apparently, people aren't too cautious with the information they share with characters in a dream.'

Alicia thought of Ryan. She would have told him anything.

'So their name goes in the book,' she said, 'and Aldous and Morna hunt them down. Is that what she's here for—Rainn? She's one of my—one of our cousins, too?'

'I don't think so. I don't think she's related, I mean, but she is working for them. That symbol, on the book, it's the Order of Chaos. That's what they call themselves, our great-grandparents, and anyone who supports their claim to Vivador.'

'That tattoo,' said Alicia, her eyes widening. 'It's a reality check. That's what she's doing when she rubs it. She's checking to see if she's awake.'

'Yes!' Gus grinned, despite the nature of their conversation; Alicia was proving to be a model student. She met his smile with narrowed eyes.

'They have my brother,' said Alicia. 'In Vivador.' *It's real.* 'He's there. I met a man—Ryan—he knows where David is. Ryan will take me to David.'

Ryan—she delivered the name like he was a dear friend. Somebody she could rely on when nobody else was there to help her.

'Alicia, you mustn't return to Vivador. This man, he'll lead you right to Aldous and Morna. You cannot trust him.'

His hands were on her shoulders now. Alicia leaned forward, her green eyes searching his.

'And I can trust you? Where's the book?'

Both heads turned to the corridor as a distant blast shattered the silence of the early morning. The pair leaped to their feet, exchanged a glance, and headed for the well.

Embers

WHORLS OF BLACK smoke drifted across the railway tracks to where Alicia had paused, leaving Gus to continue alone. Joe did not look up when his nephew reached him. Arms folded across his uniform, the police officer was lost in reverie as he stood over smouldering fragments of wood and stone. The well had been blown to pieces. All that remained was a pile of blackened bricks and a shallow hole, partly collapsed. The walls of the shed had exploded outward, the splintered panels aflame, singeing the long grass. Gus detected a smell of bleach in the air, the tell-tale sign of triacetone triperoxide: a popular explosive among the amateur and ill-equipped. He had first encountered TATP when solitary parkour adventures had landed him in the wrong crowd, who had taken to enjoying the playground at his local park by blowing bits of it up.

'Official police business?' Gus asked.

Joe watched the burning panels of the door begin to dwindle as a light rain set in. Alicia's arrival pulled his focus from the flames. She nudged a plank aside with the toe of her shoe and stepped up beside the police officer.

'Did you toss the book in there while you were at it?'

The last time their eyes had met, Sergeant Crow had stood in Alicia's front doorway, talking with Rory. Head dipped and heavy-browed, his profound sadness had made his lies no easier to swallow.

From the top step, Mr Harrington, yes. It was a clean break, painless.

A sob had escaped Rory's lips and, perhaps out of discomfort, Joe had raised his eyes over the man's shoulder and spotted Alicia on the stairs.

You're as good at lying as your nephew, she had thought before slinking up the steps.

Alicia's stance was hostile. Confident. How much did she already know?

'What book?' he asked.

She shook her head and turned to walk away, kicking a charred brick into the trees.

'I took it,' said Gus. The wood hissed as the rain intensified. A burning ember floated between the pair, reflected in the young man's feline eyes. 'I needed to know how they died.'

'My mother.' She balled her fists, swallowed, raised a finger. 'You took that book and she went straight to Melissa Lawson. And when these—our—this *Order* came to kill Melissa, they found my mum instead.'

Joe stepped in front of Gus, hands spread as if approaching a wild dog. He opened his mouth to speak but Gus pushed past him.

'My parents were in Portugal when they died. They took the Murder Book—that's what my father called it. Your mother—she was in Portugal, too. She was looking for David. They gave her the book and died at her feet.'

He raised his hands to take hers, but buried them in the front pocket of his hooded jacket. Rain plastered dark hair to his brow as he continued.

'Joe asked her to give it back. But she wouldn't. Your mother was no murderer, Alicia, and she was no coward either. She didn't kill those people. Jack, Melody—she tried to warn them.'

Embers landed in the long grass and sizzled out of existence, their heat extinguished instantly. Something Alicia had been resisting began to cool. Like a salve on scorched skin, imagined memories were rewritten: murderous images of her mother replaced with Anna Harrington's struggle to protect the innocent.

Heavy droplets pounded Joe's scalp as Alicia addressed him.

'Rainn. Was it her? Did she kill her?'

Joe remained statuesque and Gus answered: 'No. Aldous and Morna killed your mother.'

'They're here?'

'No. They're still in Portugal, Joe reckons.'

Gus attempted to engage his uncle, who had either taken a vow of silence or was attempting to wake from a nightmare.

'So how...' Alicia trailed off, her thoughts on Jack drowning in the pool. Nobody had attacked him. Nobody was there but her mother.

'At first,' said Gus. 'Aldous and Morna hunted people here, in the waking world. Once they had a name, they weren't difficult to find. People started falling off balconies and...' he studied his uncle's pained expression, recalling his words, 'drowning in riptides. But each murder put the family at risk. Each death was traceable. But now—now there's nothing to prepare. Nothing to hide. They've found a way of targeting their victims from Vivador. You could be going about your daily business and Aldous and Morna can kill you from their beds.'

In her mind's eye, Alicia watched Jack Henson sink beneath the water. Melody Wilson slid to the kitchen floor as the stove continued to burn. Anna Harrington ascended the stairs as two figures watched from another realm. She opened her mouth to challenge Melissa, but no words came out. A final breath slipped through her lips as she collapsed on the steps.

'That's how they killed my parents,' said Gus, wiping rain from his eyes. 'That's how they killed your mother. And that's how they'll kill us unless we get to them first.'

Joe finally nudged his nephew aside, a statue stirring to life.

'Alicia...' he paused, breathed, his chest heaving under the sodden uniform. When he continued his tone was deep and his teeth bared, his urgency expressed as anger. 'I did everything I could to stop her. I tried to reason with her. And when she wouldn't listen, I took the house next door.'

She searched his eyes but found no trace of deception.

'I begged her to return that book. My brother and his wife should never have taken it. Anna should never have kept it. And now Gus is going to return it before we all suffer the same fate.'

Joe faced his nephew with a depth in those blue eyes that Gus had not seen in a year. That unguarded pain reminded him of the nights his uncle had spent staring at the knotted oak of an empty table, daring it to blink. Since then, any vulnerability had been concealed beneath layers of anger.

'Losing my brother was more painful than you could ever…I will not let them take you too.'

Rain coursed his cheeks in lieu of tears. Gus's throat burned as he turned to Alicia.

'Melissa is still alive because she convinced Rainn that she can get the book from you. If I return it, maybe they'll leave her alone.'

'And what, that's it?' Alicia asked. 'We just let them get away with it?'

'No,' Gus said with a grim smile. 'Your birthday present—'

'Augustus—' Joe warned.

'—Your Mum was writing you letters. Letters that lead to Aldous and Morna. Rainn can take their precious book, it's no good to us now. But she's not leaving town with those letters.'

Undone

SOME NIGHTS ALICIA lay on her back and imagined that she did not understand a word of English. Her sleep-deprived mind struggled to harass her with unwanted thoughts when she failed to recognise the words. She closed her eyes and listened, daring the thoughts to make themselves known. Sinking beneath her eyelids into the vast cavity of her skull, she waited. In these silent moments, she slipped into sleep.

Gus had warned her against Vivador, but she saw no threat in the lucid dream she was experiencing. She devoured the details of her bedroom: the carpet layered with Post-It Notes, snatches of dreams she had managed to recall, images dragged from one state of consciousness to another. The drawer of her desk would not shut, full to bursting with half-finished paintings that were not ready for the honest opinion of her mother or the unsolicited praise of her delightfully maddening father. She lifted a framed photograph from the desk. With eyes tight and mouths open, Alicia and two friends screamed on a rollercoaster. Her best friends had tried to console her. They had encouraged her with patient smiles and silent pleas to forget David and move on. She had not spoken with them all summer.

Down the stairs, she ran her fingertips along the wooden banister and watched the muscles in her forearm flex when she gripped it. In the living room, each surface leaped for her attention. She traced her consciousness along the neural pathways in her brain, testing them as a safecracker might listen for that *click* as the wheels of the lock slide into place. Passing kitchen cupboards, she wondered if any led to Vivador. Which of these intangible structures represented a link between the material world and what lay beyond? Were she to climb inside, would she find one of these conscious pathways, through which her soul could escape her biological mind?

She reached the patio. In the middle of the garden, where the pond should have been, a well disappeared into a hillock. Her bare feet flattened wet grass. If the well was not in the clearing beyond her grandmother's cottage, would it still function as a portal? Was it the location of the well that mattered, or simply the idea of it?

Don't be an idiot, she thought, brushing a hand across the circle of weathered stone. The bricks were charred and soot settled in her fingerprints. Lucid in her dream, she considered the ride home in Joe's police car before she had crept back into bed. As the sun rose over Godalming, he had watched his nephew in the rear-view mirror, wincing visibly as Gus recounted Rainn's visit. She described her journey to Vivador and Ryan's offer to lead her to David. Joe's wet knuckles were white as he gripped the steering wheel, yet his tone remained firm:

He doesn't have your brother. He'll lead you straight to Aldous and Morna.

The most sensible decision would be to wake up and wait until they had retrieved her mother's letters. If Ryan's claim that he was taking her to David was a trap, she should not walk into it blindly.

But Ryan did not know what Gus had told her. The Order of Chaos, Aldous and Morna—she was not as blind as her guide believed. He had led her to a door and challenged her to destroy it. What lay beyond this Unbreakable Door? She leaned over the stones and gazed into the well, seduced by curiosity.

Wake up, Alicia thought before falling into darkness.

BLINKING TO THE cliff's edge, she saw a set of stone steps leading to the ground below. She could not remember seeing the steps before. It was the first of many instances in which she would wonder if such a detail existed only because she expected it to. Ryan stood with his back to the door, waiting to lead her to her brother, or perhaps her death.

With a hand against the cliff face, she descended the steps and crossed the stretch of grass to the wooden door. Arched at the top and bearing thick panels of a knotted wood, the formidable structure appeared to be missing an iron portcullis. Though both halves of the door met flush in the middle, there was no handle on either side. She made to step around the wide frame but stopped abruptly when she caught the ghost of her reflection. She raised her hand and realised that the door was embedded within a thick wall of glass, so transparent it was barely visible. The glass was cool to the touch and misty fingerprints faded when she removed her hand.

'It's a dome,' said Ryan. 'Covering the forest and the well.'

Of course, thought Alicia, the voice in her head so loud she feared he might hear it. Aldous and Morna would ask lucid dreamers for their names and then hunt them down in the waking world. If they were to return to Vivador before they had been eliminated, the avid explorers had only the forest in which to lose themselves.

Alicia placed both hands on the wooden panels. The door was so solid—so intensely present—she imagined it pressing back. Closing her eyes, she had a vague sensation of the mind, or minds, that had created it. An innate energy vibrated through her finger-tips, powerful and alive.

Taking a breath, she imagined herself on the far side of the door, visualising the structure behind her and the empty plains ahead. She willed herself beyond it, just as she had blinked to the edge of the cliff. But trying to cross this barrier through will alone felt like stretching a rubber band and it left her with a knot in her stomach.

She opened her eyes to find Ryan watching patiently.

Taking a step back, she focused on the knotted surface and adopted the meditative concentration she had summoned when raising her oak from the hilltop. A fire spread across the panels and flames licked the wood, increasing in intensity until the heat of the inferno burned her face. When she let the fire die and laid a palm upon the panels, they were resolutely cool.

The pair stepped aside as the ground trembled and a cannon rose from the soil. Inspired by the castle that this door might have fitted, Alicia's weapon comprised a wrought-iron chamber on a wooden carriage. She focused on the fuse protruding from a vent at the back of the chamber and it sparked into a flame that disappeared within the cylinder. With a resounding blast, the weapon fired. The cannonball left no dent in the wood and fell impotently to the ground.

Narrowing her eyes, Alicia watched a wick sprout from the cannonball, forming that quintessential image of a cartoon bomb. The bombs multiplied at the foot of the door until a considerable pile lay against it. Ryan and Alicia paced away as the young woman set each wick alight. There followed a tremendous blast as the agglomeration of bombs detonated, sending a sheet of soil and grass in their direction. The dirt settled and the pair uncovered their eyes to see that the bombs had merely exposed the length of these panels, continuing deep into the ground.

Frustration lined her face as Alicia turned to Ryan.

'It won't burn or crack. It won't explode—how am I supposed to destroy a door that's indestructible?'

Ryan pulled a hand from the pocket of his shorts and offered her a deck of cards. He asked her to pick one. Taking a card, Alicia took a quick glance at the six of hearts and committed it to memory, wondering why, of all the cards available, she had selected that particular one. Surely, in Vivador, chance did not exist?

'Don't tell me what it is,' Ryan said, holding up his hand. 'Now change it.'

'What do you mean?'

'Change the card. And show it to me.'

Alicia presented him with the ace of spades.

'This was always the card that you picked,' he said, taking the ace of spades and returning it to the deck.

'No, it wasn't.'

'Yes, it was,' he said tranquilly. 'There is no evidence that you picked any other card, and there never will be. All that exists is the present moment. The past, like your memory, is alterable. Anything here can be undone.'

'I remember the card I chose.' Alicia folded her arms. 'The memory exists in my mind, as real as when I'm awake. If it exists in my mind, it exists here.'

'Are memories so reliable? How certain are you that you can remember the card you chose? How certain would you be a year from now?'

Was this all part of an act?

Offer her the cards, said an elderly man with beady black eyes. *Make her question her memories.*

'I bet you chose a red six,' Ryan said with a small smile. Alicia furrowed her brow and then remembered their conversation about conscious pathways. His smile was little more than a lift of his cheeks and lowered eyelids, but she did not imagine it.

'Who are you, Ryan? Where are you from—on Earth, when you wake up?'

A shadow crossed his face, erasing the smile. She followed his gaze to the floor, where a tiny lamb nibbled at the clumps of grass littering the ground.

'I am a simulacrum,' he said. There was no lilt in his voice or lift to his cheeks. 'Conjured by the same minds that made this door.'

He lifted the animal into his arms and it nuzzled his neck.

'I am no more real than this lamb.'

The outline of the lamb began to flicker and fade and, moments later, white smoke drifted into the air. Then there was nothing. In the silence that followed, Alicia studied Ryan's glacial eyes, struggling to imagine that her great-grandparents had created them. Had his features been designed so that she would follow his every word? It felt powerfully arrogant to believe that this young man existed purely to tempt her.

He's not real.

But if Ryan was no more than a simulacrum, why did she feel pity when she met his eyes?

'Red,' said Alicia.

'Six,' said Ryan.

She smiled and he frowned. He faced the door and the chunks of soil and clumps of grass soared back into place, as the explosion reversed. A second later, the damage had been undone and the ground restored. When Ryan returned his gaze to Alicia, his lips were parted and there was a subtle complexity about his expression, as if he were deliberating.

'Have you ever had a number in your head, and wondered where it came from?' he asked.

'Is this another test?'

He shook his head. 'No, it's—come on.' He nodded at the door, his face impassive but his deep voice impatient. 'Just focus.'

She took a deep breath, acutely aware that her desire to destroy this door was not driven by the need to see her brother. She was determined to prove to Ryan that she was capable of solving this challenge. She was self-aware of how self-conscious she felt standing next to this handsome stranger. Seeking the approval of a man who did not exist.

If the Unbreakable Door would not burn or crack under cannon fire or explosives, she needed to be more creative. Aldous and Morna could not possibly have defended it against the infinite alternatives at her disposal. Laying her hands upon it, she felt that undeniable sensation of the door pushing back: a living resistance that its makers had instilled within it.

'Designed to withstand anything…any attack…what did you say?'

'The door was designed to withstand any attack that a human mind can conceive,' said Ryan, watching Alicia scan the knotted wood, searching for hidden cracks.

'Withstand any attack,' she echoed, turning the statement in her mind like a cryptic clue, holding each word to the torchlight of her attention. And with every passing second she felt him judging her, while knowing that this was false.

Alicia turned to face the simulacrum. In his eyes, she searched for a depth that was not there. Any emotion was a lie, as the playing cards had been. Like the cards, which could be interchanged without a trace, Ryan had no tangible past. All that he had done in Vivador—all that he had been—could be undone.

Anything here can be undone: those had been his words. Her eyes narrowed and she stepped back to see the Unbreakable Door in full view. With her human mind, she believed the door to be made of wood—a solid, organic structure. Focusing on the panels, she imagined the fibres of this wood, and within these fibres lay the atoms that held it together. Within these atoms lay protons, neutrons and electrons—the basis of a scientific understanding that she had never seen yet believed without question. Alicia understood at that moment that the door was as real as she expected it to be. The harder the door was attacked, the stronger her belief that the structure was real. To attack the door was to believe that it existed. How can you destroy something that is not real?

'I have no feet,' she whispered.

As Alicia held the image of the door before her eyes, she did not push against it. She did not attempt to break bonds that did not exist. Instead, she chose to deny it.

There is no door.

As though a light switch had been hit, the door was undone.

She did not have a moment to enjoy her success, for she faced a figure who had been standing on the far side of the wooden panels. The beautiful young woman wore a long sapphire dress that rippled like water in the breeze.

'Rainn,' said Alicia.

'Alicia Crow,' The woman's smile was fierce. And then her large cerulean eyes were all Alicia saw, holding her as she had held the door.

'She's not ready,' Ryan called by her side.

'We'll see.'

The pause that followed was as tense as the moment between an orchestra's finale and the tumultuous applause of the audience. A rough grip on her upper arm and Alicia pulled her eyes from Rainn's to find that Ryan had pressed something to her chest. It was the barrel of a gun. She raised her head and met his gaze, and in his eyes she saw fear. But was this any more than the mirror image of her terror?

She opened her mouth and Ryan pulled the trigger.

Breathe

AT NOON ON a Sunday, shoppers washed along the rain-battered cobbles of the high street. Mothers spilled out of charity shops and into cafés, swapping gossip over the heads of toddlers that licked glazed buns as big as their faces. Couples dodged puddles and teenagers leaned against the pink arches of the Pepperpot, ignoring the greengrocers that arranged stalls of leeks and tomatoes on the raised platform of the old town hall. Sharing jokes and umbrellas, the residents of Godalming defied the unrelenting rain. Though the downpour was heavy, their steps were light, not one of them wondering whether their great-grandparents were preparing to kill them.

At the traffic lights, Gus tugged the zip of his waterproof jacket over the rucksack pressed to his belly. Cradling the mound, he caught the attention of the elderly man to his right. The man eyed the bump, blinked, and returned to waiting for the green man.

Cars drove over a loose drain—*thud-thud, thud-thud*—drawing out the sound of Gus's heartbeat as he recalled his exchange with Joe that morning. Returning from the well, he had entered their house to see the Murder Book on the living-room table. His uncle had found it, but had not driven to Melissa's.

'Yoga—you…' Gus said, shooting Joe a quizzical look. 'You could have handed it to Rainn? You're desperate to hand it to Rainn. But you haven't.'

'That decision is not mine.'

As he stared at the symbol of an Order that had murdered his parents to protect a dream-world, a shadow in Gus's mind darkened. He approached the liquor globe and poured his uncle a drink.

Joe lowered himself into the leather armchair and accepted the drink from his nephew. He lifted a photograph of Benedict and Sylvie from beside the crow in the bay window.

'Every night I promise them I will keep you safe. But I can't.'

Gus stared at the blinds, half expecting a ghostly figure to drift through the wooden slats. Joe took a long draught, his eyes on the photograph.

'So long as Aldous and Morna live, they will hunt you and Alicia. Whether they mean to stop you before you take revenge, or convince you to join their Order, you will never be safe. Anna was right, we must find them. Not in Vivador, but here.'

'Let's hope those letters come with a map.'

'You'll return the book to Rainn,' Joe said, tipping his tumbler in Gus's direction. 'I've blown up that well—that'll please them. Nobody else can stumble across it now. You give them the Murder Book and that's that. You'll earn their trust. But let me go after those letters.'

When Gus spoke, it was not as a defiant nephew, but an equal.

'All right.'

Tapping his foot, Gus waited a full two minutes at the traffic lights before realising that the elderly man had yet to press the button. Smiling, he leaned across, reached for the button and froze when a juniper-green Jeep drove past. Melissa Lawson was alone in the car and did not spot him as she continued towards the high street. Gus crossed the junction and picked up his pace.

Melissa's house towered above the surrounding properties as if they had crowded around and taken a seat. While the neighbouring bungalows had character—walls so thick with ivy that the brick could not be seen; exposed wooden beams bisecting at uneven angles—the Lawson property was a wash of white with grey windows.

Gus slowed when he reached the driveway. Rather than Melissa's Jeep, he saw a Tesla. He had expected Melissa to be present when he handed the book to Rainn—a glimmer of trust passing between them as he returned the evidence she had vowed to retrieve. His shoulders tightened as he approached the front door.

The lights were off. Perhaps Melissa's guest had taken a stroll to Eloise's cottage to confirm the destruction of the well? Spotting an ornamental stone squirrel between two flowerpots, he wondered how much trouble he would be in if he shattered the frosted panel and unlocked the door. He was here to return the book, not hunt for the letters; but if the house was empty, why waste the opportunity? He bent to seize the squirrel and heard voices.

Licking raindrops from his lips, Gus trampled the flowerbeds from window to window. He stepped around the side of the house until he spied a kitchen at the back. Rainn and Winter sat on high stools at a breakfast bar that split the room. Keeping to the corner of the window, he leaned his head back into the branches of the fir. The window was ajar and Gus listened to the pair as water ran behind his ears and down his collar.

'—always like that?' asked Winter, her dark hair disappearing against her black dress. The broad, gold belt around her dress matched her heels, and she would not have looked out of place on a catwalk. Her appointed mentor wore a sleek turquoise dress and perched on the stool with one leg across the other. Gus envisaged a flute of champagne in Rainn's slender hand as she blew over the top of her teacup.

'Like what? The dried husk of a woman with the personality of a gargoyle and a face to match?'

Winter laughed. Her head bobbed up and down like a toy bird pecking incessantly at a glass bulb filled with water.

'Never laugh at what people say.' Rainn tilted her head to the right, studying the teenager. 'They'll think you're easy to please. And if people think you're easy to please, they'll stop trying to please you.

Just smile. Keep them guessing.'

Winter was silent for a moment.

'Consider me counselled.'

From between the branches, Gus saw Winter's desire to maintain the attention of this confident beauty. With an elbow on the marble counter, she surreptitiously checked her reflection in a glass jar filled with pasta. Rainn sipped her tea and asked a question that Gus did not hear.

'Some old woman,' Winter replied. 'Mrs Wilfred or something. Jack talked about her like she was a real person.'

'And what did he call these hallucinations? This Wilfred character, did she give it a name?'

'She called it Vivador.'

Winter did not spot the flash of alarm in the woman's eyes. Rainn opened a clutch bag on the breakfast bar and removed a packet of cigarettes. She withdrew a cigarette and flicked open a Zippo lighter of brushed sterling silver, visibly expensive. Rainn did not lift the cigarette to her mouth, but traced the flame up and down its length, watching it burn.

'Reminds me of my grandfather,' she said distantly as a sickly scent pervaded the pristine kitchen. 'I lost my grandparents when I was thirteen. The house caught fire while I slept. I never knew Jack. I can't understand your loss and I won't pretend to. But I've wasted energy chasing questions with no answers.'

The cigarette was alight from tip to butt, disintegrating beneath a golden flame. Rainn dropped it on the marble, where it continued to burn.

'*Why* is a volatile question that grows like cancer in the mind of the curious. You ought to do as I did, and move on.'

'Anna Harrington died and that well's been blown up. I'm the only one who knows that she talked to Jack about lucid dreaming. I'm the only one who believes that it's all connected. And nobody is listening to me.'

Rainn plucked the packet of cigarettes from the counter. 'Smoke?' she offered.

'No thanks.' Winter shook her head, disappointment creasing her unblemished skin.

Rainn raised her tidy brows. 'I guess I'll have to find another way to kill you.'

Winter managed not to laugh.

Gus ducked, leaning back against the wall with the rucksack on his thighs, fearful that the beat of his heart might resonate through the glass. His mind reeled at an image of Winter collapsing on the white tiles, silenced.

If he knocked on the front door, he could return the book to Rainn and ask her to leave town. Joe would find a way into Melissa's house, as he had done with Anna's, and enter with a mobile scanner from his office, copying the letters while Rainn slept.

But would Rainn let Winter live?

Keeping low, he glanced around the back of the house. Details sharpened as adrenaline electrified his body. A set of double doors opened out from the kitchen to a conservatory. Through the conservatory panes, he spotted a narrow wooden door at the far end of the back wall, presumably the original rear door before the house had been renovated beyond recognition.

This is becoming a habit, he thought.

If this door was open, he could search the house while Winter divulged her secrets and dug her own grave. If he found where the letters were hidden, it might not be necessary for Rainn to leave Godalming. In Joe's police car, he could escape to the countryside with Winter and Alicia, beyond the reach of the Order of Chaos. And from their hiding place, Anna's letters would lead them to his great-grandparents.

Not daring a dash past the conservatory, Gus tore around the front of the house and down the far side, squeezing between an overgrown hedge and the brick wall to reach the rear door. The door was open and narrow steps led to a basement beneath the house. He took a breath; it was unlikely that the letters would be anywhere but the room in which Rainn was staying. Perhaps an internal door led to the heart of the house?

With a soft click, he flicked a switch on the wall. A bulb stuttered on for a second, revealing the steps ahead, and then flickered off. Treading lightly, Gus continued down into shadow. The old bulb flickered sporadically, shedding enough light for him to spot a washing machine, a toy horse and a tartan sofa that he was not surprised Melissa had relegated to the basement. There followed a spell of darkness as he reached the concrete floor and shuffled ahead. Somewhere distant, a grandfather clock struck a hard monotone, out of sync with the chaotic patter in his chest. Light through the doorway above illuminated something on the floor: a pair of blue eyes.

A heavy chain clinked and time stopped as Gus realised that a large animal lay beside the steps he had descended. He leaped back as the sudden light of the bulb revealed what appeared to be a wolf chained to the bottom of the banister. With eyes blazing, the beast reared to its feet and drew back its lips, baring a formidable set of teeth.

Gus's eyes strayed from those jaws and eyes just long enough to determine that it was not a wolf, but a husky. The dog issued a deep growl, its head low and hackles bristling. Gus stepped back, pushing against the corner of the sofa, and the dog moved between him and the stairs. As a pair of icy blue eyes bore into his, the throaty growl became a harsh barking. The dog reared its head and strained on its chain, less than an arm's length away.

Sharp barks bounced between the four walls and carried through the house. Fangs snapped as spittle flicked upon the concrete floor. The banister moaned as the dog tugged ever more aggressively, determined to break the narrow distance to which Gus now owed his life.

'Shhh,' a voice floated down the stairs. Gus's eyes oscillated between the turquoise dress, shimmering in the light from the open doorway, and the banister post, straining visibly. It would not last for long.

Rainn bent to lift the horse from the floor. The toy consisted of a long wooden pole with a wheel at one end and the blue velvet head of a horse on the other: a hobby horse. Holding it by the pole, she drew the lighter from her bag.

At the click of the lighter, the dog barked sharply, its violent eyes on Gus. An unseen part of the banister cracked. In that moment, the intensity of the dog's bark was so fierce that Gus was certain it would kill him.

'Shhh, Sam,' Rainn soothed as the velvet head of the horse began to flame. The dog tore its eyes from Gus and faced its master.

In the blaze, Rainn's skin was golden as she crouched beside the animal, waving the toy from side to side in a hypnotic fashion.

'What are you doing here?' asked an accusatory voice. Gus tore his eyes from where Rainn appeared to be both threatening and placating the beast. Winter stood on the stairs, leaning on the banisters and glaring at Gus as if he had crashed her party.

'Announcing a pregnancy?' asked Rainn when Gus made no reply. She eyed the bump beneath his jacket. Winter descended the stairs, high heels clicking on the concrete. Rainn extended a hand and stroked the dog's silver-grey coat while holding the fire so close to the animal's face that it wrinkled its nose under the heat. She rose from her crouch, leaving the toy to burn on the floor with the dog fixated upon it.

That animal is trained to kill, thought Gus.

'I have something that belongs to you,' he said, unzipping his jacket. 'I'm here to return it.'

Eyeing the bag, Rainn stepped over the burning toy and settled on the sofa beside him, sending a cloud of dust into the air. Winter watched the fire dwindle, curious as to what the dog would do when it had burned out. She maintained her position with one foot on the bottom step.

Opening her bag, Rainn withdrew the packet of cigarettes and offered one to Gus. He wrinkled his nose.

'Kids these days.' Rainn shrugged, tipping the remainder of the cigarettes into her hand and scattering them onto the fire, followed by the empty packet. Renewed, the flames burned with a vigour reflected in the dog's eyes. Winter was as spellbound as the dog, her eyes on Rainn, drawn to the bigger personality. Gus's stomach churned as black smoke reached for the ceiling, unable to escape.

'My grandfather was a smoker,' said Rainn in a conversational tone as she returned to her seat. She lowered her eyes to where Gus was toying with the clasp of his backpack. 'Always fiddling, always agitated. Never still. I would watch him draw nicotine into his lungs and wonder: what are you so afraid of?'

Her gaze was penetrating.

'Fear,' breathed Rainn. 'That great motor that drives us from one irrational decision to the next. What drives your motor, Augustus? What are you so afraid of? Other than tattoos.'

'Questions,' said Gus as Rainn rubbed the symbol on her wrist. He undid the clasp and opened his bag. 'Not big dogs, not creepy messages written on the walls in glow-in-the-dark paint. It's the questions that keep me up at night.' He withdrew the Murder Book. 'And I'm done asking them.'

With tentative hands, Rainn lifted the book from Gus's grasp. She stood, cradling the book to her chest and tilting her head to the blackening ceiling.

'Finally, the book is mine!'

And then she cast it onto the fire.

'I'm not here for that mouldy old list, silly,' she said, reaching into her bag. 'I'm here for you.'

She tossed a handkerchief into Gus's lap with one hand and gripped a handgun in the other, letting her bag drop to the floor. Winter backed against the wall as the weapon was trained in her direction. Down the side of the gun's barrel, the words were caught in the firelight: *Glock 19 Austria.*

'That's it,' said Rainn as Gus picked up the handkerchief. 'Over your mouth.'

Gus saw fear in Winter's eyes and willed her not to charge up the stairs. He had no doubt that Rainn would pull the trigger if she attempted to escape. He lifted the handkerchief to his mouth and chloroform stung his nostrils.

Black leather twisted in the flames, a golden eye folding shut. Rainn nodded, her smile triumphant, while the grandfather clock pounded between his ears.

'Breathe.'

Headstones

ALICIA LURCHED FORWARD in bed, clutching a hand to her chest where the bullet had entered her ribcage. She drew her fingers away, expecting blood. But this was not Vivador and the expectation died in her mind. The gunshot had woken her instantly, forcing the retreat of her soul within its material cradle. So intense was the shock of adrenaline, the portal had not been necessary.

She's not ready.

He had protected her. This simulacrum, a creation of the enemy designed to do their bidding, had ensured her return to the waking world. Rainn's eyes remained like the afterimage that follows a flash of light. What might have happened had Ryan not put a bullet in her chest?

Alicia Crow.

She trod Post-it Notes into the floor, pacing her bedroom while discordant thoughts refused to form an orderly queue.

A coiled spring. A shallow breath.

Ten, nine—

No. She fought the urge to distract herself with pointless tasks. Like counting down. Or searching for those who could not be found. Or waiting for those who would never return. She had been too busy playing with fire and cannonballs to consider her place in this murderous family. Craving something concrete, her mind wandered to a marked tree in another realm.

Don't be an idiot, thought Alicia as she climbed under the covers.

Again, it was not necessary to visit the clearing behind her grandmother's cottage. In her lucid dream, Alicia raised a well through her bedroom floorboards and threw herself down it. It was the idea of this well that served as a portal, and she landed on the hilltop in Vivador.

She returned to the outermost tree of the pine forest. Ryan and Rainn were surely beneath the glass archway, discussing whatever test he believed she would fail. Should either of them materialise before her, she could return to the well in the blink of an eye.

Or shoot herself in the chest? If it was not necessary to use that portal, how else might she return? The line between Vivador and the waking world had thinned. Alicia knelt at the foot of the pine and needles pricked her skin. She knew in which realm she felt more alive.

A + E Forever. The A did not stand for Anna after all. Had her grandmother, Eloise, sat beneath this tree with Augustus Crow? Had she held his hand while he conjured a blade of glass, sharp enough to pierce the bark and mark a world where everything could be undone? Since time immemorial, the human race has strived to create something permanent in a transient world, building pyramids like sandcastles before the rising tide. Perhaps Augustus had believed that if he cut deep enough, his love for Eloise would exist beyond their shared experience.

Had he led his lover down the well and shown her the world that his parents discovered? If so, this message was all that remained of them. Anna had been eighteen when her mother died. As had Alicia.

An aching spread like poison through her projected self and pine trees bent under the wind. More than answers, more than the feel of her brother's hand in hers, Alicia had an overwhelming need to see her mother.

She was alone. Ryan and Rainn may have been on the far side of the forest, picking over the finer details of her demise, but this was the first time she had been by herself in the immaterial realm.

Scanning endless hills, she was a speck of paint on a large sheet of paper. With nobody to share it, Vivador felt as private as the landscape of her dreams. She could generate anything she desired.

'You're exposed as an artist,' her mother had said while sharing her latest creation. On the kitchen table lay a wooden sculpture of an eye, the iris filled with acrylic-sprayed petals in varying states of decay. 'You assume that people will judge you on your talent, but it's what you've chosen to create that they will question.'

Settling her focus on a flat section of grass between two hills, Alicia sent a series of walls rising from the ground. Stacking brick by brick, the walls grew higher, outlining the familiar structure of her local church. Wooden doors filled the doorways and glass filled the windows. A large tree sprouted beside the far corner of the building, leaving a narrow patch of sky between the two, so blue that it appeared to be in the foreground. The soil trembled as rows of headstones lined the ground between her and the back door of the building. She marvelled at the intricate design on the stained-glass window. How similar was her recreation to the original? How accurately had she recalled each piece of glass? Sunlight streamed inexplicably through the window from the church's interior, illuminating the headstone at her feet.

Rays of green, orange, red and blue fell in bands across Anna Harrington's name. Standing before her mother's grave, Alicia's heart thumped as turbulently as when the bullet had entered it. With each shuddering beat, a thought in her mind expanded— intoxicating, terrifying—so large that it was all she understood.

I could bring her to life.

When deciding whether to quit her teaching role and work at the art gallery on Godalming High Street, Anna had debated with Rory. Each had taken one side and then switched, to argue from both perspectives. This was proving to be an effective means of reaching a difficult decision, until Rory had fallen asleep. Alicia had stepped in to reason that her mother would be happier out of the classroom and would benefit from the extra time to paint. It had surprised them both how passionately Anna had argued that she enjoyed her teaching, inspired by the creativity of her students. Through this debate, she had realised how much she loved her job, as impractical as it may have been given the heavy demands on her time. Alicia did wonder whether Rory falling asleep had swayed her mother's view, since they relied on her stable salary.

Facing the far corner of the church, Alicia watched her own image step through that blue rectangle between the wall and the tree. This debate would be between Alicia and herself.

'I could bring her to life,' Alicia voiced the thought aloud. Her conjured self stopped behind the headstone at her feet, facing her with hard eyes as counter-arguments formed.

'It would be a simulacrum. Like Ryan. Like me. It would not be Mum.'

Hearing her own voice argue against her was as thrilling as it was unnerving.

'It would look like Mum...sound like Mum—'

'It would not be real.'

But the image before her appeared unfathomably real. Strands of dark hair played against her face in the anxious breeze that she unconsciously created. Knowledge of her green eyes with subtle flecks of brown had been drawn from every photograph of herself she had seen and every mirror she had looked in. Her lips were pursed in that serious pout her father mocked her for when she was cross. Surveying the detail in her face, Alicia did not doubt that she could look upon the animated image of her mother with equal clarity.

'I need to speak to her. I have questions, I need to know—'

'You would be asking yourself.'

Irritated by her own reasoning, Alicia's voice rose in pitch and force.

'If I can summon her here...if I can hear her voice...feel her—'
She reached out across the headstone and took the simulacrum's
forearm, running the pad of her thumb against the warm skin. 'How
could I not?'

She stared into her own eyes, trying to convince herself. Seeking
permission. A desperate heart pleaded with a logical mind. But the
simulacrum could not tell her what she wanted to hear, only what
she already knew.

'Because you would feel no more than an immaculate agony.'

Her hands trembled as the simulacrum leaned across the grave,
closing the distance between them.

'If you killed those people,'—animosity blazed in that pale face
as she delivered the final words she had called to her mother—'don't
come back.'

Green eyes filled her vision.

'She's dead,' said the simulacrum. And there it was. That which
had been lodged between the grey matter and the roof of her skull
made itself known. Alicia took a step back and her mirror image
lurched through the headstone.

'You haven't shed a single tear since your mother died.'

Faced with the truth, Alicia was frightened by the intensity of
her self-loathing.

'I have to be strong,' she uttered, weakly. 'I have to find David. I
cannot—'

'She's dead.'

'Stop it.'

'She's dead.'

'Stop it!' Alicia screamed and the simulacrum vanished. She
closed her eyes and opened them on top of the hillock before
throwing herself down the well.

She was shaking when she woke. She blinked her eyes at the

alarm clock: 14:07. The numbers shifted as if beneath the skin of a pond, but only because the walls of her dam had started to splinter. Brisk, unconscious steps carried her down the corridor, down the stairs and through the front door.

A light drizzle fell as she stood before her mother's grave. The petals of flowers she had not envisaged in Vivador quivered in the rain, echoing the tremble of her folded arms. A light in the church was on, but the coloured rays through the stained-glass window did not fall upon Anna Harrington's headstone. Alicia stumbled forward and placed her hand on the light grey stone, brushing raindrops from its surface.

As the tremor in her fingertips grew, the drizzle became a downpour, the clouds breaking with the walls of her dam. Tears streamed down her face as she fell to her knees and lowered her forehead to rest against the cold stone. With every shuddering sob, Alicia submitted to a reality that she could no longer deny.

She did not know how many hours passed as she wept at the grave, her knees sinking deeper into the waterlogged soil. The sky had started to darken when she took a slow breath and lifted her head from her mother's headstone. Like magnets, her eyes were drawn to the incomprehensible beauty of the circular window. Rays of light through the glass fragments landed on a grave a short distance away. With a sniff, she hoisted herself to her feet and followed the coloured beams to where they fell.

This grave was three years older, though the marble from which the headstone had been hewn shone as though recently polished. Alicia stepped closer and read the name that lay beneath the rays. Her heart stuttered to a halt.

Immobilised, she stood before the grave of Ryan Lawson.

MELISSA STEPPED THROUGH her front door to see a track of muddy footprints leading up the stairs. Broken glass littered the plush carpet, surrounding an ornamental stone squirrel. Without pause, she stole into the kitchen and snatched a large knife from the rack. She ascended the stairs with the knife in both hands before her chest, her breathing silent and controlled. The footprints led to the room at the end of the corridor: her bedroom. The doors on either side were closed, leaving the corridor dark. Light spilled from the room ahead through a crack in the doorway.

Shifting the knife into her right hand, Melissa raised her left to the door and gave it a firm push.

'Alicia?'

The young woman stood on Melissa's bed, muddy footprints on the pillows. With her back to the room, Alicia painted the white wall above the bed. Finishing a careful stroke, she turned and stepped aside.

The knife slipped from Melissa's hand and struck the carpet with a thud. Alicia watched her headmistress stagger back and collapse against the doorframe as she stared at the face that was painted on her wall. The hair ranged in colour from a cinnamon-brown to a tawny-gold. The eyes burned a glacial blue.

'Where is my brother?'

Ryan, age 12

ON THE NIGHT of Amira's 9th birthday I was stuffed with cake, just looking at how fat I was in the mirror. That's when I heard her screaming. I pulled down my jumper and ran downstairs and her bed was covered in spiders. There must have been about 29 of them. Of course, everybody thought it was me that put them there.

'Were you jealous that it was Amira's birthday?' Mum asked while Peter brushed the spiders into a cereal box.

The next morning, I watched Peter leave the Pagoda with the P.S. Lawson briefcase and the S reminded me of Sam and that made me cross. It was Peter who gave me the key to the attic and Peter who found me unconscious by the mirror. It was Peter who told Mum that I must have found the key in his study—another excuse for him to start working in the Pagoda.

At seven, I'd been too pleased that "Daddy" was paying me any attention to wonder why he wanted me to find an old mirror in a locked room.

'When you've a question on your mind, ask the mirror,' he had said, twirling the key like it was magic. 'The Ryan in the mirror will know what to do.'

The problem is, Peter, that Ryan is not a little kid any more. And the questions on his mind are about you.

The best thing about living in a farmhouse in the middle of nowhere is that you get to explore every inch of it when playing hide and seek. You find all sorts of things: love letters that Mum received in college, books that are not for children and lots of keys. Keys to cupboards that were thrown away, keys to padlocks that are rusted shut and spare keys that were made and then forgotten.

When Peter drove off down the driveway, I knew he would be gone all day as it takes forever to get anywhere from here. But I wasn't going to dawdle. I raced to the kitchen, took the set of keys from behind the cutlery tray and ran back out. I stopped running when I passed Amira's bedroom, since running would be too suspicious. Amira had either seen another spider or a shadow and Mum was rubbing her back while Sam searched around the bed for something to eat.

Amira didn't look up at me. I told her that I didn't put the spiders on her bed, but I think she doesn't trust me now my voice has gone all deep. Mum looked at me and smiled, but luckily she did not ask me where I was going in such a hurry. Sometimes it can be useful that she doesn't talk to me any more.

The lock on Peter's study door was ancient so I knew exactly what key to use: the one that looks just about right for a treasure chest. I unlocked the door.

It's no wonder Mum wants to clean it so bad—the room was a total mess. Books and paper everywhere and so much dust. Two bookcases, a desk and a swivel chair with a peeling leather seat: that was it. I guess the bubbling beakers and brains in jars were probably in the Pagoda, but the lock on that was new and I wasn't getting in there any time soon.

The books on the shelves had funny titles like Disorders of the Brain and Living with Phobia. I might have thought how nice it was that he had read all these books to help him with Sam's epilepsy and Amira's synaesthesia until I found the papers in the desk drawer. The papers had been printed off his computer (also in his new office) and lots of words had been highlighted in a green pen. Down the side, Peter had written in his spidery handwriting:

Fear removal vs fear creation? Fear controls us ⇒ control fear.

The jack was out of the box now. Peter had created Amira's fear of spiders. This fact left me with two questions: how and why?

I needed to get into his office in the Pagoda. There was nothing else useful in that dusty room, and it was just as I pocketed the key that I heard the front door: he was back.

When I looked down the stairs, I saw the most beautiful girl in the world, I reckon. Her hair was so straight and black it looked like Mum had ironed it. And her eyes were like two sapphires.

Rainn is fifteen years old and she is very troubled. Mum was obviously not pleased that Peter had brought home an orphan who was older than me, but Amira was so happy to have someone to share her room with.

Rainn settled into Sam's old bed and I wondered what fear Peter had in store for her.

PART TWO: THE WILL OF OTHERS

Fear will express itself in a number of curious ways. Given the same stimulus, some minds will soften, pliable as heated wax; others will harden, brittle as flint. In reflective surfaces I catch the anger on my face and find myself asking: what do you fear?

— Peter Lawson —

CHAPTER FIVE
Mother

THE GRAVE IS *empty.*

In her mind's eye, Alicia watched her headmistress hack at the soil with a shovel, the sweat on her brow glistening in the moonlight. Numb fingers prise open the decaying panels of a bare coffin. Brushing a hand across her forehead, she stares into the empty cavity with a smudge of dirt above her silver eyes. A shallow breath fogs the air as belief transmutes to truth: her son is alive.

Ryan was not a simulacrum. His flawless features had not been generated by Aldous and Morna Crow to tempt victims through a series of tests. Ryan had been created here, in the waking world—the real world—a world in which he had a history that could not be undone. And where, presently, he was held in a farmhouse in the Lake District with Alicia's brother.

Take me to him.

Alicia had kissed her sleeping father's forehead and left a note on the kitchen counter telling him not to worry, she would be back in the morning. She had considered waking him, but it would have taken as long to explain where she was going as the four-hour journey to the Lake District. She was keen to travel overnight, while the roads were quiet. She was keen to travel now.

The police car was not in the neighbouring driveway and Gus did not answer the door, so she had jumped into Melissa's Jeep and told her to drive. Melissa had needed no coercion, her hands like talons on the steering wheel as she floored the pedal and accelerated down Gardner Road as if fearful that Alicia might come to her senses and change her mind.

Standing on the bed, paintbrush in hand, Alicia had asked Melissa exactly what happened when her mother had visited. Drops of blue paint struck Melissa's pillowcase as the woman crept across the carpet, her face drawn with intense longing as she stared at the image of her son. Finding her voice, she explained that Rainn must have left the door ajar; Anna had let herself in. From her bedroom, Melissa had heard Alicia's mother call her name, and reached the top of the stairs as Anna reached the bottom. Anna wanted to know why David was held in the house where Melissa used to live. She had asked Melissa to take her to him.

I think I've found someone who can help us.

Anna had made it to the third step before she collapsed.

The tyres burned along the dual carriageway and Alicia studied Melissa's reflection in the windscreen, searching those barren eyes for fragments of what they had witnessed. She longed to walk through Melissa's memories, to see her mother's final moments: a hand clutching the banister, muscles flexing in the forearm as she prepares to ascend; her face contorting as she demands to be taken to her son. And then the muscles relax. For half a second, certainty is replaced with disorientation before her eyes glaze over and Anna Harrington folds onto the steps like a rag doll.

Alicia rested her head against the window and closed her eyes. The vibration of the engine travelled through her skull and into her chest. The cool glass reminded her of a headstone and the vibration intensified. She opened her eyes and sought distraction in two white lines running in parallel down the side of the dual carriageway. If she relaxed her eyes, the painted lines appeared to detach from the road and hover like static bands above the tarmac. Lazily, her gaze drifted to the right and sent the bands accelerating up the road. She would like to explain this curious sensation to David, as she had strived to describe so many of the details that others overlooked. Some curiosities seemed impossible to explain, but she enjoyed the challenge. There was so much of the world she was yet to share with him.

If he is in the Lake District—

She clenched her teeth, letting the hum of the engine rattle her molars, allaying the rise of that treacherous optimism. Until she laid eyes on her brother, she would not allow herself to believe that the wait could be over, and that the interminable might end.

'Do Aldous and Morna run this farmhouse?'

Melissa took her eyes from the road and stared at Alicia for a full second, her skin bleached in the glare of a passing van. Alicia knew more than Melissa had thought. The headmistress accelerated through an amber light and took a hand from the steering wheel to adjust her chignon bun. Her face was composed as she adopted a businesslike tone.

'No. Burnflower is run by a man named Peter. A psychologist, of sorts—'

'Burnflower? As in Rainn Burnflower?'

'Yes. Rainn was one of three orphans that Peter...' She paused. A flash of pain crossed her face, but she controlled it. 'Peter had an interest in phobia and fear. He believed fear—'

'Gus told me that Rainn's lesson, at school—the art lesson—it was about fear.'

'It is rude to interrupt people while they are talking.'

Alicia sat back in her seat, biting down a retort.

Melissa continued, 'Peter believed fear to be the primary motivator, reasoning that all action could be traced back to this primitive emotion: every decision made in its shadow. The creation and manipulation of fear became his life's work.'

'With orphans?' Alicia asked, her throat dry. A gentle acceleration built in her heart.

'The creation of an irrational fear is relatively easy: generate a sensory overload and expose the individual to a chosen stimulus and they will be unable to process it, developing a phobia. It's the reversal of this process that was the real challenge. The mind loves fear—we would not ride rollercoasters and watch horror movies if not for the thrill of it. And once we have latched on to a particular fear, we construct an identity around it. He experimented with hypnosis, and enjoyed some success; a fear could be lessened if not removed entirely. You see, a child will not avoid fire because they are told not to touch it. Fear supersedes reason. Control fear and you control the individual.'

Her manner was detached, lacking any emotion, primitive or otherwise, as she described experiments designed to terrorise orphaned children. Alicia watched her shift the gear stick from fourth to fifth in a movement both automatic and controlled.

'What did he want with David?'

'Peter was interested in how different minds respond to the same stimulus, to determine which areas of the brain were responsible for the psychological and physiological effects of fear. Would an aversion to certain flavours be as pronounced in a child with synaesthesia? Might—'

'Could a blind child be afraid of the dark?'

Melissa caught Alicia's eyes in the glass.

'David isn't simply blind, is he?'

A truck blasted its horn as Melissa cut across the lane to exit the dual carriageway, but Alicia's heart was already beating at full throttle. David had a rare condition known as 'blindsight'. While his mind was unable to create a mental picture of the world, he would occasionally respond to his environment as if his brain received the visual information without his knowledge. Though David had no conscious image of the table in front of him, Alicia had watched him grab the spoon as if he knew where it was. His condition had fascinated her friends, who set up tasks in which David was challenged to place a coin in the slot of the piggybank or to stamp a marker in the centre of a circle. His accuracy was inconsistent and his teenage examiners soon lost interest, speculating that it was little more than blind luck.

'Did you work for him?' asked Alicia. 'At Burnflower?'

'Peter is my husband.'

The separate fragments of an incomplete truth assembled themselves like the shattered pieces of a stained-glass window.

There was a tiny shake of Melissa's head, almost imperceptible, like she was reluctant to remember. She spoke as though addressing the road ahead.

'We adopted Sam when Ryan was young. We couldn't have another child. We wanted him to have someone to play with. And then—Amira, she came after. Taken from the same children's home. Amira with her synaesthesia, he was forever testing her.' The ghost of a nostalgic smile vanished when she swallowed. She adjusted the bun and took a sharp left at the roundabout. 'But it was Ryan that suffered the most. Through years of hypnosis, Peter ensured that his son grew up in isolation, unattached. He took my enthusiastic boy and made a monster of him. A…' She caught Alicia's eye, a flash of wariness. 'And then Rainn. She was more troubled than any child I've known. She suffers from REM sleep behaviour disorder: acting out her dreams without the sleep atonia that keeps us in our beds at night. He couldn't control her, not as he had with Ryan. He told her everything. Her disorder, her dreams—she fascinated him. And then, Ryan tried to kill her. He must—it must have been jealousy, or…' She fiddled with a hidden pin at the back of her head. 'Peter told me that he could fix him. That he could make my boy forget what he had done, to Rainn, and to…So they put him in a coma.'

I am a simulacrum. Ryan's eyes had held no sense of self. Whatever Peter had done to fix him, his memories had been obliterated, good and bad. Alicia pictured Ryan and Rainn beneath the glass archway, Ryan with no notion of what he had done to her.

'What did Ryan do?'

'It wasn't a coma,' said Melissa, ignoring the question. 'Peter had given Ryan to Aldous. They said, Peter and Rainn, they said they needed him, and I—I needed him!'—a flash of anger—'Peter told me that they needed other minds to work with. All I wanted was my Ryan back. So I did as I was told. I took the position at Valmont. If they needed other children…But two months later, Peter told me he had died.'

Melissa paused and Alicia did not fill the silence.

'It was Rainn's idea, I've no doubt. She was running my home at Peter's side and wanted me as far away as possible. But I didn't believe it, I couldn't—a mother knows if her child is still alive. Some connections exist beyond the waking world.'

Alicia had seen that look in Anna's eyes, beyond doubt and reason; beyond brittle hope lay an unshakeable certainty.

'I unearthed that empty coffin and confronted them. Rainn told me that if I wanted to see him again, I must do as instructed. I was forced to discover what a mother would do to get her child back.'

Alicia's nails were white against the door handle.

'How did they find David?'

'There is nothing that a mother wouldn't do, Alicia.'

Captive

THE FIRST SENSATION was a stinging around his nostrils as the remnants of the chloroform continued to corrode his skin. The second was a dull thudding behind his eyes. And the third, immediately more concerning, was that the seat of his pants was wet. Through a thick lethargy that sealed his eyes, Gus determined that he was sitting upright with his hands bound behind his back. At his wrists, he felt the cool metal of the pole against which he was propped. A gentle rocking, as if he were in the back of a truck on uneven ground. His chapped lips stung in the salty breeze of sea air. One by one, his dislocated senses converged to present him with his surroundings. The boat's engine hummed to his left and his heavy head rolled to the side as the vessel rose and fell over the waves.

There followed a sharper, less subtle, sensation as a finger prodded him in the back.

'Wake *up*, you thumbsucking—'

Winter fell silent as Gus groaned and leaned forward, straining against the pole. He lifted his eyelids to find a murky gloom, and his eyes captured what light they could to draw his environment into focus.

He and Winter sat back-to-back, bound by cable ties to a steel pole. This pole ran from the roof of their small cabin to the rotting planks on which they sat. He felt a modicum of relief as water sloshed past him, through his jeans, and towards the tapered end of their cabin at the front of the boat. He may have been kidnapped by the school counsellor and was bound in the shadows with one of the most self-obsessed girls he had ever met, but at least he had not wet himself.

'Where is she taking us?' Winter hissed, leaning her head against the pole. 'What the hell is going on?'

Gus ignored her as his eyes adjusted to the light and swept the small cabin. To his left was a simple counter with a sink and stove, a flight of wooden steps leading to the upper deck and a door that swung open with each wave they crested to reveal a narrow bathroom. Beyond the mournful hum of the engine, the silence was punctuated by a steady dripping of petrol that leaked from the low roof of the cabin to stain the sodden planks.

'Where is she?' Gus asked, his hoarse voice barely audible above the engine. 'Are there others?'

Metal sheets creaked overhead as somebody crossed the deck.

'She's brought that dog,' said Winter. 'And there's some creep driving the boat, but he doesn't talk. He just stares. She came down a while ago—hours ago—after we set off, but I may as well have been dead. She put that thing around your neck and walked back up the stairs without even looking at me.'

Gus's hands yanked instinctively against the pole as he became aware of something around his throat. Night was falling, and opaque clouds had made a mirror of the window running along the side of the boat, just above sea level. In the reflection he was able to discern the thin black collar that his numb senses had failed to detect. He pulled again at the cable ties binding his wrists as a claustrophobic desperation shot through him to grab at whatever had been strapped around his neck. He was particularly disturbed by the green LED light blinking intermittently on the dark band.

Pouncing on the consciousness of her fellow captive, Winter launched a barrage of questions: *Who is that woman? What does she want with us? Did she kill Jack? What was that book?*

Gus let them drift by with the passing waves as he mulled over questions of his own, occasionally snatching one of Winter's to contemplate in silence. But amid all the questions, one truth lay evident, and all else paled against it: Rainn was taking them to his family.

There was no need for Anna's letters; he was being taken exactly where he wanted to go. Aldous and Morna had not sent Rainn to retrieve the Murder Book, but to destroy the evidence. It was Gus and Alicia they wanted—the remaining Crows yet to prove their loyalty to the family. He would be offered a choice: join the Order of Chaos, or die. He had already surrendered the book. He would continue to earn their trust. He would be welcomed into the arms of the elder Crows and the murder of his parents would be avenged.

In the glass, Gus caught Winter's reflection in the window on her side of the cabin. The fear in those chestnut eyes was pitiable. Winter was a loose end, a threat. Rainn would have tried to convince her that Jack's death was the tragic mistake that the police claimed. But there was only one way to silence her now.

Rainn could have pulled the trigger and left the girl in Melissa's basement. Another murder for his uncle to cover up. Had she taken Winter along for the ride so that Aldous and Morna might decide what to do with her? Or would Gus be the one to choose? How might his loyalty be tested?

'My uncle's a policeman,' he said, catching her gaze in the reflection.

'I think I've seen his car…'

'He'll be able to track this boat. There's nothing to worry about.'

Her nostrils flared and her upper lip curled as fear burned to anger.

'Oh good. That's reassuring. I'll just settle in, try to catch a tan when the sun comes out.'

With their eyes locked in the reflection, Gus did not merely see the ire in Winter's eyes: he felt it. He was drawn to it as the embers of a fire within were stoked and burned anew. He filled his lungs, taking in the salty, petrol-laced air that stung his nostrils. But the cracks in Winter's confident façade sent a churning through his gut. Wherever Rainn was taking them, Joe would never find them before they reached the Crows.

'Vivador,' said Gus, recalling the name on Winter's notepad. 'What did Jack tell you about it?'

From the expression on her face, you would have thought she had found him rifling through her memories.

'She killed him, didn't she?'

The boat hit a wave and water sloshed across the floor, soaking through Gus's jeans and into his underwear.

'I don't think so. I think that Jack, and Anna Harrington, were killed by my great-grandparents.'

Winter said nothing. Somehow through the sound of the engine Gus could hear her breathing. And then: 'Why?'

'My family were hiding something down that well, and they found it. Everybody who found their secret was written in that book and then killed.'

'And that's where she's taking us? To your great-grandparents?'

'I think so.'

'Blackout.'

Silence followed as the pair let the enormity of their predicament press against them in the confined space.

'So, your relatives murder people and your uncle drags you around the country covering for them? No wonder you're so angry.'

The curve of a smile lifted the corner of her mouth. He had never raised his voice before her; he had never shown her any sign of anger. Only behind the closed door of his home had his uncle seen it surface. A wave struck the side of the boat and echoed through him, hot and acidic. Was the emotion that he harboured so obvious? Did he wear it on his face like some baroque theatrical mask? Turning from her piercing gaze, he met his own reflection. How freely available our faces are to others, he thought; and yet—

without a mirror—they are hidden from ourselves.

He coughed, straining against the cable ties with an unconscious desire to bring a hand to his face. He wanted to rub his eyes or scratch the corner of his chin.

'You *literally* threatened to bite me,' he said.

Winter laughed weakly and her shoulders brushed against his. She raised her head to the metal panels above, to the crack by the pole through which the petrol leaked.

'Your uncle had better get a move on,' she said, closing her eyes.

Gus surveyed his prison, small details sharpening as his eyes continued to adjust to what meagre light permeated the clouds. Screw-holes in the wooden planks around the pole appeared recent, and he imagined the table that had been removed to make room for the pair of them. It had been shortly after noon when he drew the chloroform into his lungs; and now, on the brink of nightfall, it must be around seven in the evening. How long had he been on this boat? How many hours would it take this vessel to reach Portugal? Without the pills he was accustomed to, an intense fatigue crept over him. His will faded with the last rays of daylight, and heavy eyelids fell like iron shutters. With a start, he cracked his head against the pole and his eyes snapped open. The moment he had lost consciousness, the collar had delivered an electric shock.

'Is that so?' he uttered.

If the collar prevented him from sleeping, then Rainn feared him entering Vivador. This left him one option, though it was not an inviting one.

When Winter opened her eyes, Gus's reflection was sharp against the black sky: consternation on his parted lips, studying her as if weighing up his options.

'Don't look at me like I'm already dead,' she said.

'We need to tell Alicia where we are.'

'I'll ready my carrier pigeon.'

The young man's eyes scanned the floor, watching the water slosh left and right. Bubbles in the screw-holes.

'You've got a thing for her, haven't you?' she asked.

Gus frowned. 'She's my cousin. Or something like that. We share a grandfather.'

Winter opened her mouth and then looked away, confusion playing across her face. More than confused, she was defeated: so little made sense to her now. And this was exactly where he needed her.

Above their heads, footsteps crossed the deck.

'People used to believe the Earth was flat,' said Gus. 'And not the stupid ones. Everyone did. It was a fact: the Earth was flat.'

Winter said nothing.

'Five hundred years ago, people believed that the Earth was the centre of the universe. It was common knowledge. And those who disagreed were tied to a post and set on fire.'

'Have you been drinking the petrol?'

'A hundred and fifty years ago, nobody knew that we evolved from apes. They thought the world was, like, six thousand years old and that every species was created as it is now, right out of the packet.'

'Unsubscribe,' said Winter flatly, closing her eyes in an attempt to shut him out.

'A couple hundred years from now, they will laugh at everything we think we know. Do you get that? Every single thing we think we understand about how this universe works will be a joke. History is just a string of people believing that what they know is true.'

'So?'

'So you're not going to believe what I'm about to tell you.'

Winter yawned. 'Will it get me off this boat?'

On the deck above, a dog barked. The sound reverberated down the steel pole and into their bodies, making the pair flinch, each savage warning a shock to the heart. Gus spoke between these barks, just louder than the engine, so quietly that Winter had to lean back and press her ear against the pole.

'I need you to fall asleep, enter a lucid dream, and find Alicia.'

A final bid

WHY DID YOU barbecue your phone?

'Alicia, get back in the car.'

On either side, dark woodland encroached upon the country road, heavy boughs shouldering the black scar that man had laid upon it. Alicia stood between two aspens at the roadside, her arms folded like a petulant child.

'You kidnapped my brother.'

Her voice was hard yet she sounded younger than her years. Melissa cut the engine and silence flooded the woodland. The headmistress exited her vehicle, closed the door with a soft click, and brushed creases out of her white jacket as if entering a boardroom meeting. She walked around the car to where Alicia waited on loose stones at the edge of the tarmac.

'And I would do it again if it brought me closer to Ryan.'

She was careful to meet Alicia's eyes. It was her intention to drive the point home, to present the facts. A black bird emerged from the shadows, swooping over the road and into the trees on the far side.

'Is that what this is?' Alicia asked, keeping her voice low and adult. 'An exchange?'

'Would it matter?'

Alicia dug a hand into the pocket of her jeans as though her phone might materialise if she continued to search for it.

'I'm calling the police.'

'If you thought that there was any sense in that, you would not have said it aloud.'

Their heads turned at a light in the distance. A car approached the bend that led to their stretch of the country lane, its full beam scattering through the bushes like torchlight through a colander. Melissa's gaunt face tightened.

'Why do you think I'm still alive?' she whispered.

Alicia knew why her great-grandparents had spared Melissa: she had struck a deal with the Crows. Following Anna's death, she would take Alicia under her wing, caring for her when her disabled father was unable to. She would invite Alicia into her home and into her confidence, convincing her to hand over the stolen book.

'If Rainn has Anna's letters,' Melissa continued, 'then she knows that I was trying to help your mother. There are more than cars on these roads tonight, Alicia. They know where I am heading and if they find me before I get there…'

The car turned the corner and its headlights struck the surrounding trees. Alicia expected heavy shadows to splinter into thousands of feathers: crows bursting from the boughs. But the branches were as bare as the pines in Vivador. Melissa watched the vehicle slow and spoke through clenched teeth.

'If you want me to take you to your brother, get in the car.'

Alicia had painted Ryan's image on Melissa's wall to coerce the woman into taking her to David; if her son was leading Alicia through Vivador, Melissa must know where David was held in the waking world. But Melissa was not working with Ryan. Ryan was working for the Crows and his mother's name was on their list. The headmistress had not broken speed limits and ran red lights, racing to the Lake District before Alicia came to her senses and called the police. Melissa's time was up: she was driving to her death. This was a final bid to rescue her son.

The car stopped beside them. A middle-aged man, too tall for the low roof, stooped slightly over the steering wheel and wound down his window. In the back seat, a young girl slept with her head against the door, a tangle of dark ringlets for a pillow. The driver's friendly face ducked through the window and Melissa tensed as Alicia locked eyes with the stranger.

'You ladies all right?'

What might he find in her eyes? In her dilated pupils, could he see the fear of a girl disappearing into the night with the woman who had kidnapped her brother? Did the aftershock of her mother's death linger in bloodshot corners?

Anxiety creased his homely face. Perhaps his boss had failed to recognise his efforts. Perhaps he was late for dinner. *Same mind, different problems*: so Gus had been taught by his father. Anna had taught Alicia that each of us believe our struggles to be greater than those of others. In children, this is exposed through heated tantrums at 'unfair' situations; in adults, self-awareness limits the outbursts, yet the underlying resistance remains the same. We magnify our problems until they fill our minds, consuming our thoughts and disconnecting us from those around us. Battling alone, we are unable to see that each person we encounter is suffering from the same delusion.

Alicia found no connection in those kind eyes. Whatever challenges the stranger faced, his world remained intact. How could he see that hers had ended?

'There was a spider,' she replied in a monotone.

Melissa cleared her throat and peered through the window of the Jeep.

'Oh look, it's gone.'

The man gazed from one face to the other as if watching an exceptionally poor play. Melissa thanked him for stopping and opened her door as Alicia rounded the bonnet. She had just enough time to click her seatbelt into place before Melissa accelerated towards the bend.

The woodland gave way to a large basin, revealing a sheet of black water under the overcast night sky. The twin beams of their vehicle disturbed the night like a siren through the darkness.

'Why is your name in the book?' Alicia asked.

Melissa's grey eyes narrowed, glaring at the road ahead as she unearthed the past.

'Your mother had this belief that David could be found through lucid dreaming. Peter was fascinated with dreams—he'd written a paper on it, *Dreaming: Pattern and Potential*, pillaging the content of dreams in order to map subconscious desires. Anna was struggling. That book she found at her mother's, it was a comfort. It was something. And if anyone were to believe that lucid dreaming might make the intangible tangible—that bond between mother and son...

'I slept in my car a lot last summer. Outside Burnflower, waiting. I had nothing to lose. Or so I thought. Nothing else to try. So I experimented with lucid dreaming, as Anna had suggested. I found the well. And I found Ryan.

'When I saw him there, I thought he was just—I thought I had created him. Subconsciously. He was so far away, on his back, by the trees. Watching clouds cross the sky. I made to approach him, afraid to call his name, and Rainn appeared between us. Her warning was clear: return to Vivador, and they would terminate him.

'I didn't know what to do. I never saw him at Burnflower, and started to wonder whether he was in Portugal, with Aldous and Morna. So that's where I sent Anna. I thought she might find Ryan there. Instead, she returned with that book. With my name in it.

'I panicked. I spoke to Peter and he told me that Aldous and Morna would spare me if I got it back, the book. If I convinced Anna to return it. But I—they had made a promise to me. I had already given them David, why wouldn't they give me Ryan?'

She took a hand from the wheel and ran fingers through her scalp, tucking loose strands into the chignon bun and tentatively adjusting the positions of hidden bobby pins. The ashen-blonde hair remained as taut as her skin. Her face was not merely blank like her son's had been. Ryan's face was absent of emotion; Melissa's was devoid, as though drained. All that remained in her eyes were the vestiges of a cold, hard hope, like a gambler who had lost everything and everyone and was playing their life in one final bet.

'My brother wasn't enough?'

'David was bait. It wasn't your brother they were after. It wasn't Anna. It was you.'

Leverage

WINTER HAD RIDICULED Jack over his interest in lucid dreaming. She had mocked and yawned, threatened his reputation and explained in no uncertain terms that if he bored her with one more account of his dreams, she would take a staple gun to his eyelids and leave him to it. Everybody had weird dreams and nobody wanted to hear about them.

Nobody but the art teacher.

Jack Henson had been funny, charming and attractive in a way that made the younger students stare and Winter's friends simmer with envy. When Anna Harrington had chosen dreaming as the stimulus for their summer-term projects, Winter had rolled her eyes as Jack regaled the class with his latest nocturnal adventures, and his peers had listened as though he were recounting sporting victories. She had not rolled her eyes when Mrs Harrington had asked to speak with Jack after class, but she had been surprised that the woman had taken an interest in his childish fantasies.

When he died, one police officer suspected that Jack might have had a cramp in the water. Another informed her that accidental drowning was the third most common accidental death in the world. Winter had not been reassured by this information. She wanted to know why Alicia's mother had found him in the pool that day, and she wanted to know why nobody was listening to her.

In her role as the new school counsellor, Rainn had pressed Winter to be honest when talking about Jack; Winter had affected a damaged smile, playing the role of the distraught but brave victim of an unkind world. She confided in this stranger: it had been her idea to take a walk in the woods with Jack, and she had opened the door to the shed to see what lay inside. Jack had found the well unfathomably interesting, trying to convince her that there was a unicorn skull at the bottom. The idiot. And then he dreamed of the well, and thought that he had woken up.

'He wouldn't shut up about how real it was.'

'False awakenings are a common sign of psychosis.'

Though Rainn had pretended not to believe her, she had asked to see the well. Finally—unlike the teachers; unlike the police officers; unlike her busy mother—someone was listening to her. And Rainn understood: were students to see Winter frequent the counsellor's office at school, it would spread like lice through a kindergarten. Winter had not hesitated when Rainn invited her over on a Sunday afternoon. Her stubborn belief that Anna was responsible had landed her in captivity.

What to believe now? Had her boyfriend travelled down that well in a lucid dream and found another realm? Could she blur the lines that she had drawn between fantasy and reality, the lines that separate unicorns from horses, dragons from lizards and magic from science? And, if she could believe in the world down the well, was she responsible for Jack's death?

If Gus was not as deluded as she would like to believe, then Rainn was taking them to a pair of geriatric murderers. Between the weak beats of a tired heart, she strained to organise her thoughts. Whether Gus was right or wrong, she saw no harm in attempting a lucid dream, and agreed to listen to his instructions. What followed was proving difficult.

GUS YEARNED TO rub his itchy eyeballs with the back of his hand as he waited for Winter to wake. Hours passed and he envied her slumber; each time he drifted off, a sharp shock returned him to reality. Incessantly, droplets of petrol hit the water beside him, forming a glossy sheen. He was staring at a rainbow floating in concentric circles, undisturbed by the rocking of the boat, when Winter finally stirred.

'Truthfully?' she answered through a yawn. 'I fell asleep. You were there. I punched you in the face—I'm sorry, Augustus. The heart wants what it wants.'

Gus took a deep breath and Winter imagined him drawing his hands down his face, though his fingers brushed her belt as he shifted against the pole.

'Try to stay aware of your surroundings,' he dragged the pages of *Lucid Dreaming: A Beginner's Guide* into focus. 'If you hold on to where you are, consciously aware while your body enters the sleeping state—the rocking of the boat, the petrol dripping—then you'll enter the dream lucidly.'

'Doesn't it take Buddhist monks, like, their whole lives to do this?'

'That's enlightenment. I'm not asking you to become enlightened. This is serious, Winter. They want me—but you—if my uncle doesn't—'

Winter was well aware of her predicament and did not need to be reminded. Her empty stomach lurched as they hit a wave and her throat burned like it had been left out in the sun to dry. Her underwear was soaked and, though she could not see her wrists, she imagined the red rings that the cable ties were scoring into them. These feelings coalesced in her forefingers and she prodded Gus in the small of his back.

'You think I don't know that I'm leverage—' She cut herself short, her words too large for their cabin. The sheets overhead creaked. Leaning back against the pole, she lowered her voice to a whisper. 'Jack was always looking at his watch. It drove me nuts. He told me that if he checked it in a dream, the numbers changed.

That's how you know you're dreaming.'

'Sure, but we don't have a watch,' said Gus. 'Reality checking—that's what Jack was doing. It works with writing too.'

He scanned the surroundings for anything that Winter might use for a reality check. There was a label near the sink and a fire-safety sticker peeling off the window, but it was dark and the text too small to read from a distance. His eyes turned to the stairs at the sound of footsteps.

The first thing he saw was a large husky that looked positively ravenous. The dog tugged at the leash as Rainn stepped into view wearing a white halter-neck dress. Gus pulled his feet to the right, away from the animal's reach, as Rainn tied the leash to the metal leg of the work surface.

'You poor things,' she cooed, nudging the dog out of the way with her knee as she filled a glass with water at the sink. 'You must be parched.'

Gus was too preoccupied with the straining metal leg to notice the folded sheets of paper under Rainn's arm. She stepped across the sodden planks to Winter's side of the cabin and pulled a low wooden crate through the inch of petrol-stained water. Winter watched the woman fold her legs under her dress and seat herself delicately on the crate. She lifted the glass of water to the girl's cracked lips. Winter met those cerulean eyes and could not quell a flush of gratitude as cool water spilled down her dry throat. Rainn pulled the glass away and tossed the final mouthful against the wall.

She opened what appeared to be a set of letters in her lap and lit a small white candle to illuminate the pages. A drop of petrol hit the floor inches from where they sat and Winter's body went rigid as the flame flickered.

'Vivador,' said Rainn, looking up from the letters with a twinkle in her eyes as if it were a magical word. 'What a pretty name for the new world. When we met, I only asked Jack for his name. I wonder when Melody Wilson told him about Vivador?'

The candle dripped and a droplet landed on Winter's bare thigh, just below the hem of her black dress. The white wax glowed against her dark skin. She had paid little attention to Jack's tales of the elderly woman who gave him sweets. It sounded indescribably creepy.

She lifted her eyes to her captor's, imagining Rainn's seductive smile as she asked Jack for his name before adding it to the hit list. He had never mentioned dreaming of a beautiful blue-eyed woman, though that did not surprise her; better to avoid an inquiry over his subconscious choices.

'I never went down that well,' said Winter. 'I couldn't care less about funny dreams. What do you want with me?'

'You're leverage, darling,' Rainn replied with a wink and patted Winter's thigh.

Rising from her seat, she set the candle by the sink and filled the glass with water. When she stepped up to Gus, the dog issued a low, guttural growl.

'Shhh, Sam,' Rainn soothed, 'this one's family.'

But Sam continued to growl. As Gus accepted the water, he stared into the bright-blue eyes of the husky. The dog's muzzle wrinkled as it bared its fangs. How had this animal learned such fear? Rainn left the glass in the sink and lifted the candle, waving it absentmindedly before the dog's eyes while she studied Anna's letters. The growling ceased.

'You and Alicia were born on the same day? The day Eloise Grett took her own life?'

She peered at Gus over the top of the letters, curiosity in her candlelit eyes.

'I gave you the book,' said Gus. 'I gave you what you wanted— now take this bloody thing from round my neck and let me sleep.'

'So you can have a little chat with your cousin in the immaterial realm? I think not.'

Gus shook his head and spoke with impatience. 'There's no need for this. Dragging me kicking and—I want to speak with them.'

'You want to kill them.'

Her smile was thin, knowing. Against his fingers, Winter trembled.

'Let her go and I'll do whatever you say.'

Rainn folded her arms, tapping the letters with a fingernail.

'I let her go—*splash*—and I have your word that you will behave yourself. Or, as an alternative option, I don't let her go, and you have to do whatever I say.' She wagged a finger. 'Bargaining is not your strong suit.'

'You don't need her.'

'Whether either of you come out of this alive is of little interest to me, Augustus. But take some advice from someone who has outlived the odds. If you want great granny and grandad to trust you, you'd better make them believe that you don't care what happens to this one.'

She blew out the candle, untied the dog and ushered him up the stairs.

The boat rocked, the petrol dripped and the water sloshed as the pair sat in silence. Winter's eyelids opened with each creak of the bathroom door and each footfall above. At the sound of a distant growling, she opened her eyes to see a word painted across the window, glowing before her eyes: *Liar*.

It wasn't fair, she thought: she was not a liar, she was mistaken. She would never have written that message on her teacher's bedroom wall had she known the truth. How could she possibly have known?

She turned her head from the four glowing letters, wracked with what was unmistakably guilt. Anna Harrington had lost her son. She had returned to Valmont that day to try to help Jack. And in the last week of the woman's life, Winter had accused her of murder. She tried to face the word on the window, but the writing was scrambled, unintelligible.

She was dreaming.

The cabin appeared to shrink as she ran her eyes around it, assaulted by the clarity of her surroundings. Tiny bubbles washed against her feet as the water seeped into the floorboards. If this was a dream, then she was in control. In a wave of excitement, she woke up.

'I did it,' Winter hissed, so abruptly that Gus jolted as he did each time the collar delivered a shock.

'You found her?'

'Of course not—shut up. I lucid-dreamed. Dreamed lucidly. What am I supposed to do next?'

'You need to get to Vivador,' Gus resisted adding: *Remember?* He opened his mouth to remind her of the well and then paused. Rainn knew he would try to gain their trust. She knew Winter had no collar and had visited the well with Jack; he must assume that she expected Winter's arrival in Vivador. A conversation with Joe surfaced.

'Have you been to Stonehenge?' he asked Winter.

Their vessel buffeted over the ocean waves as Gus recalled what he could on how to change the environment in a lucid dream. He had paid this chapter little attention, since he had never dreamed lucidly himself. If Winter managed to find Alicia, they could get a message to Joe that they were on a fishing boat to Portugal. Joe could put out a search for unregistered vessels entering Portuguese waters and Winter might get out of this alive.

In so many words, Winter asked Gus to keep quiet so she could sleep. With a will bent on lucid dreaming and the precarious situation making deep sleep impossible, she was soon staring at a message on the window before her: her own name, struck through with a solid line. Pondering the cruelty of her subconscious, she stepped up to the sink. The bulb of lucidity brightened and her critical-thinking skills came to the fore, analysing other inconsistencies in her surroundings, such as the full moon through the window and the fact that she was no longer tied to a post.

Despite her confidence that this was a lucid dream, Winter remained hesitant as she stepped before the narrow window and prepared to follow Gus's instructions. The ocean swelled, black under the moonlight. It was the haunting realism of those cold, dark waves that troubled her. If she was not dreaming—if she was not still tied to that pole; if she had somehow managed to wriggle free and sleepwalk to the window—then her next move would be fatal. Taking a step back, she pictured Stonehenge. With tall sandstone blocks in the forefront of her mind and Salisbury plain stretching to the corners, Winter leaped forward and threw herself through the glass.

Burnflower

THE JEEP TURNED abruptly from the road and bounced over the woodland debris, flattening ferns as it weaved between the trees. This was clearly not Melissa's first venture through the undergrowth, and her choice in vehicle was justified. The pair jolted in their seats as the headmistress stopped the Jeep and pulled up the handbrake. Without a word, she killed the lights, cut the engine and left the car. Alicia opened the door and stepped into the centre of the forest in the middle of the night with the woman who had kidnapped her brother.

Melissa checked the buttons on her jacket and marched through the trees with Alicia following a few paces behind, climbing over rotting logs and dodging brambles. Conscious of the crackle of each twig and autumnal leaf, they reached the corner of a vast clearing. The overcast night sky did little to illuminate the field before them. Keeping to the edge of the woodland, Melissa led Alicia towards the shadowy outline of a farmhouse.

Burnflower: Alicia turned the word through her mind, the name that Rainn had adopted as her own. The farmhouse had been constructed from limestone, capturing what little light penetrated the clouds. Approaching the rear of the building, they passed tidy rows of cabbages and spinach, stalks of broad beans and the red bulbs of radishes. Not a whiff of manure hung on the crisp air; were this once a farm, it no longer held livestock. Alicia could not see what lay to the front of the house. Looking down the side of the building, she saw the edge of a slope that fell to the thick woodland encircling the estate. Burnflower was perfectly disconnected from the world.

Closer now, they moved through the cover of the outer trees. It was a little after one in the morning and all the inhabitants would be fast asleep. What might lie within those walls? Anticipation tightened Alicia's chest. A coiled spring. A thread of positive energy tugging at her heart—

No: she swallowed the optimism.

Without slowing her pace, Melissa crossed the short stretch of grass to the left-hand wall of the farmhouse. Alicia joined her against the roughly hewn brickwork, an arm's length from a ground-floor window. Melissa peered through the window and Alicia crept to her side, a heartbeat in her throat as she looked through the glass.

There were two beds in the ground-floor bedroom. In the bed nearest the window slept a teenage girl. Amira lay on her back with a frown troubling her brow. Thick, black hair tumbled down olive cheeks. On a chest of drawers between the two beds sat a glass terrarium. Whatever it contained was hiding beneath a sheet of bark half-buried in the red soil. In the corner of the room, a strappy top, a pair of leggings and a dressing gown decorated the arms and seat of a wicker chair. Alicia scanned these details in half a second before fixing her eyes on the empty bed by the door.

That thread of positive energy gave way to sharp splinters of disappointment. Beside her, Melissa's impassive face was as grey as the clouds. Had she expected to find her son in that bed, or was she studying the face of the girl she had forsaken?

Through the silence, a faint music permeated the rectangular panes of the farmhouse window. Melissa raised a hand in protest as Alicia slipped her nails under the corner of the frame and pulled until the window had opened a crack. Immediately, a low feminine voice slipped into the night. Alicia recognised the voice as Rainn's and released the window frame. The crack closed and the sound muffled. She leaned back against the wall, pausing to steady her heartbeat. Melissa attempted to catch her eye, but Alicia furrowed her brow and returned to the glass. The wooden door in the far wall was ajar, but there was no adult in the doorway. Gingerly, Alicia pried the corner of the window open again and listened. It was a lullaby, playing on repeat, issued through a hidden speaker.

Time to sleep,

Go to bed.

You've got no more space for the world in your head.

Time to rest,

Get undressed.

Climb under the covers and take a deep breath.

Time to dream,

Think no more.

Close your eyes and awake now, escape now, to Vivador.

Rainn's words drifted across the bedroom like a soporific veil. Had this lullaby been recorded for sixteen-year-old Amira, or with a younger audience in mind? Alicia bent to dislodge a large stone from the long grass at the foot of the wall. She raised it to the glass and Melissa caught her wrist.

'Wait,' she hissed. Nails pressed into Alicia's skin.

'She's in Vivador. I need to wake her up. If David's here, she can tell me where he is.'

'You need to trust me.'

A shadow stirred within Alicia like a dormant beast. Facing panic in those silver eyes, she remembered a poster crumpled in blue fingers. A moment of weakness. A depth of emotion that stilled her violent heart, drawing her to what she had mistaken for empathy.

There, there.

Not empathy, but guilt. Her breath held and her mind presented her with a single image: a large stone striking Melissa's head. Denying the will of the shadow, Alicia let numb fingers slacken and the stone hit the soil. She leaned into those silver eyes and whispered:

'You took him from us.'

Melissa's grey eyes were steeled and a light within burned wild and desperate.

'I have not seen my son in three years. They have kept him from me because they needed him. They took my Ryan to get to you.' Fingernails broke the skin of Alicia's wrist. 'Now you will help me get him back. And you will have your brother. But you must listen: if Peter knows we are here, it will take a single phone call and we will be dead in minutes. We cannot break windows and doors, we must wait until morning. Amira will water the vegetables at the back of the house, and that is when we'll make our move.'

A hot silence filled Alicia's ears while the words burrowed into her logical mind, as caustic as they were inarguable. She stared at the farmhouse. How many stone walls separated her from her brother? She lifted a palm, longing to lock her mind upon those bricks and erase them like the Unbreakable Door.

If she must wait, there were other places to look. Heavy feet led her back to the forest. She climbed into the unlocked car and pulled a pillow from the back seat. Wondering how many nights Melissa had spent sleeping in this vehicle, she reclined the seat and lay her head on the pillow.

It might have been Rainn's lullaby, or the combination of a tired body and an alert mind, but Alicia was lucid dreaming in minutes. In a moonlit forest, she raised the well in the ferns beside Melissa's Jeep, wondering distantly what portal Rainn had introduced to Amira.

In Vivador, Alicia was about to close her eyes and picture a glass archway when she saw a distant building at the edge of the forest. She blinked to reappear before the church. For a moment, she was surprised to see the building before her. In the events that had followed the argument with herself, she had forgotten her replica of Anna's grave. That she could leave something so personal for anybody to stumble across left her with an uneasy feeling in her gut. The feeling thickened when Rainn entered the scene.

Riding on the back of a horse so white it appeared luminous, Rainn rounded the corner of the church with an expectant smile on her face. The unseen sun struck her hair like polished obsidian as she led the beast between the gravestones and towards Alicia. As she approached, Alicia stared into the horse's eyes: a bright, glacial blue.

She's not ready.

'Is that...' she eyed the horse and whispered, 'Ryan?'

'The horse? How funny. Wonderful idea. But no.'

'Where is he?'

'I thought you were looking for your brother?' Rainn asked tartly as she stopped the horse beside one of the headstones, where it lowered its large head to graze on the green shoots of Anna Harrington's grave.

'Ryan was leading me to him.'

'Was he now?' Her smile was malignant. 'Well, you just got upgraded.'

Rainn looked over her shoulder in the direction of the church, leading Alicia's gaze to the horse's shadow, which fell on a stretch of wall beside the back door. The shadow darkened until the brick was no longer visible. Shimmering in the light, the sharp silhouette rippled like liquid before taking on a new definition. It expanded into the third dimension, the liquid matting to hoof and hair until a fully-formed horse stepped from the wall. The steed crossed towards Alicia, hooves clip-clopping between the graves. Its coat was as dark as the large pupils in its mahogany eyes. Something lurched in her gut as the eyes reminded Alicia of her mother.

'Hop on,' said Rainn, her sapphire dress resplendent against the beast's coat.

Alicia stood motionless.

'You stole my mother's letters.'

'One of my lesser crimes. The letters lead to Aldous and Morna, and that's where we're heading. Your brother is with them, at their home in Psarnox. And since you've never been there, we're going to have to take the long way. But don't worry—' she patted the neck of her horse, '—these boys are fast.'

Rainn glanced at Alicia's steed and he stepped beside her obediently. The grass quivered and a set of three crystal steps rose to the height of her hip. Alicia's sight drifted to where the white horse continued to feed on her mother's grave. With an air of impatience, Rainn slipped from the horse and approached the grave, running her finger along the top of Anna Harrington's headstone.

'It's not real, you know,' she said, eyeing Alicia as she traced the stone. 'The church, the grave. The pain. It's only ever as real as you choose it to be.'

Rainn swept a hand across the top of the headstone and left a trail of fire behind.

'When I was thirteen, I was living with my grandparents in Singapore. They had one of their rows and,' she shrugged, 'I was sick of their fights—so fed up that I stood at the top of the stairs and yelled. I told them that if they argued one more time I would burn the house down. That night, I went to bed and had a dream. I dreamed that I had walked to the kitchen stove, turned on the gas, lit the candle on the table in the hallway and walked out of the house. The police woke me in the front garden.'

The fire on the headstone blazed. The horses stopped grazing, red flames reflected in their large eyes. And then the fire vanished.

'Do I expect your pity?' Rainn uttered. 'Do you expect mine? I couldn't care less what happened to your mother.'

With a wave of her hand, the headstone vanished. The grave was gone, dismissed.

'I don't want your pity,' said Alicia, standing between the horses, her fingers tensed, 'but if you expect me to climb crystal steps and ride shadow horses, I want the truth. Aldous and Morna kidnapped my brother and killed my mother. They used David as bait, in the real—on Earth. And Ryan here. What do they want with me? Do they really think, after everything they've done, that I'll join this Order of theirs?'

'They think you're special,' said Rainn as she stroked her horse's mane and gazed into its sapphire eyes. 'Aldous and Morna believe you may have inherited an exceptional willpower from your grandmother. The ability to break the rules set by other minds. That door was reinforced by the pair of them. Your mother could not break it. Neither could I.'

She turned, wearing a coy smile as she brushed strands of hair from her forehead. 'Honestly, Alicia, I found myself a little jealous when you passed their test.'

Rainn closed the distance between them.

'*But then I had an idea.*'

The voice in Alicia's mind sounded as a thought of her own. But it was not her voice: Rainn had projected the words within her skull. Their faces were an inch apart and Alicia took a step back.

'*Will and expectation.*' Rainn's silky tones resonated between her ears. '*Vivador is founded on these principles. If you have a willpower that exceeds their own, then you are a threat to the Order of Chaos. Aldous sent Ryan to test you so that he could determine how powerful you are. And what if you are precisely as powerful as he believes?*'

Alicia frowned.

'It would mean—'

Rainn raised a hand to silence her, and Alicia glanced left and right, expecting figures in the shadows of the nearby pines. She kept her mouth closed and formed each word carefully, looking through the woman's eyes to what lay beyond.

'*They're afraid that I'll destroy them.*'

Rainn flashed her perfect teeth.

'*Ride with me to Psarnox. You will get your brother and I will claim Vivador.*'

Alicia returned the smile, but cocked her head. The shadow stirred within as she spoke aloud: 'And what if I kill the pair of them, take my brother and leave you with nothing?'

Rainn's face darkened and her smile fell. A flicker of panic swept her eyes but she did not check their surroundings for anyone who might have overheard. She turned and leaped onto the back of her horse.

'You may be special here, Alicia,' she uttered aloud, her teeth barely parting. 'But in the material realm you are flesh and blood. Here, strength is determined by the conviction of your will. On Earth, power lies with the immoral. You may be able to break the rules in Vivador, but challenge me in the waking world and I will put a bullet in your head.'

What's your name?

THE MOMENT SHE hit solid ground, Winter knew the trick had worked. Her flight through the glass had given her brain the opportunity to restructure her surroundings. By picturing Stonehenge, she had drawn on the memories of her nine-year-old self, and these nebulous images were presented to her in magnificent detail. Facing the massive sarsen blocks of the prehistoric monument, Winter recalled her father's history lesson.

The circular formation of stones, over four thousand years old, had perplexed humanity for millennia. It was once believed that the wizard Merlin had used magic to conjure the structure; later it had been attributed to the work of Druids; and then carbon-dating had revealed that the stones were erected during the Stone Age. For eight centuries, the structure was amended and extended, and by the Bronze Age, it was the greatest temple in Britain.

Winter stood at the end of what was called the Avenue: a wide, flat path of grass believed to be the ceremonial approach to Stonehenge. Here, beside the enormous, unshaped Heel Stone, she had held her father's hand as he pointed to the spot where a second stone had stood, marking the grand entrance. At her feet, a metal arrow glinted, its head indicating the direction of the midwinter sunset.

A smile teased her lips as she recalled her father's awe, directing her gaze along the path of the arrow. The winter solstice, the shortest day of the year, had fallen on her birthday. Thousands of years ago, great feasts were held on this day, as crowds watched the sun set between two upstanding stones: a blood-red orb descending to the base of the trilithon arch in the centre of Stonehenge. In modern day, all that remained of the Great Trilithon was a single stone, over seven metres tall, topped with a blunt spike. Winter's brow furrowed as she looked beyond the outer ring of sarsen blocks. This prominent stone was missing.

She strode deeper into the memory, passing a sunken stone pitted with holes. Rainwater pooled in this horizontal block, drawing out the iron in the rock. With a penchant for the macabre, Winter's father had drawn her attention to this rusty red, after which the block had earned its name: the Slaughter Stone. It was once believed that women and children were sacrificed to the gods as religious leaders charted the seasons. As with all memories of a gruesome nature—replayed with fascination; embedded with fear— she recalled his words with the exceptional clarity that faced her now.

From the angle of her approach, the outer ring of sarsens appeared complete, though only six lintels remained on top of their upstanding stones. These enormous sandstone blocks had been hauled on wooden sledges from the Marlborough Downs—thirty kilometres away—in a labour that would have taken two hundred people a gruelling twelve days.

Stepping closer, she studied the precarious lintels, wondering if their grooves were natural or manmade? Which details were remembered, and which could be credited to her imagination?

In that garrulous mood he adopted when his wife was absent, Winter's father had indicated a ring of bluestones within the outer circle. These igneous stones had travelled nearly two hundred and fifty kilometres from the Preseli Hills of Wales. Beyond this, Winter had seen a horseshoe of trilithons, with the towering stone of the Great Trilithon at its head. But not now. Now, there were no bluestones, no trilithon arches. Amid the sarsen circle lay a large pool.

'What do I do at Stonehenge?' Winter had asked her fellow

captive and felt a shrug on the other side of the pole. Presently, a primordial urge drew her to the water. She crossed beneath a lintel, stretched her arms to brush her fingers against the upstanding stones on either side, and dived into the pool.

At first she was falling. Then, like a stone cast into the air until it reaches that balance between two forces, she was pushed and pulled at once before accelerating back up through the water.

Winter was launched from the pool and landed heavily, hip and shoulder, on flat stone. Under a black sky, the sarsen blocks surrounding her were lit by an ethereal glow that emanated from the dark water. She lay on an octagonal dais in the centre of the pool. A drum sounded, rippling the water's surface and reverberating through her bones. She leaned up on her elbows and spotted a silhouette under one of the lintels. Squinting through the glow of the pool, she was able to discern a teenage girl, a year or two her junior. She opened her mouth to call out when something wrapped around her wrists and ankles, binding her supine to the dais. Diamond-patterned scales tightened about her wrist: the body of the snake that held her down. Punctuated by the beat of the drum, her shriek echoed between the stones.

With panic-stricken eyes, she sought the figure at the water's edge. Uplit by the glow, the girl stood in a strappy top and leggings, fists balled either side of a waifish frame. Dark hair was tied in a single plait that fell over her bony shoulder. It was not with interest that she watched Winter, not curiosity, but rapt intention.

'I will *literally*—' Winter's threat died on her lips as something crawled along her leg. A tarantula crept from her knee to her thigh. Her breath was solid in her throat as she noticed the girl staring with such intensity that Winter was certain she controlled the spider's movement. Unblinking, she moved each hairy leg across Winter's bare skin.

Winter had not achieved her position at the apex of the social pyramid by playing victim to younger girls. The sickly tremor on those parted lips—in her attempt to terrify Winter, this girl had created something she loathed. Winter met her eyes, exposed the fear that lay within and delivered her most hostile glare. As with every peer that had dared to defy her, the girl's resolve crumbled. The spider disappeared.

The scaled bodies around her ankles and wrists tightened and there followed a hiss as the heads of two snakes reared into view. As red eyes gazed into her own, Winter had the profound sensation that ash lined her throat. She coughed until her eyes were watering and she struggled against her binding. The twin pairs of eyes blinked from red to blue and this change in colour altered the taste in the back of her mouth. With a tang of iron, she tasted blood.

The younger girl's mouth snapped shut and her nostrils flared impatiently. Winter's forearm stung and a cut appeared on her skin as if she had been struck with a whip. She winced under more invisible strokes as the slash-marks formed letters and the letters, words.

WAKE UP.

Winter's lips twisted into a grimace: this urchin's attempts to drive her from Vivador were clearly failing. The drum beat harder and faster, synchronising with the thudding of her heart as Winter tore her arms and legs from the snakes that bound her. Standing up, she glared at her tormentor and scanned the pool. Dark skin glistened under the violescent glow and black hair fanned across the water's surface: a dozen floating cadavers, made in her own image. Swallowing a rising nausea, she lifted a bare foot and stepped onto the back of the nearest body. The black dress shifted under her weight.

You're too heavy, she thought, her mother's voice between her ears. With tentative steps, she crossed from one body to the next, using broad gold belts as stepping stones. Her eyes were narrow and her smile maleficent when she reached the bank. She lowered her head to that thin face.

'Boo.'

The girl vanished, taking what appeared to be a dome of darkness with her. The drumbeat ended and the pool shimmered an innocent blue in the daylight.

'Blackout,' Winter said aloud, taking stock of her surroundings. In the distance to her left, a solitary mountain broke the uniform horizon. To her right lay an expansive lake, in the centre of which stood a stone tower. Her heartbeat slowed as she stepped between the blocks of Stonehenge and gazed upon this silent space. Animated and enthusiastic, Jack had exhausted her with details, desperate to convince her of his journey down the well.

You never believed him—why were the words that filled her head so accusatory? Jack had never mentioned hearing loud, angry thoughts. Or had he? She had cut him off, threatened him, changed the subject—

Why didn't you listen?

I don't like this place. She delivered her judgement with a decisive nod. Vivador would pass for the real world, were it not for an ominous silence that seemed to invite a scathing inner commentary.

You told him everything—

—What do you fear? Rainn's face lurked in a corner of her mind. And before she had found something on which to fasten her attention:

You have nobody left to talk to.

'What now then?' she asked out loud, hands on hips as she glanced from the mountain to the tower. She might have cupped her hands to her mouth and shouted Alicia's name were she not haunted by the feeling that she was being watched. Since the mountain looked an impossible distance away, Winter turned to her right. She strode from the sandstone blocks to where a simple wooden bridge stretched across the water until it reached a low platform in the centre of the lake. The building that rose from this platform resembled a Buddhist tower that had been stripped of its paint and left at the mercy of time. A network of vines twisted between thin windows and burrowed in and out of cracks in the dark, crumbling stone.

I don't like this place.

Words of caution pricked her mind as Winter crossed the bridge. After such a hostile welcome to this alien realm, she cast skittish eyes across the still waters, waiting for the emergence of some prehistoric beast. She picked up her pace, marching across the sun-bleached planks. Her footsteps fell from wood to stone as she reached the central platform and scanned the empty windows. The hexagonal walls of the tower rose seven storeys into the sky. The broad arches that lined the highest floor were empty. It was unlikely that Alicia would be waiting inside.

With nowhere else to go, she stepped under a tall archway to ascend a spiral staircase that wound along the inner wall. Through each window she saw only the lake, the standing stones encircling the small pond, the mountain on the horizon and endless fields rippling outwards. If this building held no clues as to where she might find Alicia, she would have to tell Gus that his plan had failed.

She reached the top step and entered a hexagonal chamber lined with arches stretching from floor to ceiling. In the centre of the floor, two intricately engraved stone thrones rotated back to back on a circular platform. Though the thrones were empty, she was not alone in the room.

Standing beneath one of the arches, little more than a silhouette against the brilliant sky, a man looked over the bridge. His shoulders were broad beneath a brown leather jacket, his arms crossed. He waited a moment as if to determine whether anyone else might cross the bridge and then he turned to face her.

The man was in his early forties, with pale-blue eyes in a narrow face. His beard was flecked with grey, his hair dark and ragged. A cleft in his upper lip revealed a canine, giving him a snarl not echoed in his dull eyes. His expression was profoundly unwelcome and Winter took a step back towards the staircase.

And then he spoke, and his husky voice was all she understood. It originated not from his mouth, but the centre of her mind, as if it were a thought of her own.

'*What's your name?*'

Haunted by that pale gaze, Winter was immobilised. Had a leviathan risen from the lake and seized the tower in its jaws, it might have taken her a moment to notice. What finally stirred her into motion was a searing pain in her leg. Gripping her left thigh, she fell to the floor with a vivid awareness that, in the waking world, something was savaging her. The man furrowed his brow, raised a hand and took a step across the tiles. An unveiled look of dismay crossed his face before Winter shut her eyes and the tower vanished.

Ryan, age 14

I HAVEN'T LEFT *this place, not in fourteen years. Mum teaches us all about the different countries, cities, islands, but our world has four walls, seven ponds and a tower we're basically not even allowed to look at. Rainn told me and Amira a whole bunch of things that she had at her grandparents' house in Singapore, like Television and Internet—where you can see anything that has ever existed. Ever. But all I've got are the photographs Mum prints off her computer. Photographs and dreams.*

Peter tells me that it isn't safe out there. Not after what happened with Sam. He says that people are looking for me, but Rainn says nobody has even heard of Burnflower. Not that I should believe anything that comes out of Rainn's mouth. She even told Amira that her surname is Burnflower, and that's how she found the place.

I knew it was Rainn that left the front door open that night. She does a lot of things while she's 'sleepwalking', and it's funny how many of these accidents involve my stuff—my teddy bear with the arm missing, my underwear in the cookie jar. She basically hates me and I don't even know why. Peter told me I should be nice to her, but it's a two-way street and Rainn is like a lorry ready to run me down. I overheard Mum say that Rainn was definitely going to run away because she's so troubled.

The front door was wide open and Sam was missing for the whole day. I didn't even eat. I must have walked around the house about 29 times looking for him. I wanted to search the woods but that was obviously forbidden. Peter told me that he had searched the Pagoda but I didn't believe him, so I waited until it was dark and went right to the top. *The top floor is empty with a bamboo floor that Mum used to do yoga on before Peter needed his space. There are six arches at the top and through the one at the very back you can see the lake behind the trees. I was trying to see if Sam was swimming in the lake when I heard footsteps behind me.*

Peter led Sam up the steps on his lead. Sam was so excited to see me and I was just about to run over when Rainn walked up behind them. Peter looked at me forever and then he turned to Rainn.

'I have a present for you,' he said as he offered her the lead. 'Perhaps you will take better care of him.'

I waited for Rainn to say something, but she just kneeled down and stroked him between the ears like he was the first thing she had been given in her whole life. She dragged him down the steps and I stood at the arch that faced the house. I did not want to look at Peter, so I just watched Rainn walk my dog between the ponds and waited for my lecture.

'You must never become attached to anyone or anything. It makes you weak.'

Peter is attached to nobody. He is a nasty island that exists for no reason other than to wreck ships.

The next day I snuck right back up the Pagoda, even though I knew Peter was working in his office below me. I wanted to be by myself, so I watched Amira feed the fish in the pond. Obviously, she wasn't scared of them any more. She's terrified of one thing one minute and something else the next. Snakes, spiders, cucumbers!

And me. She'll play with Sam happily enough, but when I throw the ball and join in she backs away like I'm about to do whatever Peter told her I did to Sam.

Rainn walked out with Sam on the lead, but when he saw Amira he got so excited that Rainn lost the lead and fell over on the gravel. Sam jumped up at Amira and she almost snapped in half—she's so skinny these days, I think she's scared of her food. He licked all over her face and I could hear her laughing.

'Bad dog!' Rainn hit him like he had done something wrong. And then she looked right up at me.

When I looked in the mirror that night I could see my hatred. And it made me angry. Peter thinks I'm stupid, but I know exactly why he gave my dog to Rainn. He wants Amira to be scared and he wants me to be angry. He wants me to hate Rainn. He wants me to kill her, like I killed Sam.

CHAPTER SIX
Fairy tale

ALICIA STRUGGLED TO keep Rainn in sight as she directed her horse between the pines. Riding bareback through the forest, she felt the power of the animal between her thighs, each muscular leg an extension of herself, rising and falling under her command, pounding the needles to dust. Rainn's sapphire dress was a flicker of blue, disappearing amid distant trunks while Alicia ducked low branches and leaped fallen logs. She could not recall stray branches and logs breaking the uniformity of this forest when Ryan had led her through it. Had Rainn left these obstacles in her wake? Looking four, five, six trees ahead, she willed her horse between the trunks as fast as she dared, its speed entirely dependent on her confidence. Clenching her teeth, she urged the hooves into a gallop along a straight between the rows of trunks until Rainn turned sharply to the left, forcing Alicia to slow to a more cautious canter as she rode along the sides of banks and over exposed roots.

Crystal shards scattered like glitter as Rainn ploughed through the stretch of broken glass. Alicia cleared Ryan's trial in a single leap—a thousand rainbows shimmering beneath her—and crashed through the undergrowth in pursuit of the white steed. Steeling herself at the low branch in her path, she did not duck. Accelerating through the doubt, she let the branch break against her chest, splintering into fragments and leaving her unharmed. She lowered her head until the black mane tickled her chin, looked between the horse's ears and charged onward, not around the trees, but through them. Locking on to her distant quarry, she denied the reality of the trees between them. Trunks split and needles scattered as she cleaved the forest in two, a streak of black riven through sawdust.

Approaching the spray of needles behind Rainn's horse, Alicia maintained her speed. She leaped, four hooves kicking from the forest floor, and careered over her guide, rising above the treetops at the forest's edge. She struck the lip of the cliff and kicked off with powerful hind legs, sending a sheet of rock crumbling to the steps below. The ground quaked when she landed before the glass dome and galloped through the archway to the plains beyond. Slowing into a wide arc, she turned to face the white horse trotting out to meet her. Rainn sat with her legs to one side, her chin high and hands clapping against her chest.

'Oh bravo, *bravo*,' she said, affecting a pompous air. 'Our Ryan taught you rather well.'

She's not ready.

Ryan believed himself to be a simulacrum, yet he had tried to protect her. He had defied Rainn, returning Alicia to the waking world before she was tested in a manner for which he considered her unprepared. The emotion in his eyes had not been a projection; he had feared for her safety. He was alive and, because of her, he was their captive.

'Where is he?'

Rainn trotted a circle around the black stallion.

'Here, he is held by Aldous and Morna, in Psarnox. In the material realm, he's with his father, Peter.'

So, he is at Burnflower, Alicia thought, glancing down to avoid projecting her words into Rainn's mind. The Crow family had used Ryan as bait, and now he was no longer needed.

'Is he safe?' she asked.

Rainn grinned and Alicia blushed.

'If you care whether Ryan lives or dies, then the Order will find a use for him.'

The thunder of hooves echoed across the undulating plains as

Rainn and Alicia left the archway behind. With the wind whipping at their hair, the pair accelerated between one hilltop and the next.

'There she is.'

Alicia's thoughts were interrupted by Rainn's low, silky tones. Were it possible to travel at this speed in the waking world, Rainn would have had to shout across the short distance between them to be heard over the roaring passage of air; but the words projected between Alicia's ears were as clear as thought. Rainn nodded ahead, where the tip of a mountain jutted from the horizon like a shark's tooth.

'Mount Psarnox.'

Despite the ferocious speed of their approach, the dark rock sat obstinate, refusing to grow. The distance between the well and the mountain was in itself a deterrent to any who might stumble across Vivador; to cover this blank canvas required a speed that was a direct corollary of Alicia's willpower. When later she was asked how fast she had travelled across the plains, she replied simply and truthfully that it was as fast as she could imagine.

Like bullets, a streak of white and black crossed the sea of green. As the mountain expanded into the cloudless sky, Alicia's thoughts penetrated the rock, searching what lay within. Had her grandmother and Augustus made this journey across Vivador to where Aldous and Morna had taken up residence in the immaterial realm?

'Tell me about the Order of Chaos.'

With black hair flowing behind elfin ears, Rainn adopted the manner of a storyteller. It was in the guise of a fairy tale that Alicia traced her bloodline through a history of avarice and murder.

'Aldous and Morna were teenagers in love, sharing an interest in dreams. It was their belief that through lucid dreaming they might merge their consciousnesses. Separated one summer following a holiday in the Algarve, they planned to meet in their dreams, at a lighthouse on the cliffs. Every night, they entered a lucid dream and *walked the rugged cliffs, searching for their beloved. And it was through the exploration of this Portuguese peninsula that they found an escape: slipping through the cracks in their biological shells and into Vivador.*

The pair eloped. They had discovered a world of their own beneath those cliffs, and they did not intend to share it. Without a word to their families, they stole what money they could and fled to Carvoiero, where they were married. In the years that followed, Morna gave birth to two sons. Raised between two worlds, the obedient boys became independent teenagers, and Aldous and Morna set clear boundaries: to tell another soul about Vivador was to betray the family.

But boys will be boys, am I right? Of course I am. Their eldest, Augustus, fell for your grandmother, Eloise. And how better to impress the lady than to show her a world where all her wildest dreams can come true. He defied his parents and led her down that well. The boundaries were broken and the secret was out. And it was not only Eloise who slipped down the well—other lucid dreamers were breaching their walls. And, so they founded the Order of Chaos. The choice was simple: honour the Crow's claim to Vivador, or be hunted on Earth.'

Something stirred in Alicia's chest.

'*My grandmother joined this Order?*'

Rainn shook her head bitterly. The timbre of a sullen disappointment tainted her words.

'*No. She refused. She took her baby and she tried to hide. When Aldous and Morna found her, they would have killed her had Augustus not intervened. He gave his parents the one thing that might spare her: he gave her value. He believed that Eloise had a willpower that surpassed each of theirs, fitting a legend that Aldous had recently uncovered. So they let your grandmother live, waiting to see whether*

her children might inherit this strength of will. While Eloise had refused to join the Order of Chaos, young Anna might be persuaded.'

Alicia felt the beat of the stallion's heart as it pounded blood through every muscle, every imaginary artery of its projected form.

'*That's why they took David. To lure my mother to Vivador and test her on the door. And when she failed, they sent Ryan after me. What sick minds would murder innocent people to defend a world that doesn't exist?*'

Alicia's anger was met with frigid shock: a block of ice between her ears. The emotion was solid, distorting Rainn's words as if she spoke through a wall. Ask somebody to name a favourite book or film and then criticise it, and you will be met with hostility; to offend a treasured opinion is to offend their sense of self. Rainn's identity was so grounded in Vivador that to question its existence was to challenge hers.

'*Remind me of the difference between reality and a dream?*'

'The real world—*it's permanent*,' said Alicia, having considered this a great deal over the past few days. '*It has a past. Present. Future—everything's connected by time. There are rules, like gravity. And consequences. A dream has none of these things.*'

Rainn's confidence returned and her words rang clear as crystal bells.

'*And Vivador? All that exists here can be undone, that is true. But all that exists on Earth will one day be destroyed. Everything in existence fades to nothing in the end. Whether it is the Hanging Gardens of Babylon or that Unbreakable Door, every mark made on these worlds can live on only in memory. And what are we, Alicia, other than a collection of memories, real and false? If you believe that Vivador is unreal, perhaps you need a new definition of reality.*'

In the silence that followed, Rainn's umbrage lingered in Alicia's mind. Hooves beat the ground like gunfire. Time passed until the mountain was no longer on the horizon, but embodied it. Alicia raised her head to see smoke issuing from its peak; it was not in the image of a mountain that Psarnox had been made, but a volcano.

The bare rock had all but filled the sky ahead and they were yet to reach its base. Alicia was dwarfed by the magnitude of this creation. Her mother had once said, through a cluster of anecdotes and metaphors, that the inability to comprehend the size of a mountain, ocean or night sky renders the mind speechless, creating a deep silence.

'There is great power in this silence,' Anna had whispered with her face to the heavens and a paintbrush in her hand as starlight struck the canvas. 'Primal. Thoughtless.'

Alicia understood this silence as they reached the foot of the volcano. When faced with great swathes of time and space, we are in awe of that which makes us feel insignificant. This is what her mother had strived to capture in her painting. And this is what she felt in that moment: in comparison, she was nothing.

The volcano was so vast that it was surely visible for hundreds of miles in all directions. If Aldous and Morna had generated this structure, then they had wished to make their presence known. Staring up at the bare rock face, straining to see the distant peak, she imagined ghostly figures watching her approach, like a fly before the spider's web.

'*Where now?*' asked Alicia, slowing her horse and casting her eyes across the steep cliffs, searching for the outline of paths or tunnels. The mountain looked impregnable.

'*Straight to the—*'

'*—Rainn—*'

Both horses reared as another voice entered Rainn's mind, projected to Alicia with the passage of her thoughts. The colourless voice was not confined to Alicia's skull, but resonated within every fibre of her projected being, as if she were nothing but a conduit for its deliverance.

Rainn locked eyes with Alicia and then vanished abruptly, leaving the white stallion to canter aimlessly in a circle before trotting to a halt. It lowered its head to graze at the shoots poking from beneath a large igneous boulder. Alicia held a hand to her chest to quiet the eruption within. That voice echoed between the walls of her skull, lingering as an afterthought. She sat on her horse at the foot of the mountain, trying to determine whether she was alone in her head.

Scarecrow

PURSING HER LIPS to suppress the escape of another sob, Winter stared at the tattered hem of her dress. Bloodied threads draped across her savaged thigh. The boat lurched over a wave and she stifled a moan as pain throbbed through the open wound. In the stained water sloshing across the planks, she glared at her pathetic reflection before closing her eyes.

Absent-mindedly, Gus brushed his thumb up and down the small of Winter's back, feeling as powerless now as when the captain of the boat had come down to find her sleeping. The skeletal man had shaken her shoulders wordlessly and then struck her across the cheek. When she did not stir, he had scurried up the steps and returned with the dog.

Metal sheets creaked as Rainn paced the deck. Gus had heard her receive a call, and the short, ill-tempered bursts of an argument breached their cabin. Between breaths drawn through clenched teeth, Winter explained how a teenage girl had attempted to wake her up.

'Did she have a tattoo on her wrist?' asked Gus. 'Like Rainn's?'

'I don't know, I didn't inspect her. It was dark—she had made it dark, around the pool. And I was distracted by the hundreds of dead bodies, with my dead face, staring up—stop poking me.'

Winter told Gus about the tower in the lake, where she had not found Alicia. She provided a brief autopsy of his plan, which had cost her a leg and possibly her life. Gus asked about the man in the tower.

'Just some weirdo. He was waiting for someone else to arrive—you, probably. Just staring at Stonehenge. He got as far as asking my name before I was mauled to death.'

'Aldous?'

Winter sighed. 'I don't know, he didn't introduce himself. He looked about forty-something. I know Alicia's mother was, like, twelve when she had her, so I don't know how things are done in your family, but he didn't look old enough to be anyone's great-grandfather.'

'Did he have a tattoo?'

'Would you shut up about tattoos? Next time, I'll ask them to strip, shall I? *Excuse me, tower weirdo, would you mind taking your top off and giving me a twirl?*'

Gus listened to the plop of petrol on the sodden planks as blood-stained water sloshed through his jeans. His chapped nostrils stung with the salty, petrol-laced, iron-tinged air.

'How's your leg?'

'He did have one of those—those cleft lips. You know, where there's a bit of the top lip missing. You could see some of his teeth. I would recognise him, if I saw him here.' She shuddered at the memory of those pale eyes, his voice penetrating her mind. 'If by my leg you mean the gaping hole where my leg used to be, then it's great. It's like someone stuffed a hive of fire ants—can you just stop wriggling? Please. Do you need the toilet?'

'No.'

This was a lie. He sat as still as he could and tried not to think about how much he needed to relieve himself. He hitched his attention to Rainn's argument, presumably with the man in the tower, but failed to make out any words. Day was yet to break, the windows were black, and the waves rose and fell in his mind's eye.

At Salthill Beach, he and his father had taken it in turns burying one another in the sand while his mother watched the waves. Clutching her knees to her chest and pressing her feet to the corners of a towel determined to blow away, she had described the journey of these waves as if each had its own character. Gus had visited the beach alone last December, on a night as dark as this. He had listened to the ocean and tried to imagine a time before people had learned how to think.

'He was right,' said Winter, always first to break the silence. 'Vivador looks exactly like here. You wouldn't know you were dreaming, you wouldn't know the difference, if someone wasn't pulling animals out of thin air. That spider she threw at me, it was a tarantula. I could feel every hairy leg on my skin.'

'Did it have a tattoo?'

'Oh, shut up.'

He caught her smile in the glass as she gazed into the middle distance. The smile faded and she chewed her lip in pain.

'We'll ask her for some bandages, or something,' Gus suggested quietly, knowing how absurd it sounded.

'Maybe a bow, as well? So she can gift wrap me for the serial killers. Nice one, Augustus.' She winced. 'He was right though, Jack. It's like you've woken up. Except that...except it's like you're wearing noise-cancelling headphones. No sound in the background, just you and your thoughts.'

And your fears. Her internal monologue was not as clear as in Vivador, but it was louder than before. Words danced between her ears, subtle as neon, refusing to settle down into the murk of her subconscious.

Rainn had finished on the phone and Winter's whisper was low when she spoke:

'Do you ever think about the things you should have told them?'

'Who?'

'Don't play dumb.'

'I'm not. You mean my parents?'

'Yes, your mum and dad. Doesn't it drive you crazy, thinking of all the things you never said?'

Bending her uninjured leg, she scraped at the wood with a high heel and waited for Gus to respond. He fixed his eyes to the sheen of light on the tap. It was not a big deal, his sexuality. What did it matter if he had told them? Would they have cared?

You don't seem very—

Would his parents have been as dismissive as Joe? Perhaps he should have made it more obvious, though he wasn't sure how. There were a lot of things that his parents had not known about him. They never knew he had eaten half of his eleventh birthday cake in the middle of the night and hidden the evidence in the wheelie bin; Sylvie assumed she had left it at the store. There were so many secrets that the pair of them had never known. Why did some secrets feel like lies?

Winter stopped scraping the wood. When she spoke, her words were quick: 'I talk to Jack. I just—I tell him I'm sorry. For never listening. For never letting him pick the film. Or the food. Or his nose. For that stupid postcard…'

'I'd say he saw the funny side in that.' Gus forced a smile as he recalled Winter's joke: *Wish you were dead.* 'He was dating you—he must have had a sense of humour.'

And when Winter said nothing, he added: 'I talk to mine too, sometimes.'

'What do you tell them? That you're mental?'

The stairs creaked and the captain walked down as far as the bottom step. The man was a scarecrow: sallow eyes and sunken cheeks in an unshaven face. He lifted his arm to the wall, either to steady himself or lean upon it, and a greying cuff slipped down to reveal the tattoo on his wrist. He craned his neck and looked first at Gus, long enough for the light on his collar to blink, and then at Winter. Satisfied that both were awake, he turned back up the steps, freezing when Gus called after him.

'She needs a tourniquet or she'll bleed out. They won't be happy if she's not—if she's too tired to talk to them. Aldous and Morna need to interrogate her. They'll be angry with you.'

The scarecrow paused for a moment without looking back, and then continued up the stairs. Winter's breathing was laboured and she continued to scrape her heel through the inch of water, dissecting oily rainbows.

'I think we should tell each other things before we die,' she uttered.

'Have you been drinking the petrol?'

'What would you say to them if you had another chance?'

Gus chewed his lip. What was Winter so keen to share? He was considering what truths he might part with when Rainn came down the steps.

'How are my little detainees?'

'She needs a—'

'Oh shut up, Gus.' Winter elbowed him, as if the embarrassment of his request was harder to bear than the pain in her leg. A phone rang in the bag on Rainn's shoulder. She dropped the bag on the counter, unclipped the fastener and stared at the name on the screen. Gus was reminded of Melissa's face in her office when she had received Rainn's call.

The woman hoisted her lips into a smile and answered: 'Hello, Aldous.' She leaned back against the sink with the phone pressed to her ear and drew the lighter from her bag.

'Yes, cheeky little wastrel. Now you see why I sent Amira to the portal.' She flicked the lighter on and off, and the intermittent firelight made a grimace of her smile. 'Well, no, but that's because she projects her own fears. If you were to grant Peter and me access to…if we had a means of following them—of doing our homework, shall we say—these protective measures could be personalised. Then it would be child's play.'

Rainn stopped playing with the lighter. She nodded and rubbed a fist against her brow.

'Well, she won't be sleeping anytime soon, Aldous.'

Her expression shifted in the shadows like a cloud crossing the moon. Her nostrils flared and her lips were tight. When she spoke, her voice was terse.

'I only had one collar. I can't be in two places at once. I was—yes, I understand, but—I instructed him to use the dog if he was unable to wake her.'

She cast her eyes across the water.

'We're nearly there. Well, if that's—I can kill her now?'

Gus felt Winter stiffen against the pole as a drawer opened and Rainn sifted through its contents. She withdrew a knife with a serrated blade.

'Yes, I understand.'

Rainn hung up and dropped her phone into the empty sink. She lifted Anna's letters from the bag and tucked them under her arm before approaching Winter with the lighter in one hand and the knife in the other. A low horn sounded on the upper deck and Rainn paused midway to sitting on the small crate. With swift movements, she left the letters by the sink and climbed the steps. A bold light panned through the window, breaking the darkness. It was the beam of a lighthouse.

White orchid

ALICIA PLACED A palm on the igneous rock. She brushed her thumb against its rough surface, wondering whether the warmth that emanated from its volcanic depths existed outside her imagination. Stepping back, she sized up the steep incline that shot tens of kilometres into the sky, tapering to a peak beyond her sightline. This was a mountain with no foothills and no vegetation, nothing but an impenetrable wall of rock.

The shade of the stone was unmistakable: a burnt maroon, almost black against the eggshell blue of the sky. She had seen this shade in her parents' bedroom. From her approach on horseback, she had seen a single peak, while on her mother's canvas there were two. In the landscape painting, a higher peak on the right dipped with the gentle curve of a hammock to a lower peak on the left of the crater. To the right of the higher peak, the mountainside fell at a moderate decline, sweeping to the ground and almost reaching the edge of Anna's canvas. The lower peak on the left dropped in a considerably steeper bank, almost vertical in comparison. In her mind's eye, Alicia visualised the shape of the volcano as roughly that of a shoe, and was confident that she now faced its heel.

It was conceivable that Mount Psarnox was a replica of a volcano in existence on Earth and, by coincidence, her mother had found inspiration in this same volcano. Yet Alicia was again in the position where the fantastical option was the more plausible: her mother had also laid eyes on Aldous and Morna's creation in the immaterial realm, but had approached it from another angle. In painting the volcano on her canvas, Anna had taken something from Vivador and reproduced it in the waking world: the immaterial made material.

'So, Mum,' Alicia said aloud. 'What next?'

Rainn's words surfaced: *Straight to the—*

'To the top, then.'

Alicia mounted her horse and urged him into a wide arc across the grass, creating a distance between her and the foot of the mountain. Lowering her eyes between black velvet ears, she kicked the beast into a gallop.

A thunderous crack rent the air as hooves leaped from grass to rock. The gradient was impossible from the outset and Alicia glanced over her shoulder to see the plains fall away beneath her. She was riding vertically up sheer cliff face. Loosening her grip on the horse's neck, she let her fear dissolve. For there was no volcano. There was no horse. She was not defying gravity, but denying it. She released her grip, spread her arms outward and accelerated up the wall of rock, soaring toward the sky.

The mountainside quaked under the formidable strength of the black stallion. Did the pounding hooves resonate through the volcano to those awaiting her? With a crunch underfoot, the terrain shifted from rock to scree. The gradient declined and Alicia saw a second peak on the far side of an enormous crater. Sending sheets of gravel and ash in her wake, she reached the lower peak, beyond which tendrils of smoke rose to a thin cloud overhead.

On a narrow ridge, she slowed the stallion to a trot and rode along the lip of the crater. The horse navigated the uneven rock with the agility of a mountain goat, clip-clopping over fissures that breathed steam against Alicia's bare feet. As she surveyed Vivador from this tremendous height, vertigo plunged through her like frigid water.

Casting her eyes over the plains they had crossed, she was just able to discern a blurred fringe on the horizon—all that was visible of the pine forest. It thrilled her to consider that she might close her eyes to reappear at the well beyond that forest and then return to this ridge in a blink, crossing that continent of green in a heartbeat, as if the space between these two points did not exist. From her vantage point upon the lower of the two peaks, Alicia saw what lay beyond the volcano—behind the image on her mother's canvas. Spilling out from the foot of the mountain was a rainforest, suffusing mist from the canopies of a million trees. The tropical expanse was broken by the light brown cliffs of a gorge that twisted to the left. Towards the horizon, a river issued from the gorge until it met a cerulean band, darker than the sky. She narrowed her eyes at the distant shore, wondering whether it marked Vivador's edge, or the beginning of an ocean larger than all that she had seen.

'Not a bad sight for blind eyes.'

She spun on her horse to find Rainn looking down at her from the highest point of the ridge. She stood with hands on hips, a smile on her face and a distracted look in her eyes. Alicia hopped from the back of her horse and sent him trotting off along the rim of the massive crater.

'What did Aldous want with you?'

Rainn's eyes flickered, her expression as treacherous as the craggy terrain. With graceful steps, she joined Alicia on the flat section of the ridge.

'Don't get cocky, Alicia. It's unbecoming.'

Sweeping the sapphire dress beneath her, Rainn perched on the edge of a flat rock that was nearly the width of the ridge and motioned for Alicia to sit on the far side. The warmth of the volcano rose through Alicia's jeans. Here the rock was a dark grey, rough as pumice and glistening with the lustre of a thousand tiny minerals embedded throughout. Rainn gazed into the space between them and her thin eyebrows shifted infinitesimally. Between two bands of iron red, the dark rock split like the hatching shell of an egg and a green shoot rose from the cracks. The plant matured into a white orchid and Rainn met Alicia's eyes.

'It is your wish for the flower to be blue and my wish for it to be red.'

Rainn lowered her eyes to the head of the flower and the petals snapped to red without blush or transition. It was as though a light switch had been flicked and the white petals cast under a ruby filter. Settling herself on the rock and leaning a fraction closer, Alicia focused on the petals and willed for the colour to change from red to blue. As with the Unbreakable Door, the moment she laid her mind on Rainn's creation she felt a strong conscious resistance. Unlike the pines, which had been raised in an instant and crumbled before her, the flower was imbued with a persistent will. This living intention that embodied the flower head felt different to the one that Alicia had encountered when placing her palms on the door. Like a flavour, or perhaps a tone or timbre, the resistance resembled the emotion she had felt when Rainn projected words into her mind. She would later wonder on the timbre of her own thoughts.

Clenching her teeth, Alicia willed the petals to blue, flooding them from the centre to the tip until all red had been driven from them. There followed a jarring sensation, like travelling at high speed and hitting a bump, as Rainn snapped the flower head back to red.

Blue.

Red.

The petals fluctuated furiously, faster and faster, until the flower head flickered violet.

Gripping the warm rock and focusing on the head of the orchid until it was all she could see, Alicia set the full force of her mind upon it and the petals trembled a deep blue. There remained a moment of pause in which the blue orchid stood resolute before bursting into flame and withering to ash.

Alicia unlocked her eyes and blinked, acknowledging the truth:

her will was stronger than Rainn's. With a nostalgic smile, Rainn stared at the empty space and said: 'That's how Peter taught me.'

'Taught you what?'

Rainn looked up as if surprised that she was not alone. The corner of her mouth twitched.

'When his son tried to kill me, Peter brought me here. He needed to protect me from what Ryan had become.'

Alicia found it hard to imagine Rainn requiring protection from anyone, let alone that lost young man with tranquil eyes. What had Peter done to Ryan? Had he really raised his son as a killer?

'Taught you what?' Alicia repeated.

Rainn stood and faced the crater. The steam rising from below played with the ends of her hair.

'Ryan tested you with the shards of glass—to rise above expectation and deny the natural pain response of your projected body. With the Unbreakable Door, you demonstrated an ability to break rules. Expectation and will, Alicia. Expect a breeze and a breeze will blow, will it to rain and the rain will fall. But then, there is the will of others.'

Alicia stepped beside Rainn until her toes met the edge of the cliff. Eddies of wind tousled her hair and filled her ears with violence: the clash of metal and the stutter of gunfire. The vast crater of Psarnox stretched before them, bearing a lake of lava that bubbled and spat. In the centre of the crater was a large circular platform, rotating slowly with the churning of the molten rock. This sheet of obsidian caught the rays of light permeating the smoky cloud and glistened like polished marble. On the platform, so distant that they appeared no larger than insects, two figures were engaged in combat.

Alicia cast her vision deeper into the volcano and the distant platform magnified before her. With the blast of laser beams and an explosion that rocked the platform on its viscous bed, two teenage girls fought to return one another to the waking world. These girls were identical: olive skin and black hair plaited over the left shoulder. Amira was battling her simulacrum.

'Welcome to the Playground,' said Rainn.

Blowhole

WE'RE NEARLY THERE.

The beam of the lighthouse swept the cabin, playing through Gus's mind like a silent alarm. It must have been half an hour since the horn had summoned Rainn to the deck, and she had yet to return. Unable to reassure Winter, Gus trawled his imagination for a plan that might buy them more time.

'Winter, are you...?' he whispered.

'Awake? Alive? None of the above.'

'I'm going to pretend I'm dreaming, all right? When she comes down, tell her that the water shorted the collar and it's broken.'

In their reflection, her eyes narrowed on the green light blinking insolently on his collar, but neither commented on the flaw in his plan.

'You'll say that I've gone to speak with the man in the tower. That I want to strike a deal. And when she thinks I'm in Vivador...Winter!'

Her head was back at an awkward angle and the sound of droplets hitting the floor had ceased. She was taking the petrol into her mouth.

'What are you—stop it. We can get out of this.'

It was his turn to prod her roughly in the back, but she continued to catch the drops of liquid falling through the rusted crack in the ceiling. Before Gus could protest any further, steps on the staircase signalled Rainn's return.

'Sorry to keep you waiting,' said Rainn with an exasperated sigh as she lifted the letters from the work surface. 'Busy night!'

She settled herself on the small wooden crate, flicked on the lighter and rifled through the letters.

'Ah, here we are.' She spread the letters flat across her thigh and placed the knife on the crate beside her. '*Melody spoke fondly of Jack, having met him down the well.* Fancy that.' She caught Winter's gaze and shook her head distastefully. 'Your boyfriend kisses you goodnight and then goes home to share his dreams with an elderly woman. Each to their own, I suppose.'

Winter said nothing. A tense pause followed and Gus wondered how much of the petrol she had swallowed. Rainn pouted, her shoulders lowering as she flicked the lighter on and off.

'I would have liked you as a protégé. When you painted that message on Anna Harrington's wall—threatening a woman while she searched for her kidnapped son—I saw potential. Pride, confidence and humour are a lethal combination when guided by the right hands. Perhaps I saw in you what Peter had seen in me. But there's no use in crying over what could never be.' She brushed the point of the blade across Winter's lower eyelashes to collect a single tear. 'People like us don't make friends, we make allies. And when you play our game, all allies are enemies in the end.'

She lifted the knife and ran the flame along the serrated blade. When it reached the tip, the teardrop shrivelled on the heated metal.

'Any last words?'

Winter opened her mouth and sent a spray of petrol into Rainn's lap. A scream rent the cabin as the liquid crossed the open flame and the pages caught alight. Leaping to her feet, Rainn emptied her hands and beat the flames climbing her white dress. Screams ricocheted between the metal walls as the woman hurled her blazing self up the narrow steps.

Anna's letters burned readily on the small crate. The fire inched down the wood towards the petrol-soaked panels. Kicking the lighter aside, Winter used the heel of her shoe to scrape at the fallen knife.

Silently, his mouth open, Gus watched the fire in the window, waiting for a stray flame to lick the contaminated water that soaked their clothes. Winter screamed as she used the full force of her mauled leg to kick the knife towards her. There was a clink as it struck the pole. Working together, the pair shimmied lower until Gus caught the knife with straining fingertips. The corner of a burning page fluttered from the crate and sizzled impotently in the water, missing its mark. The glossy sheen of petrol rocked between Winter's bare calves.

Gus spun the handle of the knife and began to hack blindly at the cable ties. Rainn's screams had stopped and with every passing second he waited for footsteps to reach the stairs or fire to strike the petrol. Winter gasped as her hands fell free of the pole. Twisting around, she snatched the knife from Gus and slashed at the plastic ties that bound him. Large splinters of wood dropped from the edges of the crate, still burning as they drifted across the water. With a snap, the cable tie gave way and Winter stuffed the knife into her belt. She clambered up the stairs after Gus, gritting her teeth as searing pains shot through her leg. As the pair emerged, they were met with a gust of sea air and the empty expanse of an overcast sky. A roar filled the cabin below as fire claimed the petrol-soaked panels.

They were at the stern of the boat, facing the sea. Gus turned and ran his gaze from the dark windows of the captain's cabin to the bow, where the loose flaps of a tethered sail buffeted in the breeze. The cabin obstructed his view and if Rainn was on the deck beyond, he could not see her. Winter gripped his arm as the door to the cabin opened and a scarecrow emerged from its dim interior. A pair of empty eyes. A rifle raised. Without hesitation, Gus yanked Winter to the edge of the boat and the pair leaped into the black water.

There was no sound of gunfire. They kicked through the waves, the jagged rocks of the shore just metres away, yet the distance seemed interminable beneath the sight of a gun. Gus disappeared under the waves and Winter followed his lead, urging her savaged leg to kick through the freezing water.

Nearing the shore, Gus raised his head to glance back at the boat. The fire was no longer contained below, but crept up the mast, feeding on the exposed flaps of the sail. Pain stabbed his knee as he struck something sharp and proceeded to haul himself out of the water. A wave crashed overhead, knocking the pair against the rocks. With fingers numb and bleeding, they struggled to their feet and dragged themselves from the unrelenting waves.

Winter steadied herself against Gus's shoulder, ready to haul her body from the rocks to the bank, when she saw the scarecrow silhouetted against the flames of his blazing vessel. Fingernails dug into Gus's collar as the rifle was levelled in their direction.

'No!'

A desperate scream sounded from the rocks to their left. Soaked, with her bare navel showing through a blackened dress, Rainn cried out to the captain as Gus and Winter gripped the rock and awaited the gunshot. The man's face was impassive as he lowered his eyes to the sight of the gun and fingered the trigger.

With a resounding blast, the boat exploded. Flaming debris was jettisoned into the sky before landing in the waves. Rainn stared in horror as the decimated vessel teetered and sank beneath the dark water. Gus tugged at Winter's arm and the pair scrambled up the bank to where it flattened. They had reached a pinnacle of rock, with nothing but woodland ahead and a lighthouse standing defiant at the end of the world. Gus cast one final glance at the shoreline to watch a husky dog pull itself from the water and onto the rocks. Rainn had slipped from view.

The beam of the lighthouse swept overhead as Gus and Winter plunged into the strip of woodland that truncated this peninsula. Conscious of the sheer cliff on either side, Winter dragged her leg through the underbrush and the pair navigated the shadows until a flat expanse lay before them. The barren peninsula widened over hundreds of metres before joining the distant mainland. From over the trees, the beam of the lighthouse swept the rock like the flash of a prison guard's torch. Winter yelped in pain as she tripped over a root and Gus hooked her arm around his shoulders, taking her weight as he led her out into the open. Under an overcast sky, they could see little ahead; the passing beam illuminated no more than a series of craggy cliffs and crude paths leading to higher ground. They crossed the unsheltered stretch, exposed, wondering if eyes followed their hobbled progress.

The beam delivered a half-second of light and Winter shrieked, pulling Gus to a halt. They were a step away from the edge of a large hole in the rock. The water below sloshed and gurgled, and Gus peered into the blowhole. Tireless waves had bored a tunnel into the cliff face and broken through to the surface. He steered Winter around its edge and they raced to the left, wary of other pitfalls.

Thunder rippled overhead and the clouds broke, casting sheets of rain on them. As the beam swept his back, Gus peered over the cliff to spot a ledge below. He helped Winter down to the narrow path and they made their way along stony ground, steadying themselves against the rock face until they reached a stretch where the sheer cliff fell away under a rocky overhang. Gus ducked inside the recess and out of the rain. He twisted in the shallow space and sat with his back against the wall. Winter kicked sharply at his protruding feet with her good leg.

'Get up! I'm not dying in some hole on this miserable rock. Not with you.'

'If they're expecting us, we'll not go limping into their arms.' Gus thumbed to the right, where the peninsula joined the mainland. 'At least let them think we might have made it—let them widen the net. Give me that knife.'

Winter tugged the blade from her belt and kneeled beside him, flicking sodden hair over her shoulders and wincing through the pain. Gus caught her eye as she slid the serrated blade between his neck and the collar.

'Alicia isn't there,' said Winter as the collar fell to the floor.

Gus snatched it and cast it over the cliff. 'I'm going to talk to that man—' He recalled Rainn's conversation with Aldous. '—Peter. Find out what he wants. He doesn't know where we are. If Aldous and Morna want to speak to me that badly, it will be on my terms.'

Winter slumped against the wall of their cave, her dark skin ashen and her wet hair violescent.

'You'd better come back,' she said, 'or I'm rolling you into the sea.'

Finally removing her high heels, she stared out across the grey ocean with no expression in her eyes. Gus wondered if she was thinking about the scarecrow that had just been blown to oblivion.

But Gus had no time to think. He closed his eyes. For a year, he had resisted; each night, natural sleep had been forbidden. Resting his head against the rock, he released his consciousness like a feather in a gale-force wind. As rain lashed the cliffs, Gus left a soaked and battered body in the waking world.

The Playground

A FINE BLACK smoke rose like a veil against the eggshell blue of Vivador's sky. Through this veil, Alicia trained her telescopic vision and studied the battle that raged below. On the obsidian platform, Amira seemed intent on spending what was left of the night in ceaseless combat with her simulacrum. Rainn had excused herself with a sly smile, disappearing to 'attend to something' in the waking world. Or was this a test? Alicia scanned the rock shelves lining the crater's inner wall to see if Rainn was watching from one of the many tunnels. She resisted the urge to interrupt the fight and question Amira before she woke.

Alicia's eyes flitted from one furious face to the other, unable to determine which was the original. The mirror image on the left cast her hands forward, palms open and joined at the wrists, to send a torrent of laser beams at her opponent. The girl on the right stepped effortlessly to the side and the beams passed under her arm, crossing the lake of lava to strike the wall of the crater.

Having argued with her mirror image, Alicia understood that it could teach you nothing that you did not already know. In dreams, the subconscious could devise unexpected characters and objects; but, unlike that bullet in Alicia's heart, Amira's simulacrum was unable to provoke a shot of adrenaline powerful enough to wake her. So, she experimented, testing out weapons and ferocious animals, and Alicia wondered what she was preparing for.

The scream of a chainsaw and the crack of an electric whip were silenced as two identical faces raised their eyes to the rock shelves. Previously empty, these shelves now teemed with thousands of translucent figures: the onion-skin image of a jubilant crowd. In dresses that glistened with rubies and amethysts, the ghostly simulacrums were made in Rainn's image. Cries of delight filled the volcano and Alicia followed the gaze of ten thousand faces to a distant figure travelling along the rim of the crater. Projecting her vision across the expanse, Alicia watched Rainn back-flipping along the rocky precipice to the gasps and whistles of her onion-skin audience.

The whistles became screams, and the screams chants, as Rainn deftly navigated the uneven rock, travelling at a remarkable speed. When she was below the higher of Psarnox's two peaks, a section of the cliff fell away and a waterfall of lava surged into the volcanic depths. Rainn sprang from a backflip and launched herself down the waterfall, landing on a board that materialised above the cascading lava. To screams of adoration, Rainn rode her board down the waterfall, plummeting towards the lake of molten rock.

The cries were tumultuous as she struck the lava to surf upon a great viscous wave. Brighter than the gem-studded gowns of the translucent crowd, the sapphires in her leotard reflected the light of the bubbling lava. She manipulated not only the board but the wave itself, drawn to a great height and then lowered to a modest crest as she approached the platform. She hopped from the board to the obsidian disc and Amira's simulacrum vanished.

With a pair of flaming scimitars, Rainn twisted towards Amira, who shielded herself with an icy broadsword. Such was Rainn's ferocity and speed, she appeared not only to be demonstrating prowess, but venting fury.

The fight was brutal. There were moments when the crater trembled and the pair were knocked back against the edges of the disc, skidding to a halt before the lava. They paused to stare at one another and Alicia watched emotion play across Amira's face. The girl's lip trembled, she blinked thick lashes and inclined her head at the threat or criticism driven between her ears.

Once a new attack had been introduced, it surfaced in the repertoire of the attacked. But ideas were not cloned, they were amended. Improved. And, so, the battle evolved, with each imitation more devastating than the last. Alicia watched the seamless transmission of ideas, progressing at a tremendous rate, unparalleled in the waking world. This battle would end only through the deployment of an attack so novel and unpredictable that the opponent was unable to stop it.

The platform tipped gently as Rainn landed on its edge and cast a stream of missiles into the sky to shower down upon her younger opponent. Amira vanished beneath the explosion, but when the smoke dissipated, she remained.

There were boos and hisses from the onion-skin audience, and then a playful gasp as the tunnels behind them whooped and howled. Amira spun on the spot, casting wide eyes across the walls of the crater as a troupe of macaques hurled themselves over the burning lake. Her brows furrowed in determination and she raised her palms defensively. The first three monkeys to land on the platform petrified instantly, lining the edge of the obsidian as grotesque statues. But the monkeys continued to pour from the ledges, more numerous now. The girl tried to cast each to stone, but within moments she was overpowered and disappeared beneath an amorphous mass of grey-brown fur. The attack was swift and savage—tooth and claw—and then the whooping ceased as Amira returned to the waking world.

Rainn's crowd disappeared and the Playground was empty.

'*What are you waiting for?*' growled a voice in Alicia's head. She withdrew her vision from the bare platform and turned to find Rainn beside her. The woman's sapphire leotard glistened like the crystal-encrusted rock beneath their feet. Her eyes glowered. '*A push?*'

It seemed unnecessarily intrusive for Rainn to force her words into Alicia's mind when she could have said them aloud. From the timbre of her voice, Alicia knew she was struggling to maintain her cool composure. Whatever havoc Rainn was wreaking elsewhere, something was troubling her.

'Nice show,' said Alicia.

'Oh, please.' Rainn waved a hand. 'I could have ended it in a heartbeat. I thought you could use some inspiration.'

'If I win—if I wake this girl up, what will that prove?'

Rainn's words entered Alicia's head as a cool whisper.

'When Aldous and Morna look into your eyes, there won't be anyone to put a bullet in your chest. Show me what you're made of, and I will take you to them.'

Amira appeared in the centre of the platform, scanning the shelves.

Alicia asked, 'How do I get down?'

Rainn raised her eyebrows and Alicia nodded with a thin smile. Gripping the rock and bowing her head like a bird of prey, she launched herself from the edge and into the crater.

Sol

GUS STOOD IN his dormitory at school, aware that his environment was fictional. He brushed the back of a finger against loose threads hanging from the corner of his mattress, permitting himself a moment to marvel at the fraying cotton, before turning to the window. The outdoor swimming pool—an adequate form of punishment in an Irish boarding school—was vacant, and the placid water glimmered in the sunlight. It was more than the uncommon weather that prompted Gus to register his surroundings as false; he was conscious that his body lay on the cliffs in Portugal. He swept his eyes around the contents of his mind. What had lain forgotten on the ghostly shelves of his mental library now stood before him in arresting detail.

He ran hands down his thighs, over his black jeans—how good it felt to be dry!—and took two paces back. He crossed his arms before his face and sprinted at the window. In a blur of broken glass, the landscape shifted under his intention and he lowered his fists to see the plains before Stonehenge. Quick steps carried him over the shallow ditch, his bare feet flattening the long grass at the bottom. He approached the low-lying stones, collapsed and sunken, where the outer circle was broken. As Winter had described, the stones within this sarsen ring were missing.

While the great sandstone blocks, with pale-green lichen fused to a pockmarked surface, were testament to the depths of his memory, Gus could not begin to fathom the arrangement replaced by the pool. Had the stones within been smaller? Bigger? Rounder? He had not paid attention to the summer-camp teacher, wheezing her facts; he had busied himself proving to another boy that it was possible to slip on a banana peel.

Chuckling inwardly at the memory, he raced between the stones. He dived into the water and hijacked the conscious pathway of the unknown lucid dreamer who had established this portal between the realms. Landing on his backside on a stone dais in the middle of a pool, Gus Crow entered Vivador.

No teenage girl waited between the stones. The sky above, as the water below, was an innocent blue. Turning bare feet on the dais, he scanned the sarsen blocks and set the focus of his attention on the horizontal stones that lay precariously on top of the others. Under his direction, six lintels rose into the air. The blocks drifted higher until Gus allowed their weight—all thirty-five tonnes—to return and sent them crashing down. With a rumble that disturbed the surface of the water, the structure collapsed around him.

He crossed the pool in a leap and landed on a fallen stone to gaze at the distant mountain, where tendrils of smoke rose between two peaks. Had Alicia's mother seen the volcano here in Vivador and painted it on waking, or had she painted it first in the material world and then conjured it in Vivador? Which was the original and which the reconstruction?

Beyond the fallen monument, a tower stood in the centre of a great lake. In comparison, the pool between the broken blocks was little more than a garden pond. Catlike in speed and agility, Gus leaped across the length of the pool, landed in a crouch on a sunken stone and sprang forward to reach the end of the bridge. He paused for a second, stared across the wooden planks that led to Rainn's accomplice, and broke into a run. He ran because Winter lay beside him, biting down the pain as she bled to death. He ran because he had no time to think. No time to consider the holes in his plan.

Stone steps blurred beneath his feet and narrow windows passed like the slits along a zoetrope. He slowed only when the room opened up to reveal two empty thrones rotating at its centre.

Standing in an archway, having doubtlessly watched that desperate sprint across the bridge, a man waited with his back to the room.

'Hello, Peter,' said Gus, his voice level.

The man ran his eyes from Gus's bare feet to his unkempt hair, dark as his monochrome jeans and T-shirt. Peter's hands were in the pockets of his trousers, his white shirt carefully tucked under a leather belt that matched his open jacket. The sleeves of the jacket were long, no tattoos visible. His waxwork face revealed nothing; this man had no intention of confirming or denying his identity. Gus took a step closer.

'Rainn lost us. We got away, me and the girl. Winter.' He slowed down, controlling his breathing. 'And if you don't do exactly as I say, you'll have to tell Aldous we're gone, and I've a feeling he won't be too happy about that. Not after everything he's done to get me to Portugal. Winter is bleeding to death. I'll send her back to the lighthouse, alone, and Rainn will take her to a hospital. And when Winter is safe, she'll meet me here in Vivador, at a location we've discussed, and she'll tell me that you've done as you were told. And then—and only then—will I return to meet my family.'

Peter inclined his head, pinched his hooked nose between his thumb and forefinger, and folded his arms.

'I met your father once,' he said, in a voice as rough as stone. 'He was not like you. There was a certain charm about him. A confidence he acquired having mastered his emotions. How disappointing, when sons fall short of expectations.'

Gus held his body rigid as his chest tightened.

'I didn't ask about my father. Do we have a deal?'

With his head down, Peter trod the hexagonal tiles to the revolving dais. He unfolded his arms and brushed a finger against the stone arm of a passing throne.

'Take a seat.'

Gus did not move. He could read nothing in those pale eyes. At first, they reminded him of the captain: empty as the lens of a camera; yet while that scarecrow had moved as if hypnotised, Peter's eyes were empty through his own design. He had willed them clear of emotion, his deception absolute.

'I don't know how Benedict found me at Burnflower last summer. He told me he planned to surprise Aldous and Morna. That, on your seventeenth birthday, you would meet them for the first time. He was convincing—more so than you—and I gave him the key to their home. I warned Aldous, of course; he was expecting them.'

Peter paused and Gus strove to mirror that unfathomable expression. He had unwittingly displayed his anger about Winter; he would not let this man know his agony. He would bury his need to understand how they died. He would change the subject.

'Who are you? Why did you have a key to their home?'

'Aldous told me what happened when your parents reached their bedside,' Peter cocked his head and continued as if Gus had not spoken. 'How he and Morna watched them deliberating. They saw no reason to return to their bodies when Benedict pulled the knife from his bag. The hesitation on his face—no intervention was necessary. He was not going to kill them. There was a weakness about him, not visible in the waking world. His energy, how did Aldous describe it?' He drew a thumbnail through his short grey beard. 'A dying bulb. Sylvie grabbed the book at the bedside and, mirroring his cowardice, she ran.'

They let them live: as heavy as stone thrones, the words hung between Gus's ears. Thoughts laced with disappointment. His father could have ended the pair of them. Anna Harrington, Jack Henson, Melody Wilson—how many others might still be alive?

'It's harder than you imagine.' Peter stepped around the thrones, closer to Gus. 'To take the life of a blood relative goes against nature. Ingrained through evolution, there is a need to protect the family. True strength,' he said, raising his eyebrows, 'lies in the ability to break the rules that we inherit through nature's cradle. To overcome our biological flaws. When faced with difficult choices, weaker minds will fail to do what is in their best interests.'

You're here for Winter.

'I see the anger in you.' Peter searched his eyes. 'Born out of the murder of your parents, nurtured by fear and yearning to feed itself through vengeance. Aldous and Morna do not expect forgiveness. They offer you the chance to break the cycle. Must they die like the others?'

As Peter continued, faces entered Gus's mind. The images held such clarity that he was certain they were delivered with each word reverberating between his ears.

'*Joseph. Alicia. Winter.* More innocent lives, more collateral damage, victims of a struggle that need not concern them. But there is a solution, Augustus. Take a seat.'

Again, Peter gestured to the throne revolving past him. Again, Gus heard a clamour between his ears.

A rehearsed speech—

You're here for Winter.

—written by Aldous.

Through the maelstrom of his thoughts, Gus spotted something around Peter's neck: a silver chain just visible beneath his unbuttoned collar. On the end of the chain, glinting in the light that streamed ubiquitously through the arches, a thin disc bore the symbol of the Order of Chaos.

He's not listening to you—

—make him listen.

Gus raised a hand as though to ask a question, then lowered three fingers until the index remained, pointed at the ceiling. Peter leaped backwards and raised his arms as the roof of the tower was blown skyward. Heavy chunks of stone fell like meteorites into the lake.

Gus swept his arm to point at the thrones. Peter tensed, his long-fingered hands before him.

'You wouldn't like that,' said Gus, nodding at the throne without taking his eyes off Peter, 'would you?'

Peter straightened up, pushed his hands into his pockets and restored a mask of nonchalance. He opened his mouth to speak, but Gus beat him to it.

'What happens when I sit on this throne?'

A brick slid from one of the broken arches and cracked a tile on the floor. Peter cleared his throat and ran a hand through his dark hair.

'It is commonly understood that the energy that drives us in the physical realm—'

'In your own words,' said Gus. 'You're their puppet—I get that. You've been practising, standing at that arch, watching the portal. Waiting for your big moment. Tell me in your own words, not his.'

Though the waxwork mask did not change, Peter's fury radiated through the tiles, heating the soles of Gus's feet.

'Solar energy—photosynthesis, plants, food.' His lips barely moved. 'That's what makes our bodies move. Our material bodies. But there's another energy. The energy right here.' He spread his hands. 'Aldous and Morna spent decades in Vivador seeking the origin of the soul. And they found it. While our physical bodies are driven by the light of the sun, our immaterial bodies are powered by the stars. Every human on Earth is linked to a different star.'

Peter paused as if anticipating scorn at the fantastical statement; but Gus did not blink. Conversing with a stranger in the immaterial realm while his body lay under a rocky overhang in Portugal, he would have found nothing unbelievable at that moment. The anger that blazed in his projected body was no less real than the air he breathed into his lungs on Earth. He had never considered its origin.

When Gus made no comment, Peter continued. 'The strength of

a person's soul depends on the strength of their star, and its proximity to Earth. This puts the individual linked to our closest star, the sun, at an unfair advantage—deriving from it both material and immaterial sustenance. This individual would have a conviction of will unparalleled by any other. They call this power the Sol.'

As he continued, Peter kept his hand on the arm of a throne, completing a revolution of the dais.

'Your grandfather, Augustus; he found what his parents were looking for. He fell in love with the Sol, in the guise of Eloise. She couldn't handle it. Eloise sat on this throne and took her life on the day that two children were born: Alicia and yourself. Aldous and Morna want to know which of you inherited her strength of will.'

The twin seats were identical, casting shifting shadows. The rock was as white as bone, every inch carved with a tessellating pattern of triangles. Which seat was he expected to take, or was this the test? A throne passed and he imagined the ghostly apparition of Eloise sitting upon it, lifting a gun to her temple so that he or Alicia might inherit a responsibility that she was unable to live with.

Gus frowned. 'Eloise is Alicia's grandmother, not mine. Why would I inherit anything from her?'

'A fact I have raised with Aldous more than once.' Peter nodded as if conceding a point. 'He believes it to be more complicated than that. And here we are—to prove, perhaps, that you do not have what they seek.'

Gus hesitated and his soles burned with Peter's impatience.

'I will…' he said, gesturing at the passing throne, 'park myself on this stone seat if you get Winter to a hospital. Once I know she's safe, and—'

Rainn appeared between a pair of crumbling pillars where an arch had stood. She raised her eyes to the sky and then glanced from Gus to Peter.

'This is a waste of time,' she said. 'It's Alicia we need, not him.'

A snarl issued through Peter's lips, the cleft exposing a canine.

'A good dog does not leave its post.'

Peter and Rainn glared at one another and Gus caught a flush in her cheeks before she willed them pale.

'He sleeps,' she said, lifting a hand to gesture at Gus.

But Gus was gone.

Ryan, age 16

I MEMORISED THE position of each sheet of paper on the desk, so I would know where to put them back. I held my breath, partly to concentrate and partly to listen for the sound of Peter's motorbike. Rainn said he would be gone all day and I wondered if he would be back with another dress for her.

Underneath printouts of medical journals I saw a photograph of a boy who looked maybe ten years old. Another orphan? On top of the bookcase behind the desk was a plastic tub filled with about 29 rubber snakes, and a small cardboard box labelled anti-venom. I didn't want him to bring another kid to Burnflower.

'Bingo,' said Rainn as she lifted a file from the top drawer of the metal cabinet behind the door. I saw my name on a printed label on the corner of the file. She looked at me like she was thinking about handing it over, but she leaned against the cabinet, crossed her feet and opened it. I had come to expect this from Rainn: if there was a 'right thing to do', she would do the opposite. The only thing she loved more than stroking Sam in front of me was 'training' him. She would smack him for dropping the cricket ball at my feet, but then stroke him for growling at Amira when she walked too close to his food while he was eating. I told Mum she wasn't treating him properly. She said that jealousy was an ugly trait.

Mum is jealous of Rainn. She's 19 now and Mum said she could have left Burnflower and found a home of her own, but she chooses to stay here. I used to think it was only Amira that interested Peter, and whatever phobia she had that week, but he spends most of his time with Rainn. I hear them arguing sometimes, in the Pagoda. She's the *only person who's allowed to shout at him. Last night, I kept my bedroom window open and her shouts raced across the field: 'She's not your secret!'*

Who is 'she'?

It's not like I could ask Rainn. The only reason she talks to me is to torment me. Accusing me of watching her change into her nightgown. Telling Amira I had drawn a picture of her, and Rainn had burned it because it was so cruel. So, I didn't jump up and bow when she walked into my room after breakfast this morning. But she had a key in her hand—the key that Peter wears on a chain around his neck. How did she even get it?

There wasn't much in the office: file boxes on the shelves filled with printouts from journals and a desk drowning in paper. A rectangle of wood where the laptop sat—he had taken it with him, like he always did. An old printer on the floor under the window. Rainn had gone straight for the filing cabinet.

I leaned against the edge of the desk, careful not to disturb the papers, and I watched her read my file.

'He's been studying you.'

'Ground breaking.'

'Egoic-association…targeted cathexis…attachment.' She smiled that cold, beautiful smile. 'You're his special subject. He's training you.'

'For what?'

But I knew. I had known for years. That mirror was like a test tube in a lab. Isolated and unloved, he was growing a killer.

Peter—my father—had controlled every variable in my life to make sure I had no attachments. He had nurtured an anger inside me so strong that I had murdered Sam out of jealousy. My life had been an experiment and my personality a product of his design. How many of my actions, from dropping that dollhouse to the death of Sam, had been under his direction? Had I made any of these choices?

Had I made any choices at all?

I walked up to Rainn and she held the file to her chest, smiling like she did when she pushed Sam's ball down her top. It wasn't my file I reached for; it was hers. I knew why Peter found her interesting: he's fascinated by her REM behaviour disorder. I wanted to know how he planned to use it.

I pulled out her file and opened it on the desk. There wasn't much inside, not half as much as mine—I guess he keeps most of it on his laptop now. Along with some old school reports, a couple of magazine articles on RBD and an advert for a Sleep Clinic in Singapore, there was a sheet of paper filled with names. The names were in little boxes joined with lines—it was a family tree.

My finger stung as Rainn ripped the paper from my hands. She dropped my file on the floor and walked out of the office. This was obviously what she had come for, and I thought she would take it back to her room, but she turned left out the door and headed up the steps that spiralled to the top of the Pagoda. I sucked my papercut and followed her up the stairs.

Rainn sat down in the archway that faces the house with her legs over the edge of the bamboo floor. I didn't like it—Mum was round the back of the house, picking rhubarb with Amira, and if they walked down the side they'd see us right away. There were six arches, why not sit in the one facing the forest?

But I didn't say anything. I wanted to know what Peter wasn't telling her, so I walked up behind Rainn and studied the paper in her hands. Two names at the top: Aldous and Morna. Beneath them, two more: Augustus and Marcus. Augustus was linked to two women, one on either side. From a horizontal line joining him with Eloise, a vertical line went down to Anna. Anna was linked to Rory, and they had two kids: Alicia and David. On the other side of Augustus was Blithe, and they had two boys: Benedict and Joseph. Joseph wasn't linked to anyone else, but Benedict was linked to Sylvie, and they had named their boy Augustus.

It was the other side of the tree that had me holding my breath again. The woman linked to Marcus had a full name: Hazel Burnflower. Marcus and Hazel had a daughter.

'Rainn Crow?' I read aloud.

Rainn looked up at me and I took a step back, but she didn't look cross. She folded the paper and held it out for me.

'Put this in your pocket.'

'Why?'

'You'll need your hands.'

I did as I was told. I wanted to tidy up the office before Peter got back. But Rainn did not get up. She turned and lowered herself over the edge of the floor, hanging out the archway, gripping the bamboo. Then she screamed.

She screamed so loud that I took another step back and almost covered my ears. So loud that Mum came running down the side of the house with the basket of rhubarb in her hands.

'Help!' Rainn shouted, but she wasn't asking me. She was trying to look over her shoulder. Mum dropped the basket on the patio.

'What are you doing?' I held out my hand, but she screamed even louder.

'He pushed me!'

Mum was running down the gravel path between the ponds. Rainn looked in my eyes and I knew this was another game. She waited until Mum entered the Pagoda and then she asked me to help her up. I grabbed her arms and pulled and she made it up to her knees. She leaned against me, hands on my shoulders, and then she pulled me forwards and I lost my balance.

I don't remember hitting the ground. The last thing I remember is the sound of a motorbike.

CHAPTER SEVEN

Patience

ALICIA LANDED IN the centre of the platform with such force that the surface of the obsidian split. Startled, Amira stepped back, her eyeline falling to the crack between her feet, and it occurred to Alicia that the creator of this platform had deemed it unbreakable. The younger girl looked up, eyes roving the tunnels and ledges higher up the crater until her telescopic vision found Rainn on the distant rim. A face in shadow inclined as the woman nodded.

The rock shelves filled with an onion-skin audience, ten thousand simulacrums of Amira. Unlike the girl on the platform, these translucent figures did not wear a baggy, cable-knit jumper, hanging from a scrawny frame like a shirt caught on a fencepost; they gleamed in neon Lycra. Unlike Amira, these girls looked comfortable in their own skin. With hands to their mouths, they chanted her name, and Amira tugged at the ends of her jumper, squirming at their immodesty. She faced Alicia with humiliation in her eyes.

Amira cast a hand behind her and from it flowed a long, silver whip. With a hiss, the whip flew through the air, splitting into two tendrils that snapped either side of Alicia's face. As the girl toyed with the weapon, casting it from behind her lean figure to snap at Alicia's left and right, its movement appeared organic. Each tendril unfurled and cracked independently, like the tentacles of an octopus. On the fourth strike, the whip cracked so close to Alicia's ear that the air around her shifted. She raised a finger to her stinging cheek and blood smeared the tip. A cheer echoed around the crater, primal as the amphitheatres of ancient Rome.

Amira cracked the whip again and the two tendrils split into four, curling around Alicia's wrists and ankles. The silver hardened as the whip became a metal chain. The girl's eyes narrowed and Alicia's scream filled the crater as the metal burned.

I have no body.

As with the shards of glass, Alicia tore her mind from the matter, closing her eyes to deny her body and resist the scent of burning flesh that threatened to wake her.

'*I didn't bring you here to practise your defence,*' a caustic voice sounded in her head. Alicia opened her eyes and sought the silhouette against the sky.

'*Patience, Rainn,*' she fired back as the metal continued to sear her wrists and ankles.

'*Patience is for those with low expectations. If you want your brother, fight for him.*'

Alicia was fighting. She was resisting the belief that the pain was real. But she could not win this battle—she could not succeed in this realm—by denying it. Fire in her wrists, white heat scorching her ankles, and beneath this: intention. Focusing on the heat, Alicia hijacked Amira's desire to burn her. She filled her projected body with a brilliant fire, fuelled by the girl's will, rising to a temperature as intense as the magma beneath her. And then, like an electric charge, she sent this heat back along the whip, delivering it into the girl's hands with such ferocity that she was blown into the air.

Skinny feet skidded to the edge of the disc and wet eyes shone through a tangle of dark curls that had fallen from her plait. She was on the edge of tears; what words of encouragement might Rainn be offering? Amira's lips hardened and she stretched one hand before her and the other behind, palms down, in the stance of a surfer. From her palms, what appeared to be smoke poured outward and encircled her.

A cheer rose from the simulacrum crowd as she thrust her palms forward, issuing the cloud before her, a cloud not consisting of particles of smoke, but thousands of tiny piranha. As the shoal drifted through the air, reflected in the volcanic glass, Alicia raised a single palm. The silver cloud slowed as it crossed the distance between them. When the first of the fish were inches from Alicia's outstretched palm, the shoal froze. She slowly lowered her hand, holding the cloud of fish in her mind and resisting their approach. Thousands of tiny mouths snapped at thin air a moment longer and then all was still. Resting her hands on her thighs, Alicia cast her mind through the shoal in its entirety, feeling Amira's struggle to regain control of her creation. But the piranhas were under Alicia's command. The fish burst to life, continuing their journey through the air and whipping around Alicia in a spiral of silver scales and needle teeth. Amira watched on, helpless, as Alicia lifted the spiral skyward before sending it plummeting into the lava. The platform rocked and rumbled. Amira's bare feet faltered and she steadied herself, glancing left and right to guess from which direction the fish would emerge. When, finally, the shoal burst into the air, dripping with lava from the molten bed, the thousands had coalesced in a tight formation, taking the shape of a great white shark. The shark twisted through the air, the scales of each individual piranha glimmering in the glow of the lava. Amira drew her arms before her face as the shark opened its mouth ready to engulf her. The jaws snapped shut, striking at empty space as Amira woke.

Alicia glanced up with the misguided idea that Rainn might show approval, but there was no one on the crater's edge. Rainn had returned to whatever battle she was facing in the physical realm.

Uncomfortable before the sea of silent faces, Alicia cleared the audience. She had not a moment to herself before Amira returned. With her back to Alicia, the girl searched the crater's rim for Rainn, awaiting further instruction. Alicia locked upon the back of her head.

'*Amira.*'

The girl spun at the sound of a voice in her skull. Her eyes were wide, her mouth gaping. Alicia spoke hurriedly.

'*I know you're at Burnflower. I'm looking for—*'

Amira stumbled backwards and dived into the lava.

Drinking from shoes

THE RAIN HAD not abated. Tripping over roots and slipping down streams of water that coursed along the moss-lined banks, Gus crossed the strip of woodland to where the sky began to lighten. He had just discerned the outline of the lighthouse through a gap in the trees when the bushes to his right rustled. From the leaves emerged the head of a large dog. The animal tensed before lowering into a crouch, silver-grey fur dripping on the sodden soil. Gus backed against a tree as the dog inched towards him. He held the rough bark between his hands and lowered his body, levelling his eyes with the beast.

'Easy boy.' His breath escaped as mist into the cold morning air.

Teeth bared, the husky sniffed gingerly at the torn and ragged jeans before raising his blue eyes to meet Gus's. He turned and padded off into the trees.

Steadying his pounding heart, Gus continued towards the lighthouse, avoiding any semblance of a path until he reached a crop of bushes between the outlying trees. The structure towered on the cliff's edge, the stone black against a platinum sky. Rainn leaned in the open doorway with her head resting against the wall and the captain's rifle by her side. Water cascaded from the red cupola roof, hit the barrel of the gun and split like a curtain. Rainn's clothes were soaked, with a large hole around her navel where the fire had burned through the white dress.

Gus crouched in the bushes and watched her eyelids fall. He waited a moment before emerging, ready to charge through the curtain of water and seize the weapon. But Rainn's eyes snapped open and swept the clearing, narrowly missing Gus as he ducked behind the nearest tree. He maintained his position for several minutes, snatching glances of a pattern as Rainn blinked in and out of consciousness. So adept at lucid dreaming, she entered the state almost instantly, and took no more than a couple of seconds to visualise whatever portal she used before blinking to the tower. She monitored both the lighthouse and the thrones, spending less time in Vivador than it would take for Gus to dash across the clearing and grab the rifle.

Defeated, Gus crept into the woodland and made his way back to the plateau. Weak morning light outlined a path that wound from the sheet of rock to the mainland above, and before this lay the blowhole, its edges barely visible in the centre of the peninsula. There was no sign of the dog.

Gus hopped down to the ledge that ran along the cliffside and lifted his shoe to inspect the canine print beneath. He raced along the uneven path, tripping twice and steadying himself against the rock as his mind provoked him with images of what he might find in the shallow cave. Scrambling along the ledge, scattering small stones into the ocean below and calling Winter's name as loud as he dared, he reached the overhang to see a grey tail poking from their shelter. With his heart in his throat, Gus peered inside to find Sam beside Winter. The dog's shaggy head rested on the girl's lap. Winter raised her eyebrows expectantly as he approached, stroking the beast that had savaged her.

'She's guarding the lighthouse,' said Gus. The dog eyed him cautiously as he stepped over its tail. 'She's alone, I reckon. We'll head for the mainland.'

Winter brushed a thumb between the dog's ears.

'If Peter wants her guarding the lighthouse, that's where you should go.'

Gus narrowed his eyes, taken aback. Cold rain streamed down his cheeks. Winter had protested vehemently against waiting on the peninsula, and he had been reluctant to leave her when he woke. Her lips were tight, her face hard, and whether she was suffering or had simply resigned to her fate, he could not tell.

'She'll only sleep when I'm in Vivador—'

'You can't go back!' Winter barked, loud enough for Sam to raise his head. She stroked him reassuringly and shifted her position so that he did not rest on her wounded thigh. 'You can't sit on that throne. This power—your soul—you would give it to them?'

Thunder rent the ocean as the pair stared into each other's eyes.

'It's Alicia that has this power—'

'You don't know that.'

Gus scratched the back of his head and spoke tentatively. 'Maybe if I sleep again, I could distract them in Vivador. You could head to the lighthouse and look for a phone...'

He trailed off. When recounting his conversation with Peter, Gus had not told Winter of his offer, which relied on her making it to the lighthouse alone. In her state, she would be lucky to cross the ledge without stumbling into the sea. And while it might energise her to demolish his plan, he would not frustrate her with it. With Rainn straddling sleep, awaiting him in both realms, he had no means of contacting his uncle and no time to search Vivador for Alicia.

He ducked under the overhang and leaned across Sam, who pricked his ears. He lifted one of Winter's shoes from beside her, held it under the rain and let it fill with water.

'You're disgusting,' she said as he offered her the water. He brought the golden heel to her mouth and she opened her lips to drink from the tattered rim.

'I need to get you to a hospital,' he said, sitting on his knees, his eyes drifting between the pallor of her lips and the bloodstained strip of dress that he had tied above the wound. His jacket did not appear to have warmed her.

'You're going to carry me? With those skinny arms of yours?'

Gus looked down at his arms, frowned, and leaned back against the rock. The rain fell in sheets from the overhang, separating them from the outside world. Splitting their cave from reality. Staring at the falling water, Gus thought of the dripping petrol, the fire, and Anna's letters reduced to ash. What secrets had Alicia's mother uncovered? Had she climbed that tower and laid her eyes on those spinning thrones? Had she made it into the lighthouse, as his parents had done? With bare elbows on wet knees, he ran his fingers against his temples, his head throbbing with all the unknown wisdom that Anna Harrington might have left behind.

'You're eighteen, right?' asked Winter. 'An adult? Your childhood is dead?'

'All right, Hallmark.'

'What have you learned? What do you know now that you didn't when you were a kid?'

'Aside from lucid dreaming leading to another realm—'

'No, I mean about life. The real world.'

Gus cupped his head in his hands and stared through the rain at the ocean, his eyes distant.

'When you're standing at a pedestrian crossing, never assume the person beside you has pushed the button.'

'You're an idiot.'

He grinned and picked up the shoe. The downpour was starting to lighten and the sheets of rain had become thin streams that funnelled between the overhanging rocks. Winter watched him fill the high heel until water spilled over the rim, and then tipped it away with trembling fingers. Gus tossed the shoe into the corner behind him and studied her out of the corner of his eye. She had admitted speaking to her dead boyfriend. In what might have been her final hour, she had been honest with him. What else did she need to confess?

'Go on then, humour me,' he said. 'What have you learned?'

She looked away and a distant flash of lightning lit the ocean. When her eyes returned they were filled with reluctance, as if pressed for the truth.

'My dad was scared of everything. Mum, mostly, of course—but everything else too. He'd make excuses not to go out with friends and he'd put things off till the last minute—afraid to call up the plumber when the bathroom taps were installed backwards. He was always apologising. Always trying to please, even when someone had messed him about. He was such a psycho...sicko...'

'Sycophant?'

'It drove me nuts, listening to him. Watching him shrink smaller than everyone he met, like cats that roll over to submit to the boss—'

'I think that's dogs—'

'He started getting these nightmares about losing his job at the post office. It drove him to drink.'

The rain pattered against the rock at their feet.

'What happened?'

'He went to work drunk and got fired.'

Gus leaned forward and laughed into the rain.

'I'm sorry,' he said, wiping his eyes.

'It's not funny,' said Winter, unable to suppress a grin that exposed her flawless teeth.

'It's not funny,' Gus agreed and Winter traced his face with her chestnut eyes, searching for creases of humour.

'When he died, my dad, I told myself I'd never be scared. Never shrink like he did around other people.' She shook her head and drops of rain flicked from the ends of her hair, landing on Sam's twitching ears. 'And guess what, Augustus? I've been scared every bloody day. I can hear them now—the voices. Warning me: *don't tell him anything that...*' She blinked slowly. 'It's so obvious, when you can hear it. So stupid. We don't even know we're listening to it.'

Gus watched her pinch at the droplets of rain between the dog's ears, a mask of dejection on her ashen face.

'You talked to Jack about your dad? Before, I mean.'

She nodded and turned to look at him.

'Who do you talk to?'

Gus shrugged, and rubbed his eyes. When he spoke, his voice was jovial: 'I guess that's why old people are so fearless, right? They don't give a damn any more, about what people think. They know it doesn't matter.'

Winter released a breath, disappointed at his attempt to deflect the attention from himself.

'You know what I've learned.' Gus cleared his throat. 'I've learned you're not as stupid as you pretend to be. That trick with the petrol? You got us off that boat. Methinks the sprout hath brains.'

'If you call me a sprout one more time—'

'You will literally bite me?'

'I will *literally* set this ferocious beast at your throat.'

Gus grinned, reaching out to scratch beneath a furry ear. Sam looked up sharply and then closed his eyes as Gus rubbed a spot on his neck.

'I killed him,' Winter uttered the thought aloud.

In both their minds, a scarecrow levelled a rifle in their direction and disappeared beneath explosion.

'You didn't know he would die. He could have jumped off the boat like the rest of us.'

She made no response. Whether it had been her intention or not, the captain was dead because of her. If not murder, it was manslaughter. The rain had finally ceased and Gus watched drops fall from the overhang as the peninsula drained. He watched his father stand at the bedside of his great-grandparents. Benedict Crow pulled a knife from his bag and faced the ancient figures as they dreamed their murderous dreams. In that situation, would Gus have the—

The what? The strength? The courage? The cold-blooded resolution to do what his father could not?

When faced with difficult choices, weaker minds will fail to do what is in their best interests.

He scratched the bare rock with a fingernail as heat filled his chest. There was no uncertainty as to what must be done. When he faced Aldous and Morna, he would succeed where his parents had failed.

Winter saw his face darken.

'She's right, you know. That pyromaniac has a point. About fear, I mean—that motor, driving us. My dad's fear made him a sycophant, but yours is different. It makes you angry. We're only angry when we're afraid we can't change the situation, my mum says. What are you so afraid of?'

Back from Vivador, Gus could hear his thoughts. Paranoid and defensive, they urged him to keep his mouth shut. Avoid judgement. Disappointment. Above the dog's collar, Winter's hand shifted against his and he met her eyes. In their isolated enclosure on this barren peninsula, they might have been the only two people in the waking world. Brown eyes glistened in the half-light as Winter closed the distance between them.

'Winter.' Gus leaned back a fraction. 'I'm into guys.'

'Blackout.'

Gus let out a chuckle, gazing across the ocean.

'Don't laugh, you tapeworm. I'm spending my last moments on Earth drinking from shoes and hitting on gay guys.'

Gus laughed again, his body shaking by Sam's side. The dog let out a yawn that escaped its formidable jaws as an irritable groan, and Winter surrendered to the laughter in her chest. Light and indefensible, their mirth carried across the waves to where cirrus clouds were tainted pink by the first rays of the morning sun.

'I'm not going to die scared,' Winter whispered, stroking Sam's fur and staring into the dawn of her final day.

Betrayal

THE WEIGHT OF the rifle lingered on her collarbone as Rainn cast her eyes across the hexagonal tiles. Gus's head emerged from the stairwell and she released her grip on the material realm. Grounded in Vivador, she leaned against the arch, and the pull of that wet strap evaporated, replaced by the tactile sensation of crumbling stone beneath her fingertips.

The young man stepped into the throne room. His green eyes flitted between Peter and Rainn, waiting in opposite arches. Without a glance at the restored ceiling, Gus crossed the tiles toward the thrones. The curl in Peter's cleft lip parodied a smile.

'His will is stronger than his father's,' grunted Peter to Rainn, folding his arms and leaving his position under the arch. 'Perhaps he will surprise us.'

Wordlessly, Gus stepped onto the revolving platform and stood before a throne. The pair watched him complete one full rotation, staring at the white seat.

'This is not surrender,' Peter continued. 'You choose to end this. To end the uncertainty. The hunt that has cost so many lives.'

With stiff limbs, Gus lowered himself upon the throne.

Peter unfolded his arms and strode across the floor, dark hair ruffled by an impatient breeze that whipped between the arches. He stopped mid-stride as Rainn vanished from her archway to reappear on the empty throne. She raised her chin, her chiseled cheekbones white as the stone beneath her. Cerulean eyes strafed leftwards, following Peter as she drifted past him.

Her mouth did not move when she spoke. A low voice filled the chamber: 'Should we not summon Aldous?'

Her emerald dress scattered the light, and green shadows played across the floor as she circled back into view. Her words had not been delivered between Peter's ears, but out loud, available to those unseen. For the first time, she saw fear on his face.

'Or...' she mused, 'perhaps you intend to claim the Sol for yourself?'

Rainn spun out of Peter's view, her defiance exchanged for Gus's white-eyed bewilderment. Peter spoke calm words over his head.

'As members of the Order, we are here to determine whether Gus is in possession of the Sol. Not to claim it.'

Rainn's nostrils flared, her expression regal. 'You have trained me, tested me, analysed me like one of your stolen children...' she scoffed. 'Like a child. Another experiment for Aldous. Mighty Aldous. You would think he discovered this place alone. You would think he founded the Order alone. Aldous this and Aldous that— Morna might bend to her husband's will, bend the knee to this patriarchy, but this realm was built by no man, built for no man, and will be commanded by no man. Not once, Peter—not in one iteration of this moment, did you consider that I might take the throne. That I might inherit this power. Have you forgotten that I am a Crow?'

Peter's eyes were as vacant as his son's, observing her patiently. No intention to respond. No desire to intervene.

Rainn closed her eyes.

'Let's see what my cousin is made of.'

The chamber froze. Each strand of hair on Peter's head, the silver chain about his neck, the playful hem of Rainn's dress—each lay unwavering as a still image. All that remained in motion were the revolving thrones.

And then, nothing.

'Well,' said Rainn, her tone clipped. 'I guess the Sol doesn't lie with a man after all. As I said, it's Alicia we need.'

'Or…' rumbled Peter, 'that is not Augustus.'

Rainn revolved away and the second throne passed into Peter's view. Winter lounged upon it.

Rainn staggered from the platform, her footing uncertain as she crossed the tiles. She stretched out her hands, reaching for Peter's support, but he disappeared. She fell against the archway and turned to stare at the imposter. Winter's smile was defiant, not a trace of fear in her chestnut eyes.

Champagne

MELISSA WAS AGITATED. She ploughed through fern and bramble on an unwavering path towards Burnflower. Alicia watched her stumble on a low ridge of grass at the woodland's edge and glare at the green shoots, scolding their insolence.

Ten minutes earlier, Alicia had woken in the Jeep to find Melissa leaning across her legs. The headmistress had stuffed a small cardboard box and a pair of gloves in the compartment under the dashboard and then straightened up, her face flustered and her hair in disarray. Shadows beneath her eyes suggested a sleepless night.

The sun had risen, marking the end of Sunday night and the start of Monday morning. For eighteen years, Alicia had woken to little more than fuzzy slivers of an incoherent narrative, and while her time in Vivador had energised her physically, she struggled to compress the night's events within six hours of sleep. From her journey on horseback to the battle with Amira, she needed to process her nocturnal adventures. Branches twanged in Melissa's wake and Alicia shielded herself while attempting to describe the battle in the crater. She received no response.

'I think Rainn's training her to defend the portals,' said Alicia as they reached the back of the vegetable patch. She scanned the rows of crops—bulbous pods of broad beans wet with dew—and fixed her eyes on the farmhouse. The windows were black in the daylight shadows. 'Is she up? Amira? Did you see—'

'I couldn't find him anywhere,' said Melissa.

'You broke in?'

She marched Alicia through the outer trees until they stood in line with Amira's bedroom window.

'It's my house. I know the weak spots. Ryan is not here.' A quick glance left and right, and Melissa left the trees. 'But look.'

She nodded at the window and Alicia's heart did a somersault: the bed by the door was no longer empty. A block of morning light fell through the open doorway and upon a mound of covers that stretched across the pillow, concealing the figure beneath. Whoever lay within appeared to have curled into a ball with no hands or feet protruding from the white duvet. Alicia's fingers found the cool glass of the window and her breath spilled on the pane. Amira remained on her back with her eyes closed, and Alicia was torn between a desire to launch a rock through the glass, and to drop to the ground and return to Vivador, where David might be fighting in the crater.

'One phone call,' Melissa warned.

'And we'll be dead in minutes,' said Alicia.

The block of light was disturbed as a man walked past the doorway. Melissa dropped to a crouch and Alicia followed her along the wall to the bushes at the back of the house. Not daring to disturb the leaves, they peered through the kitchen window. Peter Lawson stood beside the sink, regarding a bottle of champagne on the work surface.

Ryan's father did not match the image in Alicia's mind. Unlike his wife and son, Peter was dark-haired, with a short beard around a prominent jaw. While Melissa wore dry-cleaned suits, Peter's leather jacket was cracked with age, stretched across the broad shoulders that Ryan had inherited. Tugging his hooked nose, he glared at a tag about the bottle's neck: *Rainn, Happy Birthday, Peter.*

With quick, angry movements, Peter tore at the label, tossed it to the floor and stamped on it twice. He rested his hands either side of the sink, lowered his head, and then turned abruptly to walk back through the doorway. A second later, he reappeared, snatched the bottle from the work surface and unlocked the back door. Behind the bushes, Alicia and Melissa held their breath. Peter stood in the doorway and raised the bottle over his head, preparing to launch it at the vegetable patch. His shoulders sagged and he stepped inside, planting the bottle beside the sink and exiting the kitchen.

Alicia released her breath. 'Does he have a weapon?'

Melissa watched the kitchen doorway, waiting for Peter to return, her concentration so intense that she had not noticed the fly crawling along her temple.

'No. Rainn has the gun.'

Alicia's eyes flicked from the open back door to the champagne bottle.

'I have an idea.' She leaned to whisper into Melissa's ear: 'We go through that door and take the bottle, shake it, loosen the cork…wait until he rounds the corner and then release it.'

'Destroying Rainn's birthday present may seem like poetic justice, but—'

'It's a distraction. I'll release the cork, you go for his pockets, take his phone…Melissa?'

Melissa had left the bushes. With swift and silent steps, Alicia followed her through the back door. Rainn's lullaby was no longer playing and the silence thickened as they trod muddy footprints across the slate tiles. With her shoe on the discarded label, Melissa reached for the bottle of champagne.

'Just loosen—' Alicia whispered, but Melissa passed into the corridor. Alicia cursed under her breath and drew a kitchen knife from a wooden block beside the fridge before following her headmistress. Her eyes snapped feverishly between the foot of the stairs to their left, the entrance hallway ahead and the front door. Melissa paused before the doorway to the right, peering into Amira's bedroom. Alicia crept up behind her and reached for her shoulder, but her fingers grasped the air as Melissa entered the room. With a crash, she brought the bottle down on the corner of a bedpost.

Alicia stepped into the doorway as Melissa ran at Peter. The man was standing by Amira's beside, cradling a brass bowl in his left arm and holding a small wooden mallet in his right. His lips parted as the woman crossed the floor, brandishing the broken neck of the bottle. The bowl struck the lid of the terrarium with a clang and the mallet rolled beneath Amira's bed. Melissa lifted the dripping green shard to Peter's throat and a thin smile broke his sombre face.

'A bold move, Melissa. Desperate times?'

Champagne bubbles popped on her trembling hand as she waved the sharp corner of the bottle's neck before her husband's jugular.

'I gave you David,' she hissed through clenched teeth. 'And now—' still brandishing the bottle, she thumbed over her shoulder to the figure in the doorway. 'Now her. Now give me my son!'

Peter's predatory eyes left Melissa's and locked upon Alicia. His lips fell, his languid gaze was penetrated by a fascination so intense that it bordered on fear. Alicia squeezed the handle of the kitchen knife and Peter's curious smile returned, the cleft in his lip revealing a canine.

'Alicia Crow,' he nodded slowly, reverently, his voice a low rumble. 'I was about to wake Amira here, so that we might arrange a meeting. Thanks to my loving wife, that won't be necessary.' He spoke genially while his loving wife held broken glass to his neck. 'Rainn tells me you have been cooperative. That you have shown patience, passing each of our tests. No doubt, you will be relieved to hear there is just one more. And then we can make an exchange.'

Alicia eyed the bed to her left and Peter drew a hand to his mouth, barely concealing a smile that would take up permanent residence in her memory banks.

'Oh, you didn't think...?'

Alicia tore the bedcovers aside to reveal a large teddy bear. She blinked, as if to close her eyes might change the world around her.

But nothing changed. She watched Melissa avert her eyes, unable to meet her gaze. She watched Melissa sneak into her former home and slip a bear beneath the covers, baiting her trap. Her final bid.

The knife slipped through Alicia's fingers and the strength left her legs. She slumped onto the bed, gripping the shoulder of the bear and looking at Peter through blurred eyes.

'Where is he?'

'David is in Portugal with Aldous. And Morna. Under lock and key.' Peter brushed the glass at his throat aside, as if it were a bouquet of flowers, and tucked a hand down the top of his shirt to withdraw a long iron key at the end of a silver chain. 'A key that I am prepared to part with, *if* you do as you are told.'

Kill the lamb.

The glistening shard of the broken bottle reminded Alicia of the glass blade of a dagger. Ryan was built like his father. Built by his father. Engineered to murder. Warped to a point where his mother had no option but to hand him over to be fixed. Ryan believed himself a simulacrum, spared the horror of his past. In that moment, Alicia envied him.

Kill him, she thought, urging Melissa to drive the glass into Peter's neck so she might break that chain and take the key. With both hands, she gripped the bear, breathing through her nostrils. No sound escaped her lips.

Melissa's resolve appeared to have softened, and she lifted a hand to steady the heavy broken bottle.

'And Ryan?'

Peter returned his pale eyes to Melissa, remembering that she was there. He tucked the key under his shirt and placed a hand on her shoulder.

'In the Pagoda. Come.' He pushed past her. Melissa's eyes lingered on the terrarium, as if fearful that whatever lurked inside had been woken by the clamour. Her expression was resigned as she trod the carpet behind her husband, holding the bottle awkwardly at her side.

Peter stopped at the foot of the bed upon which Alicia sat. She considered reaching for the knife on the floor, but lacked the strength to move. Peter followed her eyeline and nudged the blade with the toe of his shoe.

'We won't be long,' he said. 'Stay here. Eyes open. When I'm back, I'll show you where your grandmother died. And what she left behind.'

He kicked the knife under the bed and Melissa followed him from the room.

Piñata

SHE WAS A piñata. Strung up to be beaten until she broke. She could attempt to hold herself together, strengthening the unseen bonds that kept her whole for as long as possible, but to what end? Was it not in the best interests of the piñata to let itself fall apart? To let greedy hands take what they want and to endure as little suffering as possible?

Alicia sat on the bed and clutched the bear in her arms, its soft white fur reminiscent of the lamb. The bear had been designed, manufactured and purchased to bring comfort. She ran a finger around the loop of the tartan ribbon about its neck. The fabric was frayed and she considered its age. Loose stitching around the left shoulder suggested that the arm had once been reattached. Had Ryan held the bear as she did now, in lieu of someone to love? Had Melissa snuck into her son's bedroom higher in the house, found nothing but this bear in his bed and decided to put it to a new use? The bear was designed to be hugged; she was designed to be—

Enough.

Melissa had seen Alicia at her weakest, dissolving in self-pity. She was an adult now, and would not allow herself to wallow. She had allowed herself to hope and now she must suffer the consequences. Hope was a drug, designed by wanting minds to make things feel temporarily better and then infinitely worse. For two years, she had drugged herself with hope and it had brought nothing but pain.

She rose from the mattress with the bear in her arms and studied the glass terrarium at Amira's beside. It was too deep for the pine chest of drawers, hanging half an inch over the front and back, such that the chest did not lie flush against the wall. A sheet of cardboard—the back of a cereal box—had been leaned against it on Amira's side, covered in a scribbled rota for cooking, cleaning and tending to the vegetables. Should Amira look up from her pillow, the cardboard would obscure anything that pressed itself against the glass. Melissa had glanced at the terrarium with what Alicia had believed to be trepidation, perhaps fearing that whatever lurked within had been disturbed when the mallet struck the lid. Yet the snake that lay across the red soil was made of rubber.

This was not the first time that Alicia had misread Melissa's emotions. Crying in the snow with the poster in her fingers, she had mistaken guilt for empathy; perhaps it was with guilt that Melissa had regarded the terrarium, eyeing the object used to torment the girl she had forsaken. She had told Alicia the experiments were Peter's, but how complicit had Melissa been?

One hour and I will tell you everything. Those had been Anna's parting words. If Alicia's mother had asked to be driven to Burnflower, she would not have been back within an hour. What had she wanted from Melissa? Alicia's finger slipped between the bear's neck and the tartan ribbon as she considered the lies used to bait her.

She pulled her attention from the tightness in her chest to the wooden mallet on the floor by Amira's bedpost. Beside it lay the upended brass bowl that Peter had planned to use to wake Amira, so that he might arrange a meeting with Alicia. But why not ask Rainn? She thought of Peter tearing the label from Rainn's birthday present and wondered what she had done to upset him. As his wife had buried her guilt, he had swallowed his rage, wearing an insidious smile as he brandished the key to a door in Portugal. Fixating on that silver chain, Alicia's finger tightened against the tartan collar. Had she come so far and waited so long only to find that David was in—

Five. She silenced the thought.

Four. She steadied her breathing.

Three. Rainn had offered to take her to Aldous and Morna when she defeated Amira.

Two. She had defeated Amira; she did not have to wait.

One. Peter would lead Melissa to Ryan, and Ryan would—

Snap. The ribbon broke beneath her finger. Ryan would retrieve the key and Gus the letters that led to a locked door. With a soft smile, Alicia carried the bear to the empty bed and closed her eyes.

Will and expectation: her world was not built on hope.

DOWN THE WELL, Alicia blinked to Psarnox. Eddies of wind lifted strands of hair from her forehead as she gazed over the edge of the crater. Amira rode a burning wave around the platform, on a board identical to the one Rainn had conjured. What was surely a simulacrum stood in the centre of the obsidian disc—how else to explain the image of Winter? Rainn had dressed her in a white linen shirt and black trousers, with a broad leather belt about her waist. Her face was the picture of disdain.

Alicia scanned the peaks, the rim, the shelves and tunnel entrances, but could not see the puppeteer. Armed only with that hostile glare, Winter's simulacrum lowered her palms to her sides, and from them issued a white vapour. The heavy mist drifted across the obsidian, which crackled like cubes of ice dropped into a cold drink. Rolling outward and beyond the platform, the mist cooled the lava from red to grey and the molten lake solidified, each bubble on its surface trapped as a crisp hissing filled the crater. The platform ground to a halt and Amira met the simulacrum's eyes as the lava around her board froze solid, the wood trapped and crushed as the ice expanded. The mist continued to emanate from those down-facing palms, driving the heat from the volcano as Alicia had driven the red from the petals of the orchid.

This was no simulacrum. Alicia had seen that expression on Winter's face a dozen times before, when overconfident girls in junior years had the audacity to approach her in the school canteen. Desperate to seek the approval of the larger ego, they had broken ranks, only to be playfully dismissed. Alicia gazed upon a crystal wasteland with Winter at its frozen heart. Had Rainn found someone else to pull the wings off her flies?

Amira's dark eyes were wide and uncertain as she took tentative steps across the frozen lava, her bare feet leaving misty footprints. She stepped onto the platform and vanished immediately, not for fear of Winter, but because Alicia had blinked to its edge. Evidently, only two were permitted to fight at once.

'What are you doing here?' Alicia fired. To Winter's credit, it took no more than a second for her to compose herself, her shock returning to disdain. A scathing tone resonated between Alicia's ears, as Winter replied: '*Distracting her.*'

Rainn leaned against the entrance to a tunnel, beneath where Alicia had stood on the rim.

'I won't let you kill me,' Winter seethed aloud, an edge of panic in her voice. She lifted a bare foot from the platform and a single blade rose lengthways through the skin of her sole.

'*Threaten me, you idiot,*' said Winter. '*Tell me you hate me.*'

Alicia forced a scowl. 'I won't let you torture that girl. It's time you got what you deserved.'

'*This isn't a drama class,*' projected Winter.

Not taking her eyes off Alicia, Winter began to skate across the ice. A cheer echoed around the Playground. The shelves were filled with translucent facsimiles of Winter in short black dresses and gold belts.

'*Really?*' said Alicia.

'*That wasn't me,*' said Winter. '*That was her. Would you actually do something, please?'*

Winter's words thronged with impatience, stinging Alicia's skull as if she had swallowed a chunk of ice. With leather skating boots tight on her feet, Alicia joined her. The pair circled the edge of the platform, eyes locked across the distance as they continued their private exchange.

Winter began, '*She told me you're here to kill me. She wants me to prove myself, so you'd better—*'

Rainn's words drowned out Winter's, filling Alicia's mind: '*They're watching you, Alicia. Aldous and Morna. Amira is weak; they see no triumph in her defeat. But Winter...she considers your mother responsible for the death of the only boy who knew her secrets. She will never let you beat her. Wake her up, and you will prove your value.*'

When Rainn had finished speaking, Alicia did not search the onion-skin audience for her great-grandparents. She did not hunt for hidden eyes, but relayed Rainn's message to Winter as they circled the platform. The fury in Winter's chestnut eyes was genuine as she spoke aloud: 'We'll see if you're as pathetic as you look.'

'*What are you doing here? Why are you distracting her?*' asked Alicia.

'*She kidnapped me and Gus. We're in Portugal, I think. He's—*'

'*Kidnapped? How?*'

'*Yes, shut up. Say something!*'

'You're all talk,' said Alicia, gliding across the ice. 'You'll need more than words to burn me here.'

'*Terrifying,*' Winter projected through a scowl. '*Gus is looking for a phone. I'm keeping her here while he finds it. She told me if I can wake you up—*'

The connection broke, and Alicia was alone in her head as Rainn projected words to Winter. The pair continued to skate, carving circles around the edge of the disc, like grooves in a vinyl record. Alicia waited, not daring to continue their exchange, in case her words travelled to Rainn's ears.

'*She's getting impatient,*' projected Winter. '*She's asked me to attack.*'

'*Do it. They're watching me, and if I beat you, she'll take me to David. But you need to put up a fight. Make it real. Guns, and bombs, and—*'

'This is for Jack,' said Winter aloud. Captivated by that hateful expression, Alicia did not see the storm clouds materialise overhead. Droplets hit the frozen platform with a sizzle and Alicia glanced up at the dark clouds. The rain fell harder and she felt it burn.

Tibetan bowl

THE WHITE BEAR rose and fell on Alicia's chest, and Amira tightened her grip on the kitchen knife. Waking to find a stranger in her bedroom, she had reached for a long shard of glass on the damp carpet and saw the blade poking out from beneath the bed. She had assumed it was Rainn who had blinked into combat, embarrassed by her failure, forcing her to wake when she stepped onto the platform. Now she knew who had taken her place on the obsidian disc. The young woman slept with one arm around the bear's throat. The tartan ribbon, torn from its neck, lay crumpled on the floor.

I know you're at Burnflower. I'm looking for—

Ryan? Amira shuddered. The dread thickened as she recalled Rainn's warning.

This girl has come to kill us. For once, Amira, prove your value.

On the wicker chair, the cord of her dressing gown twisted in a breeze that nipped at her exposed ankles. Since the bedroom window was shut, the front or back door must have been left open. The knife trembled in Amira's hand as she stepped around the sleeping stranger to see muddy shoes discarded by the lower half of a champagne bottle. The end of a shoelace had fallen into a broken corner, drawing liquid from a small pool. Her bedroom smelled of alcohol and dirt. Folding her arms across her undersized pyjamas, she peered into the hallway. The front door was open.

'Peter?' she called up the stairs, loud enough to fill the house but not beyond it. He was presumably in the Pagoda, where he spent his waking hours. Had he forgotten to shut the door or had this intruder forced it open? The breeze was cold and she stole back into her bedroom and crept past the stranger, avoiding wet patches that darkened the teal carpet. She threaded the knife through the arm of her dressing gown and sunlight caught an overturned brass bowl at the foot of her bed: Peter's Tibetan singing bowl. Had this girl tried to wake her?

She shot a glance through the open front doorway, beyond the patio to the thicket of bulrushes by the nearest pond and then turned for the stairs. She carried the mallet and bowl because Peter would want her to return them. She would ask him what they were—she had not heard him on the phone to Rainn while she pretended to sleep.

After a peek in Ryan's bedroom to check it was empty, swift steps led her down the corridor—Peter would want her to return his items quickly. Her dressing gown flowed behind her as she marched up to the master bedroom and knocked firmly on the door.

'Peter?'

No answer. Down the corridor she tried his study and, when there was no response, she stood with her back to it. Facing the door to the attic, she could no longer pretend why she held the bowl and mallet. She swallowed her heartbeat, bent to lift the edge of the carpet by the doorframe and took the key. She forced the reluctant key into the lock and turned it and opened the door and stepped inside and closed it behind her. And breathed.

Cobwebs wavered, thrilled by movement in the stale air. She tightened her gown, pinching her waist, fearful that the hem might catch on cobwebs on either side of the wooden staircase. Her body tensed as she ascended the narrow steps, assaulted with eight-legged memories. Promising to desensitise Amira, Rainn had lined the volcanic shelves with species known and imagined. Amira was not to wake until she had touched them all.

'It worked!' Amira had lied, forcing the corners of her mouth into her cheeks.

At the top of the stairs, she placed a tentative foot on the wooden floorboards. Ryan lay on a mattress in the middle of the attic, a grey-white sheet covering his grey-blue skin, pale as a cadaver.

Out of habit, her eyes searched the wooden rafters for spiders alive or dead.

Stop it, she scolded, her voice as firm as Rainn's. *Prove your value, Amira, for once.*

Every inch of the rafters as high as she could reach bore repeated carvings of the same number. She had carved them secretly at first, when she believed that Peter ventured into the attic. On the back of beams and on the inner drawers of old cabinets, she had scratched Ryan's favourite number with an iron nail. She would show him, secretly, when he woke.

Every day, he had set *29* as the volume on his cassette player and rolled dice until he totalled it.

Do you ever get numbers stuck in your head? he had asked her as the dice tumbled through the classroom door and into the kitchen. *And wonder where they come from?*

For three years, Vivador had sustained him. He had lain on that mattress while his soul inhabited another realm, somehow managing to replenish his physical body. Wherever he was in Vivador, he needed no food or water. No comfort. When Amira started to suspect she was the only one who visited him, she left the key under the carpet at a certain angle, so she would know if Peter had used it. But Peter never visited his son, and she had taken the long nail to the bricks and beams, so that Ryan would see the number when he woke.

She didn't know if Peter was in the Pagoda, or what that stranger was doing in her bedroom, and she had no time to waste. She carried the mallet and bowl to Ryan's side. Her eyes flitted to the sheet at the end of the room, covering the mirror, and her knees stopped wobbling when she sat cross-legged by Ryan's waxwork head.

The thoughts that made her weak returned—louder now.

What if he pushed her?

What if he killed Sam?

The questions were carved into her mind like the numbers on the beams, tattooed through repetition. The sheet stretched across Ryan's chest as he filled his lungs, reminding her that he was still living. Alive and alone.

Rainn had cried and Melissa had cried and Peter had shaken his head. And she had believed them. Ryan was safer here, and there: his body locked in the attic, his soul trapped in the immaterial realm.

When she had left the bathroom late one night, she saw Peter fiddling with the carpet and she had decided to test herself. She wanted to be brave, to prove her value—just once—to nobody but herself. She had dared herself to look, just once. And then she had returned. She would desensitise herself, in her own time, to the boy they called a murderer. She watched him sleeping in the dark, bloodless skin on his handsome cheeks, and wondered if he really led his brother here one night. Did he really push Rainn from the Pagoda? And if he did, was his punishment to lie alone under the cobwebs, forever?

She looked at the thick wooden mallet. It resembled the truncated end of a broom handle.

Just be confident, Amira!

She lifted the mallet to the bowl and circled the rim until a low hum reached her ears. The sound haunted the room and she dropped the mallet, which landed in the bowl with a dull clang.

Cursing her clumsiness, she picked it up and set her teeth together. She sat up on her knees and promised herself that she would not fail again.

At first, the sound was orange. Timid and warm. But as she continued to run the mallet around the rim of the bowl, the colour changed from orange to blue. Not any blue, but the bright, glacial blue she had seen in happy, unpredictable eyes across the breakfast table. The eyes of a boy with a smile at odds with the acts he had committed.

The hum grew louder and she raised her eyes to the skylight above, certain that the glass was trembling. The blue intensified until it had embodied the air around her, from the carved beams to the marrow of her bones. Willing his eyes to open, Amira studied the scar on his face: the jagged white line that ran from the corner of his left eye halfway to his ear. After he murdered Sam, Ryan had fallen and hit the corner of the mirror.

The scar twitched and Amira dropped the mallet. This time, it landed on Ryan's chest. It did not roll onto the floor but settled on his sternum.

The scar had not twitched: she had imagined it. She sat back, defeated and afraid. The Tibetan bowl had not worked when Peter tried it before, though that was when Amira had pretended to sleep. He had phoned Rainn and Amira held her breath to hear fragments of an explanation: it would work on Ryan, but not Amira.

She's not between the mirrors.

Amira looked from the mirror covered with the sheet to the stairs at the end of the attic. If Ryan was between mirrors, where was the other one?

She placed the bowl beside his head and stood. If she rushed to the Playground while the stranger slept and Peter worked in the Pagoda, she might trick Rainn. She could say that Peter had asked her to wake Ryan, and Rainn might tell her where the other mirror was hidden.

Satisfied with an excuse to leave the attic (or at least to defer her failure) Amira scampered down the stairs. While the sound of her footsteps was audible, the thrumming of the bowl continued to resonate, too low for her to hear.

She closed the door and Ryan opened his eyes.

CHAPTER EIGHT
Rewrite

THERE HAD BEEN complications with Ryan's birth; Melissa and Peter would be unable to have a second child. Both were keen for their son to grow up with other children, and Sam's adoption had seemed a fine solution. But as the boys grew, Melissa started to question her husband's interest in the epileptic child.

At university, she had been drawn to Peter's passion. It was not a passion for her—it was never a passion for her—but for his postdoctoral work. While her friends lost interest in his fanciful ideas on how to cheat the subconscious and conquer fear, she found herself enrapt. Quiet, but never shy, he was often frustrated by people's indifference to the nature of their lives. He shook his head dismissively when the topic of conversation drifted back to sports, celebrities or the weather. In bed at night, he would tell her how sheep were selectively bred to lack curiosity, and that her friends were no different, daydreaming through their lives.

'He's very intense,' said her elderly mother. That's what Melissa had liked about him.

Now, she followed her estranged husband down the gravel path that branched from the patio to fork between the seven ponds, and she wondered how she had ever loved him. Patches of weed spread through the gravel like mould, and the pond borders were wild. Peter's pace was unhurried as he led her towards the Pagoda. The morning sky was cloudless, a brilliant blue paling at the edges. The central pond was the largest and deepest; her father had once convinced her that his old car lay at the bottom, though the circular pool would struggle to conceal more than a motorbike. She recalled

Ryan and Sam on the edge of this pond, standing in their under-pants as they fished with sticks and string tied around Haribo rings until the backs of their necks were red. Ryan had raced inside, declaring in a high-pitched voice that Sam had eaten his sweet straight out of the pond.

Peter had talked at length of his concerns that Ryan was jealous of Sam, and the effect this might have on their son's development. If the boy feared that his biological parents loved the adopted child more, would Ryan be able to form a healthy relationship with him?

Melissa started to wonder whether Peter was not simply observing the boys' behaviour patterns but creating them. Did he pay such attention to Sam to further his research into epilepsy, or was he deliberately trying to make Ryan envy his brother?

Sam had a fatal epileptic attack in the attic and Melissa tried to convince herself it was an accident. Ryan had only been playing with the torch; he had meant no harm. Whispers in the bathroom mirror became a daily mantra, and Melissa grew adept at lying to herself. She wrote the narrative that absolved her of guilt.

Amira was chosen for her synaesthesia. Driving from Sunny Climes children's home, Melissa had watched the six-year-old in her rear-view mirror. A little rat sleeping on its way to the lab. The girl would giggle when Peter presented her with cuddly snakes, dyed different colours, and asked her what they tasted of. The experiments were amusing, and Melissa smiled at the spring in her husband's step as he set off between the ponds to devise another set of harmless tests.

As a growing pressure will transform carbon to diamond, her suspicion hardened to belief. When Amira's bed was filled with spiders, she questioned Ryan, but not Peter. The patterns fitted the theory, but they were not proof. She might have asked him whether he had taken to experimenting on the girl while she slept; but there was no need when she had the spare key to his study. Why confront him when she could unlock the door and read his files first-hand?

When the opportunity arose and Peter left for a weekend, Melissa did not seize it. She convinced herself that she was scared of her husband. She convinced herself that to challenge him was a threat to Ryan's safety. But it was not Peter that she feared; she left that key at the back of the kitchen drawer because her theory remained unproven. If she knew the truth—if she raided his files and learned the extent of her husband's experiments—then she would have no choice but to act on it.

Enter Rainn. The fifteen-year-old who had set fire to her grandparents' house while sleepwalking. The orphan that Peter had ostensibly found because she shared the name he had given their home. The orphan who was not an orphan, but a girl who had fled her British father and moved to England to find out what had happened to her Singaporean mother.

The seventh pond curled around the uneven ground like one of Dali's clocks. Melissa raised her gaze to the Pagoda, up the hexagonal walls that rose twenty feet to the bamboo roof supported by floor-to-ceiling arches.

'A place to think,' Peter had said, in one of the rare moments he spent with her in the first year of their marriage. She had plenty of time to think, since he spent every waking hour building the tower by hand, making his mark on her parents' land. And when it was finished, he renamed their home.

'Burnflower? Isn't that the name of the girl in your year at university? The one who died?' she had not asked him. When he had completed the tower, a heaviness in his shoulders had lifted, and she chose to enjoy his buoyant mood rather than dwell on the reasons behind it.

In the glare of the morning light, her fatigued mind played tricks on her: the ghost of Rainn, legs dangling beneath the arch, risking her life so Melissa would believe that Ryan had tried to kill her. Leaking from the eyes and nose, the young woman had sobbed on Melissa's shoulder, asking why Ryan had done it. Why had he pushed her off and then jumped?

There, there, Melissa had soothed, saying no more as Ryan lay comatose in his bed. She knew why her son had done it. First Sam, and now Rainn: the victims of his envy.

Shaped like a kidney bean, the outer pond was bordered by chrysanthemum, peony and a thicket of weeds. Brushing past, Melissa caught her reflection in the water. 'Stoneface,' the students called her, but she had not always been this hard. She had comforted Amira when she trembled at the shadows of fish in the water, or pushed the slices of cucumber from her plate with the butt of her knife. Tears wet her neck as the girl pressed her head to Melissa's shoulder, craving a mother's protection.

But she had known why the tears had fallen. What was overwritten was never lost. Denied, repressed, her guilt had festered, hollowing her from within to leave nothing but a hardened shell— nothing but a woman capable of luring a blind child into her car.

Rewrite, she thought savagely, clenching her teeth at the magnitude of her self-deception.

The path extended beyond the seventh pond to the Pagoda, ran in a straight line through uncut grass and down a gentle slope that fell to the trees. Checking the buttons on her jacket, Melissa stared at the back of Peter's head. She did not need to see his face to read his expression. After twenty years of marriage, she knew it like her own: cool and purposeful. A wolf stalking its prey. She had provided him with the land he needed to conduct his experiments and the children on which to conduct them; he had wanted no more from her. She had long given up yearning for affection, vying for his attention or demanding his respect. And while she did not respect her husband, she envied what he had: an unshakeable peace of mind. How much easier it must be to write your chosen narrative without that querulous voice of reason in your mind.

The path ended in the flagstones beside a patch of long grass where she had found her fallen son. The glass of the broken bottle was warm in her hands, a heartbeat in her thumb, as she remembered the folded paper that had poked from his pockets. She took a breath and followed Peter under the archway.

To the right, spiralling steps led to his office and the uppermost floor. To the left stood the wooden door to the cellar. A curt glance over his shoulder, and Peter blocked Melissa with his back as he entered a code into the padlock on the door.

Peter opened the door and light spilled on the steps that wound along the wall to the ground below. The cellar beneath the tower was hewn from a light stone, so rough and bare it resembled a large well. The circular space was wide enough to accommodate a single mattress at the foot of the steps, three wine barrels that had once been filled with her father's vintage, crates of foreign lager and an array of rusted garden tools perched against the wall. Peter stepped aside and Melissa took the first two steps, just enough to see that the boy on the mattress was David Harrington.

The throes of agony

WINTER WINCED WHEN Alicia screamed. As the droplets seared her skin, Alicia sent her will strong and metallic along the outline of her body, rendering herself invulnerable to the acid rain. Winter stood unharmed beneath the downpour. With her focus on the attack, she withdrew her influence on the frozen volcano. Were it Aldous or Morna, Peter or Rainn, who had set the platform rotating on a bed of lava, their will persisted and the ice began to crack.

Holding her body together like a piñata, Alicia was consumed by her defence. In this state, it would take just one strike to defeat her. Leaving enough strength in her body to resist the burning rain, she felt for the melting platform. In great tendrils, she buried her will in the volcanic glass beneath her feet.

The platform trembled, lava seeped through the cracks and Winter waited for the revolutions to resume. Alicia held the platform in her mind and let her body go. As the acid burned, she ripped through the frozen obsidian, tearing it to pieces. The ground detonated and Winter was launched into the air. Through conscious or unconscious design, both of them landed on a chunk of black ice that bobbed in the molten rock.

Alicia steadied herself on the block, shifting her heels against grooves in the ice. Winter rose skyward on a frozen pillar and Alicia joined her rival, extending the block from the surface of the lake. The pair stood tall on top of their pillars, facing one another from opposing sides of the crater. The dark storm cloud stretched across the sky, rippling with lightning. Thunder reverberated through the air and Psarnox trembled.

A green glow lit the gloom: capital letters tattooed across the walls of the crater. From the surface of the bubbling lake to the jagged rim, a thousand copies of a single word.

MURDERER.

With a hand to her chest, Alicia's gaze raced between the slanted messages, broken by tunnels and fissures, warped by translucent forms with hands to their mouths, stifling giggles. Around her ribcage, a coil tightened, braced to snap. Then, there was an anomaly in the identical crowd: Amira emerging from the tunnel where Rainn had stood, her eyes transfixed by the writing on the wall. On Winter's face, a hateful grin—

A lie. These blazing letters were not a taunt, but an apology.

'*I didn't know—I never would have...I'm so sorry.*' The words hummed between Alicia's ears like the mournful note of a violin. Not pity, but authenticity. She met those chestnut eyes and knew that in another realm, tears slid down a sleeping face.

'*I need to see my brother,*' Alicia stated. '*Don't hold back.*'

Winter mimicked the surfer's stance, raising one hand to the sky and the other before her, fingers splayed. Alicia marvelled at the intensity of the storm above, so thick with thunderbolts that the light was a strobe upon them. Lightning left the cloud at multiple locations to land on Winter's waiting hand. Channelling the great energy through her body, she sent the lightning along her outstretched arm, through her nails, and blasting across the crater.

In the throes of agony, people speak of a white-hot pain. A flame will burn red, orange and blue before transitioning to white. Alicia had seen nothing as bright, felt nothing as hot and experienced nothing as painful as the energy that coursed through her, tearing at every unreal atom of her projected body. She was gripping an electric fence. Blinded. To let go was to wake.

And then it ended. In the shadow of the storm cloud, ten thousand pairs of eyes glinted from the shelves, awaiting Alicia's move. But what to do when the options are endless? She could stab and slash, blast and burn; she could send an infinite number of horrors to maim and maul Winter's body. Wracking her mind for an original assault, Alicia spotted a familiar face on the rim of the crater. Lightning played across the cloud beyond her.

'*Winter fears no attack on her body because her body does not exist,*' hissed Rainn. '*You must attack what lies before you.*'

Whether Aldous and Morna watched from the shelves, or whether that was another lie, Alicia knew that Rainn was right about Winter. Those projected words had been tainted with guilt, but not fear. Winter understood this for the game it was. Alicia needed to prove to Rainn that she was ready to face her family.

'*I need to wake you up now,*' said Alicia to Winter. '*Don't worry about the phone—tell Gus I'll send Joe.*'

A flicker of protest might have crossed Winter's face. It might have been the lightning.

'*I hope you find him,*' Winter replied, her scowl unbroken.

A chanting rose as the simulacrum army called Winter's name, urging her to finish this battle and drive Alicia from the Playground. Winter relaxed into the role, raising her chin in a supercilious manner.

'*Can you see it?*' Rainn asked Alicia. '*Now seize it.*'

Alicia reached across the crater with her mind's eye. When she reached Winter's projected body, she sought what lay within. Looking beyond her eyes, she fastened on that which Ryan had lacked: the ego. Winter's perfect smile faltered.

Lightning struck the crater's rim and rock cascaded into the lake as Alicia held Winter in her grasp. It was not Winter's body that she strove to drive from Vivador, but her soul. The young woman began to flicker, passing through each colour of the spectrum as she lost her definition. For a split second, she was no more than a glassy outline and then the pillar was empty.

It might have felt like victory had every simulacrum not dropped to their knees and screamed.

Matricide

MELISSA DROPPED THE broken bottle at Peter's feet and raised her hands to her face. She hurried down the steps to the mattress at the bottom. David lay on his back, his head on a pillow with no case. His blue lips and pale cheeks matched the stripes on his pyjamas, and she might have thought him dead had his chest not risen and fallen beneath the cotton. The light shifted as Peter crouched to retrieve the broken bottle. Wearing a mask of surprise, Melissa turned to face him.

'Another lie,' she whispered. 'You told me that you needed other minds to fix Ryan, and I did not question it. I took that position at Valmont and I would have done anything you asked of me. Anything. This—' she spread her arms, gesturing at the cellar, '—*tell her he's here, lock the door, problem solved!* This I understand. But why tell me that he died?'

Peter descended the stairs. Light strained through the grass outside, through brick vents near the ceiling and caught the jagged glass in his hands, curling green shadows along the wall. On the farthest of the three barrels lay a black tin, slightly larger than a lunchbox. A finger of green light caressed the tin and Melissa steered her eyes to Peter's face.

'In Psarnox, Aldous has a pair of mirrors,' Peter growled. 'Suspended between these mirrors, a person is unable to separate their true self from the infinite reflections. In this state, the self will erode, deteriorating in its search for identity amid illusion. Between these mirrors, Ryan lost himself. He was a clean slate.'

'That's what I asked for. That's what you promised me. You should have returned him to me. You didn't send me to Valmont for other minds, Peter. You sent me for the Harrington family—and I would have given them to you. What sense was there in telling me that he had died?'

Peter drew the glass against the wall as he reached the bottom step, scraping a chalky line into the brick. He put down the broken bottle and stood by the barrel. Melissa did not permit herself to look at the tin.

'Only in Vivador is the memory wiped. In the waking world, history returns. Here, he would know nothing other than his ruinous past. What he did to Sam,' he said, scratching the cleft in his upper lip, 'such things cannot be undone. We could not give you what you wanted, Aldous and I. So, he cleared the mirrors for David and took Ryan as a simulacrum.'

'You couldn't fix him, so you used him as bait,' she said bitterly, tightening the knot at the back of her head. 'When I found that grave empty, did I rush to the police? No. I took David for you. And if it was Anna or Alicia you were after, I would have taken them too.'

'I read her letters.'

Melissa swallowed.

'You sent her to Portugal,' Peter continued. 'You sent her to Aldous and Morna. If it weren't for you, that book would never have ended up in her—'

'And I would have got it back! I said I would get it back. There was no need to send Rainn to my house!'

'It is rude to interrupt people while they are talking.' Peter closed his eyes and pinched his nose, his expression weary. 'Do you have any idea how much easier it would have been to let them kill you? I set you up in that school. Played the long game. Just to give you purpose. I gave you value in their eyes. You are alive because of me.'

'You killed me when you broke our son,' said Melissa. Blinking back tears, she let her eyeline hover on the screw in the wall where the gardening gloves had hung. She sniffed, straightened up and adopted a forceful tone.

'Lock me in, go on. Go ahead. You shut that door, and I'll enter Vivador. I'll wait in that tower.' She pointed a finger to the ceiling, as if twin thrones revolved between the arches on the upper floor. 'And when Alicia returns, I will tell her where her brother is.'

She held her breath. She need only endure that arrogant smile for as long as it took him to open the tin. He picked it up. Fingered the clasp. Ready to brandish a collar before her eyes and let her know that he had beaten her. Again.

Peter opened the clasp, lifted the lid and Melissa absorbed the change in his face. He did not scream when he dropped it. Two rubber collars bounced across the concrete floor and a snake slithered between the barrels.

He held his right hand in his left, pinching the bite mark. Their eyes locked just long enough for Melissa to witness her husband's fear: his weapon of choice used against him.

Peter darted through the door. Melissa followed. She reached his office to find him struggling with the padlock. Nudging him aside, she entered the four digits that she had used on both locks earlier that morning. Peter knew what he would find when his wife let him into the office: an empty space on the shelf where the box of anti-venom had been kept.

'Where is it?' he asked, eyes flicking along the shelf to the tub of rubber snakes.

'Far enough,' she replied.

Peter walked around the desk and settled in his chair. With his bitten hand raised near his chin, he opened the drawer and withdrew a mobile phone, surprised that Melissa had not removed it.

'You should probably call an ambulance,' said Melissa in a

monotone. 'But what was it that you said to Amira when you presented her with that tank, and placed it by her bedside? Twenty minutes?'

In the theatre of Peter's imagination, his wife replaced the snake in the terrarium with a rubber toy and hid the reptile in the box of collars.

Melissa opened the filing cabinet and pulled out the file she had read three hours before. The chair creaked as Peter leaned back, watching her read his notes on Ryan. She sifted through the pages, conscious of her husband watching her skim material she had already absorbed; letting him know what she knew. When climbing into bed late at night, having returned from a day in the Pagoda, had he watched her sleeping as he dreamed these plans?

'Matricide,' he uttered, as if his eyes were in her head. As if he knew what page she had settled on. 'Do you know how difficult it is to break the bond between mother and son?'

She returned the file and tugged Rainn's from the drawer. Rainn: the final playing piece in his twisted game. Ryan was to fall in love with her, and Melissa would send her away. Ryan would hate her for it. But her son had not fallen for Rainn; he had pushed her. Ryan was unable to love.

'Is that what my murder would prove?' she asked curiously, her eyes unable to focus on the page. 'That love could be destroyed? Like your love for Hazel?'

Melissa withdrew the family tree she had found in Ryan's pocket. Her husband's motorbike had roared in her ears as she scanned its contents, and quickly put it back. The bike had dropped to the floor as he ran to his son's side. A moment later, she was lifting Ryan into her arms and Peter was locking the door to his office.

Her eyes now lingered on the name on the paper: Hazel Burnflower. Rainn's mother. The dead woman after whom he had renamed her parents' home. Peter watched his wife, her face taut with conflict, and imagined her keying a date into his padlocks.

'2001,' he breathed.

Melissa rested the file on top of the cabinet. Words slipped from her unsmiling mouth: 'The year we met.'

'The year she died. You cracked it.'

She shook her head. Before taking the bear from Ryan's bedroom last night, she had tried the door to the attic and found it locked. Had she tried to force it open, Peter might have woken. She would have to wait for him to unlock it for her. Or take the key from around his neck—the key that he claimed was to a door in Portugal.

The Pagoda did not require a key; after Ryan broke into his office, Peter had replaced the keyholes with padlocks.

'There are ten thousand possible combinations to a four-digit padlock,' said Melissa, arms hanging at her sides, lacking the energy to fold them. 'Lucky the first digit was a two. It took me under an hour.'

'You were always lucky,' said Peter.

She laughed and he smiled, surprising them both. Sweat had broken on his brow and his breathing was laboured. He would die in that chair. Her eyes drifted from the silver chain along his clavicle to the phone clasped in his unbitten hand.

'What did she do? Rainn?'

Peter's thoughts flickered: a torn label stamped into the floor.

'Nothing that I didn't expect of her.'

'It didn't look like you expected it.'

'It can be disappointing to learn that you were right.'

She nodded. 'That's something we can agree on.' She stepped up to the desk and leaned on it, as he had leaned on the kitchen counter, all the weight in her hands and frustration in her eyes. 'I wanted to give you the chance to tell me he was in the attic. One last chance to tell me something true. But I knew that you would lead me here.'

Peter swallowed and a bead of sweat slipped down his forehead, along the crease between his brows and into his eye. He blinked.

'Fear and hatred will always triumph over love.'

'I don't know love,' said Melissa, turning from the room. She heard him key a number into his phone as she went down to the cellar, her steps quickening. Where might she find the snake?

Active Nothing

UNABLE TO DISSUADE her, Gus had resigned himself to Winter's plan. He had left her in their shallow cave and dashed along the ledge towards the lighthouse. Cautious as a cat, he stalked from the bushes to the empty doorframe. A staircase to his right wound up the inner wall to the upper level, where the light was housed. The staircase was accessible only via a perforated metal door, which itself was blocked by a figure sleeping on her feet. Gus braced himself for the flutter of Rainn's eyelids, but she did not stir when he prised the rifle from her grasp. Her attention was elsewhere, her mind engaged in Vivador. His finger found the trigger and he trained the weapon at her chest, ready to shoot the woman while she slept. He hesitated. Were it Aldous or Morna in front of him, he might have been able to convince himself: taking vengeance for the murder of his parents. But Rainn was not his target.

He brushed the deadly thoughts aside and slung the strap of the rifle over his shoulder. There was no phone on the walls. He eyed the padlock on the steel door and considered searching Rainn for the key, but chose to investigate the door to his left. He found what might have been a storage room, now bare, with an open hatch in the centre of the concrete floor. With one last glance at Rainn, he stepped on the rusting ladder and descended into the dark.

Like mole rats, Aldous and Morna's hired hands had dug out a crude tunnel under the lighthouse which twisted beneath the crop of woodland and deeper into the peninsula. Gus ran his hands along rotting timber supports, his fingers slick with a slime that lined the rock. He had no time to waste. The ruse might end at any moment, as Peter and Rainn realised that an imposter stood before them. His walk became a jog, the rifle bouncing against his back. If he could reach his great-grandparents before Rainn woke, he would finish what his parents had set out to do on his seventeenth birthday.

Gus ran into a door. The rifle clattered to the floor and his hands searched the surface before him. Finding a keyhole, he stooped to peer through it, but saw nothing. The door would have fitted an old prison cell and the tunnel was barely broad enough to accommodate it. He slammed his shoulder against it with all the strength he could muster, but the iron did not give. In almost total darkness, he tripped over something on the ground, heavier than the rifle. Fingers grazed the rusting blade of a large axe. He pulled it upright, lifting the weapon over his shoulder and bringing it down upon the door. A loud clang issued back along the tunnel, but this axe was on the floor for a reason: whoever had last attempted to break this door had failed.

Seized by blind panic, Gus struck the door repeatedly. Each impotent strike reverberated down his arms, chipping away at nothing but his own resolve. They would know by now that Winter had deceived them. If he returned to the lighthouse to search for the key to unlock the door to find the phone, Rainn would be ready for him. Cursing in frustration, he slammed the axe against the door a final time and let the weapon drop from his hands.

Exhausted by his efforts, Gus took a couple of steps back and aimed the head of the rifle in the direction of the lock. He was standing in the pitch black, wondering how stupid a move this might be, when an agonised wail issued from the lighthouse. Taking this as a sign to abandon his efforts, he raced back along the tunnel. He climbed the ladder, through the hatch. Rainn's post was empty. A second scream spilled down the stairs and through the metal doorway. An image of Winter flooded his mind as he shouldered the rifle and charged up the steps.

The light spun in a sad and futile manner, straining against the daylight to cast its beam across the rocks. Rainn was sitting on the metal walkway with her back to the curved glass window, gazing at the rotating bulb. The spiral cord of a telephone stretched from her lap to a bracket on the wall behind her. Rainn's face was lined with tears and the passing beam lit her pupils. She did not raise her head when Gus approached.

'This is not how it was meant to be.' Her voice was flat, staring into the beam each time it struck her face. Gus gripped the rifle in both hands.

'What happened?'

Rainn looked up as the beam swept past and her face was contorted with emotion.

'She killed her.'

'Who?'

'Melissa killed Winter.'

Gus ran. Tripping down the spiralling steps, he burst from the building and into the woodland. Along the barren rock he raced, with the beam of the lighthouse against his back. He stumbled along the ledge, balancing himself with the rifle until he saw Sam's tail poking from the underhang. He slowed to a halt as the dog sniffed Winter's body.

He threw the rifle to the floor, shook her shoulders, shouted her name; but that beautiful face resisted his attention as defiantly as she had in life. Barks and growls punctuated desperate pleas. Sam paced the ledge, padding either side of Winter's legs, his tail shaking in agitation.

Barks and cries gave way to whining, and then to silence.

A GREY SEA undulated beneath the bleak, lifeless sky. Each wave gave the false impression of a journey to the shore as the sea rose and fell, creating the illusion of the water's progress. With his toes flush to the edge of the cliff, Gus followed the futile journey of a wave from its birth on the horizon to a certain death upon the jagged rocks of an unforgiving shore. When the white spray had bled away, the wave disappeared with no trace that it had ever been.

No furnace burned in Gus's chest. In the void of his anger lay a profound emptiness. That burning vengeance had led him to a locked door; Winter had sacrificed herself for nothing. The grey waves swelled hypnotically, waiting to swallow him. Distantly, he heard the clatter of pebbles dropping down the cliff face and heard the approach of footsteps. He blinked and ducked beneath the overhang, feeling a surge in his chest as the vacuum filled. He reached for the knife as Rainn walked around the corner.

Morning light caught the serrated edge of the blade as Gus held the knife to Rainn's throat. Rainn's heels shifted against the jagged lip of the cliff and loose stones fell silently into the ocean. A growl issued between Sam's teeth, but he remained by Winter's side, blue eyes moving between the pair.

'Lies,' Gus uttered with a tremble that ran from his lips to the knifepoint, 'your words. Your tears. You brought her here to die. You're done.'

'The man in the tower, Peter.' Rainn's voice was calm and certain, her cheeks dry. 'He is Melissa's husband. Melissa has struck a deal with Aldous in return for her son, Ryan. She has killed Winter. She will kill Alicia. Aldous believes that Alicia has the Sol, and she will die for it. Unless you stop Melissa.'

Ryan will take me to David.

Gus choked back a breath, his thoughts jumping between shelves in his mental library. Alicia's guide: Melissa's son.

'You told Peter that Alicia has the Sol—that he was wasting his time with me. If Melissa is after her, that's your doing. If Alicia dies, you've killed the pair of them.'

'I told Peter that Alicia has the Sol because I did not want you on that throne. I did not want them to take what you have.' Her throat shifted as she swallowed. 'Alicia destroyed the Unbreakable Door—that is why they think she inherited Eloise's willpower. But I don't. Why would I kidnap you, why would I come here, unarmed, if I did not believe that you had what they were after? Your parents knew. That's why they flew to Portugal. That's why they died here, up there…' She nodded beyond the overhang, in the direction of the woodland. Gus fought the urge to follow her gaze. 'They did not want the Order taking what you have. The Sol lies with you, Augustus. And I can show you how to use it against them.'

Gus searched those eyes for fragments of truth amid layers of deception. He could end her now, and who would know? Who would mourn her?

'Anna's letters lead to Psarnox,' Rainn continued. 'To their home in Vivador. But she could not reach them. They hide beyond a chasm, and that is where Alicia's mother failed. I have read the letters—I can take you to this chasm. If you have the Sol, you will cross it, and on the far side you will find their greatest weapon. That is the only way you can reach Melissa before she kills Alicia.'

Gus inched closer, moving the knife just millimetres. Rainn's foot slipped and she lurched forward to grip his shoulder with one hand and his wrist with the other.

'I am a liar and a murderer,' she said. 'One push and you will rid this world of me. One push, and you lose your only chance of saving your cousin.'

Rainn felt the knife falter. Holding Gus's gaze, she eased his wrist aside and stepped from the cliff's edge. He watched her duck beneath the overhang and lie on the ground. On her back, resting on her elbows, she patted the ground twice in invitation.

He ignored the growls of the husky, settled beside Winter and closed his eyes. Through the rush of the wind, Rainn whispered in his ear and Gus drifted into an uneasy sleep. Lucid footsteps under a starry sky carried him to the blowhole in the centre of the peninsula. As Rainn had described, a green vapour rose from the depths of the weathered hole as if it were a cauldron in the rock. It was through this portal that his great-grandparents had discovered the immaterial realm over sixty years before. With tendrils of green mist snaking around his ankles, Gus stepped over the edge and fell into Vivador.

He lay on the floor in a large, dark cavern lit by shafts of light that permeated the rock high above. He ran his eyes across the ceiling in search of the blowhole, but saw only the cracks through which the light fell. The underground chamber stretched to walls on his left and right so distant that he struggled to see them. Apart from the crystals glistening underfoot, the environment was unremarkable. He might have believed he was still on Earth, were it not for the luminescent green dress that Rainn wore.

She stood with her back to him on the edge of a wide chasm. Gus walked over, narrowing his eyes as he strained to see the far edge. It looked as if the cavern had been cleaved in two and set fifty metres apart. When Gus reached her side, Rainn swept a hand from behind her and drew a branch into view. The branch ignited, casting a shuddering light on their surroundings, though the light had no effect on the abyss before them. Slowly, Rainn extended her arm. As the burning torch crossed the cliff's edge, it disappeared as if it had passed through a curtain, leaving Rainn with nothing but a blunt stick in her hand. She drew her hand towards her and the branch reappeared to cast the pair in firelight.

Gus stepped cautiously to the edge of the abyss. He held his hand before him and turned to Rainn, who nodded. He inched his fingers over the edge and watched them vanish, passing into a perfect darkness. Gently, he withdrew his hand and flexed his fingers.

'What is it?'

'Active Nothing. Aldous and Morna decreed that nothing can exist here. Anna could not cross it. Neither can I.'

She turned from the chasm and observed him. As Gus stared into the void, he felt the weight of her expectation. All that remained was to determine whether he, and not Alicia, had inherited the Sol.

'*If you can cross this chasm,*' Rainn projected within his skull. '*You will find the portal that Aldous used to kill your parents. Through this portal, you can reach Melissa before she finds Alicia.*'

'And then what?' Gus asked aloud.

Rainn whispered into the void.

'You cannot let her live.'

Who is Ryan?

RYAN RAN A finger through the dust, tracing the number on the low beam. The 2 and 9 had been scored in straight lines along and against the grain of the wood, resembling figures on a digital clock. He lifted an iron nail from the floor beside the mattress and swept his eyes across dozens of 29s engraved into the beams and the floorboards, the exposed brick between the attic floor and the raftered roof, and the discarded, cobwebbed furniture.

Amira's tongue poked between her teeth as she drew the number 2, boxy and right-angled on the paper, dragging the blue crayon with uncertain, infant strokes.

The nail slipped through Ryan's fingers as the memory ghosted into focus like fragments of a dream: the six-year-old girl lying on her tummy on his bedroom floor; the deconstructed cereal box covered in numbers. He turned his face to the shaft of morning light that fell through the window in the slanted roof. Wearing only boxer shorts, he felt the sunlight warm his clammy skin and burn the retinas through his closed lids, scattering the ghosts.

He lowered his eyes to the blunt wooden mallet that had rolled off his chest when he woke. Beside this was an empty brass bowl. Like the needle of a record player, his eyes circled the rim of the bowl and a hum rang between his ears. The haunting sound brought forth a second memory, more recent yet more distant than the last. A pair of black eyes observed him distastefully as he hung suspended between two opposing panes of glass. He attempted to reconstruct the face that held those eyes, but the humming between his ears continued to grow, drawing him from the memory as it had pulled him from between the mirrors. Melting into that liquid sound, his soul had been lured from the immaterial realm and returned to his body.

Ryan tore his eyes from the bowl. For how many months, or years, had he lain upon that mattress? Trying to fathom how he had ended up in the attic was like trying to recall his own birth. Staring at the aged sheet, he searched for memories. It was like fishing for a plug in cloudy water, reaching deeper but finding nothing.

An innate urge pulled his gaze to the back of the room, where a bedsheet covered the mirror. Crossing the floorboards, he looked beyond the material to what lay beneath: brown-spotted glass and rusted leaves bordering an iron frame. With each step he took, his heartbeat increased, the pounding of blood in his ears grew as deafening as the ethereal hum that had woken him. He lifted a hand to the grey-white cotton and watched his fingers tremble.

A torch flickered on and off in the dollhouse windows—

—'Melissa!'

Each memory bubbling through the murky waters harboured a passenger: an emotion heavier than anxiety but less defined than regret. His fingertips brushed the edge of the bedsheet.

'Stop it!'

Stop what? His chest tightened and a weight pressed him from all sides as a tyranny of emotion coursed through his veins. To uncover the mirror would be to look into his eyes and see what they had seen. One tug of the sheet and he would face his past. He wrung his hands together against his chest, took a deep breath and turned from the mirror, rejecting the memories that sang for his attention.

At the foot of the attic stairs, Ryan faced his father's study. Staring at the Leave-It door, he recalled a flash of spidery handwriting: *Fear removal vs fear creation—*

—a briefcase: P.S. Lawson.

He steadied himself against the door, hands on the frame, forehead against the wood. The letter *S* lingered in his mind, significant and painful. On the back of his eyelids, a sheen on black leather glinted like obsidian eyes. Watching him. Waiting for him to be undone.

You are a simulacrum.

Retreating down the corridor, Ryan considered the burden of thought. As a simulacrum, he had been free from the shackles of consequence and time, his actions dictated by Aldous and Morna, his purpose to do their bidding. He had to contend with neither the regrets of past decisions nor the anxieties over future choices. He had lived without guilt or fear.

She's not ready.

Had he not intervened, Rainn would have extinguished Alicia's soul. The test was unfair: regardless of whether Alicia was as powerful as Aldous and Morna believed, she would not have known how to prevent the attack. So, the simulacrum had taken action, firing a bullet into Alicia's heart.

And the simulacrum was punished, placed between the mirrors that no longer held David. Ryan had waited for those obsidian eyes to latch upon his body, like Alicia had held the Unbreakable Door.

But he was not a simulacrum, and could not be undone. He was a person, with a history, and to have history was to have all the mistakes of your past rolled out before you like a stained rug. He followed this rug to his bedroom, where the door was ajar.

On his bed lay Amira. She was thinner than when he had last seen her; the duvet barely creased under her waifish frame. She was older too, by a couple of years at least. Her face appeared troubled, even in sleep, and he wondered why she slept in his bed and where her soul lay. Drawn to that fragile form, he wanted to lie on the floor and join her in Vivador, to meet her eyes and ask for her help to navigate his memories. But now he had escaped the immaterial realm, could he willingly return to it?

He opened the wardrobe in the corner of the room and dressed slowly, pulling on a pair of black jeans and sliding his arms into a cream jumper, enjoying the sensation of the wool against his cold skin.

You're distracting yourself.

He did not want to fish for memories. They no longer lurked at the bottom of murky waters, but darted like sharks beneath the surface. Moments ago, he had believed himself to be a simulacrum: a mental projection born from the imagination of Aldous Crow. As an isolated fragment, he had questioned nothing; now he was connected to a history so vast it overwhelmed him.

In Vivador, a rock might be conjured in an instant, originating in the mind of its creator. Through will or expectation, the rock would be obliterated, leaving no trace behind but the memories of those who had seen it. In his bedroom, everything that Ryan saw existed in a sliver of time between an infinite past and an infinite future. To trace the origin of an object, he would have to look beyond its construction to the creation of the materials from which it was made.

Near the foot of the bed, a table lay beneath the window. On four short legs sat a disc of pine an inch thick. Though the surface was bare, he recalled a dollhouse that had once sat in its centre. Blue wooden panels, cracked. Tinged with guilt. He pushed the memory aside, reaching deeper into obscurity. Before the dollhouse, a Turkish lamp had scattered multicoloured rays against the white wall. Bathed in these rays, he had read in bed, his eyes on the pages of the book in his lap while his father's voice carried up the stairs as he read to Amira in her bedroom below.

Amira? Or someone else?

Jealousy coloured the memory and Ryan tried to picture what had lain on the table before the lamp. He pondered the contents of a past that existed outside his memory. In how many rooms—in how many houses—had this table served its stoic purpose in the corner?

And before this, on what sunlit hill or sunken valley had grown the pine from which it had been hewn?

—not her bedroom—

Ryan ignored the memories that thrashed beneath the surface. He focused on the table: this inanimate object driving deep roots into a history that dwarfed his own. Twenty years ago, when the molecules in his body inhabited other organisms, had this table existed as he saw it now? In decades to come, when his body returned to the soil and his atoms found new homes, would this table remain standing, defiant against the other uses this world might find for its parts? He kneeled to study the marks on the table legs and recalled a husky puppy gnawing on the wood, wagging its tail.

Sam. The dog's name was Sam. Guilt and jealousy twisted into pain, and he reeled from the name that resounded through his mind. Again, he latched his attention to something safe: the blank patch of wall above his bed where coloured rays had fallen. Heightened by emotion, a succession of memories overrode his perception of the bedroom, more real than his surroundings.

'You're my special boy,' his mother whispered, a proud, protective glint in her silver eyes as she squeezed his hand, lying in bed beside him with a picture book on her chest.

The image shifted and the memory stung.

His mother caught his eye as he passed the bedroom doorway. Her face was blank, her eyes wide and untrusting.

He blinked fiercely, beating down the memories and grounding himself in the waking world. He stuffed his hands into the pockets of his jeans. If his eyes unlocked evocative moments from such innocuous surfaces, he dared not lay his hands on anything.

Yet, as a child might lift a finger to a static surface, knowing they will suffer a shock, his curiosity wrestled his fear, and his eyes found Amira's face. From her coy smile rose the colours of the rainbow: a

313

string of numbers sang tunelessly as she folded her arms across the wooden desk. He smiled at the bedside, enjoying the memory of his mother's laughter, while keeping Amira's face in focus, not allowing the images to consume him—

A bed filled with spiders. A mess of twitching legs on the sheets, the pillows. There must have been 29 of them—

—'Were you jealous that it was Amira's birthday?'

Fear on Amira's face, and he was the source. She blamed him for the spiders. Not just the spiders. There was more. He staggered backwards until his heel met the wardrobe, and he raised his hands in front of him. What forgotten crimes had they committed?

Who is Ryan?

In Vivador, hours had passed as he followed the chaotic tumble of a waterfall or the gentle passage of a cloud. He had waited for Alicia without impatience, allowing time to flow with his surroundings, passing through him effortlessly. Now the weight of history pressed upon him as he studied the face on the pillow. Mirrored in Amira's angelic innocence, Ryan saw himself reversed. He was a demon, guilty. A shoal of thoughts jostled for his attention, fins breaching the surface. And these thoughts carried different weights. Like a great white shark, his father's voice weaved through his attention, scattering all else in its wake.

Ryan is a murderer.

'Dad?'—a female voice, outside his mind. Downstairs. Ryan fled his bedroom and looked over the banister to the hallway below. Alicia Harrington stood by the front door with a phone pressed to her ear and a look of abject desolation on her face.

29

'DAD?'

'Alicia?'

Pain pricked her dry throat at the sound of her father's voice.

'I need you—' *Winter's face flickered, translucent as stained glass.* '—I need you to come and get me.'

She cut through Rory's urgent questions, describing the location of Burnflower as best as she could and assuring him that she was physically unharmed.

'Have you...' his voice was a tentative whisper. 'Is David...?'

'No. Bring Joe Crow.'

Alicia returned the phone to the bracket on the wall and stared at it for a moment before her peripheral vision alerted her to the figure at the top of the stairs. It was not a simulacrum that stood in black jeans and a woollen jumper. It was the young man who had pressed a gun to her chest and pulled the trigger. The living, breathing Ryan walked down the stairs. He appeared bigger in the real world, taller and broader, perhaps because she had, until now, only seen him against a backdrop of rolling hills and innumerable pines. She had, until now, only known him in another realm.

'What happened?' he asked, his voice husky and lethargic. And when she did not answer: 'Alicia?'

She pictured the headstone near her mother's grave on which his name was etched. Her lips quivered and she swallowed.

'I think I just killed someone.'

His eyes darted to the ceiling, to the bedroom above, and then to the bedroom behind her.

'Who?'

'No.' She shook her head. *Not someone you love.* 'You don't…she was a…'—*a friend? An enemy?*—'it was Winter.' Her voice caught as she delivered the name that meant nothing to him and would forevermore mean everything to her. His confusion thickened and she averted her eyes. 'I thought I was waking her up.'

Winter disappeared, leaving the pillar bare. Amid the simulacrums that wailed and clawed at the ledges, Amira stood beside the entrance to a tunnel. One look at that horror-stricken face and Alicia knew that Winter would not wake. She slid from the ice and let those wretched screams envelop her as she fell towards the lava.

'I was trying to wake her up.'

Alicia shrank when Ryan raised his arms. And then he held her in a tight embrace. Holding her together. With a palm against the back of her head, he drew her into his shoulder, into a wordless hug, firm enough for her to understand that he too was lost. He did not press her to his chest because she was innocent; he held her because nobody had held him, and because she needed to be held.

She broke, weeping against the soft jumper and gripping him as she had gripped the bear. Too soon, he relaxed his grip. She watched him stare through Amira's bedroom doorway. Where once his eyes had been as placid as a lake, an ocean of thought surged within them.

'How do you live with them?' he whispered, shutting his eyes for a full second as if willing a migraine to pass.

'With who?'

'The voices.'

She wiped her eyes to better see him trying to make sense of this new world.

'You are the voices.'

A scar ran from the corner of his left eye towards his ear, just over an inch long. That jagged thread, a brilliant white against the fair skin, was one of the most beautiful things she had ever seen.

What was more real than imperfection? Suddenly repelled by her desire to hold him—to accept his attempt to ease the pain that she deserved—Alicia withdrew from the embrace.

'I'm sorry I shot you,' he said in earnest. Concern furrowed his brow. 'Rainn was about to extinguish you—to try, anyway, and I think she might have...'

His explanation continued: how she was not ready for this test; how he had to force her to wake; but the word 'extinguish' expanded between Alicia's ears as Rainn's cerulean eyes stretched to the corners of her mind.

Had Winter's vision filled with green eyes when Alicia reached inside and seized her soul?

Ryan lunged forward to catch her by the shoulders as her knees buckled. The truth pressed in on her, pushing her, and she staggered out of his reach, creating a distance between herself and the comfort she craved. Not a simulacrum, but still a stranger, he stood with strong arms ready to catch her and she knew that his desire to hold her was as urgent as her desire to be held. She fought the temptation of those open arms to lure her from the epicentre of a pain that she had authored.

'Melissa,' she said, 'your mum, she's in the Pagoda. With your dad.'

The pair looked through the open front doorway, across the paths and ponds to the tower in the trees. A squirrel crossed from a branch to the roof of the Pagoda, pelted along the bamboo and disappeared into branches on the far side. Alicia shot a final glance at Ryan, caught the longing in his eyes as he sought the face of the mother that awaited him, and a fierce jealousy tore at her throat.

She fixed her gaze to the wooden fence at the bottom of the sloping field. Only the odd beam was visible amid the browning leaves of the bushes. Beyond the fence, the trees were perfectly still. Not a breath of wind disturbed the branches. She stepped onto the patio, staring at the silent woodland. Were this Vivador, her mental state would have driven a gale through those trees, uprooting all in its path. How could this world remain so utterly indifferent to the emotion that ravaged her?

For a full second, she closed her eyes and the world disappeared.

And reappeared. Solid and impervious to will or expectation. An intense pain shot through her chest and her vision blurred. In that moment, it was not her brother that she needed. She closed her eyes and dropped to the ground.

ALICIA LAY ON the patio, her head inches from a birdbath that Ryan had once filled with frogspawn. He wanted to cross the mossy flagstones and rouse her, to check that she was breathing. He wanted to shift her awkward limbs into a more comfortable position that might resemble someone sleeping, rather than a corpse.

But she had shrunk from his touch. She had slipped from his embrace. She had looked into his eyes and seen what he was too afraid to face, and then withdrawn from him.

Without another look at the Pagoda, he turned for the bedroom that had not always been Amira's. On a chest of drawers between the beds lay a glass terrarium—and before this, a dollhouse with tiny panes of glass, uncracked: a coveted birthday present. On the bed beneath the window lay a white bear—and before this, Sam.

Footsteps on the carpet, fingers reaching for the dollhouse.

'*It's at the top of the house,*' he whispered in Sam's ear as curly hair tickled his cheek. '*I'll show you.*'

The light of a torch flicked on and off.

Sam: the orphan. The adopted brother. The eight-year-old boy who died in the attic.

'*He had an epileptic fit. It wasn't your fault.*'—his mother's explanation tasted like a lie. He cradled his head in his hands, trying to remember what had happened in the attic. How was it possible for a mind to crave a truth so desperately while knowing that it might destroy you?

He returned to the front doorway. Gravel paths stretched like running tracks, set for him to tear between the ponds, down to the tower and into his mother's arms. But his legs would not move.

Your mother finds it hard to love you after what you did to Sam.

What if he found her and she pulled away, scared of the secrets in his eyes? Steeling himself, he turned for the stairs. Whatever had happened in the attic, the memory had been locked away, sequestered in a hidden file for his own protection.

When you've a question on your mind, ask the mirror.

Repression leaves scars, Ryan thought; 29 of them, if he remembered correctly. A song on the radio can transport you to the time and place that you last heard it; a smell can evoke the memory of a deceased relative. All he needed to unlock his past was to look in that mirror and find the truth in his eyes.

Taking the steps two at a time, he shook cowardly voices that urged him to let it be. Like a lamb to the slaughter, he stepped through the attic doorway, ready to spear himself upon an irrevocable truth. Rising through the fear, he reached the top step and strode between the numbers carved by a girl who feared him.

He gripped the grey-white sheet and his chest tightened. He had yet to connect a violent thumping to the beating of his heart. Incessant mental chatter screamed for his attention as he braced himself to face all that he had seen and all that he had done. With a sharp tug of the bedsheet, he uncovered the mirror.

'*Those eyes will get you in trouble one day.*' *His mother gave him a wink and he licked the ice cream from his fingers, wondering what she meant.*

Will and expectation: he would find the truth in his eyes because that is precisely what he feared. He looked into that fear and searched for the cause that lay beneath it. He caught snatches of truths that he already knew: Peter whispering through permanently-clenched teeth that friends should share secrets. He had wanted to share his secret mirror with Sam. He had not wanted to hurt him. He could not remember wanting to hurt him.

Frustrated, Ryan pulled his eyes from those cloudy depths and cast them across the reflected room, willing the memory to surface. Dust motes hovered in the shaft of light that fell upon his mattress, but his memories remained locked in the shadows.

A large *29* caught his attention, engraved into the nearest beam. In the mirror, these digits reversed and the air in his lungs petrified. Every inch of the attic walls as high as Amira could reach was covered with two letters: PS.

P.S. Lawson—the gold lettering of the briefcase flickered violently under the light of the torch in Peter's hand.

'Stop it!' Ryan shouted as Sam collapsed on the floor. He tried to turn to his friend, but rough hands gripped his shoulders. He was thrown forward and a light exploded in his head as he struck the corner of the iron frame.

'Ryan is a murderer,' whispered the voice in his ear as all went dark.

Paralysed by the enormity of his father's deception, he slid to his knees and drew a thumb along the white scar that ran down his cheek. Beyond the horror that made pinpricks of his pupils, Ryan found innocence.

CHAPTER NINE
Frieze

A PILLAR OF rock rose from the ground like the trunk of a redwood tree. Over fifty metres high, it was nearing the ceiling of the cavern when Gus halted its growth. A resounding crack echoed between the walls as the rock split at its base and proceeded to topple forward. But as the falling pillar crossed the edge of the chasm, it disappeared into the darkness, leaving nothing but a blunt stump that hit the ground with a quaking thud. The base of the pillar rolled to the cliff's edge, where it lay flush against the Active Nothing as though sliced with the beam of a laser.

No light fell on the chasm, yet Gus was able to discern the ghostly outline of its far edge. Had Aldous and Morna granted passage to those meagre rays of light touching the distant cliff, so that Gus would see the side he could not reach?

'No thing that you create can exist here,' Rainn had said before disappearing as abruptly as his failed creations. Had she given up on him? Since he was unable to generate a structure spanning the abyss, Gus assumed that Rainn had left in search of Alicia. He inched his hand forward again, focusing on his fingertips and willing them to exist where nothing could. They vanished.

Only you can cross it. Gus found new meaning in Rainn's words as he stared into the void. He had no fingers. These were mere projections, as real as the pillar of rock. If he were to believe that he held a unique energy capable of overcoming the will of others, then it was this energy alone that could cross the Active Nothing.

But what was it? What exactly was he supposed to command? What intangible element of himself was he expected to draw from?

Impatience stoked the fire in his chest. He resented the imaginary heart that pumped imaginary blood through his imaginary body. In his mind's eye, Rainn overlooked his physical body on the cliffs, preparing to roll that dead weight into the ocean. Melissa pursued Alicia, tightening the knot at the back of her head as she readied herself to do whatever it took to recover her son. And he glared at an empty void, paralysed by his own failure.

Rainn reappeared and the air thickened, enveloping Gus with a viscous emotion that she struggled to repress. He recalled her vulnerable form, cradling the telephone as a beam of light swept her vacant eyes. Who had she spoken to? Winter's death meant nothing to Rainn: this was not the news she had received.

But whatever had happened, he thought, wherever she had been, at least she had not rolled him off the cliff.

Gus's face was intense as he edged his hand forward, focusing not on his fingers, but the energy within them.

'*Your parents only wanted to protect you.*' Her whisper crackled through his skull. '*In their attempt to save you, they lost their lives.*'

A violent undercurrent stirred her words and the edge of his nails glowed like a blade in sunlight. As his nails crossed an invisible line, this light remained.

'*If you fail to stop Melissa, Alicia will die.*'

Like breath across a burning coal, Rainn's words filled him with a bright vengeance and the tips of his fingers glowed.

'*Surrender to the fire,*' she hissed. '*Let it burn.*'

Gus moved forwards, feeding himself into the void as he drew on all that he was. Inching over the abyss, he had no hands or feet. He controlled no body and saw with no eyes. As fear and anger and hatred, he crossed the Active Nothing.

Feet met rock and he collapsed to the ground, letting unreal air fill his projected lungs. His mind reeled as if he had been squeezed through a garlic press. Rolling over, he glanced back across the chasm to see an unbroken gloom. He was alone.

Like the teeth of a gargantuan beast, stalactites hung from the ceiling of the cavern while stalagmites rose to meet them from the gently inclining floor. Slender beams of golden light fell through cracks in the ceiling to strike rock pillars like dappled sunlight upon a petrified forest.

The ceiling lowered and the gradient of the floor continued to rise until, ten feet apart, they met the far wall of the cavern. Etched upon the volcanic rock were engravings that ran in a long band, stretching to the left and right like the Parthenon Frieze. Images on the far left depicted a man and woman sleeping hand in hand, facing one another in bed. Gus stepped closer to the engraving as something caught his eye. The rock that formed the characters' eyelids twitched perceptibly like the shell of a hermit crab, revealing obsidian eyes beneath. In the image on the right, the outline of a volcano had been cast into the wall. As he looked at it, the rock above the crater split and sealed repeatedly, giving the impression of an eruption.

Scanning the animated carvings, Gus saw the history of Aldous and Morna. The furnace inside him burned and a flush of contempt heated his cheeks as he witnessed the arrogance—the glorification of a tale that ended in the slaughter of innocents.

Stepping to the right, he followed their story, with each static scene stirring to life under his attention. Lightning bolts snaked down the rock in jagged cracks to strike at raised boulders. Tornadoes and car crashes—several of the events he did not understand. Others, he recognised immediately: a golden eye unfolding on the cover of a book. He ran his eyes across the dynamic engravings, searching for meaning.

A woman climbed upon a throne and plunged a crystal dagger into her chest. Eloise Grett took her life so that her granddaughter might inherit a responsibility she had been unable to face. Gus's breath spilled like mist from his open mouth, clouding the tiny crystal dagger as a coldness gripped him. He had crossed the Active Nothing; had Eloise's power passed to him?

Outside a lighthouse, two figures handed a book to a third before collapsing to the ground. Gus sank to his knees, tracing his fingers along the arm that his father had slung around his mother's body. As the rock split and sealed, it pinched his skin and he brushed the pad of a bloodied fingertip across his mother's fallen face. The image reset, with his parents emerging from the lighthouse, and he watched them collapse twice more before struggling to his feet and remembering his purpose.

The death of his parents last summer was the final scene of this animated frieze; the section to the right was blank. But as the bare rock received his attention, it shifted like quicksand, presenting him with a new image. Light fell over his shoulder from a hole in the ceiling and struck the rock in a horizontal line, forming a bridge across a dark recess. The figure of a woman drifted across this bridge. Gus leaned closer, following the single green stone that travelled through the rock: the eye of the woman who had crossed the Active Nothing. The figure drifted between pillars towards a cloaked individual that had materialised on the igneous canvas with a bead of obsidian for an eye. The woman raised her palm and the figure disappeared.

On a cliff in another realm, his heart clenched. This was not history, but a premonition: the elimination of Aldous by a woman with green eyes. Did the patriarch of the Crow family await Alicia Harrington? Had he surrendered to his fate, ready to face a weapon that he would be unable to withstand?

But Aldous was wrong, and the premonition false: Gus had crossed the Active Nothing.

A high cawing sounded behind him and he turned to see a crow perched on a stalagmite, watching him with a cocked head. The bird took flight and Gus followed its passage between the pillars, leading him deeper into the cavern. Dark wings fluttered silently between the shafts of light and he was beginning to tire of chasing shadows when he heard a roaring in the distance.

The petrified forest gave way to a clearing as large as a football pitch, with a low basin and a high ceiling. The tremendous roar came from a hole in the roof of the cavern. Gus wandered down to where a wide shaft of light through the circular opening struck a single boulder in the centre of the basin. Unlike the dark igneous rock, this boulder was of a light stone, almost white beneath the falling beam. The boulder was massive, over twice his height, and its flat surface had been carved with the lines of a poem. Gus's thoughts returned to the animated frieze as he studied the scorched letters, burned into the rock by bolts of lightning.

The greatest war that man shall fight will not lie on the plain.
No spear or gun, no atom bomb, no enemy terrain.
The foe long sought, this evil fought, will share his given name.
The war between and war within will be one and the same.
From fear inane, projected blame: to seek is not to find.
The greatest war that man shall fight will lie within his mind.

Gripping a lone stalagmite with leathery talons, the bird watched Gus approach, its eyes dark and knowing. Stepping into the light, he saw that the opening above was a tunnel, stretching higher into the rock than he could fathom. He was not surprised that this tunnel matched the diameter of the blowhole on Earth; but unlike the jagged blowhole, carved by decades of erosion from the ocean waves, the shaft above was smoothed by a tornado that whipped along its length. This was the tunnel through which Aldous and Morna had first accessed Vivador. This was the portal through which they hunted the souls of their defenceless victims. Twelve months ago, his great-grandparents had stood as he did now before launching themselves through that portal and after his fleeing parents.

Gus stared into the eye of the tornado and leaped from the rock.

Kill the bad guy

MELISSA STAGGERED DOWN the gravel path with a tin under her left arm and a key in her right fist. She had searched the cellar for the snake, pulling at the wine barrels, shifting the dusty crates of lager from the wall and peering in the musty bag of the broken lawnmower. Thrumming with anxiety, she had cast a thousandth glance at David and seen movement in the creases of his pyjama top. For a terrible moment, she thought the snake had slid beneath his clothes and across his chest. But then: a flicker of brown scales. The animal slithered down the side of the mattress behind David's head.

Overwriting rational thought, Melissa had seized the snake, wrestled it back into the tin and clipped the clasp shut; but not before sustaining bites on her thumb and forearm. She held her arm up, hissed between clenched teeth, and stared at the deadly puncture wounds, wondering how long it would take her to reach the Jeep. The creases in David's pyjamas thickened and thinned, blue folding over white as he slept on unawares.

Passing the nearest pond, she pressed her injured arm against her chest to better grip the tin, squeezing tight, as if to prevent the writhing reptile from breaking free. A passionate agony in her left arm migrated through her body. Each crunch of her feet on the uneven stones sent bright splinters along her nerves. Maintaining her balance with a forward gaze, she saw two figures on the patio. On the flagstones by the birdbath, Alicia slept in Amira's shadow. Amira passed a kitchen knife from one hand to the other, wiping a palm on her dressing gown. At the sight of that severe expression, Melissa urged her legs into a sprint.

'Amira,' she called. The girl looked up and the colour drained from her face. Tattered and bleeding, hair straggling wild down her cheeks, Melissa came at her like a banshee.

'Amira?' she repeated as a pulse of agony shot from her heels to her skull. 'What are you doing?'

The girl's lips quivered and her brown eyes glowered. In her hand, the knife trembled.

'She killed…' Amira coughed and returned her gaze to Alicia, who lay with her arms by her sides and one leg tucked beneath the other like a discarded puppet. 'She murdered a girl. In Vivador.'

Melissa crossed from the gravel to the patio flagstones, firing questions—*Killed who? How?*—but Amira stared at Alicia's face, reliving what she had witnessed. The girl's olive skin was taut with determination, her lips pursed and her brow furrowed, and Melissa remembered the night before Ryan's tenth birthday. Young Amira had trembled with the need to make it right, biting her lip when she poured too many sprinkles on the cake. Though Amira had not uttered a sound, Melissa had read the curses on her face, berating herself for making a mistake. Now she watched the girl wrestle with what she believed to be weakness: her reluctance to stab a sleeping stranger.

What has he done to you? Her thought was white-hot as Melissa viewed the outcome of her husband's experiments. Then, the heat cooled: *what did you let him do to her?*

This thought was not rewritten. David was the second child she had stolen; Amira was the first. After Sam, they could not return to Sunny Climes children's home. They would not be able to adopt again. But Peter had convinced Melissa that Ryan must not grow up alone. While the children played in the fields beyond the children's home, Melissa approached the six-year-old with a fistful of daisies. The little girl with synaesthesia, who Peter insisted was not getting the treatment she required in that underfunded place. The little girl had not said no to the kindly woman offering to help her make a daisy chain. She had not said no when the kindly woman offered to adopt her.

With Peter dead, Melissa was the last living parent that Amira should never have had. She pocketed the key and crossed the flagstones, holding out her hand.

'Give it to me,' she demanded in the authoritative tone she had used when the puppy ran off with her hairbrush. Amira looked from the knife to the tear that slipped down Alicia's cheek. The droplet fell and hung on a blade of grass that poked between the paving slabs.

'She's dangerous,' Amira muttered, arms deflating to her sides as she struggled to maintain her fragile resolve. 'A killer. I can't...in Vivador, I can't stop her. I have to stop her.'

Amira raised the weapon.

'I killed Peter,' Melissa whispered.

Amira's eyes snapped to hers. Melissa saw a dead body slumped in a desk chair, head back and eyes wide. She had pulled the key from beneath her husband's collar and tossed the chain to the floor. His hand rested on the desk, fingers gripping the phone, and she had wondered whether it was Rainn he had called, or Aldous. Or both. Wherever Rainn might be, Melissa knew she would head for Burnflower. Before leaving the Pagoda, she had locked the cellar door.

'He's dead?' Amira's gaze drifted to the Pagoda, as if Peter's ghost might hover in the arches.

'I was too afraid to do anything,' Melissa stated. 'To stop him. I should have stopped him. But he's gone now, Amira. He's gone. And you...' She clenched her teeth, unable to speak to this girl as a mother should. Her voice hardened. 'I lost everything to that man. My son, my home. My hope. And I got my revenge.'

Amira saw the swollen skin around Melissa's left hand and forearm. Redness spread around two puncture wounds as the blood panicked.

'Mambo?'

Melissa nodded, and her stomach lurched at hearing Ryan's name for the black mamba. It was her son's attempt to humanise the present that Amira would not look at. She softened her tone.

'That anger inside—the one screaming that it isn't fair. The one that makes you want to seize something valuable and crush it in your hands. I thought it would help. I thought that getting my revenge would make the anger go away.'

Beneath the black hair that curled against her forehead, Amira's dark eyes lingered on the teardrop hanging from the blade of grass, splitting the light of the morning sun. She could not look at Alicia's face any longer, though the knife was steady in her hand. She opened her mouth to speak and a bead of perspiration dropped from her lower lip.

'It's not revenge. She hasn't killed a friend—I don't have...I didn't know that girl. I tried to wake Ryan, but I can't. She's going to kill him.'

Melissa's mouth hung open, but she shook her head, which swam as if filled with liquid.

'No. She wouldn't. Not everyone kills to get what they want. That's not...' The tin was too heavy to hold, and she placed it by Alicia's feet. A wistful look came upon her. 'Remember those superhero comics we gave Ryan one Christmas?'

Amira nodded. She and Ryan had taken it in turns reading the speech bubbles. He had been eleven, she had been eight. He had used different voices for the villains and she had tried to copy him. It was the Christmas before the spiders.

'Kill the bad guy,' Melissa continued. 'That's what they teach us. That's what they want us to believe. The books, the films. The news. But the bad guy never really dies, he just changes. He changes into you.'

Melissa held out her palm again as her husband's voice swam through her liquid mind: *Fear and hatred will always triumph over love.* It was the final thought that she rewrote.

'Alicia is good, Amira. And so are you. You've always been good.'

Amira passed the knife to Melissa, who received it as if it were a great weight and fell to her knees, her adrenaline exhausted. Fifteen minutes must have passed since the snake had bitten her, and she would not make it to the Jeep before losing consciousness.

She tapped the tin and blinked heavily, trying to keep Amira in focus.

'The snake is in this box. There are gloves in my car, in the— over—' she gestured to the back of the house. 'Put Mambo back. Her brother is in the cellar. And the attic—I have the key. He says it's for Portugal. But he lied.'

In her jacket pocket, her fingers slipped around the key. Might she make it up the stairs, just to see his face? She tilted her head to the windows above and saw—a hallucination? She lifted the knife, raising a hand to shield her gaze, and met Ryan's eyes through his bedroom window.

Ghost

AS RAINN HAD instructed, Gus held an image in his mind: a wakeboard cleaving the surface of Lake Windermere. The deafening howl of the tornado ceased and an expanse of water lay below him. His surroundings shifted in and out of focus, flickering between different shades of green as if viewed through the facets of an emerald. Suspended in the air, he tried to comprehend the immensity of this experience. Through his great-grandparents' portal, the conscious element of his self had left Vivador without returning to his body on the cliff in Portugal. He had entered the material world as spirit alone. He was a ghost.

Reaching out a spectral hand, he urged this curious form across the water. A fine golden energy threaded through his fingers, making not a ripple when he passed his hand beneath the surface. He lifted from the lake and shot across the width of a slender isle to twist between the boats of Bowness Bay. He commanded his soul across the lead-covered roof of a church and through quiet roads empty of residents this early in the day. He had been on holiday in Windermere with his parents and uncle in the spring before Blithe died. Through chance or memory, he veered left, gliding over slate tiles, not knowing what he was looking for, until he saw the cottage at the end of the lane.

Returning from the lake, he and his father had parked the car, turned that corner and found Joe and Sylvie playing cards on the terrace. Gus set his attention on the empty chairs as he had focused on the animated frieze, willing memories to stir. He heard his mother's boisterous laugh. He smelled the acrid fumes from Joe's pipe. His mother tossed a winning card onto the pile; Joe toyed with his fashionable moustache and accused her of cheating. The wry grin on his uncle's face was as alien as his surroundings. The seats below were empty, but this was not fantasy: the memory was true.

Haunted by his uncle's grin, Gus lost himself in thought. Had he never been born, Joe would not have been left alone to care for Blithe. Had he never been born, Joe would not have received a call from the Portuguese authorities informing him that his twin brother was dead.

And I was left with the child that they were never supposed to have.

The terrace trembled and Gus remembered himself. He shot into the sky with a sudden urgency until Windermere was visible in its entirety. Still rising, he scanned the Lake District, latching his attention to tiny details—a falling leaf; the swish of a horse's tail—anchoring himself to the landscape. At this height, the great lakes were garden ponds, with Windermere a narrow crack through the south-east of the National Park. Recalling instructions that had seemed so unnecessary while he struggled to cross the Active Nothing, Gus searched emerald ridges until he spotted the lake matching Rainn's description.

He soared through the air with a sea of trees beneath him, as inert as the landscape of a model train set. Lowering himself, hungry to connect, he glided first through the treetops and then along the surface of a dirt track before rising again, his gaze searching the farthest shore of the lake for a farmhouse visible only from the sky. From his vantage point high above the lake, he saw a bamboo roof poking through the leaves.

Gus fixed his attention to the tower in the trees and reeled himself towards it. A fish on the line, he did not slow when he passed through leaves, branches, trunks—stopping only when faced with stone arches. Though the tower in Vivador reached seven storeys high, and this Pagoda only three; while the roof in Vivador was made of stone rather than bamboo, there was no doubt that one of these structures had inspired the other.

No thrones rotated on the bamboo matting. No figure awaited his approach. If this was where Melissa hid, where was she? He willed his body through the floor and there followed a moment of darkness before the room below stuttered into focus. Silver light fell through two narrow windows, converging on the upturned face of a man seated at his desk. Peter was still, gazing at the ceiling with eyes that were not the pale blue he had seen in Vivador, but an olive green. Death had set a permanent sneer on his cleft lip. In his hand, he clutched a phone.

This is not how it was meant to be—lifeless eyes as Rainn cradled the phone in her lap. Gus surveyed the room: the open filing cabinet, the files on the desk, the tub of rubber snakes on the shelf; but no blood, no weapons, no sign of a fight. How had Melissa killed her husband?

He left the second corpse he had found that morning and drifted through the door. Had Alicia even left Godalming, or had Rainn sent him to avenge the death of her only ally? In search of other clues, he followed spiral steps to a padlocked door and urged his ghostly form through green panels.

The steps continued along the wall and down into a cellar, lit by weak shafts of light that breached vents in the ground-level bricks. The light fell through him; he cast no shadow on the mattress by the wine barrels. On this mattress lay a boy, his eyes closed in sleep or death. Gus drifted down the steps and recognised the freckled face of David Harrington. He studied Alicia's brother just long enough to watch his chest rise and fall, and then he gazed around the cellar. There were no empty trays, no flask of water, not even a bucket. Had Vivador sustained him for two years?

An urge to find Alicia drove him through the ceiling, through the office, through the roof, and he might have launched into space had he not hooked his attention to the farmhouse. A path ran in a straight line towards seven ponds that glinted in the light of a silver sun cresting the trees to his right. Like capillaries, the paths diverged to link the ponds and then converged again, drawing his attention to two silver lights on the patio.

He soared through wild grass along the inclining slope, darted over path and pond and slowed when he reached the patio. A thin-faced girl he did not recognise leaned over Alicia's body to hand a knife to Melissa. While their bodies glowed, Alicia's was devoid of light—like Peter's. He scanned her fallen form for signs of trauma; but she was breathing. Perhaps, like her brother, Alicia's physical body was empty because her soul was in Vivador.

Melissa dropped to her knees and Gus veered to her side, mesmerised by the light that emanated from her. Tendrils of silver energy weaved through her limbs, so bright her skin was translucent. Brighter still was the light in her skull. The spectral outline of his hand appeared in his vision, rising subconsciously, riding a visceral desire to reach out and connect with that brilliant energy burning in the woman's mind. Melissa's lips moved as she spoke to the girl, her words inaudible.

A jade blade glistened in the sunlight. He drifted in front of her, through a birdbath by Alicia's head, but Melissa saw nothing. She heard nothing when he called her name. Was she responsible for Winter's death? If he did not strike, would she drive that knife into Alicia's chest? Rainn had given no further instructions, yet it was a primal urge that commanded him now. Golden sparks flooded his fingertips, and he hesitated. Just like his father.

When faced with difficult choices, weaker minds will fail to do what is in their best interests.

Melissa raised the knife and a frenzied emotion lit her face. Gus stretched out his hand, forced his golden fingers into that burning light and closed his fist within the woman's mind. A violent flash of colour and Melissa collapsed on the flagstones.

Light and shadow

WITH HER BACK against her mother's headstone, Alicia followed the streams of coloured light to their source. High in the church wall, the circular window held each diaphanous shard of glass in place. Each fragment was a piece of a puzzle. If she were able to reassemble it, to lay the disordered pieces down side by side, she might unlock their secrets and order the chaos.

Her thoughts were frenetic. Again, she considered conjuring her mother's image, if only to scream at that hopeful face for leaving her to deal with this insufferable mess. A cold wind drew gooseflesh on her bare arms and she found comfort in the lie, absorbing every inch of the fiction that surrounded her. She turned to kneel before the grave and glared at the palindromic *ANNA* as if it were her mother's face.

'You never believed in chaos,' she said out loud. 'Everything happens for a reason, doesn't it, Mum? It's all part of a grand design. So, tell me, was this my fate?'

Dark and violent, the shadow stirred within her. What had lain dormant now rose, tightening her throat and clenching her jaw. She glared upon the lettering, indulging in the knowledge that this environment was as false as the eyes that beheld it. All that was real was the current of fury accelerating through her self.

'What am I supposed to do now?' she hissed, gripping each side of the headstone until cracks appeared beneath her thumbs. Fragments of unsolicited advice cycled through her mind.

Look at all those challenges, Anna had said as Alicia chewed her lip, thumbing buttons on the gaming controller. *It's just a game, Mum.* But that's what her mother had wanted her to see: win or lose, it did not matter. It was all just a game that we chose to play each day. Alicia had lost against the boss, tossed the controller to the floor and accused her mother of distracting her—of trying to make a lesson out of everything.

She had shielded herself from her mother's suggestions, each tailored to infuriate her. She had shut her ears and rolled her eyes. Now, with ears open, she knelt on the grave and listened to the silence, squeezing the granite and longing for words of wisdom.

The letters rippled as though beneath water and then hardened into new forms, and Anna Harrington became Winter Hazelby. Gingerly, Alicia pressed her palms either side of the name, and then harder, straining against the polished stone as she had the panels of the Unbreakable Door. But Winter's death was no fiction, and Alicia's actions could not be undone.

Before she might question this cruel trick of a troubled mind, the coloured rays were disturbed and she turned to see a silhouette in the window. A figure stood behind the glass.

Alicia stepped through the back door of the church and scanned the empty pews. A mezzanine ran overhead: a walkway linking the organ with a row of vestibules on the far side. For someone's shadow to fall on the stained glass, they must have been standing in the centre of this mezzanine, directly overhead. Bare feet padded across cold stone as Alicia ascended the steps.

Rainn leaned against the wooden railing, appearing to contemplate the chaotic pattern of glass. She did not turn when Alicia approached. A beam of light that fell through a tiny, clear window in the front wall widened across the church and lit the stained glass. The rays caught the back of Rainn's head like a corona, generating a soft, golden glow.

You must attack what lies before you.

Alicia launched herself at Rainn, splintering the wooden railing. The pair flew through the air to strike the stained glass with a hideous crack. In a kaleidoscope of colour, they disappeared through the window.

Shards of green, orange, red and blue littered the rough rock as Alicia rose to her knees. She was on the lip of the volcanic crater, alone. Staggering to her feet, she watched the obsidian platform revolving undisturbed on its magma bed. She was unable to track her thoughts, unable to determine whether she or Rainn had chosen this change in scene. She chastised herself as she scanned the empty shelves of rock: Rainn had altered the name on the grave, cast her shadow upon it and stood awaiting Alicia's attack—this was her game.

In the exact spot where Amira's abject terror had confirmed Alicia's crime, Rainn waited for her pawn. A wink, and she turned down the tunnel, disappearing into Psarnox.

You're not in control. Anxious thoughts urged Alicia to count down from one hundred, to give herself time to think. Time to reason. If she noticed it, why couldn't she stop it? In her chest, a coiled spring. Before her eyes, the spot where Winter had flickered. The coil tightened.

One hundred—

She shut her eyes, gritted her teeth, blinked to the shelf and marched after Rainn.

Alicia's fingers brushed the warm rock, tracing crystals that glistened in the darkness. The tunnel curved to the right and continued downwards at an increasing decline before opening out into a subterranean expanse. Shafts of light permeated the ceiling to illuminate the chamber. Given the curve of this passage, she must be beneath the crater, and she tried to understand how the light reached her through the lake of lava. But this was Vivador, where the laws of nature did not apply.

The chamber stretched twice the distance she could throw and then the floor fell away at the edge of an abyss. Halfway to this abyss,

Rainn waited with a hand on her hip and a smile in her eyes. Alicia did not question why Rainn had led her here. She did not think or reason. She listened only to the darkness in her chest.

A heartbeat later, she stood before Rainn with her hands like talons. A gust of wind blasted the woman across the cavern and she struck the rock with a thunderous crack that echoed between the distant walls. Alicia reappeared before her, palms outstretched and fingers trembling. Rainn rose higher up the rock, which splintered under the force of Alicia's wrath. Weak, blunt phrases tumbled through her mind as she stared at the face of the woman who had handed her a gun without telling her it was loaded. Words poured from her open mouth like a gale.

'You let me kill her.'

Crushed against the rock, Rainn twisted beneath the strength of Alicia's will. Each strand of her black hair fanned against the crystalline surface. With her head to the side, her arms spread and one knee raised, she lay against the stone as if in crucifixion. Numerous shafts of light cast Alicia's shadows on the wall and in these shadows her thoughts lay bare, shifting before her eyes as they made themselves known. The dark forms moved independently of her projected body, rippling like the black stallion and growing into the third dimension. A dozen arms reached from the wall and in their hands were knives and spears, axes and swords, poised and ready to destroy the enemy.

But Alicia did not need weapons, for she was one. She drew the shadows from the wall and let them coalesce within her, surrendering to their fury. Closing the distance, she lifted her head so that Rainn might look down the barrel of the gun.

Alicia saw no fear in those cerulean eyes. Instead, they radiated victory and malice.

'You are ready.'

Alicia screamed and flung her hands to the right, hurling Rainn in the direction of the abyss. The woman landed on her feet and Alicia was before her, hands raised, using the force of her will to drive the woman closer to the edge. The rock slid beneath Rainn's feet and Alicia felt the strain in that confident sneer.

'Push me into the Active Nothing and I will simply return to the lighthouse with your cousin,' said Rainn, though her voice was noticeably weaker. 'You cannot bring yourself to kill me because I am not the target of your hatred.' And within Alicia's mind, she added: '*Right now, the only person you hate more than yourself lies across this chasm.*'

Rainn slowed to a halt with her heels at the edge of the abyss. One more push and she would be swallowed by the impenetrable gloom. Alicia narrowed her eyes and then her lips parted as the darkness beyond Rainn was illuminated. Where only emptiness had existed, a bridge of light now stretched across the chasm. Like sunbeams glancing the surface of a pond, a wide pathway cut through the shadow beyond Rainn's heels. Rainn placed the sole of her foot upon the white rays and raised an eyebrow at Alicia.

'*And he waits for you.*'

Over Rainn's shoulder, Alicia saw a figure at the far end of the bridge, striding towards them. Alerted by the panic in Alicia's eyes, Rainn shrank from the bridge and, for the first time, Alicia watched terror twist the corners of her mouth.

The figure neared their end of the bridge and the white rays lit the contours of Gus's face. Alicia took tentative steps to meet her cousin, a frown of disbelief creasing her brow as if he had emerged from the underworld. He did not rush to greet her. His eyes were unsmiling, haunted by secrets, reminding Alicia of her mother's absent gaze on the morning of her final day.

In Alicia's eyes, something had hardened. Crystallised. The pair faced one another with questions on their lips, unable to recount the events that had ruptured their former selves and changed them irrevocably.

'I found him,' said Gus, seizing her forearms. 'David is in that tower at the bottom of the garden—the one with the arches. He's in the cellar.'

Alicia's spine stiffened but she managed to step out of his arms.

'The Pagoda? Are you—'

'Yes,' Gus nodded profusely. 'He's there, Alicia. Wake up.'

A frigid energy radiated from Rainn.

'They won't be the last,' she breathed, her eyes flitting between the pair. 'Winter…Melissa…Who will be next?'

Gus and Alicia hardened at the names. They exchanged a fearful glance, wondering what the other knew.

'Cross that bridge now,' Rainn ordered aloud, taking a step closer to Alicia, 'and put an end to this.'

Gus stepped between them, his stance protective.

'There's nothing but death across that chasm.'

Alicia sidestepped Gus and studied the insistence in Rainn's expression: the desperation that aged her heart-shaped face, stretching porcelain skin over high cheekbones in a severe manner reminiscent of Melissa. Through that beautiful mirage, Rainn's motives were exposed as she urged the pawn to do her bidding. Peter had trained her to kill Aldous, but Rainn lacked the willpower to destroy their enemy. So, she had taken an apprentice of her own. Training Alicia as Peter had trained her, Rainn had nurtured a shadow violent enough for Alicia to succeed where she had failed.

Alicia trod small steps across the rock and craned her head to whisper into Rainn's elfin ear.

'I have no more hate to give you.'

She dived into the abyss.

Another door

ON THE PATIO lay a kitchen knife and a metal tin that Alicia had not noticed when she woke. She had hurtled down the gravel paths without a backward glance. She had seen nobody since returning from Vivador. No living body; only Peter's corpse in his office chair. Her hands throbbed from beating the cellar door, her voice was hoarse from calling David's name, and the joints in her fingers ached from tearing at the padlock.

The blade of the knife was thin. If she took it to the lock, it would only bend. With no sign of Ryan or Amira through the open doorway, she bent to pick up the tin. The clasp was open and she pulled at the lid and then leaped upright, alerted by a distant crack. A police car ploughed through the wooden gate at the bottom of the field and tore up the grass as it veered around the ponds. She shielded her brow to see Joe's determined scowl through the windshield and the shape of her father in the passenger seat. Reaching the corner of the patio, Joe slammed the brakes and Rory lurched forward, caught by his seatbelt. He fell back and his head rolled to the side in sleep.

The empty tin clattered on the flagstones and Alicia ran to the vehicle as Joe stepped out. It had been little over three hours since she had called her father, and the police officer huffed as if he had powered the vehicle from Godalming through willpower alone. The midday sun lit his bald scalp as he tucked his thumbs into his belt and surveyed Burnflower.

'Please,' said Alicia, drawing his attention from the farmhouse windows. 'He's over there—my brother, he's in that tower.'

'Calm down.'

Joe rounded the bonnet, disturbing crickets in the long grass, and Alicia took a step back when he raised his arms to her shoulders. She frowned at the accusation that she was anything but calm.

'Breathe,' he said.

In breathless fragments, she told him about the padlock on the cellar door; her hunt for the combination in the office; Melissa's husband dead at his desk; and the silver chain on the floor.

'There was a key on the chain. It's a combination, the lock, but he might keep it in the desk—the code. He said David was in Portugal, but that's—he wanted me here while he took Melissa to the Pagoda. He wanted her out of the way.'

'Who's up there?' Joe nodded at the house. A shadow shifted in the window, obscured by the glare of the sun. A fist clenched around Alicia's heart as she remembered the names that Rainn had uttered.

'Melissa's son, Ryan. And a girl, Amira. And…' she raked fingers through her hair. Had Melissa found her son? 'Melissa was here, she drove me here. She was in the Pagoda, but she's not there. I don't know.'

Joe entered the farmhouse with his hand hovering near the illegal firearm in his belt. Alicia crossed the flagstones, ready to charge after him, to search the house for anything with which to break the lock. Then she saw her father's cheek pressed into the seatbelt. She opened the passenger door and manoeuvred Rory's head into a more comfortable position.

'Wake up,' she said, shaking his shoulders. She wrapped her arms around him and whispered urgently in his ear: 'He's here, Dad.'

Finding no comfort in his limp arms, Alicia straightened up and shut the door. Joe exited the farmhouse, offered her a nod and started down the path between the ponds. Brushing against the bulrushes, Alicia hurried beside him and Joe recounted what he had found upstairs.

'Melissa's dead.'

In the master bedroom, he had found the headmistress on the covers of a four-poster bed. In quiet, disjointed phrases, her nineteen-year-old son had explained how his mother had fallen face-down at Alicia's side. Amira had offered more: indicating two snakebites on Melissa's left arm, and telling him how she had slurred before collapsing. The girl still wore the gardening gloves she had used to return the black mamba to its terrarium.

Ryan had ducked beneath the draped swags and lifted a key from Melissa's jacket pocket. Given the expression on the young man's face, Joe doubted he held the snake responsible for his mother's death.

'Where is it?' Alicia eyed his empty hands. 'The key?'

'That key is for another door,' said Joe. In his mind, an axe struck an iron sheet, quaking through his arms, showering sparks into the darkness. Ryan had not surrendered the key and Joe had not pressed him on it.

'Did they know the code?' Alicia asked, leading him under the archway at the foot of the Pagoda.

'No.'

She frowned, unable to comprehend why he had left the house without an axe, a chainsaw or a medieval cannon. She stepped aside, gesturing at the cellar door.

'You're going to kick it down?'

Joe ran his fingers down the edges of the lintel, knocking at the heavy wood to determine its thickness. He weighed the padlock in his hand and gave it a perfunctory tug.

'This is no garden shed,' he said, chin in hand. 'I've as much chance of breaking my leg as I have of kicking this door off its hinges.'

'But you'll try?'

Alicia drove the full force of her insistence into those bullet-hole eyes. Her long gaze broke at the sound of crunching gravel.

'Oh, Alicia,' Rory murmured as she flung her arms around his neck. She buried her chin in his shoulder and closed her eyes. In her chest, a coil loosened enough to let her breathe. Her father's hands were tight against her shoulder blades—how satisfying to embrace him while he was conscious! She allowed herself another breath before drawing back to see his face. With shrunken eyes, he resembled a gopher, moments from hibernation.

'He's in there,' she said. 'David's in there. And Joe—' she fixed the police officer a commanding look, '—he's about to shoot the lock.'

Joe buried his hands in his trouser pockets, attempting to neutralise her urgency with patience. He spoke to Rory as if outlining the rules to a puzzle he had just devised.

'It's a combination padlock. Four digits. I know a number of common entries, but it could take a while. In the house, there might be a crowbar, or something we could use to prise it off.'

Rory did not appear to be listening. Unable to take cautious eyes off his daughter, he gripped her shoulder and spun her attention to him. 'Alicia, are you—what happened?' He lifted a hand to her cheek and she turned into it involuntarily. 'On the phone, you sounded so—'

'Can you find something, Dad?' She stepped back, her heart wild with adrenaline. In her chest, what had loosened now tightened, and if she started to explain—or even think—about what had happened in the crater, something was going to snap.

Rory nodded warily, peering up the spiral steps. He headed up to the office and Alicia might have protested had she the energy— the last thing she needed was him tumbling down the stairs. But she reserved the remainder of her resolve for Joe as he twisted the padlock back and forth, inspecting it from different angles.

'Shoot it.'

'I'll try some combinations. People aren't as inventive as you'd think. You head back to the house, see if you can get your hands on a—No.' He caught her wrist as she lunged for his gun.

'Just shoot the lock,' she ordered, her impatience growing. Her breath held underwater.

'There's more chance of the bullet ricocheting—stop that.'

She tried to seize the weapon with her other wrist and he held them firm in his calloused hands. Her breath was shallow and her eyes wild: striving to force her urgency into his skull.

'2001,' called a voice from above. Rory descended with an identical padlock in his hand. 'Try 2001.'

With slow, methodical fingers, Joe twisted the numbered dials. Click. Blink. Alicia could not breathe. Her throat had closed. She kicked towards the water's surface, fearing that she might not make it. Hands at her face, she opened her mouth to scream for him to finish it. Click, and the lock fell open.

Alicia leaped forward as Joe leaped back to catch Rory, who appeared to have lost consciousness through sheer exhilaration. As Joe supported her sleeping father, Alicia bolted down the steps.

Sunlight flooded the vents and fell upon all that lay within the cellar: barrels of wine, gardening tools, crates of lager and a lost boy on a threadbare mattress.

Alicia seized her brother like oxygen into suffocating lungs. With his head in both hands, she brushed her thumbs across the freckles on his cheeks and they did not shift beneath her gaze. His face had thinned and his closed eyes were more sunken than she remembered; but he was otherwise unchanged. When those features softened through her tears, she brushed the back of her hand against her streaming eyes and his definition returned. She drew him into her arms, laid his heavy head on her shoulder and squeezed his body as Ryan had squeezed hers, so tight that his heart beat against her chest. In deep, shuddering breaths, she breathed him in, surrendering to all the hope she had denied and all the pain she had endured. This was not memory or fantasy; it was not a simulacrum she held. Her brother was real and solid, here and now.

Through a blurred world, she watched Joe carry her father's sleeping body down the stairs. She sat on the thin mattress, lifted David's head into her lap and brushed a hand through his hair.

'I've found your body, little brother. Now to find your soul,' she said quietly. Joe lowered Rory to the ground, positioning him so that his head was on the mattress by Alicia's knee. Feeling as if his presence was an intrusion, Joe cast narrowed eyes around the cellar and bent to lift a rubber collar from the floor.

'Gus is in a lighthouse in Portugal,' said Alicia, catching Joe's eye. He dropped the collar on the top of a barrel.

'He phoned me, from the lighthouse,' said Joe. 'I've contacted the station in Carvoeiro and they're on their way to arrest Rainn. But I'm going there myself—to get Gus. And when we're back...' he trailed off and Alicia understood why he could not say any more out loud. There was only one way that Gus could have been certain that David was in this cellar. Beyond that chasm, he had found a means of travelling here, in the same form that Aldous and Morna had taken when they had killed Alicia's mother and Gus's parents. Joe's eyes were fixed on the vents, wondering who might be listening.

'We'll talk,' said Alicia.

Talking could wait. Thinking could wait. The name that Gus must have shared with his uncle—that could wait. A storm raged in her past and future, but this—her brother's heartbeat against her knee; his freckled face unchanging—this was her moment. With nothing left to count down to, she anchored herself in the eye of the storm.

Joe turned for the stairs, scratched his nose and turned back. He crouched to Alicia's level.

'I needed to protect him,' he said, his hard eyes now locked on hers. 'I let Rainn take your mother's letters. I wanted her to leave. To get them off our backs. You know what they're capable of, my—our family. But your mother, my half-sister.' He attempted a smile, thin and pained. 'She had courage. She came to see me, in Galway. Showed me that book, and I...' He barely moved his lips when he continued: 'I told her to burn it. After Ben, I just...I was lost. Anna told me Melissa Lawson had sent her to that lighthouse, so I looked her up. Melissa said they'd taken her son. She wanted the book—she wanted to give it back to them. An exchange. But Anna...When I refused to help her, she turned to Melissa. And they ripped her.'

Ripped—the word plunged through Alicia like a spectral fist. Is that what the Order called it, to tear a soul from its body?

'Why?' she asked.

'Because she was fearless. Because they didn't need her any more, not with Ryan leading you to them. And because Anna had...ideas.'

He wanted to tell her why her mother had gone to see Melissa that day. What would Alicia make of her mother's plan to overthrow the Crows? Wind ruffled the long grass outside the vents, brushing feathery shadows across the walls.

It could wait.

He rose from the crouch and stretched his legs. Golden rays struck his cheek.

'They asked for my help. Both of them. Your mother and Melissa. And I couldn't—I didn't help them. But you...you don't have to be brave any more, Alicia. Aldous and Morna want you, you know that. They won't harm you, they need you alive. Just stay out of Vivador, and you'll be safe.'

He nodded to the stairs.

'Is there anything I can do, before I...?'

'A cup of tea would be nice,' said Alicia. His eyes narrowed and she shook her head. 'Leave us.' Her voice was firm but not unkind.

'Bring him home. I have everything I need.'

She managed a smile, with one hand on her father's shoulder and the other on her brother's brow. Bathed in sunlight, there was nothing but a profound serenity in her malachite eyes. Joe nodded and climbed the steps. He was halfway to the door when she called his name.

'He needs more than your protection, Sergeant Crow.'

Moonrise

THE EARTH CONTINUED its ceaseless rotation, creating the illusion of the moon rising over the ocean. The rays of a hidden sun struck the surface of the moon like a mirror before bouncing over the ocean waves, up through the glass of the lighthouse and into Gus's pupils, where the light stimulated receptors in the back of his eyes to generate an image in his mind that looked nothing like anything on which he gazed. The moonrise was steady but certain, unhurried but unstoppable, and in the great white face of the moon Gus found a haunting beauty. A timeless indifference to the drama of his little life.

Sam lifted his head at footsteps on the stairs. The husky watched Rainn reach the raised metal walkway and then lowered his head back down on Winter's thigh and continued to stare at the rotating bulb.

Rainn's small nose wrinkled with distaste as she lifted her heel to step over Winter's bare feet. She reached Gus with twin moons reflected in her eyes.

'You think you've saved her, but she'll return to Vivador.' Rainn scratched a fingernail through the rust on the metal cage that protected the bulb. 'You haven't spared your cousin, only delayed the inevitable.'

She folded her arms, waiting for him to challenge her. He was exhausted to the bone and tired of her games.

'She'll have no reason to go back.'

He chose his words carefully. He saw nothing beyond the curved glass but the silver light upon the waves and a broken mast battered against the rocks. But what souls might have left their beds below to hover before his unseeing eyes?

'You think you can kill them, don't you?' said Rainn, giving his cheek a sharp pinch. 'So cute. While Aldous and Morna are in Vivador, you cannot rip them. And you won't find them in the immaterial realm unless they want you to.'

'I crossed that chasm,' Gus whispered, the mark on his pale cheek reddening. 'I have the Sol.'

'But do you, though?' She winked, her smile devious. 'You think you're the only one who crossed the Active Nothing?'

Her face was so close that Gus caught his open-mouthed reflection in her eyes. When Alicia had vanished into the void, Rainn had eyed the bridge of light and Gus had cast it away immediately, so that she would be unable to cross it.

'You said—'

'What you needed to hear. The Active Nothing: an idea vulnerable only to one with the Sol. That's what Peter told me—that's what he had been told by Aldous. But you see, young Augustus, an idea is only as strong as those who believe it. Aldous and Morna do not possess the Sol, so how could they have generated an idea any more powerful than themselves? Will and expectation: to cross that chasm, you need only believe that it is possible.'

'If you could cross it, why didn't you go after Melissa yourself? I saw Peter. He called you, didn't he? Before he died.'

Rainn toyed with a blackened thread that draped across her navel. She then straightened up, with her hand on her hip.

'I gave you what you wanted. Revenge, for that—' She flicked a thumb over her shoulder at the dead body behind her. 'And you didn't need much of a push, did you? Came rather easily, didn't it?'

She shook her head, flashing a smile, her teeth opaline in the moonlight. 'At Burnflower, I learned a lot from Peter. He taught me that fear is the great catalyst that drives us through our lives. But he failed to see that it comes in so many different flavours. Such different intensities. He created fear through hatred and hatred through fear—Ryan ran that vicious cycle like a hamster in a wheel, and Peter almost got what he wanted. But hatred will only get you so far. Vengeance, yes, and enough anger to drive a misled little boy across an empty void. But if you want real fear—top grade, eternal, all-consuming—you need love. Alicia loves her brother, and behind that love is an unbearable fear that she will lose him again. Now that she has found him, now that you have reunited the pair of them, what would she do to protect him?'

'The police...' Gus hesitated. When ghosting through Burnflower, he had been unable to hear the words spoken between Melissa and the girl. He edged closer, leaning into Rainn's ear, and cupped a hand to his mouth so that his lips could not be read by spectral observers.

'The police are on their way. Joe will find the key for that door and we will finish this. You have no use for Alicia. Get out of here, and leave us.'

'That won't be necessary,' said Rainn. 'The show's not over yet. I think I'll stick around. Joe will take the key from Burnflower and Aldous will rip him before he even reaches the door. Devastated, you will beg Alicia to return to Vivador. And she won't need much convincing, since only Morna can wake her brother. But those are events waiting to happen. Steps along a path already laid. It's the unpredictable that interests me. What will our Ryan do when he finds out who killed his mother?'

Gus closed his dry throat. He leaned back a fraction and did not cover his mouth when he spoke.

'I told my uncle that Aldous and Morna killed Melissa.'

A siren wailed. Red and blue lights lit the surrounding glass as a police boat rounded the corner of the peninsula. Rainn pushed the sunglasses over her eyes and patted Gus gently on the cheek. It took him a moment to register the emotion. It was a maternal pride.

'Welcome to the family.'

EPILOGUE

WITH A LOOK of undisguised disdain, Agent Oliveira surveyed the woman on the far side of the front desk. This was the third time in as many months that the French woman had visited Caroeiro's small police post, and this time she had brought her cat. In broken English, the woman explained her grievance with the town florist, and Agent Oliveira shifted his weight from one leg to the other, drawing fingertips down his neat beard and biting back the urge to remind her that he had endured these details twice already. The woman had moved into a coastal property earlier that year and was adamant that the florist was lifting begonias from her hanging baskets and replacing them with withering plants, so that he could sell her healthy specimens at his stall in the town centre. The cat had, allegedly, scratched the perpetrator during his previous attempt to rob her, and hissed wildly whenever the man passed her on the street. The languorous animal lay boneless in the woman's arms, and the officer could not imagine it stirring into action even if it were dropped onto a nest of rats.

'You ask him in, this moment,' said the woman. Her skin was weathered, her hair tangled by the sea spray, her eyes quick and mistrusting. 'You call him now.' She prodded the phone on the desk with her finger, and her sudden movement caused the cat's ears to prick irritably. 'And I show you how she hisses.'

'A cat is not a witness.'

There followed a snort of laughter from the bench against the far wall of the small and narrow room. Two of his colleagues watched the exchange with a twist of amusement about their otherwise bored expressions. Unlike this pair, Agent Oliveira had a good grasp of English, which meant he was often landed with the complaints of tourists and expatriates. The men were idle, waiting for the superintendent, who was on the phone in an adjoining room to a British police officer. The young woman they had brought in had winked at Agent Oliveira as they led her, handcuffed, through the open doorway. The superintendent had taken a look at her to verify the description he had received, and asked his men to wait with her before returning to his call. She had stretched out along the length of the steel bench and fallen asleep immediately, wrists handcuffed in her lap. Having failed to wake her, the policemen perched on either side of the bench, the larger of the two half-submerged in the leaves of a potted plant.

The French woman spoke a fierce diatribe, slowing only when struggling to translate curse words. Agent Oliveira folded his arms and enjoyed a deep yawn. The animal's amber eyes mirrored his indifference.

The cat turned its head towards the open door and delivered a loud hiss, halting the woman's rant. The three police officers watched the animal wriggle, twist and scratch the woman's bare arm, drawing blood. With an offended shriek, the woman opened her arms and let the animal drop to the floor. It arched its back and continued to stare at the doorway. Its black head moved slowly to the right, as if following the passage of a fly so small the humans were unable to see it.

'You must take him outside,' said Agent Oliveira, his patience spent. 'Or we will have no choice but to arrest him.'

Recovering from the behaviour of her pet, the woman opened her mouth to correct him on the animal's gender when the police officer rolled his eyes. She took a breath, readied herself for a fresh rebuke and Agent Oliveira dropped to the desk. His head struck the telephone, knocking the handset from its base, which followed him to the floor in a tangle of cables.

His colleagues bolted upright, calling his name. The leaner of the two approached the desk and dropped as abruptly, collapsing like a puppet with severed strings. The remaining police officer emerged from the leaves of the potted plant, staring at the wild woman as if she had cast some spell on them. A second hiss issued from the cat and the policeman's eyes glazed over, his jaw falling slack. He fell back into the plant and slid down the wall to settle with his chin against his chest.

On the bench beside him, the woman stirred, opening her eyes and blinking lazily. She let out a satisfied moan as she stretched her handcuffed wrists over her head and shifted upright. She met the woman's startled gaze, nodded to a set of keys that hung from the policeman's belt and held out her handcuffs.

'If you wouldn't mind?'

Author's Note

I'm a new author, and this book will disappear into the ether without reviews. If you can spare a minute to write a line or two, I would greatly appreciate a review on Amazon.

Now let's play a game.

Which of the five below is fictional?

> ➤ Blindsight
> ➤ Godalming
> ➤ Mt Psarnox
> ➤ REM behaviour disorder
> ➤ Lucid dreaming

All of them? None of them? Somewhere in between? Let's find out...

Blindsight: David may be fictional, but his condition is not. Incredibly, studies have shown that participants with blindsight are capable of interacting with their environment as if they can see it, despite having no conscious image of the world. When asked to describe what lies in front of them, they cannot. When asked to place a dot in the centre of a circle, a part of their mind will tell them where it is.

Godalming: It may sound like somewhere out of *The Lord of the Rings*, but Godalming is a town in Surrey. I celebrated the turning of the millennium inside the Pepperpot, in fact.

Mt Psarnox: Much of the description of Psarnox was inspired by

Mt Rinjani in Lombok, Indonesia. Aldous and Morna did not recreate a volcano they had seen in the waking world, for Psarnox does not exist.

REM behaviour disorder: This is real. Terrifying, right? When we sleep, our muscles are inhibited, so we can go for a walk or have a little dance and our bodies remain safely under the covers. For people with RBD, this inhibition doesn't happen, and they literally act out their dreams. The disorder can be managed with medication, but there is currently no cure.

Lucid dreaming: As far as I'm aware, it isn't possible to access another realm while you sleep; but the act of becoming conscious within the dream, of altering the dreamscape and facing your subconscious, is not only possible but every bit as exhilarating as it sounds. It's such a weird phenomenon that a handful of my closest friends—those who knew I'd been writing the trilogy for almost a decade—asked: "You can actually *do* that?". Like many others, they assumed that lucid dreaming was pure fantasy.

For those interested in lucid dreaming, I've written a short guide, available to download for free at **benjhenry.com** – why not give it a try this month?

The website also contains a little more about the trilogy, blogs on lucid dreaming, and the opportunity to stay in touch by joining the *Chaos Readers Club*. I email members on the first Friday of every month, with lucid dreaming tips and updates on the trilogy.

Stay in Touch

Join the *Chaos Readers Club* and get a free guide to lucid dreaming. As a member of the Club, you'll get an email on the first Friday of every month, with updates on new releases, behind-the-scenes information on the development of the trilogy and, of course, the latest tips for lucid dreaming. Find out more at **benjhenry.com**.

The Trilogy

The Order of Chaos is the first in a trilogy. *Burnflower* is set for release in December 2021, and *Catalyst* will follow in 2022. For more information, visit **benjhenry.com**.

Thanks

A huge thank you to Mum, who helped me to edit the early drafts. This book was finished during a particularly challenging time of my life, and I'm eternally grateful to those who got me through it—you know who you are.

Thank you to Victoria Lee, for her incredible attention to detail during the final edits, and to the Faber Academy for providing such encouraging support while I revised the manuscript. I would also like to thank Jericho Writers and David Gaughran, whose sage advice helped me to navigate the world of self-publishing.

Copyright

Printed in Great Britain
by Amazon